GASCOYNE, THE SANDAL WOOD TRADER

GASCOYNE, THE SANDAL WOOD TRADER

R. M. BALLANTYNE

WILDSIDE PRESS

BOOK INFORMATION

Published by Wildside Press, LLC
www.wildsidebooks.com

CHAPTER I

THE SCHOONER

The great Pacific is the scene of our story. On a beautiful morning, many years ago, a little schooner might have been seen floating, light and graceful as a seamew, on the breast of the slumbering ocean. She was one of those low, black-hulled vessels, with raking, taper masts, trimly-cut sails, and elegant form, which we are accustomed to associate with the idea of a yacht or a pirate.

She might have been the former, as far as appearance went; for the sails and deck were white as snow, and every portion of brass and copper above her water-line shone in the hot sun with dazzling brilliancy. But pleasure-seekers were not wont, in those days, to take such distant flights, or to venture into such dangerous seas,—dangerous alike from the savage character of the islanders, and the numerous coral reefs that lie hidden a few feet below the surface of the waves.

Still less probable did it seem that the vessel in question could belong to the lawless class of craft to which we have referred; for, although she had what may be styled a wicked aspect, and was evidently adapted for swift sailing, neither large guns nor small arms of any kind were visible.

Whatever her nature or her object, she was reduced, at the time we introduce her to the reader, to a state of inaction by the dead calm which prevailed. The sea resembled a sheet of clear glass. Not a cloud broke the softness of the sky, in which the sun glowed hotter and hotter as it rose towards the zenith. The sails of the schooner hung idly from the yards; her reflected image was distorted, but scarcely broken, by the long, gentle swell; her crew, with the exception of the watch, were asleep either on deck or down below; and so deep was the universal silence, that, as the vessel rose and fell with a slow, quiet motion, the pattering of the reef-points on her sails forcibly attracted the listener's attention, as does the ticking of a clock in the deep silence of night. A few sea-birds rested on the water, as if in the enjoyment of the profound peace that reigned around; and far away on the horizon might be seen the tops of the palm trees that grow on one of those coral islands which lie scattered in thousands, like beautiful gems, on the surface of that bright blue sea.

Among the men who lay sleeping in various easy, off-hand attitudes on the schooner's deck, was one who merits special attention—not only because of the grotesque appearance of his person, but also because he is one of the principal actors in our tale.

He was a large, powerful man, of that rugged build and hairy aspect that might have suggested the idea that he would be difficult to kill. He was a fair man, with red hair, and a deeply sun-burned face, on which jovial good humor sat almost perpetually enthroned. At the moment when we introduce him to the reader, however, that expression happened to be modified in consequence of his having laid him down to sleep in a sprawling manner on his back—the place as well as the position being, apparently, one of studied discomfort. His legs lay over the heel of the bowsprit, his big body reposed on a confused heap of blocks and cordage, and his neck rested on the stock of an anchor so that his head hung down over it, presenting the face to view with the large mouth wide open, in an upside-down position. The man was evidently on the verge of choking, but, being a strong man, and a rugged man, and a healthy man, he did not care. He seemed to prefer choking to the trouble of rousing himself and improving his position.

How long he would have lain in this state of felicity it is impossible to say, for his slumbers were rudely interrupted by a slight lurch of the schooner, which caused the blocks and cordage attached to the sheet of the jib to sweep slowly, but with rasping asperity, across his face. Any ordinary man would have been seriously damaged—at least in appearance—by such an accident; but this particular sea-dog was tough in the skin,—he was only awakened by it—nothing more. He yawned, raised himself lazily, and gazed round with that vacant stare of unreasonable surprise which is common to man on passing from a state of somnolence to that of wakefulness.

Gradually the expression of habitual good-humor settled on his visage, as he looked from one to another of his sleeping comrades, and at last, with a bland smile, he broke forth into the following soliloquy:

"Wot a goose, wot a grampus you've bin, John Bumpus: firstly, for goin' to sea; secondly, for remainin' at sea; thirdly, for not forsakin' the sea; fourthly, for bein' worried about it at all, now that you've made up your mind to retire from the sea; and fifthly—"

Here John Bumpus paused as if to meditate on the full depth and meaning of these polite remarks, or to invent some new and powerful expression wherewith to deliver his fifth head. His mental efforts seemed to fail, however; for, instead of concluding the sentence, he hummed the following lines, which, we may suppose, were expressive of his feelings, as well as his intentions:—

"So good-by to the mighty ocean,
And adoo to the rollin' sea.
For it's nobody has no notion
Wot a grief it has bin to me."

"Ease off the sheets and square the topsail yards," was at that moment said, or rather murmured, by a bass voice so deep and rich that, although scarcely raised above a whisper, it was distinctly heard over the whole deck.

John Bumpus raised his bulky form with a degree of lithe activity that proved him to be not less agile than athletic, and, with several others, sprang to obey the order. A few seconds later the sails were swelled out by a light breeze, and the schooner moved through the water at a rate which seemed scarcely possible under the influence of so gentle a puff of air. Presently the breeze increased, the vessel cut through the blue water like a knife, leaving a long track of foam in her wake as she headed for the coral-island before referred to. The outer reef or barrier of coral which guarded the island was soon reached. The narrow opening in this natural bulwark was passed. The schooner stood across the belt of perfectly still water that lay between the reef and the shore, and entered a small bay, where the cairn water reflected the strip of white sand, green palm, and tropical plants that skirted its margin, as well as the purple hills of the interior.

Here she swept round in a sudden but graceful curve, until all her canvas fluttered in the breeze, and then dropped anchor in about six fathoms water.

CHAPTER II

BUMPUS IS FIERY AND PHILOSOPHICAL— MURDEROUS DESIGNS FRUSTRATED

The captain of the schooner, whose deep voice had so suddenly terminated the meditations of John Bumpus, was one of those men who seem to have been formed for the special purpose of leading and commanding their fellows.

He was not only unusually tall and powerful,—physical qualities which, in themselves, are by no means sufficient to command respect,—but, as we have said, he possessed a deep, full-toned bass voice, in which there seemed to lie a species of fascination; for its softest tones riveted attention, and when it thundered forth commands in the fiercest storms, it inspired confidence and a feeling of security in all who heard it. The countenance of the captain, however, was that which induced men to accord to him a position of superiority in whatever sphere of action he chanced to move. It was not so much a handsome as a manly and singularly grave face, in every line of which was written inflexible determination. His hair was short, black, and curly. A small mustache darkened his upper lip, but the rest of his face was closely shaven, so that his large chin and iron jaw were fully displayed. His eyes were of that indescribable blue color which can exhibit the intensest passion, or the most melting tenderness.

He wore a somber but somewhat picturesque costume,—a dark-colored flannel shirt and trousers, which latter were gathered in close round his lower limbs by a species of drab gaiter that appeared somewhat incongruous with the profession of the man. The only bit of bright color about him was a scarlet belt round his waist, from the side of which depended a long knife in a brown leather sheath. A pair of light shoes, and a small round cap resembling what is styled in these days a pork-pie, completed his costume. He was about forty years of age.

Such was the commander, or captain, or skipper of this suspicious-looking schooner,—a man pre-eminently fitted for the accomplishment of much good, or the perpetration of great evil.

As soon as the anchor touched the ground, the captain ordered a small boat to be lowered, and, leaping into it with two men, one of whom was our friend John Bumpus, rowed toward the shore.

"Have you brought your kit with you, John?" inquired the captain, as the little boat shot over the smooth waters of the bay.

"Wot's of it, sir," replied our rugged seaman, holding up a small bundle tied in a red cotton handkerchief, "I s'pose our cruise ashore won't be a long one."

"It will be long for you, my man,—at least as far as the schooner is concerned, for I do not mean to take you aboard again."

"Not take me aboard agin!" exclaimed the sailor, with a look of surprise which quickly degenerated into an angry frown and thereafter gradually relaxed into a broad grin as he continued: "Why, capting, wot *do* you mean to do with me then? for I'm a heavy piece of goods, d'ye see, and can't be easily moved about without a small touch o' my own consent, you know."

Jo Bumpus, as he was fond of styling himself, said this with a serio-comic air of sarcasm, for he was an exception to the general rule of his fellows. He had little respect for, and no fear of, his commander. Indeed, to say truth (for truth must be told, even though the character of our rugged friend should suffer), Jo entertained a most profound belief in the immense advantage of muscular strength and vigor in general, and of his own prowess in particular.

Although not quite so gigantic a man as his captain, he was nearly so, and, being a bold, self-reliant fellow, he felt persuaded in his own mind that he could thrash him, if need were. In fact,

Jo was convinced that there was no living creature under the sun, human or otherwise, that walked upon two legs, that he could not pommel to death, with more or less ease, by means of his fists alone. And in this conviction he was not far wrong. Yet it must not be supposed that Jo Bumpus was a boastful man or a bully. Far from it. He was so thoroughly persuaded of his invincibility that he felt there was no occasion to prove it. He therefore followed the natural bent of his inclinations, which led him at all times to exhibit a mild, amiable, and gentle aspect,— except, of course, when he was roused. As occasion for being roused was not wanting in the South Seas in those days, Jo's amiability was frequently put to the test. He sojourned, while there, in a condition of alternate calm and storm; but riotous joviality ran, like a rich vein, through all his checkered life, and lit up its most somber phases like gleams of light on an April day.

"You entered my service with your own consent," replied the captain to Jo's last remark, "and you may leave it, with the same consent, whenever you choose; but you will please to remember that I did not engage you to serve on board the schooner. Back there you do not go either with or without your consent, my fine fellow, and if you are bent on going to sea on your own account.—you've got a pair of good arms and legs,—you can swim! Besides," continued the captain, dropping the tone of sarcasm in which this was said, and assuming a more careless and good-natured air, "you were singing something not long since, if I mistake not, about 'farewell to the rolling sea,' which leads me to think you will not object to a short cruise on shore for a change, especially on such a beautiful island as this is."

"I'm your man, capting," cried the impulsive seaman, at the same time giving his oar a pull that well-nigh spun the boat round. "And, to say wot's the plain truth, d'ye see, I'm not sorry to ha' done with your schooner; for, although she is as tight a little craft as any man could wish for to go to sea in, I can't say much for the crew,—saving your presence, Dick," he added, glancing over his shoulder at the surly-looking man who pulled the bow oar. "Of all the rascally set I ever clapped eyes on, they seems to me the worst. If I didn't know you for a sandal-wood trader, I do believe I'd take ye for a pirate."

"Don't speak ill of your messmates behind their backs, Jo," said the captain, with a slight frown. "No good and true man ever does that."

"No more I do," replied John Bumpus, while a deep red color suffused his bronzed countenance. "No more I do, leastwise if they wos here I'd say it to their faces; for they're a set of as ill-tongued villains as I ever had the misfortune to—"

"Silence!" exclaimed the captain, suddenly, in a voice of thunder.

Few men would have ventured to disobey the command given by such a man, but John Bumpus was one of those few. He did indeed remain silent for two seconds, but it was the silence of astonishment.

"Capting," said he, seriously, "I don't mean no offense, but I'd have you to know that I engaged to work for you, not to hold my tongue at your bidding, d'ye see? There ain't the man living as'll make Jo Bumpus shut up w'en he's got a mind to—"

The captain put an abrupt end to the remarks of his refractory seaman by starting up suddenly in fierce anger and seizing the tiller, apparently with the intent to fell him. He checked himself, however, as suddenly, and breaking into a loud laugh, cried:—

"Come, Jo, you must admit that there is at least one living man who has made you 'shut up' before you had finished what you'd got to say."

John Bumpus, who had thrown up his left arm to ward off the anticipated blow, and dropped his oar in order to clench his right fist, quietly resumed his oar, and shook his head gravely for nearly a minute, after which he made the following observation:—

"Capting, I've seed, in my experience o' life, that there are some constitootions as don't agree with jokin'; an' yours is one on 'em. Now, if you'd take the advice of a plain man, you'd never try it on. You're a grave man by natur', and you're so bad at a joke that a feller can't quite tell w'en you're a-doin' of it. See, now! I do declare I wos as near drivin' you right over the stern o' your own boat as could be, only by good luck I seed the twinkle in your eye in time."

"Pull away, my lad," said the captain, in the softest tones of his deep voice, at the same time looking his reprover straight in the face.

There was something in the tone in which that simple command was given, and in the look by which it was accompanied, that effectually quelled John Bumpus in spite of himself. Violence had no effect on John, because in most cases he was able to meet it with superior violence, and in all cases he was willing to try. But to be put down in this mild way was perplexing. The words were familiar, the look straightforward and common enough. He could not understand it at all, and being naturally of a philosophical turn of mind, he spent the next three minutes in a futile endeavor to analyze his own feelings. Before he had come to any satisfactory conclusion on the subject, the boat's keel grated on the white sand of the shore.

Now, while all that we have been describing in the last and present chapters was going on, a very different series of events was taking place on the coral-island; for there, under the pleasant shade of the cocoanut palms, a tall, fair, and handsome youth was walking lightly down the green slopes toward the shore in anticipation of the arrival of the schooner, and a naked, dark-skinned savage was dogging his steps, winding like a hideous snake among the bushes, and apparently seeking an opportunity to launch the short spear he carried in his hand at his unsuspecting victim.

As the youth and the savage descended the mountain-side

together, the former frequently paused when an opening in the rich foliage peculiar to these beautiful isles enabled him to obtain a clear view of the magnificent bay and its fringing coral reef, on which the swell of the great Pacific—so calm and undulating out beyond—fell in tremendous breakers, with a long, low, solemn roar like distant thunder. As yet no object broke the surface of the mirror-like bay within the reef.

Each time the youth paused the savage stopped also, and more than once he poised his deadly spear, while his glaring eyeballs shone amid the green foliage like those of a tiger. Yet upon each occasion he exhibited signs of hesitation, and finally lowered the weapon, and crouched into the underwood.

To any one ignorant of the actors in this scene, the indecision of the savage would have appeared unaccountable; for there could be no doubt of his desire to slay the fair youth—still less doubt of his ability to dart his formidable spear with precision. Nevertheless, there was good reason for his hesitating; for young Henry Stuart was well known, alike by settlers and savages, as possessing the swiftest foot, the strongest arm, and the boldest heart in the island, and Keona was not celebrated for the possession of these qualities in any degree above the average of his fellows, although he did undoubtedly exceed them in revenge, hatred, and the like. On one occasion young Stuart had, while defending his mother's house against an attack of the savages, felled Keona with a well-directed blow of his fist. It was doubtless out of revenge for this that the latter now dogged the former through the lonely recesses of the mountain-pass by which he had crossed the island from the little settlement in which was his home, and gained the sequestered bay in which he expected to find the schooner. Up to this point, however, the savage had not summoned courage to make the attack, although, with the exception of a hunting-knife, his enemy was altogether unarmed; for he knew that in the event of missing his mark the young man's speed of foot would enable him to outstrip him, while his strength of frame would quickly terminate a single combat.

As the youth gained the more open land near the beach, the possibility of making a successful cast of the spear became more and doubtful. Finally the savage shrunk into the bushes, and abandoned the pursuit.

"Not here yet, Master Gascoyne," muttered Henry, as he sat down on a rock to rest; for, although the six miles of country he had crossed was a trifle, as regarded distance, to a lad of nineteen, the rugged mountain-path by which he had come would have tried the muscles of a Red Indian, and the nerve of a goat. "You were wont to keep to time better in days gone by. Truly it seems to me a strange thing that I should thus be made a sort of walking post between my mother's house and this bay, all for the benefit of a man who seems to me no better than he should be, and whom I don't like, and yet whom I *do* like in some unaccountable fashion that I don't understand."

Whatever the youth's thoughts were after giving vent to the foregoing soliloquy, he kept them to himself. They did not at first appear to be of an agreeable nature; for he frowned once or twice, and struck his thigh with his clenched hand; but gradually a pleasant expression lit up his manly face, as he gazed out upon the sleeping sea and watched the gorgeous clouds that soon began to rise and cluster round the sun.

After an hour or so spent in wandering on the beach picking up shells, and gazing wistfully out to sea, Henry Stuart appeared to grow tired of waiting; for he laid himself down on the shore, turned his back on the ocean, pillowed his head on a tuft of grass, and deliberately went to sleep.

Now was the time for the savage to wreak his vengeance on his enemy; but, fortunately, that villain, despite his subtlety and cunning, had not conceived the possibility of the youth indulging in such an unnatural recreation as a nap in the forenoon. He had, therefore, retired to his native jungle, and during the hour in which Henry was buried in repose, and in which he might have accomplished his end without danger or uncertainty, he was seated in a dark, cave, moodily resolving in his mind future plans of villainy, and, indulging the hope that on the youth's returning homeward be would be more successful in finding a favorable opportunity to take his life.

During this same hour it was that our low-hulled little schooner hove in sight on the horizon, ran swiftly down before the breeze, cast anchor in the bay, and sent her boat ashore, as we have seen, with the captain, the surly man called Dick, and our friend John Bumpus.

It happened that, just as the boat ran under the shelter of a rocky point and touched the strand, Keona left his cave for the purpose of observing what young Stuart was about. He knew that he could not have retraced his homeward way without passing within sight of his place of concealment.

A glance of surprise crossed his dark visage as he crept to the edge of the underwood and saw the schooner at anchor in the bay. This was succeeded by a fiendish grin of exultation as his eye fell on the slumbering form of the youth. He instantly took advantage of the opportunity; and so deeply was he engrossed with his murderous intention, that he did not observe the captain of the schooner as he turned a projecting rock, and suddenly appeared upon the scene. The captain, however, saw the savage, and instantly drew back, signing, at the same time, to his two men to keep under cover.

A second glance showed him the sleeping form of Henry, and, almost before he had time to suspect that foul play was going on, he saw the savage glide from the bushes to the side of the sleeper, raise his spear, and poise it for one moment, as if to make sure of sending it straight to the youth's heart.

There was not a moment to lose. The captain carried a short carbine in his hand, with which he took aim at the savage,— going down on one knee to make a surer shot, for the carbine of those days was not to be depended on at a distance much beyond a hundred yards; and as the actors in this scene were separated by even more than that distance, there was a considerable chance of missing the savage and hitting the young man.

This, however, was not a moment to calculate chances. The captain pulled the trigger, and the crash of the shot was followed by a howl from the savage, as his uplifted arm dropped to his side, and the spear fell across the face of the sleeper. Henry instantly awoke, and sprang up with the agility of a panther. Before he could observe what had occurred, Keona leaped into the bushes disappeared. Henry at once bounded after him; and the captain, giving vent to a lusty cheer, rushed across the beach, and sprang into the forest, closely followed by surly Diet and John Bumpus, whose united cheers of excitement and shouts of defiance awoke the echoes of the place with clamorous discords.

CHAPTER III

A BOUGH WALK ENLIVENED BY RAMBLING
TALK—BUMPUS IS "AGREEABLE"

It is said, in the proverbial philosophy of nautical men, that "a stern chase is a long one." The present instance was an exception to the general rule. Keona was wounded. Young Stuart was fleet as the antelope, and strong as a young lion. In these circumstances it is not surprising that, after a run of less than a quarter of a mile, he succeeded in laying his hands on the neck of the savage and hurling him to the ground, where he lay panting and helpless, looking up in the face of his conqueror with an expression of hopeless despair; for savages and wicked men generally are wont to judge of others by themselves, and to expect to receive such treatment from their enemies as they themselves would in similar circumstances accord.

The fear of instant death was before his eyes, and the teeth of Keona chattered in his head, while his face grew more hideous than ever, by reason of its becoming livid.

His fears were groundless. Henry Stuart was not a savage. He was humane by nature; and, in addition to this, he had been trained under the influence of that Book which teaches us that the most philosophical, because the most effective, method of procedure in this world is to "overcome evil with good."

"So you scoundrel," said Henry, placing his knee on Keona's chest, and compressing his throat with his left hand, while with his right he drew forth a long glittering knife, and raised it in the air,—"so you are not satisfied with what I gave you the last time we met, but you must need take the trouble to cross my path a second time, and get a taste of cold steel, must you?"

Although Keona could speak no English, he understood it sufficiently to appreciate the drift of the youth's words, even though he had failed to comprehend the meaning of the angry frown and the glittering knife. But, however much, he might have wished to reply to the question, Henry took care to render the attempt impossible, by compressing his windpipe until he became blue in the face, and then black. At the same time, he let the sharp point of his knife touch the skin just over the region of the heart.

Having thus convinced his vanquished foe that death was at the door, he suddenly relaxed his iron grip, arose, sheathed his knife, and bade the savage get up. The miserable creature did so, with some difficulty, just as the captain and his men arrived on the scene.

"Well met, Henry," cried the former, extending his hand to the youth; "had I been a moment later, my lad, I fear that your life's blood would have been on the sea-shore."

"Then it was you who fired the shot, Captain Gascoyne? This is the second time I have to thank you for saving my life," said the young man, returning the grasp of the captain's hand.

"Truly, it is but a small matter to have to thank me for. Doubtless, if my stout man John Bumpus had carried the carbine, he would have done you as good service. And methinks, Henry, that you would have preferred to owe your life to either of my men rather than to me, if I may judge by your looks."

"You should not judge by looks, captain," replied the youth quickly,—"especially the looks of a man who has just had a hand-to-hand tussle with a savage. But, to tell the plain truth, Captain Gascoyne, I would indeed rather have had to thank your worthy man John Bumpus than yourself for coming to my aid; for although I owe you no grudge, and do not count you an enemy, I had rather see your back than your face; and you know the reason why."

"You give me credit, boy, for more knowledge than I possess," replied Gascoyne, while an angry frown gathered for a moment on his brow, but passed away almost as quickly as it came. "I know not the cause of your unreasonable dislike to one who has never done you an injury."

"Never done me an injury!" cried Henry, starting and turning with a look of passion on his companion; then, checking himself by a strong effort, he added, in a milder tone, "But a truce to such talk; and I ask your forgiveness for my sharp words just after your rendering me such good service in the hour of need. You and I differ in our notions on one or two points—that is all; there is no need for quarreling. See, here is a note from my mother, who sent me to the bay to meet you."

During this colloquy, Dick and Bumpus had mounted guard over the wounded savage, just out of ear-shot of their captain.

Neither of the sailors ventured to hold their prisoner, because they deemed it an unmanly advantage to take of one who was so completely (as they imagined) in their power. They kept a watchful eye on him, however; and while they affected an easy indifference of attitude, held themselves in readiness to pounce upon him if he should attempt to escape. But nothing seemed farther from the mind of Keona than such an attempt. He appeared to be thoroughly exhausted by his recent struggle and loss of blood, and his body was bent as if he were about to sink down to the ground. There was, however, a peculiar glance in his dark eyes that induced John Bumpus to be more on his guard than appearances seemed to warrant.

While Gascoyne was reading the letter to which we have referred, Keona suddenly placed his left leg behind surly Dick, and, with his unwounded fist, hit that morose individual such a tremendous back-handed blow on the nose that he instantly measured his length on the ground. John Bumpus made a sudden plunge at the savage on seeing this, but the latter ducked his head, passed like an eel under the very arms of the sailor, and went off into the forest like a deer.

"Hold!" shouted Captain Gascoyne, as John turned, in a state of mingled amazement and anger, to pursue. "Hold on, Bumpus; let the miserable rascal go."

John stopped, looked over his shoulder, hesitated, and finally came back, with a rolling air of nautical indifference, and his hands thrust into his breeches pockets.

"You know best, capting," said he; "but I think it a pity to let sich a dirty varmint go clear off, to dodge about in the bushes, and mayhap treat us to a poisoned arrow, or a spear thrust on the sly. Howsomedever, it ain't no consarn wotever to Jo Bumpus. How's your beak, Dick, my boy?"

"None the better for your askin'," replied the surly mariner, who was tenderly stroking the injured member of his face with the fingers of both hands.

"Come, Dick, it is none the worse of being inquired after," said Henry, laughing. "But 'tis as well to let the fellow go. He knows best how to cure his wound, by the application of a few simples; and by thus making off has relieved us of the trouble and responsibility of trying our hands at civilized doctoring. Besides, John Bumpus (if that's your name,—though I do think your father might have found you a better), your long legs would never have brought you within a mile of the savage."

"Young man," retorted Jo, gravely, "I'd have you to know that the family of the Bumpuses is an old and a honorable one. They comed over with the Conkerer to Ireland, where they picked up a deal o' their good manners, after which they settled at last on their own estates in Yorkshire. Though they *have* comed down in the world, and the last of the Bumpuses—that's me—is takin' a pleasure-trip round the world before the mast, I won't stand by and hear my name made game of, d'ye see: and I'd have ye to know, further, my buck, that the Bumpuses has a pecooliar gift for fightin'; and although you *are* a strappin' young feller, you'd better not cause me for to prove that you're conkerable."

Having delivered himself of this oration, the last of the Bumpuses frowned portentously on the youth who had dared to risk his anger, and turning with a bland smile to surly Dick, asked him "if his beak was any better *now.*"

"There seems to be bad news in the letter, I think," observed Henry, as Captain Gascoyne perused the epistle with evident signs of displeasure.

"Bad enough in these times of war, boy," replied the other, folding the note and placing it in a pouch inside the breast of his flannel shirt. "It seems that that pestiferous British frigate, the Talisman, lies at anchor in the bay on the other side of the island."

"Nothing in that to cause uneasiness to an honest trader," said Henry, leading the way up the steep path by which he had descended from the mountain region of the interior.

"That speech only shows your ignorance of the usages of ships-of-war. Know you not that the nature of the trade in which I am engaged requires me to be strong-handed, and that the opinion of a commander in the British navy as to how many hands are sufficient for the navigation of a trading-schooner does not accord with mine?—a difference of opinion which may possibly result in his relieving me of a few of my best men when I can ill afford to spare them. And, by the way," said Gascoyne, pausing as they gained the brow of an eminence that commanded a view of the rich woodland on one side and the sea on the other, "I had better take precautions against such a mischance. Here, Dick" (taking the man aside and whispering to him), "go back to the schooner, my lad, and tell the mate to send ten of the best hands ashore with provisions and arms. Let them squat where they choose on land, only let them see to it that they keep well out of sight and hearing until I want them. And now, Master Henry, lead the way; John Bumpus and I will follow at your heel like a couple of faithful dogs."

The scene through which young Henry Stuart now led his seafaring companions was of that rich, varied, and beautiful character which is strikingly characteristic of those islands of the Pacific which owe their origin to volcanic agency. Unlike the low coral islets, this island presented every variety of the boldest mountain scenery, and yet, like them, it displayed all the gorgeous beauty of a rich tropical vegetation. In some places the ground had been cracked and riven into great fissures and uncouth caverns of the wildest description, by volcanoes apparently long since extinct. In others the landscape presented the soft beauty of undulating, grove-like scenery, in which, amid a profusion of bright green herbage, there rose conspicuous the tall stems and waving plumes of the cocoanut palm; the superb and umbrageous ko-a, with its laurel-green leaves and sweet blossoms; the *kukui*, or candlenut tree; the fragrant sandal-wood, and a variety of other trees and shrubs for which there are no English names.

Hundreds of green paroquets with blue heads and red breasts, turtle-doves, wood-pigeons, and other birds enlivened the groves with sound, if not with melody, and the various lakelets and pools were alive with wild ducks and water-hens.

The route by which the party traveled led them first across a country of varied and beautiful aspect; then it conducted them into wild mountain fastnesses, among which they clambered, at times with considerable difficulty. Ere long they passed into a dreary region where the ancient fires that upheaved the island from the deep seemed to have scorched the land into a condition of perpetual desolation. Blackened and bare lava rocks, steep volcanic ridges and gorges, irregular truncated cones, deep-mouthed caves and fissures, overhanging arches, natural bridges, great tunnels and ravines, surrounded them on every side, and so concealed the softer features of the country that it was scarcely possible to believe in the reality of the verdant region out of which they had just passed. In another hour this chaotic scenery was left behind; the highest ridge of the mountains was crossed, and the travelers began to descend the green slopes on the other side of the island. These slopes terminated in a beach of white sand, while beyond lay the calm waters of the enclosed lagoon, the coral reef with its breakers, and the mighty sea.

"'Tis a pretty spot?" said Henry, interrogatively, as the party halted on the edge of a precipice, whence they obtained an uninterrupted view of the whole of that side of the island.

"Ay, pretty enough," replied Gascoyne, in a somewhat sad tone of voice: "I had hoped to have led a quiet life here once, but that was not to be. How say you, Bumpus; could you make up your mind to cast anchor here for a year or so?"

"Wot's that you say, capting?" inquired honest John, who was evidently lost in admiration of the magnificent scene that lay spread out before him.

"I ask if you have no objection to come to an anchor here for a time," repeated the captain.

"Objection! I'll tell ye wot it is, capting, I never seed sich a place afore in all my born days. Why, it's a slice out o' paradise. I do believe if Adam and Eve wos here they'd think they'd got back again into Eden. It's more beautifuller than the blue ocean, by a long chalk; an' if you wants a feller that's handy at a'most anything after a fashion,—a jack-of-all-trades and master of-none (except seamanship, which ain't o' no use here),—Jo Bumpus is your man!"

"I'm glad to hear you say that, Jo," said Henry, laughing, "for we are greatly in need of white men of your stamp in these times, when the savages are so fierce against each other that they are like to eat us up altogether, merely by way of keeping their hands in practise."

"*White* men of my stamp!" remarked Bumpus, surveying complacently his deeply-bronzed hands, which were only a shade darker than his visage; "well, I would like to know what ye call black if I'm a white man."

"Blood, and not skin, is what stamps the color of the man, Jo. If it were agreeable to Captain Gascoyne to let you off your engagement to him, I think I could make it worth your while to engage with me, and would find you plenty of work of all kinds, including a little of that same fighting for which the Bumpuses are said to be so famous."

"Gentlemen," said Jo, gravely, "I am agreeable to become a good and chattel for this occasion only, as the playbills say, and hold myself up to the highest bidder."

"Nay, you are sold to me, Bumpus," said Gascoyne, "and must do as I bid you."

"Wery good, then bid away as fast as you like."

"Come, captain, don't be hard," said Henry: "what will you take for him?"

"I cannot afford to sell him at any price," replied the other, "for I have brought him here expressly as a gift to a certain Mary Stuart, queen of women, if not of Scotland,—a widow who dwells in Sandy Cove—"

"What, my mother?" interrupted Henry, while a shade of displeasure crossed his countenance at what he deemed the insolent familiarity with which Gascoyne mentioned her name.

"The same. On my last visit I promised to get her a man-servant who could do her some service in keeping off the savages when they take a fancy to trouble the settlement; and if Bumpus is willing to try his luck on shore, I promise him he'll find her a good mistress, and her house pleasant quarters."

"So," exclaimed the stout seaman, stopping short in his rolling walk, and gazing earnestly into his captain's face, "I'm to be sold to a woman?"

"With your own consent entirely, Master Bumpus," said Gascoyne, with a smile.

"Come, Jo," cried. Henry, gaily, "I see you like the prospect, and feel assured that you and; I shall be good friends. Give us your flipper, my boy!"

John Bumpus allowed the youth to seize and shake a "flipper," which would have done credit to a walrus, both in regard to shape and size. After a short pause he said, "Whether you and me shall be good friends, young man, depends entirely on the respect which you show to the family of the Bumpuses—said family havin' comed over to Ireland with the Conkerer in the year—, ah! I misremember the year, but that don't matter, bein' a subject of no consarn wotiver, 'xcept to schoolboys who'll get their licks if they can't tell, and sarve 'em right too. But if you're willin' I'm agreeable, and there's an end o' the whole affair."

So saying, John Bumpus suffered a bland smile to light up his ruddy countenance, and resumed his march in the "wake," as he expressed it, of his companions.

Half an hour later they arrived at Sandy Cove, a small native settlement and mission station, and were soon seated at the hospitable board of Widow Stuart.

CHAPTER IV
THE MISSIONARY—SUSPICIONS, SURPRISES, AND SURMISES

Sandy Cove was a small settlement, inhabited partly by native converts to Christianity, and partly by a few European traders, who, having found that the place was in the usual track of South-Sea whalers, and frequently visited by that class of vessels as well as by other ships, had established several stores or trading-houses, and had taken up their permanent abode there.

The island was one of those the natives of which were early induced to agree to the introduction of the gospel. At the time of which we write, it was in that transition state which renders the work of the missionary one of anxiety, toil, and extreme danger, as well as one of love.

But the Rev. Frederick Mason was a man eminently fitted to fill the post which he had selected as his sphere of labor. Bold and manly in the extreme, he was more like a soldier in outward aspect than a missionary. Yet the gentleness of the lamb dwelt in his breast and beamed in his eye; and to a naturally indomitable and enthusiastic disposition was added burning zeal in the cause of his beloved Master.

Six years previous to the opening of our tale, he had come to Sandy Cove with his wife and child, the latter a girl of six years of age at that time. In one year death bereaved the missionary of his wife, and, about the same time, war broke out in the island between the chiefs who clung to the idolatrous rites and bloody practises peculiar to the inhabitants of the South Sea Islands, and those chiefs who were inclined to favor Christianity. This war continued to rage more or less violently for several years, frequently slumbering, sometimes breaking out with sudden violence, like the fitful eruptions of the still unextinct volcanoes in those distant, regions.

During all this period of bloodshed and alarms, the missionary stuck to his post. The obstinacy of hatred was being gradually overcome by the superior pertinacity of zeal in a good cause, and the invariable practise—so incomprehensible to the savage mind—of returning good for evil. The result was that the Sabbath bell still sent its tinkling sound over the verdant slopes above Sandy Cove, and the hymn of praise still arose, morning and evening, from the little church, which, composed partly of wood, partly of coral rock, had been erected under the eye, and, to a large extent, by the hands, of the missionary.

But false friends within the camp were more dangerous and troublesome to Mr. Mason than avowed enemies without. Some of the European traders, especially, who settled on the island a few years after the missionary had made it habitable, were the worst foes he had to contend with.

In the same vessel that brought the missionary to the island, there came a widow, Mrs. Stuart, with her son Henry, then a stout lad of thirteen. The widow was not, however, a member of the missionary's household. She came there to settle with her son, who soon built her a rudely-constructed but sufficiently habitable hut, which, in after years, was inclosed, and greatly improved; so that it at last assumed the dimensions of a rambling picturesque cottage, whitewashed, brilliant, and neat in its setting of bright green.

The widow, although not an official assistant to the missionary, was nevertheless a most efficient one. She taught in his schools, being familiar with the native tongue; and, when the settlement grew in numbers, both of white and black, she became known as the good angel of the place,—the one who was ever ready with sympathy for the sorrowful, and comfort for the dying. She was fair and fragile, and had been exceedingly beautiful; but care had stamped his mark deeply in her brow. Neither care nor time, however, could mar the noble outline of her fine features, or equal the love that beamed in her gentle eyes.

The widow was a great mystery to the gossips of Sandy Cove; for there are gossips even in the most distant isles of the sea. Some men (we refer, of course, to white men) thought that she must have been the wife of an admiral at least, and had fallen into distressed circumstances, and gone to these islands to hide her poverty. Others said she was a female Jesuit in disguise, sent there to counteract the preaching of the gospel by the missionary. A few even ventured to hint their opinion that she was an outlaw, "or something of that sort," and shrewdly suspected that Mr. Mason knew more about her than he was pleased to tell. But no one, either by word or look, had ever ventured to express an opinion of any kind to herself, or in the hearing of her son. The latter, indeed, displayed such uncommon breadth of shoulders, and such unusual development of muscle, that it was seldom necessary for him—even in those savage regions and wild times—to display anything else in order to make men respectful.

While our three friends were doing justice to the bacon and breadfruit set before them by Widow Stuart, the widow herself was endeavoring to repress some strong feeling, which caused her breast to heave more than once, and induced her to turn to some trifling piece of household duty to conceal her emotion. These symptoms were not lost upon her son, whose suspicions and anger had been aroused by the familiarity of Gascoyne. Making some excuse for leaving the room, towards the conclusion of the meal, he followed his mother to an outhouse, whither she had gone to fetch some fresh milk.

"Mother," said Henry, respectfully, yet with an unwonted touch of sternness in his voice; "there is some mystery connected with this man Gascoyne that I feel convinced you can clear up—"

"Dear Henry," interrupted the widow, and her cheek grew pale as she spoke, "do not, I beseech you, press me on this subject. I cannot clear it up."

"Say you *will* not, mother," answered Henry, in a tone of disappointment.

"I would if I dared," continued the widow. "The time may come when I—"

"But why not now," urged the youth, hastily. "I am old enough, surely, to be trusted. During the four visits this man has paid to us, I have observed a degree of familiarity on his part which no man has a right to exhibit towards you; and which, did I not see that you permit it, no man would *dare* to show. Why do you allow him to call you 'Mary?' No one else in the settlement does so."

"He is a very old friend," replied the widow, sadly. "I have known him from childhood. We were playmates long ago."

"Humph, that's some sort of reason, no doubt; but you don't appear to like him, and his presence always seems to give you pain. Why do you suffer yourself to be annoyed by him? Only say the word, mother, and I'll kick him out of the house, neck and crop—"

"Hush, boy; you are too violent."

"Too violent! Why, it would make a coward violent to see his mother tormented as you are by this fellow, and not to be allowed to put a stop to it. I suspect—"

"Henry," said the widow, again interrupting her exasperated son, "do you think your mother would do what is wrong?"

"Mother," exclaimed the youth, seizing her hand, and kissing her brow almost violently, "I would as soon think that the angels above would do wrong; but I firmly believe that you are suffering wrong to be done *to you*; and—just listen to the fellow! I do not believe he's howling for more bacon at this moment!"

There could be no doubt whatever about the fact; for just then the deep tones of Gascoyne's voice rang through the cottage, as he reiterated the name of the widow, who hastened away, followed by her son. Henry scarcely took the trouble to conceal the frown that darkened his brow as he re-entered the apartment where his companions were seated.

"Why, Mary, your bacon surpasses anything I have tasted for the last six months; let's have another rasher, like a good woman. That mountain air sharpens the appetite amazingly; especially of men who are more accustomed to mount the rigging of a ship than the hills on shore. What say you, John Bumpus?"

John Bumpus could not at that moment say anything, in consequence of his mouth being so full of the bacon referred to that there was no room for a single word to pass his lips. In the height of his good-humor, however, he did his best by signs to express his entire approval of the widow's provender, and even *attempted* to speak. In so doing he choked himself, and continued in convulsions for the next five minutes, to the immense delight of the captain, who vowed he had never before seen such a blue face in the whole course of his life.

While this scene was enacting, and ere Jo Bumpus had effectually wiped away the tears from his eyes, and cleared the bacon out of his windpipe, the door opened, and the commander of H.M.S. Talisman entered.

Edmund Montague was a young man to hold such a responsible position in the navy; but he was a bold, vigorous little Englishman,—a sort of gentlemanly and well-educated John Bull terrier; a frank address, agreeable manners, and an utterly reckless temperament, which was qualified and curbed, however, by good sense and hard-earned experience.

"Good-day to you, Mrs. Stuart; I trust you will forgive my abrupt intrusion, but urgent business must be my excuse. I have called to have a little further conversation with your son respecting that rascally pirate who has given me so much trouble. If he will have the good ness to take a short walk with me, I shall be much indebted."

"By all means," said Henry, rising and putting on his cap.

"Perhaps," said Gascoyne, as they were about to leave the

room, "if the commander of the Talisman would condescend to take a little information from a stranger, he might learn something to the purpose regarding the pirate Durward; for he it is, I presume, of whom you are in search."

"I shall be happy to gain information from any source," replied Montague, eying the captain narrowly, "Are you a resident in this island?"

"No, I am not; my home is on the sea, and has been since I was a lad."

"Ah! you have fallen in with this pirate, then, on your native ocean, I fancy, and have disagreeable cause to remember him, perchance," said Montague, smiling. "Has he given you much trouble?"

"Aye, that he has," replied Gascoyne, with a sudden scowl of ferocity. "No one in these seas has received so much annoyance from him as I have. Any one who could rid them of his presence would do good service to the cause of humanity. But," he added, while a grim smile overspread his handsome face, "it is said that few vessels can cope with his schooner in speed, and I can answer for it that he is a bold man, fond of fighting, with plenty of reckless cut-throats to back him, and more likely to give chase to a sloop-of-war than to show her his heels. I trust you are well manned and armed, Captain Montague; for this Durward is a desperate fellow, I assure you."

The young commander's countenance flushed as he replied, "Your anxiety on my account, sir, is quite uncalled for. Had I nothing but my own longboat wherewith to attack this pirate, it would be my duty to do so. I had scarcely expected to find unmanly fears exhibited in one so stalwart in appearance as you are. Perhaps it may relieve you to know that I am both well manned and armed. It is not usual for a British man-of-war to cruise in distant seas in a less suitable condition to protect her flag. And yet, methinks, one who has spent so many years of his life on salt water might know the difference between a frigate and a sloop-of-war."

"Be not so hasty, young man," answered Gascoyne, gravely; "you are not on your own quarter-deck just now. There ought to be civility between strangers. I may, indeed, be very ignorant of the cut and rig of British war vessels, seeing that I am but a plain trader in seas where ships of war are not often wont to unfurl their flags, but there can be no harm, and there was meant no offense, in warning you to be on your guard."

A tinge of sarcasm still lingered in Captain Montague's tone as he replied, "Well, I thank you for the caution. But to come to the point, what know you of this pirate,—this Durward, as he calls himself; though I have no doubt he has sailed under so many aliases that he may have forgotten his real name."

"I know him to be a villain," replied Gascoyne.

"That much I know as well as you," said Montague.

"And yet it is said he takes fits of remorse at times, and would fain change his way of life if he could," continued Gascoyne.

"That I might guess," returned the other; "most wicked men have their seasons of remorse. Can you tell me nothing of him more definite than this, friend?"

"I can tell you that he is the very bane of my existence," said Gascoyne, the angry expression again flitting for a moment across his countenance, "He not only pursues and haunts me like my own shadow, but he gets me into scrapes by passing his schooner off for mine when he is caught."

The young officer glanced in surprise at the speaker as he uttered these words.

"Indeed," said he, "that is a strange confusion of ideas. So, then, the two schooners bear so strong a resemblance as to be easily mistaken for each other?"

"They are twins. They were built at the same time, from the same molds, and were intended for the sandal-wood trade between these islands and Calcutta, Manila, and Australia. One of them, the Avenger, was seized on her first voyage by this

Durward, then mate of the schooner, and has ever since scoured the South Seas as a pirate; the other, named the Foam, which I have the misfortune to command, still continues the traffic for which she was originally built."

"Ha!" exclaimed Montague, turning suddenly round with an inquiring gaze at the stalwart figure of the sandal-wood trader; "it is most fortunate that I have met with you, Mr. Gascoyne. I doubt not that you can conduct me to this vessel of yours, so that I may know the pirate when I fall in with him. If the two vessels resemble each other so closely, a sight of the Foam will be of great service to me in my search after the Avenger."

"You are most welcome to a sight of my craft," replied Gascoyne. "The only difference between the two is, that the figurehead of the pirate is a griffin's head, painted scarlet; that of my schooner is a female, painted white. There is also a red streak round the sides of the pirate; the hull of the Foam is entirely black."

"Will you come on board my vessel, and accompany me in one of my boats to yours?" inquired Montague.

"That is impossible," replied Gascoyne. "I came here on urgent business, which will not brook delay; but my schooner lies on the other side of the island. If you pull round, my mate will receive you. You will find him a most intelligent and hospitable man. He will conduct you over the vessel, and give you all the information you may desire. Meanwhile," added the captain of the Foam, rising and putting on his cap, "I must bid you adieu."

"Nay, but you have not yet told me when or where you last saw or heard of this remarkable pirate, who is so clever at representing other people; perhaps I should rather say misrepresenting them," said Montague, with a meaning smile.

"I saw him no longer ago than this morning," replied Gascoyne, gravely. "He is now in these waters, with what intent I know not, unless from his unnatural delight in persecuting me, or, perhaps, because fate has led him into the very jaws of the lion."

"Humph! he will find that I bite before I roar, if he does get between my teeth," said the young officer.

"Surely you are mistaken, Gascoyne," interposed Henry Stuart, who, along with John Bumpus, had hitherto been silent listeners to the foregoing conversation. "Several of our people have been out fishing among the islands, and have neither seen nor heard of this redoubted pirate."

"That is possible enough, boy; but I have seen him, nevertheless, and I shall be much surprised if you do not see and hear more of him than you desire before many days are out. That villain does not sail the seas for pastime, you may depend on it."

As Gascoyne said this, the outer door of the house was burst violently open, and the loud voice of a boy was heard in the porch or short passage that intervened between it and the principal apartment of the cottage shouting wildly—"Ho! hallo! hurrah! I says Widow Stuart! Henry! here's a business—sich fun! only think, the pirate's turned up at last, and murdered half the niggers in—"

There was an abrupt stoppage both of the voice and the muscular action of this juvenile tornado as he threw open the door with a crash, and, instead of the widow or her son, met the gaze of so many strangers. The boy stood for a few seconds on the threshold, with his curly brown hair disheveled, and his dark eyes staring in surprise, first at one, then at another of the party, until at length they alighted on John Bumpus. The mouth which up to that moment had formed a round O of astonishment, relaxed into a broad grin, and, with sudden energy, exclaimed: "*What* a grampus!"

Having uttered this complimentary remark, the urchin was about to retreat, when Henry made a sudden dart at him, and caught him by the collar.

"Where got you the news, Will Corrie?" said Henry giving

the boy a squeeze with his strong hand.

"Oh, please, be merciful, Henry, and I'll tell you all about it. But, pray, don't give me over to that grampus," cried the lad, pretending to whimper. "I got the news from a feller, that said he'd got it from a feller, that saw a feller, who said he'd heard a feller tell another feller, that he saw a *black* feller in the bush, somewhere or other 'tween this and the other end o' the island, with a shot-hole in his right arm, running like a cogolampus, with ten pirates in full chase. Ah! oh! have mercy, Henry; really, my constitution will break down if you—"

"Silence, you chatter-box! and give me a reasonable account of what you have heard or seen, if you can."

The volatile urchin, who might have been about thirteen years of age, became preternaturally grave all of a sudden, and, looking up earnestly in his questioner's face, said, "Really, Henry, you are becoming unreasonable in your old age, to ask me to give you a reasonable account of a thing, and at the same time to be silent!"

"I'll tell you what, Corrie, I'll throttle you if you don't speak," said Henry.

"Ah! you *couldn't*," pleaded Corrie, in a tone of deep pathos.

"P'raps," observed John Bumpus, "p'raps if you hand over the young gen'l'm'n to the 'grampus,' *he'll* make him speak."

On hearing this, the boy set up a howl of affected despair, and suffered Henry to lead him unresistingly to within a few feet of Bumpus; but, just as he was within an inch of the huge fist of that nautical monster, he suddenly wrenched his collar out of his captor's grasp, darted to the door, turned round on the threshold, hit the side of his own nose a sounding slap with the forefinger of his right hand, uttered an unexpressively savage yell, vanished from the scene, and,

> *"Like the baseless fabric of a vision,*
> *Left not a wreck behind,"*

except the wreck of the milk-saucer of the household cat, which sagacious creature had wisely taken to flight at the first symptom of war.

The boy was instantly followed by Henry, but so light was his foot, that the fastest runner in the settlement had to penetrate the woods immediately behind his mother's house for a quarter of a mile before he succeeded in again laying hold of the refractory lad's collar.

"What do you mean, Corrie, by such conduct?" said his captor, shaking him vigorously. "I have half a mind to give you a walloping."

"Never do anything by halves, Henry," said the boy, mildly. "*I* never do. It's a bad habit; always go the whole length or none. Now that we are alone, I'll give you a reasonable account of what I know, if you'll remove your hand from my collar. You forget that I am growing, and that, when I am big enough, the day of reckoning between us will surely come!"

"But why would you not give me the information I want in the house. The people you saw there are as much interested in it as I am."

"Oh! are they?" returned Corrie, with a glance of peculiar meaning; "perhaps they are *more* interested than you are."

"How so?"

"Why, how do I know, and how do you know, that these fellows are not pirates in disguise?"

"Because," said Henry, "one of them is an old friend,—that is, an acquaintance—at least a sort of intimate, who has been many and many a time at our house before, and my mother knows him well. I can't say I like him,—that is to say, I don't exactly like some of his ways,—though I don't dislike the man himself."

"A most unsatisfactory style of reply, Henry, for a man—ah, beg pardon, a boy—of your straightforward character. Which o' the three are you speaking of—the grampus?"

"No, the other big, handsome-looking fellow."

"And you're sure you've known him long?" continued the boy, while an expression of perplexity flitted over his face.

"Quite sure;—why?"

"Because *I* have seen you often enough, and your house and your mother,—not to mention your cat and your pigs, and hens; but I've never seen *him* before to-day."

"That's because he usually comes at night, and seldom stays more than an hour or two."

"A most uncomfortable style of acquaintance," said Corrie, trying to look wise, which was an utterly futile effort, seeing that his countenance was fat and round and rosy, and very much the reverse of philosophical. "But how do you know that the grampus is not the pirate?"

"Because he is one of Gascoyne's men."

"Oh! his name is Gascoyne, is it?—a most piratical name it is. However, since he is your friend, Henry, it's all right; what's t'other's name?"

"Bumpus—John Bumpus."

On hearing this, the boy clapped both hands to his sides, expanded his eyes and mouth, showed his teeth, and finally gave vent to roars of uncontrollable laughter, swaying his body about the while as if in agony.

"Oh dear!" he cried, after a time, "John Bumpus, ha! ha! the grampus—why, it's magnicicent, ha! ha!" and again the boy gave free vent to his merriment, while his companion looked on with a quiet grin of amusement.

Presently Corrie became grave, and said, "But what of the third, the little chap, all over gold lace? P'r'aps he's the pirate. He looked bold enough a'most for any thing."

"Why, you goose, that's the commander of his Britannic Majesty's frigate Talisman."

"Indeed? I hope his Britannic Majesty has many more like

him."

"Plenty more like him. But come, boy; what have you heard of this pirate, and what do you mean about a wounded nigger?"

"I just mean this," answered the lad, suddenly becoming serious, "that when I was out on the mountain this morning, I thought I would cross the ridge, and when I did so, the first thing I saw was a schooner lying in the bay at the foot of the hill, where you and I have so often gone chasing pigs together. Well, being curious to know what sort of a craft she was, I went down the hill, intendin' to go aboard; but before I'd got half way through the cocoanut grove, I heard a horrible yell of a savage. So, thinks I, here comes them blackguard pagans again, to attack the settlement; and before I could hide out of the way, a naked savage almost ran into my arms. He was sea-green in the face with fright, and blood was running over his right arm.

"The moment he saw me, instead of splitting me up with his knife and eating me alive, as these fellers are so fond of doin', he gave a start, and another great cry, and doubled on his track like a hare. His cry was answered by a shout from half a dozen sailors, who burst out of the thicket at that moment, and I saw they were in pursuit of him. Down I went at once behind a thick bush, and the whole lot o' the blind bats passed right on in full cry, within half an inch of my nose. And never saw sich a set o' piratical-looking villains since I was born. I felt quite sure that yon schooner is the pirate that has been doing so much mischief hereabouts; so I came back as fast as my legs could carry me, to tell you what I had seen. There, you have got all that I know of the matter now."

"You are wrong, boy. The schooner you saw is not the pirate; it is the Foam. Strange, very strange!" muttered Henry.

"What's strange," inquired the lad.

"Not the appearance of the wounded nigger," answered the other; "I can explain all about him, but the sailors—that puzzles me."

Henry then related the morning's adventure to his young companion.

"But," continued he, after detailing all that the reader already knows, "I cannot comprehend how the pirates you speak of could have landed without their vessel being in sight; and that nothing is to be seen from the mountain-tops except the Talisman on the one side of the island and the Foam on the other, I can vouch for. Boats might lie concealed among the rocks on the shore, no doubt. But no boats would venture to put ashore with hostile intentions, unless the ship to which they belonged were within sight. As for the crew of the Foam, they are ordinary seamen, and not likely to amuse themselves chasing wounded savages, even if they were allowed to go ashore, which I think is not likely; for Gascoyne knows well enough that that side of the island is inhabited by the pagans, who would as soon kill and eat a man as they would a pig."

"Sooner,—the monsters!" exclaimed the boy, indignantly; for he had, on more than one occasion, been an eyewitness of the horrible practise of cannibalism which prevails, even at the present day, among some of the South Sea islanders.

"There is a mystery here," said Henry, starting up, "and the sooner we alarm the people of the settlement, the better. Come, Corrie, we shall return to the house, and let the British officer hear what you have told me."

When the lad had finished relating his adventure to the party in Widow Stuart's cottage, Gascoyne said quietly, "I would advise you, Captain Montague, to return to your ship and make your preparations for capturing this pirate, for that he is even now almost within range of your guns, I have not the slightest doubt. As to the men appearing piratical-looking fellows to this boy, I don't wonder at that; most men are wild enough when their blood is up. Some of my own men are as savage to look at as one would desire. But I gave strict orders this morning that only a few were to go ashore, and these were to keep well out of sight of the settlement of the savages. Doubtless they are all aboard by this time. If you decide upon anything like a hunt among the mountains, I can lend you a few hands."

"Thank you. I may perhaps require some of your hands," said Montague, with a dash of sarcasm in his tone; "meanwhile, since you will not favor me with your company on board, I shall bid you good afternoon."

He bowed stiffly, and leaving the cottage, hastened on board his ship where the shrill notes of the boatswain's whistle, and the deep hoarse tones of that officer's gruff voice, quickly announced to the people on shore that orders had been promptly given, and were in course of being as promptly obeyed.

During the hour that followed these events, the captain of the Foam was closeted with Widow Stuart and her son, and the youthful Corrie was engaged in laying the foundations of a never-to-die friendship with John Bumpus, or, as that eccentric youngster preferred to style him, Jo Grampus.

CHAPTER V

THE PASTOR'S HOUSEHOLD — PREPARATIONS FOR WAR

When the conference in the widow's cottage closed, Henry Stuart and Gascoyne hastened into the woods together, and followed a narrow foot-path which led towards the interior of the island. Arriving at a spot where this path branched into two, Henry took the one that ran round the outskirts of the settlement towards the residence of Mr. Mason, while his companion pursued the other which struck into the recesses of the mountains.

"Come in," cried the missionary, as Henry knocked at the door of his study. "Ah, Henry, I'm glad to see you. You were in my thoughts this moment. I have come to a difficulty in my drawings of the spire of our new church, and I want your fertile imagination to devise some plan whereby we may overcome it. But of that I shall speak presently. I see from your looks that more important matters have brought you hither. Nothing wrong at the cottage, I trust?"

"No, nothing—that is to say, not exactly wrong; but things, I fear, are not altogether right in the settlement. I have had an unfortunate rencounter this morning with one of the savages, which is likely to lead to mischief; for blood was drawn, and I know the fellow to be revengeful. In addition to this, it is suspected that Durward, the pirate, is hovering among the islands, and meditates a descent on us. How much truth there may be in the report I cannot pretend to guess; but Gascoyne, the captain of the Foam, has been over at our cottage, and says he has seen the pirate, and that there is no saying what he may venture to attempt; for he is a bold fellow, and, as you know, cannot have a good will to missionary settlements."

"I'm not so sure of that," said the pastor, in answer to the last remark. "It is well known that wherever a Christian settlement is founded in these islands, that place becomes a safe port for vessels of all sorts, pirates as well as others, if they sail under false colors and pretend to be honest traders,—while in all the other islands, it is equally well known, the only safety one can count on, in landing, is superior force. But I am grieved to hear of your affray with the native. I hope that life will not be sacrificed."

"No fear of that; the rascal got only a flesh-wound."

Here the young man related his adventure of the morning, and finished by asking what the pastor advised should be done in the way of precaution.

"It seems to me," said Mr. Mason, gravely, "that our chief difficulty will be to save ourselves from our friends—"

"Would friends harm us, father?" asked a sweet, soft voice at the pastor's elbow. Next moment Alice Mason was seated on her father's knee, gazing up in his face with an expression of undisguised amazement.

Alice was a fair, delicate, gentle child. Twelve summers and winters had passed over her little head without a cloud to obscure the sunshine of her life save one; but that one was a terribly dark one, and its shadow lingered over her for many years. When Alice lost her mother, she lost the joy and delight of her existence, and although six years had passed since that awful day, and a fond Christian father had done his best to impress on her young mind that the beloved one was not lost forever, but would one day be found sitting at the feet of Jesus in a bright and beautiful world, the poor child could not recover her former elasticity of spirits. Doubtless her isolated position, and the want of suitable companions, had something to do with the prolonged sadness of her little heart.

It is almost unnecessary to say that her love for her father was boundless. This was natural, but it did not seem by any means so natural that the delicate child should give the next place in her heart to a wild little boy, a black girl, and a ragged little dog! Yet so it was, and it would have been difficult for the closest observer to tell which of these three Alice liked best.

No one could so frequently draw forth the merry laugh that in former days had rung so sweetly over the hillsides of the verdant isle as our young friend Will Corrie. Nothing could delight the heart of the child so much as to witness the mad gambols, not to mention the mischievous deeds, of that ragged little piece of an old door-mat, which, in virtue of its being possessed of animal life, was named Toozle. And when Alice wished to talk quietly,—to pour out her heart, and sometimes her tears,—the bosom she sought on which to lay her head, next to her father's, was that of her useful nursery-maid, a good, kind, and gentle, but an awfully stupid native girl, named Kekupoopi.

This name was, of course, reduced in its fair proportions by little Alice, who, however, retained the latter part thereof in preference to the former, and styled her maid Poopy. Young Master Corrie, on the other hand, called her Kickup or Puppy, indifferently, according to the humor he chanced to be in when he met her, or to the word that rose most readily to his lips.

Mr. Mason replied to the question put by Alice, at the beginning of this somewhat lengthy digression, "No, my lamb, friends would not willingly do us harm; but there are those who call themselves friends who do not deserve the name, who pretend to be such, but who are in reality secret enemies. But go, dearest, to your room; I am busy just now talking with Henry: he, at least, is a trusty friend. When I have done, you shall come back to me."

Alice kissed her father, and, getting off his knee, went at once in search of her friend Poopy.

That dark-skinned and curly black-headed domestic was in the kitchen, seated on the bottom of an overturned iron pot, inside the dingy niche in which the domestic fire was wont to burn when anything of a culinary nature was going on. At the time when her mistress entered, nothing of the kind was in progress, and the fire had subsided to extinction.

The girl, who might have been any age between twelve and sixteen,—nearer the latter, perhaps, than the former,—was gazing with expressionless eyes straight before her, and thinking, evidently, of—nothing. She was clothed in a white tunic, from which her black legs, arms, neck, and head protruded—forming a startling contrast therewith.

"O Poopy! what a bad girl you are!" cried Alice, laughing, as she observed where her maid was seated.

Poopy's visage at once beamed with a look of good-humor, a wide gash suddenly appeared somewhere near her chin, displaying a double row of brilliant teeth surrounded by red gums; at the same time the whites of her eyes disappeared, because, being very plump, it was a physical impossibility that she should laugh and keep them uncovered.

"Hee! hee!" exclaimed Poopy.

We are really sorry to give the reader a false impression, as we feel that we have done, of our friend Kekupoopi, but a regard for truth compels us to show the worst of her character first. She was not demonstrative; and the few words and signs by which she endeavored to communicate the state of her feelings to the outward world were not easily interpreted except by those who knew her well. There is no doubt whatever that Poopy was—we scarcely like to use the expression, but we know of no other more appropriate—a donkey! We hasten to guard ourselves from misconstruction here. That word, if used in an ill-natured and passionate manner, is a bad one, and by no means to be countenanced; but, as surgeons may cut off legs at times, without thereby sanctioning the indiscriminate practise of amputation in a miscellaneous sort of way as a pastime, so this otherwise objectionable word may, we think, be used to bring out a certain trait of character in full force. Holding this opinion, and begging the reader to observe that we make the statement gravely and in an entirely philosophical, way, we repeat that Poopy was, figuratively speaking, a donkey!

Yet she was an amiable, affectionate, good girl for all that, with an amount of love in her heart for her young mistress which words cannot convey, and which it is no wonder, therefore, that Poopy herself could not adequately express either by word or look.

"It's all very well for you to sit there and say 'Hee! hee!'" cried Alice, advancing to the fireplace; "but you must have made a dreadful mark on your clean white frock. Get up and turn round."

"Hee! hee!" exclaimed the girl, as she obeyed the mandate.

The "Oh! oh!! oh!!!" that burst from Alice, on observing the pattern of the pot neatly printed off on Poopy's garment, was so emphatic that the girl became impressed with the fact that she had done something wrong, and twisted her head and neck in a most alarming manner in a series of vain attempts to behold the extent of the damage.

"*What* a figure!" exclaimed Alice, on recovering from the first shock.

"It vill vash," said Poopy, in a deprecatory tone.

"I hope it will," replied Alice, shaking her head doubtfully; for her experience in the laundry had not yet been so extensive as to enable her to pronounce at once on the eradicability of such a frightfully deep impression. While she was still shaking her head in dubiety on this point, and while Poopy was still making futile attempts to obtain a view of the spot, the door of the kitchen opened, and Master Corrie swaggered in, with his hands thrust into the outer pockets of his jacket, his shirt collar thrown very much open, and his round straw hat placed very much on the back of his head; for, having seen some of the crew of the Talisman, he had been smitten with a strong desire to imitate a man-of-war's-man in aspect and gait.

At his heels came that scampering mass of ragged door-mat

Toozle, who, feeling that a sensation of some kind or other was being got up for his amusement, joined heartily in the shout of delight that burst from the youthful Corrie when he beheld the extraordinary figure in the fireplace.

"Well, I say, Kickup," cried the youth, picking up his hat, which had fallen off in the convulsion, and drying his tears, "you're a sweet-lookin' creetur, you are! Is this a new frock you've got to go to church with? Come, I rather like that pattern; but there's not quite enough of 'em. Suppose I lend a hand and print a few more all over you? There's plenty of pots and pans here to do it; and if Alice will bring down her white frock I'll give it a touch-up too."

"How can you talk such nonsense, Corrie!" said Alice, laughing. "Down, Toozle; silence, sir. Go, my dear Poopy, and put on another frock; and make haste, for I have something to say to you."

Thus admonished, the girl ran to a small apartment that opened off the kitchen, and speedily reappeared in another tunic. Meanwhile, Corrie had seated himself on the floor, with Toozle between his knees and Alice on a stool at his side. Poopy, in a fit of absence of mind, was about to resume her seat on the iron pot, when a simultaneous shriek, bark, and roar recalled her scattered faculties, produced a "hee! hee!" varied with a faint "ho!" and induced her to sit down on the floor beside her mistress.

"Now, tell me, Poopy," said Alice, "did you ever hear of friends who were not really friends, but enemies?"

The girl stared with a vacant countenance at the bright, intelligent face of the child, and shook her head slowly.

"Why don't you ask *me*?" inquired Corrie. "You might as well ask Toozle as that potato Kickup. Eh? Puppy, don't you confess that you are no better than a vegetable? Come, now, be honest."

"Hee! hee!" replied Poopy.

"Humph! I thought so. But that's an odd question of yours, Alice. What do you mean by it?"

"I mean that my papa thinks there are friends in the settlement who are enemies."

"Does he, though? Now that's mysterious," said the boy, becoming suddenly grave. "That requires to be looked to. Come, Alice, tell me all the particulars. Don't omit anything—our lives may depend on it."

The deeply serious manner in which Corrie said this so impressed and solemnized the child, that she related, word for word, the brief conversation she had had with her father, and all that she had heard of the previous converse between him and Henry.

When she had concluded, Master Corrie threw a still more grave and profoundly philosophical expression into his chubby face, and asked, in a hollow tone of voice, "Your father didn't say anything against the Grampus, did he?"

"The what?" inquired Alice.

"The Grampus,—the man, at least, whom *I* call the Grampus, and who calls hisself Jo Bumpus."

"I did not hear such names mentioned; but Henry spoke of a wounded nigger."

"Aye, they're all a set of false rascals together," said Corrie.

"Niggers ob dis here settlement is good mans, ebery von," said Poopy, promptly.

"Hallo! Kickup, wot's wrong? I never heard you say so much at one time since I came to this place."

"Niggers is good peepils," reiterated the girl.

"So they are, Puppy, and you're the best of 'em; but I was speakin' of the fellers on the other side of the island,—d'ye see?"

"Hee! hee!" ejaculated the girl.

"Well, but what makes you so anxious?" said Alice, looking earnestly into the boy's face.

Corrie laid his hand on her head and stroked her fair hair as he replied:

"This is a serious matter, Alice; I must go at once and see your father about it."

He rose with an air of importance, as if about to leave the kitchen.

"Oh! but please don't go till you have told me what it is; I'm so frightened," said, Alice; "do stay and tell me about it before you go to papa."

"Well, I don't mind if I do," said the boy, sitting down again. "You must know, then, that it's reported there are pirates on the island."

"Oh!" exclaimed Alice.

"D'ye know what pirates are, Puppy?"

"Hee! hee!" answered the girl.

"I do believe she don't know nothin'," said the boy, looking at her with an air of compassion; "wot a sad thing it is to belong to a lower species of human natur! Well, I s'pose it can't be helped. A pirate, Kickup, is a sea-robber. D'ye understand?"

"Ho! ho!"

"Aye, I thought so. Well, Alice, I am told that there's been a lot of them landed on the island and took to chasin' and killin' the niggers, and Henry was all but killed by one o' the niggers this very morning, an' was saved by a big feller that's a mystery to me, and by the Grampus, who is the best feller I ever met,—a regular trump, he is; and there's all sorts o' doubts, and fears, and rumors, and things of that sort, with a captain of the British navy, that you and I have read so much about, trying to find this pirate out, and suspectin' everybody he meets is him. I only hope he won't take it into his stupid head to mistake *me* for him,—not so unlikely a thing, after all." And the youthful Corrie shook his head with much gravity, as he surveyed his rotund little legs complacently.

"What are you laughing at?" he added, suddenly, on observing that a bright smile had overspread Alice's face.

"At the idea of you being taken for a pirate," said the child.

"Hee! hee! ho! ho!" remarked Poopy.

"Silence, you lump of black putty!" thundered the aspiring youth.

"Come, don't be cross to my maid," said Alice, quickly.

Corrie laughed, and was about to continue his discourse on the events and rumors of the day, when Mr. Mason's voice was heard at the other end of the house.

"Ho! Corrie."

"That's me," cried the boy, promptly springing up and rushing out of the room.

"Here, my boy; I thought I heard your voice. I want you to go a message for me. Run down, like a good lad, to Ole Thorwald, and tell him to come up here as soon as he conveniently can. There are matters to consult about which will not brook delay."

"Ay, ay, sir," answered Corrie, sailor fashion, as he touched his forelock and bounded from the room.

"Off on pressing business," cried the sanguine youth, as he dashed through the kitchen, frightening Alice, and throwing Toozle into convulsions of delight,—"horribly important business, that 'won't brook delay;' but what *brook* means is more than I can guess."

Before the sentence was finished, Corrie was far down the hill, leaping over every obstacle like a deer. On passing through a small field he observed a native bending down, as if picking weeds, with his back towards him. Going softly up behind, he hit the semi-naked savage a sounding slap, and exclaimed, as he passed on, "Hallo! Jackolu; important business, my boy—hurrah!"

The native to whom this rough salutation was given was a tall, stalwart young fellow, who had for some years been one of the best-behaved and most active members of Frederick Mason's dark-skinned congregation. He stood erect for some time, with a broad grin on his swarthy face and a twinkle in his eye, as he gazed after the young hopeful, muttering to himself, "Ho! yes—bery wicked boy dat, bery; but hims capital chap, for all dat."

A few minutes later, Master Corrie burst in upon the sturdy middle-aged merchant, named Ole Thorwald, a Norwegian, who had resided much in England, and spoke the English language well, and who prided himself on being entitled to claim descent from the old Norwegian sea-kings. This man was uncle and protector to Corrie.

"Ho! Uncle Ole; here's a business. Sich a to-do—wounds, blood, and murder! or at least an attempt at it;—the whole settlement in arms, and the parson sends for you to take command!"

"What means the boy!" exclaimed Ole Thorwald, who, in virtue of his having once been a private in a regiment of militia, had been appointed to the chief command of the military department of the settlement. This consisted of about thirty white men, armed with fourteen fowling-pieces, twenty daggers, fifteen swords, and eight cavalry pistols; and about two hundred native Christians, who, when the assaults of their unconverted brethren were made, armed themselves—as they were wont to do in days gone by—with formidable clubs, stone hatchets, and spears. "What means the boy!" exclaimed Ole, laying down a book which he had been reading, and thrusting his spectacles up on his broad bald forehead.

"Exactly what the boy says," replied Master Corrie.

"Then add something more to it, pray."

Thorwald said this in a mild tone; but he suddenly seized the handle of an old pewter mug which the lad knew, from experience, would certainly reach his head before he could gain the door if he did not behave; so he became polite, and condescended to explain his errand more fully.

"So, so," observed the descendant of the sea-kings, as he rose and slowly buckled on a huge old cavalry saber; "there is double mischief brewing this time. Well, we shall see—we shall see.

Go, Corrie, my boy, and rouse up Terrence and Hugh, and—"

"The whole army, in short," cried the boy, hastily; "you're so awfully slow, uncle, you should have been born in the last century I think."

Further remark was cut short by the sudden discharge of the pewter mug, which, however, fell harmlessly on the panel of the closing door as the impertinent Corrie sped forth to call the settlement to arms.

CHAPTER VI
SUSPICIONS ALLAYED AND REAWAKENED

Gascoyne, followed by his man Jo Bumpus, sped over the rugged mountains, and descended the slopes on the opposite side of the island soon after nightfall, and long before Captain Montague, in his large and well-manned boat, could pull half way round in the direction of the sequestered bay where the Foam lay quietly at anchor.

There was not a breath of wind to ruffle the surface of the glassy sea, as the captain of the sandal-wood trader reached the shore and uttered a low cry like the hoot of an owl. The cry was instantly replied to, and in a few minutes a boat crept noiselessly towards the shore, seeming, in the uncertain light, more like a shadow than a reality. It was rowed by a single man. When within a few yards of the shore, the oars ceased to move, and the deep stillness of the night was scarcely broken by the low voice of surly Dick, demanding, "Who goes there?"

"All right, pull in," replied Gascoyne, whose deep bass voice sounded sepulchral in the almost unearthly stillness. It was one of those dark, oppressively quiet nights which make one feel a powerful sensation of loneliness, and a peculiar disinclination, by word or act, to disturb the prevailing quiescence of nature,— such a night as suggests the idea of a coming storm to those who are at sea, or of impending evil to those on land.

"Is the mate aboard?" inquired Gascoyne.

"He is, sir."

"Are any of the hands on shore?"

"More than half of 'em, sir."

Nothing more was said; and in a few minutes Gascoyne was slowly pacing the quarter-deck of his little vessel in earnest consultation with his first mate. There seemed to be some difference of opinion between the captain and his officer; for their words, which, at first were low, at length became audible.

"I tell you, Manton, it won't do," said Gascoyne, sternly.

"I can only suggest what I believe to be for the good of the ship," replied the other, coldly.

"Even if you succeed in your attempt, you will be certain to lose some of our hands; for although the best of them are on, shore, the commander of the Talisman will think those that remain too numerous for a sandal-wood trader, and you are aware that we are sufficiently short-handed in such dangerous seas."

The latter part of this speech was uttered in a slightly sarcastic tone.

"What would you have me do, then?" demanded Gascoyne, whose usual decision of character seemed to have deserted him under the influence of conflicting feelings, which the first mate could plainly perceive agitated the breast of his commander, but which he could by no means account for. Certainly he had no sympathy with them, for Manton's was a hard, stern nature— not given to the melting mood.

"Do?" exclaimed the mate, vehemently, "I would mount the red, and get out the sweeps. An hour's pull will place the schooner on the other side of the reef. A shot from Long Tom will sink the best boat in the service of his Britannic Majesty, and we could be off and away with the land breeze before morning."

"What! sink a man-of-war's boats!" exclaimed Gascoyne; "why, that would make them set us down as pirates at once, and we should have to run the gauntlet of half the British navy before this time next year."

Manton received this remark with a loud laugh, which harshly disturbed the silence of the night.

"That is true," said he; "yet I scarcely expected to see Captain Gascoyne show the white feather."

"Possibly not," retorted the other, grimly; "yet methinks that he who counsels flight shows more of the white feather than he who would shove his head into the very jaws of the lion. It won't do, Manton; I have my own reasons for remaining here. The white lady must in the meantime smile on the British commander. Besides, it would be difficult, if not impossible, to do all this and get our fellows on board again before morning. The land breeze will serve to fill the sails of the Talisman just as well as those of the Foam; and they're sure to trip their anchor to-night; for, you'll scarcely believe it, this mad little fellow Montague actually suspects me to be the pirate Durward!"

Again the harsh laugh of Manton disturbed the peaceful calm, and this time he was joined by Gascoyne, who seemed at length to have overcome the objections of his mate; for their tones again sank into inaudible whispers.

Shortly after this conversation the moon broke out from behind a bank of clouds, and shone brightly down on land and sea, throwing into bold relief the precipices, pinnacles, and gorges of the one, and covering the other with rippling streaks of silver. About the same time the oars of the man-of-war's boat were heard, and in less than half an hour Captain Montague ascended the side of the Foam, where, to his great surprise, he was politely received by Gascoyne.

"Captain Gascoyne has reason to be proud of his pedestrian powers," said the young commander; "he must have had urgent reason, for making such good use of his legs since we last met."

"To do the honors of his own ship, when he expects a visit from a British officer, is surely sufficient reason to induce a poor skipper to take an extra walk of a fine evening," replied Gascoyne, blandly. "Besides, I know that men-of-war are apt to take a fancy to the crews of merchantmen sometimes, and I thought my presence might be necessary here to-night."

"How?" exclaimed Montague, quickly. "Do you fancy that your single arm, stout though it be, could avail to prevent this evil that you dread if I think proper to act according to established usage in time of war?"

"Nay, that were extreme vanity indeed," returned the other; "but I would fain hope that the explanations which I can give of the danger of our peculiar trade, and the necessity we have for a strong crew, will induce Captain Montague to forego his undoubted privilege and right on this occasion."

"I'm not so sure of that," replied Montague; "it will depend much on your explanations being satisfactory. How many men have you?"

"Twenty-two."

"So many! That is much more than enough to work so small a vessel."

"But not more than enough to defend my vessel from a swarm of bloody savages."

"Perhaps not," returned Montague, on whom the urbanity and candor of the captain of the Foam were beginning to have a softening influence. "You have no objection to let me see your papers, and examine your ship, I suppose."

"None in the world," replied Gascoyne, smiling; "and if I had, it would make little difference, I should imagine, to one who is so well able to insist on having his will obeyed." (He glanced at the boat full of armed men as he spoke.) "Pray, come below with me."

In the examination that ensued, Captain Montague was exceedingly strict, although the strength of his first suspicions had been somewhat abated by the truthful tone and aspect of Gascoyne, and the apparent reasonableness of all he said; but he failed to detect anything in the papers, or in the general arrangements of the Foam, that could warrant his treating her otherwise than as an honest trader.

"So," said he, on returning to the deck; "this is the counterpart of the noted pirate, is it? You must pardon my having suspected you, sir, of being this same Durward, sailing under false colors. Come, let me see the points of difference between you, else if we happen to meet on the high seas I may chance to make an unfortunate hole in your timbers."

"The sides of my schooner are altogether black, as you see," returned Gascoyne. "I have already explained that a narrow streak of red distinguishes the pirate; and this fair lady" (leading Montague to the bow) "guides the Foam over the waves with smiling countenance, while a scarlet griffin is the more appropriate figurehead of Durward's vessel."

As he spoke, the low boom of a far distant gun was heard. Montague started, and glanced inquiringly in the face of his companion, whose looks expressed a slight degree of surprise.

"What was that, think you?" said Montague, after a momentary pause.

"The commander of the Talisman ought, I think, to be the best judge of the sound of his own guns."

"True," returned the young officer, somewhat disconcerted; "but you forget that I am not familiar with the eruptions of those volcanic mountains of yours; and, at so great a distance from my ship, with such hills of rock and lava between us, I may well be excused feeling a little doubt as to the bark of my own bull-dogs. But that signal betokens something unusual. I must shorten my visit to you, I fear."

"Pray do not mention it," said Gascoyne, with a peculiar smile; "under the circumstances I am bound to excuse you."

"But," continued Montague, with emphasis, "I should be sorry indeed to part without some memorial of my visit. Be so good as to order your men to come aft."

"By all means," said Gascoyne, giving the requisite order promptly; for, having sent all his best men on shore, he did not much mind the loss of a few of those remaining.

When they were mustered, the British commander inspected them carefully, and then he singled out surly Dick, and ordered him into the boat. A slight frown rested for a moment on Gascoyne's countenance, as he observed the look of ill-concealed triumph with which the man obeyed the order. The expression of surly Dick, however, was instantly exchanged for one of dismay as his captain strode up to him, and looked in his face for one moment with a piercing glance, at the same time thrusting his left hand into the breast of his red shirt.

"Good-by," he said, suddenly, in a cheerful tone, extending his right hand and grasping that of the sailor. "Good-by, lad: if you serve the king as well as you have served me, he'll have reason to be proud of you."

Gascoyne turned on his heel, and the man slunk into the boat with an aspect very unlike that of a bold British seaman.

"Here is another man I want," said Montague, laying his hand on the shoulder of John Bumpus.

"I trust, sir, that you will not take that man," said Gascoyne, earnestly. "I cannot afford to lose him; I would rather you should take any three of the others."

"Your liberality leads me to think that you could without much difficulty supply the place of the men I take: but three are too many. I shall be satisfied with this one. Go into the boat, my lad."

Poor John Bumpus, whose heart had been captivated by the beauties of the island, obeyed the order with a rueful countenance; and Gascoyne bit his lip and turned aside to conceal his anger. In two minutes more the boat was rowed away from the schooner's side.

Not a word was spoken by any one in the boat until a mile had separated it from the schooner. They had just turned a point which shut the vessel out of view, when surly Dick suddenly recovered his self-possession and his tongue, and, starting up in an excited manner, exclaimed to Montague: "The schooner you have just left, sir, is a pirate. I tell the truth, though I should swing for it."

The crew of the boat ceased rowing, and glanced at each other in surprise on hearing this.

"Ha! say you so?" exclaimed Montague, quickly.

"It's a fact, sir. Ask my comrade there, and he'll tell you the same thing."

"He'll do nothin' o' the sort," sharply returned honest Bumpus, who, having been only a short time previously engaged by Gascoyne, could perceive neither pleasure nor justice in the idea of being hanged for a pirate, and who attributed Dick's speech to an ill-natured desire to get his late commander into trouble.

"Which of you am I to believe?" said Montague, hastily.

"W'ichever you please," observed Bumpus, with an air of indifference.

"It's no business o' mine," said Dick, sulkily; "if you choose to let the blackguard escape, that's your own lookout."

"Silence, you scoundrel!" cried Montague, who was as much nettled by a feeling of uncertainty how to act as by the impertinence of the man.

Before he could decide as to the course he ought to pursue, the report of one of the guns of his own vessel boomed loud and distinct in the distance. It was almost immediately followed by another.

"Ha! that settles the question; give way, my lads, give way."

In another moment the boat was cleaving her way swiftly through the dark water in the direction of the Talisman.

CHAPTER VII

MASTER CORRIE CAUGHT NAPPING — SNAKES IN THE GRASS

The Sabbath morning which succeeded the events we have just narrated dawned on the settlement of Sandy Cove in unclouded splendor, and the deep repose of nature was still unbroken by the angry passions and the violent strife of man; although from the active preparations of the previous night it might have been expected that those who dwelt on the island would not have an opportunity of enjoying the rest of that day.

Everything in and about the settlement was eminently suggestive of peace. The cattle lay sleepily in the shade of the trees; the sea was still calm like glass. Men had ceased from their daily toil; and the only sounds that broke the quiet of the morning were the chattering of the parrots and other birds in the cocoanut groves, and the cries of sea-fowl, as they circled in the air, or dropped on the surface of the sea in quest of fish.

The British frigate lay at anchor in the same place which she had hitherto occupied, and the Foam still floated in the sequestered bay on the other side of the island. In neither vessel was there the slightest symptom of preparation; and to one who knew not the true state of matters, the idea of war being about to break forth was the last that would have occurred.

But this deceitful quiet was only the calm that precedes the storm. On every hand men were busily engaged in making preparations to break that Sabbath day in the most frightful manner, or were calmly, but resolutely, awaiting attack. On board the ship-of-war, indeed, there was little doing; for, her business being to fight, she was always in a state of readiness for action. Her signal guns, fired the previous night, had recalled Montague to tell him of the threatened attack by the savages. A few brief orders were given, and they were prepared for whatever might occur. In the village, too, the arrangements to repel attack having been made, white men and native converts alike rested with their arms placed in convenient proximity to their hands.

In a wild and densely-wooded part of the island far removed from those portions which we have yet had occasion to describe, a band of fiendish-looking men were making arrangements for one of those unprovoked assaults which savages are so prone to make on those who settle near them.

They were all of them in a state of almost complete nudity; but the complicated tattooing on their dark skins gave them the appearance of being more clothed than they really were. Their arms consisted chiefly of enormous clubs of hard wood, spears, and bows; and, in order to facilitate their escape should they chance to be grasped in a hand-to-hand conflict, they had covered their bodies with oil, which glistened in the sunshine as they moved about their village.

Conspicuous among these truly savage warriors was the form of Keona, with his right arm bound up in a sort of sling. Pain and disappointed revenge had rendered this man's face more than unusually diabolical as he went about among his fellows, inciting them to revenge the insult and injury done to them through his person by the whites. There was some reluctance, however, on the part of a few of the chiefs to renew a war that had been terminated, or rather been slumbering, only for a few months.

Keona's influence, too, was not great among his kindred, and had it not been that one or two influential chiefs sided with him, his own efforts to relight the still smoking torch of war would have been unavailing.

As it was, the natives soon worked themselves up into a suffi-ciently excited state to engage in any desperate expedition. It was while all this was doing in the native camp that Keona, having gone to the nearest mountain-top to observe what was going on in the settlement, had fallen in with and been chased by some of those men belonging to the Foam, who had been sent on shore to escape being pressed into the service of the King of England.

The solitary exception to this general state of preparation for war was the household of Frederick Mason. Having taken such precautionary steps the night before as he deemed expedient, and having consulted with Ole Thorwald, the general commanding, who had posted scouts in all the mountain passes, and had seen the war-canoes drawn up in a row on the strand, the pastor retired to his study, and spent the greater part of the night in preparing to preach the gospel of peace on the morrow, and in committing the care of his flock and his household to Him who is the "God of battles" as well as the "Prince of peace."

It is not to be supposed that Mr. Mason contemplated the probable renewal of hostilities without great anxiety. For himself, we need scarcely say, he had no fears; but his heart sank when he thought of his gentle Alice falling into the hands of savages. As the night passed away without any alarms, his anxiety began to subside, and when Sunday morning dawned, he lay down on a couch to snatch a few hours' repose before the labors of the day.

The first object that greeted the pastor's eyes on awaking in the morning was a black visage, and a pair of glittering eyes gazing at him through the half-open door with an expression of the utmost astonishment.

He leaped up with lightning speed and darted towards the intruder, but checked himself suddenly, and smiled, as poor Poopy uttered a scream, and, falling on her knees, implored for mercy.

"My poor girl, I fear I have frightened you by my violence," said he, sitting down on his couch and yawning sleepily; "but I was dreaming, Poopy; and when I saw your black face peeping at me, I took you at first for one of the wild fellows on the other side of the mountains. You have come to sweep and arrange my study, I suppose."

"Why, mass'r, you no hab go to bed yet," said Poopy, still feeling and expressing surprise at her master's unwonted irregularity. "Is you ill?"

"Not at all, my good girl; only a little tired. It is not a time for me to take much rest when the savages are said to be about to attack us."

"When is they coming?" inquired the girl, meekly.

The pastor smiled as he replied, "That is best known to themselves, Poopy. Do you think it likely that murderers or thieves would send to let us know when they were coming."

"Hee! hee!" laughed Poopy, with an immense display of teeth and gums.

"Is Alice awake?" inquired Mr. Mason.

"No; her be sound 'sleep wid her two eye shut tight up, dis fashion, and her mout' wide open—so."

The representation of Alice's condition, as given by her maid, although hideously unlike the beautiful object they were meant to call up to her father's mind, were sufficiently expressive and comprehensible.

"Go wake her, my girl, and let us have breakfast as soon as you can. Has Will Corrie been here this morning?"

"Hims bin here all night," replied the girl, with a broad grin (and the breadth of Poopy's *broad* grin was almost appalling).

"What mean you,—has he slept in this house all night?"

"Yes—eh! no," said Poopy.

"Yes, no!" exclaimed Mr. Mason. "Come, Poopy, don't be stupid, explain yourself."

"Hee! hee! hee! yes, ho! ho! ho!" laughed Poopy, as if the idea of explaining herself was about the richest joke she had listened to since she was born. "Hee! hee! me no can 'xplain; but you com here an' see."

So saying, she conducted her wondering master to the front door of the cottage, where, across the threshold, directly under the porch, lay the form of the redoubted Corrie, fast asleep, and armed to the teeth!

In order to explain the cause of this remarkable apparition, we think it justifiable to state to the reader, in confidence, that young Master Corrie was deeply in love with the fair Alice. With all his reckless drollery of disposition, the boy was intensely romantic and enthusiastic; and, feeling that the unsettled condition of the times endangered the welfare of his lady-love, he resolved, like a true knight, to arm himself and guard the threshold of her door with his own body.

In the deep silence of the night he buckled on a saber, the blade of which, by reason of its having been broken, was barely eight inches long, and the hilt whereof was battered and rusty. He also stuck a huge brass-mounted cavalry pistol in his belt, in the virtue of which he had great faith, having only two days before shot with it a green-headed parrot at a distance of two yards. The distance was not great, to be sure, but it was enough for his purpose—intending, as he did, to meet his foe, when the moment of action should come, in close conflict, and thrust the muzzle of his weapon down the said foe's throat before condescending to draw the trigger.

Thus prepared for the worst, he sallied out on tiptoe, intending to mount guard at the missionary's door, and return to his own proper couch before the break of day.

But alas for poor Corrie's powers of endurance! No sooner had he extended his chubby form on the door-mat, earnestly wishing, but not expecting, that Alice would come out and find him there, than he fell fast asleep, while engaged in the hopeless task of counting the starry host—a duty which he had imposed on himself in the hope that he might thereby be kept awake. Once asleep he slept on, as a matter of course, with his broad little chest heaving gently; his round little visage beaming upwards like a terrestrial moon; his left arm under his head in lieu of a pillow (by consequence of which *it* was fast asleep also), and his right hand grasping the hilt of the broken saber.

As for Corrie's prostrate body affording protection to Alice, the entire savage population might have stepped across it, one by one, and might have stepped back again, bearing away into slavery the fair maiden, with her father and all the household furniture to boot, without in the least disturbing the deep slumbers of the youthful knight. At least we may safely come to this conclusion from the fact that Mr. Mason shook him, first gently and then violently, for full five minutes, before he could get him to speak; and even then he only gave utterance, in very sleepy tones, and half-formed words, to the remark—

"Oh! don' borer me. It ain't b'kfust-t'm' yet?"

"Ho! Corrie, Corrie," shouted Mr. Mason, giving the victim a shake that threatened to dislocate his neck, "get up, my boy— rouse up!"

"Hallo! hy! murder! Come on you vill—eh! Mr. Mason—I beg pardon, sir," stammered Corrie, as he at length became aware of his condition, and blushed deeply; "I—I—really, Mr. Mason, I merely came to watch while you were all asleep, as there are savages about, you know, and—ha! ha! ha!—oh! dear me!" (Corrie exploded at this point, unable to contain himself at the sight of the missionary's gaze of astonishment.) "Wot a sight, for a Sunday mornin' too!"

The hilarity of the boy was catching, for at this point a vociferous "hee! hee" burst from the sable Poopy; the clear laugh of Alice, too, came ringing through the passage, and Mr. Mason himself finally joined in the chorus.

"Come, sir knight," exclaimed the latter, on recovering his gravity, "this is no guise for a respectable man to be seen in on Sunday morning; come in and lay down your arms. You have done very well as a soldier for this occasion; let us see if you can do your duty equally well as a church officer. Have you the keys?"

"No; they are at home."

"Then run and get them, my boy, and leave your pistol behind, you. I dare say the savages won't attack during the daytime."

Corrie did as he was desired, and the pastor went, after breakfast, to spend a short time with Alice on a neighboring eminence, from which could be obtained a fine view of the settlement with its little church, and the calm bay, on which floated the frigate, sheltered by the encircling coral reef from the swell of the ocean.

Here it was Mr. Mason's wont to saunter with Alice every Sunday morning, to read a chapter of the Bible to her, and converse about that happy land where one so dear to both of them now dwelt with their Saviour. Here, also, the child's maid was sometimes privileged to join them. On this particular morning, however, they were not the only spectators of the beautiful view from that hill; for, closely hidden in the bushes—not fifty yards from the spot where they sat—lay a band of armed savages who had escaped the vigilance of the scouts, and had come by an unguarded pass to the settlement.

They might easily have slain or secured the missionary and his household without alarming the people in the village, but their plan of attack forbade such a premature proceeding. The trio therefore finished their chapter and their morning prayer undisturbed, little dreaming of the number of glittering eyes that watched their proceedings.

CHAPTER VIII

A SURPRISE—A BATTLE AND A FIRE

The sound of the Sabbath bell fell sweetly on the pastor's ear as he descended to his dwelling to make a few final preparations for the duties of the day; and from every hut in Sandy Cove trooped forth the native Christians, young and old, to assemble in the house of God.

With great labor and much pains had this church been built, and pastor and people alike were not a little proud of their handiwork. The former had drawn the plans and given the measurements, leaving it to Henry Stuart to see them properly carried out in detail, while the latter did the work. They cut and squared the timbers, gathered the coral, burnt it for lime, and plastered the building. The women and children carried the lime from the beach in baskets, and the men dragged the heavy logs from the mountains,—in some cases for several miles,—the timber in the immediate neighborhood not being sufficiently large for their purpose.

The poor natives worked with heart and soul; for love, and the desire to please and be pleased, had been awakened within them. Besides this, the work had for them all the zest of novelty. They wrought at it with somewhat of the feelings of children at play,—pausing frequently in the midst of their toil to gaze in wonder and admiration at the growing edifice, which would have done no little credit to a professional architect and to more skilled workmen.

The white men of the place also lent a willing hand; for although some of them were bad men, yet they were constrained to respect the consistent character and blameless life of the missionary, who not unfrequently experienced the fulfilment of that word: "When a man's ways please the Lord, he maketh even his enemies to be at peace with him." Besides this, all of them, however unwilling they might be to accept Christianity for themselves, were fully alive to the advantages they derived from its introduction among the natives.

With so many willing hands at work, the little church was soon finished; and, at the time when the events we are describing occurred, there was nothing to be done to it except some trifling arrangements connected with the steeple, and the glazing of the windows. This latter piece of work was, in such a climate, of little importance.

Long before the bell had ceased to toll, the church was full of natives, whose dark, eager faces were turned towards the door, in expectation of the appearance of their pastor. The building was so full that many of the people were content to cluster round the door, or the outside of the unglazed windows. On this particular Sunday there were strangers there, who roused the curiosity and attracted the attention of the congregation. Before Mr. Mason arrived, there was a slight bustle at the door as Captain Montague, with several of his officers and men, entered, and were shown to the missionary's seat by Master Corrie, who, with his round visage elongated as much as possible, and his found eyes expressing a look of inhuman solemnity, in consequence of his attempt to affect a virtue which he did not possess, performed the duties of doorkeeper. Montague had come on shore to ascertain from Mr. Mason what likelihood there was of an early attack by the natives.

"Where's Alice?" whispered the boy to Poopy, as the girl entered the church, and seated herself beside a little midshipman, who looked at her with a mingled expression of disgust and contempt, and edged away.

"Got a little headache,—hee! hee!"

"Don't laugh in church, you monster," said Corrie, with a frown.

"I'se not larfin," retorted Poopy, with an injured look.

Just then the boy caught sight of a gigantic figure entering the church, and darted away to usher the stranger into the pastor's seat; but Gascoyne (for it was he) took no notice of him. He passed steadily up the center of the church, and sat down beside the Widow Stuart, whose face expressed anxiety and surprise the moment she observed who was seated there. The countenance of Henry, who sat on the other side of his mother, flushed, and he turned with an angry glance towards the captain of the Foam. But the look was thrown away; for Gascoyne had placed his arms on the back of the seat in front of him, and rested his head on them; in which position he continued to remain without motion while the service was going on.

Mr. Mason began with a short, earnest prayer in English; then he read out a hymn in the native tongue, which was sung in good tune, and with great energy, by the whole congregation. This was followed by a chapter in the New Testament, and another prayer; but all the service, with the exception of the first prayer, was conducted in the native language. The text was then read out: "Though thy sins be as scarlet, they shall be white as snow; though they be red like crimson, they shall be white as wool."

Frederick Mason possessed the power of chaining the attention of an audience; and a deep, breathless silence prevailed, as he labored, with intense fervor, to convince his hearers of the love of God, and the willingness and ability of Jesus Christ to save even the chief of sinners. During one part of the service, a deep, low groan startled the congregation; but no one could tell who had uttered it. As it was not repeated, it was soon forgotten by most of the people.

While the pastor was thus engaged, a pistol-shot was heard, and immediately after, a loud, fierce yell burst from the forest, causing the ears of those who heard it to tingle, and their hearts for a moment to quail. In less than ten minutes, the church was empty, and the males of the congregation were engaged in a desperate hand-to-hand conflict with the savages, who, having availed themselves of the one unguarded pass, had quietly eluded the vigilance of the scouts, and assembled in force on the outskirts of the settlement.

Fortunately for the worshipers that morning, the anxiety of Master Corrie for the welfare of his fair Alice induced him to slip out of the church just after the sermon began. Hastening to the pastor's house, he found the child sound asleep on a sofa, and a savage standing over her with a spear in his hand. The boy had approached so stealthily that the savage did not hear him. Remembering that he had left his pistol on the kitchen table, he darted round to the back door of the house, and secured it just as Alice awoke with a scream of surprise and terror, on beholding who was near her.

Next moment Corrie was at her side, and before the savage could seize the child, he leveled the pistol at his head and fired. The aim was sufficiently true to cause the ball to graze the man's forehead, while the smoke and fire partially blinded him.

It was this shot that first alarmed the natives in church, and it was the yell uttered by the wounded man, as he fell stunned on the floor, that called forth the answering yell from the savage host, and precipitated the attack.

It was sufficiently premature to give the people of the settlement time to seize their arms; which, as has been said, they had placed so as to be available at a moment's notice.

The fight that ensued was a desperate, and almost indiscriminate, mêlée. The attacking party had been so sure of taking the people by surprise that they formed no plan of attack; but simply arranged that, at a given signal from their chief, a united rush should be made upon the church, and a general massacre ensue. As we have seen, Corrie's pistol drew forth the signal sooner than had been intended. In the rush that immediately ensued, a party dashed through the house, the boy was overturned, and a savage gave him a passing blow with a club that would have scattered his brains on the floor had it taken full effect; but it was hastily delivered; it glanced off his head, and spent its force on the shoulder of the chief, who was thus unfortunate enough to be wounded by friends as well as foes.

On the first alarm, Gascoyne sprang up, and darted through the door. He was closely followed by Henry Stuart, and the captain of the Talisman, with his handful of officers and men, who were all armed, as a matter of course.

"Sit where you are," cried Henry to his trembling mother, as he sprang after Gascoyne; "the church is the safest place you'll find."

The widow fell on her knees, and prayed to God while the fight raged without.

Among the first to leave the church was the pastor. The thought of his child having been left in the house unprotected filled him with an agony of fear. He sought no weapon of war, but darted unarmed straight into the midst of the savage host that stood between him and the object of his affection. His rush was so impetuous, that he fairly overturned several of his opponents by dashing against them. The numbers that surrounded him, however, soon arrested his progress; but he had pressed so close in amongst them, that they were actually too closely packed, for a few seconds, to be able to use their heavy clubs and long spears with effect.

It was well for the poor missionary, at that moment, that he had learned the art of boxing when a boy. The knowledge so acquired had never induced him to engage in dishonorable and vulgar strife; but it had taught him how and where to deliver a straightforward blow with effect; and he now struck out with tremendous energy, knocking down an adversary at every blow; for the thought of Alice lent additional strength to his powerful arm. Success in such warfare, however, was not to be expected. Still, Mr. Mason's activity and vigor averted his own destruction for a few minutes; and these minutes were precious, for they afforded time for Captain Montague and his officers to cut their way to the spot where he fought, just as a murderous club was about to descend on his head from behind. Montague's sword unstrung the arm that upheld it, and the next instant the pastor was surrounded by friends.

Among their number was John Bumpus, who was one of the crew of Montague's boat, and who now rushed upon the savages with a howl peculiarly his own, felling one with a blow of his fist, and another with a slash of his cutlass.

"You must retire," said Montague, hastily, to Frederick Mason, who stood panting and inactive for a few moments in order to recover breath. "You are unarmed, sir; besides, your profession forbids you taking part in such work as this. There are men of war enough here to keep these fellows in play."

Montague spoke somewhat sharply; for he erroneously fancied that the missionary's love of fighting had led him into the fray.

"My profession does not forbid me to save my child," exclaimed the pastor, wildly.

He turned in the direction of his cottage, which was full in view; and at that moment smoke burst from the roof and windows. With a cry of despair, Mr. Mason once more launched himself on the host of savages; but these were now so numerous that, instead of making head against them, the little knot of sailors who opposed them at that particular place found it was as much as they could do to keep them at bay.

The issue of the conflict was still doubtful, when a large accession to their numbers gave the savages additional power and courage. They made a sudden onset, and bore back the small band of white men. In the rush the pastor was overthrown, and rendered for a time insensible.

While this was going on in one part of the field, in another, stout Ole Thorwald, with several of the white settlers and the greater part of the native force, was guarding the principal approach to the church against immensely superior numbers.

And nobly did the descendant of the Norse sea-kings maintain the credit of his warlike ancestors that day. With a sword that might have matched that of Goliath of Gath, he swept the way before him wherever he went, and more than once by a furious onset turned the tide of war in favor of his party when it seemed about to overwhelm them.

In a more distant part of the field, on the banks of a small stream, which was spanned by a bridge about fifty paces further down, Gascoyne and Henry Stuart contended, almost alone, with about thirty savages. These two had rushed forward with such impetuosity at the first onset as to have been separated from their friends, and with four Christian natives, had been surrounded. Henry was armed with a heavy claymore, the edge of which betokened that it had once seen much service in the wars of the youth's Scottish ancestors. Gascoyne, not anticipating this attack, had returned to the settlement armed only with his knife. He had seized the first weapon that came to hand, which chanced to be an enormous iron shovel, and with this terrific implement the giant carried all before him.

It was quite unintentionally that he and Henry had come together. But the nature and power of the two men being somewhat similar, they had singled out the same point of danger, and had made their attack with the same overwhelming vehemence. The muscles of both seemed to be made of iron; for, as increasing numbers pressed upon them, they appeared to deliver their terrible blows with increasing rapidity and vigor, and the savages, despite their numbers, began to quail before them.

Just then Keona—who, although wounded, hovered about doing as much mischief as he could with his left hand (which, by the way, seemed to be almost as efficient as his right)—caught sight of this group of combatants on the banks of the stream. He, with a party, had succeeded in forcing the bridge, and now uttering a shout of wild delight at the sight of his two greatest enemies within his power, as he thought, he rushed towards them, and darted his spear with unerring aim and terrible violence. The man's anger defeated his purpose; for the shout attracted the attention of Gascoyne, who saw the spear coming straight towards Henry's breast. He interposed the shovel instantly, and the spear fell harmless to the ground. At the same time, with a back-handed sweep, he brained a gigantic savage who at the moment was engaging Henry's undivided attention. Bounding forward with a burst of anger, Gascoyne sought to close with Keona. He succeeded but too well, however; for he could not check himself sufficiently to deliver an effective blow, but went crashing against his enemy, and the two fell to the ground.

In an instant a rush was made on the fallen man, but Henry leaped forward, and sweeping down two opponents with one cut of his claymore, afforded his companion time to leap up.

"Come, we are quits," said Henry, with a grim smile, as the two darted again on the foe.

At that moment Ole Thorwald, having scattered the party he first engaged, came tearing down towards the bridge, whirling the great sword round his head, and shouting "victory" in the voice of a Stentor.

"Ha! here is more work," he cried, as his eye fell on Gascoyne's figure. "Thorwald to the rescue,—hurrah!"

In another moment the savages were flying pell-mell across the bridge with Gascoyne and Henry close on their heels, and the stout merchant panting after them, with his victorious band, as fast as his less agile limbs could carry him.

It was at this moment that Gascoyne and Henry noticed the attack made on the small party of sailors, and observed the fall of Mr. Mason.

"Thorwald to the rescue!" shouted Gascoyne, in a voice that rolled deep and loud over the whole field like the roar of a lion.

"Aye, aye, my noisy stranger; it's easy for your tough limbs to carry you up the hill," gasped Ole; "but the weight of ten or fifteen years will change your step. Hurrah!"

The cry of the bold Norseman, coupled with that of Gascoyne, had the double effect of checking the onset of the enemy, and of collecting their own scattered forces around them. The battle was now drawing to a point. Men who were skirmishing in various places left off and hastened to the spot on which the closing scene was now evidently to be enacted; and for a few minutes the contending parties paused, as if by mutual consent, to breathe and scan each other before making the final attack.

It must not be supposed that, during the fight which we have described, the crew of the Talisman were idle. At the first sign of disturbance on shore, the boats were lowered, and a well-armed force rowed for the landing-place as swiftly as the strong and willing arms of the men could pull. But the distance between the vessel and the shore was considerable, and the events we have recounted were quickly enacted; so that before the boats had proceeded half the distance the fight was nearly over, and the settlement seemed about to be overwhelmed.

These facts were not lost upon the first lieutenant of the *Talisman*, Mr. Mulroy, who, with telescope in hand, watched the progress of the fight with great anxiety. He saw that it was impossible for the boats to reach the shore in time to render efficient aid. He also observed that a fresh band of savages were hastening to reinforce their comrades, and that the united band would be so overpoweringly strong as to render the chances of a successful resistance on the part of the settlers very doubtful indeed—almost hopeless.

In these circumstances he adopted a course which was as bold as it was dangerous. Observing that the savages mustered for the final onset in a dense mass on an eminence which just raised their heads a little above those of the party they were about to attack, he at once loaded three of the largest guns with round shot and pointed, them at the mass of human beings with the utmost possible care. There was the greatest danger of hitting friends instead of foes; but Mr. Mulroy thought it his duty to incur the responsibility of running the risk.

Montague, to whom the command of the band of united settlers had been given by general consent, had thrown them rapidly into some sort of order, and was about to give the word to charge, when the savage host suddenly began to pour down the hill with frantic yells.

Mulroy did not hear the shouts, but he perceived the movement. Suddenly, as if a thunder storm had burst over the island, the echoes of the hills were startled by the roar of heavy artillery, and, one after another, the three guns hurled their deadly contents into the center of the rushing mass, through which three broad lanes were cut in quick succession.

The horrible noise and the dreadful slaughter in their ranks seemed to render the affrighted creatures incapable of action, for they came to a dead halt.

"Well done, Mulroy!" shouted Montague; "forward, boys,—charge!"

A true British cheer burst from the tars and white settlers, which served further to strike terror into the hearts of the enemy. In another moment they rushed up the hill, led on by Montague, Gascoyne, Henry, and Thorwald. But the savages did not await the shock. Seized with a complete panic, they turned and fled in utter confusion.

Just as this occurred, Mr. Mason began to recover consciousness. Recollecting suddenly what had occurred, he started up and followed his friends, who were now in hot pursuit of the foe in the direction of his own cottage. Quickly though they ran, the anxious father overtook and passed them; but he soon perceived that his dwelling was wrapped in flames from end to end.

Darting through the smoke and fire to his daughter's room, he shouted her name; but no voice replied. He sprang to the bed,—it was empty. With a cry of despair, and blinded by smoke, he dashed about the room, grasping wildly at objects in the hope that he might find his child. As he did so he stumbled over a prostrate form, which he instantly seized, raised in his arms, and bore out of the blazing house, round which a number of the people were now assembled.

The form he had thus plucked from destruction was that of the poor boy, who would willingly have given his life to rescue Alice, and who still lay in the state of insensibility into which he had been thrown by the blow from a gun or heavy club.

The missionary dropped his burden, turned wildly round, and was about to plunge once again into the heart of the blazing ruin, when he was seized in the strong arms of Henry Stuart, who, with the assistance of Ole Thorwald, forcibly prevented him from doing that which would have resulted in almost certain death.

The pastor's head sunk on his breast. The excitement of action and hope no longer sustained him. With a deep groan, he fell to the earth insensible.

CHAPTER IX

BAFFLED AND PERPLEXED — PLANS FOR A RESCUE

While the men assembled round the prostrate form of Mr. Mason were attempting to rescue him from his state of stupor, poor Corrie began to show symptoms of returning vitality. A can of water, poured over him by Henry, did much to restore him. But no sooner was he enabled to understand what was going on, and to recall what had happened, than he sprang up with a wild cry of despair, and rushed towards the blazing house. Again Henry's quick arm arrested a friend in his mad career.

"Oh! she's there!—Alice is *there*!" shrieked the boy, as he struggled passionately to free himself.

"You can do nothing, Corrie," said Henry, trying to soothe him.

"Coward!" gasped the boy, in a paroxysm of rage, as he clenched his fist and struck his captor on the chest with all his force.

"Hold him," said Henry, turning to John Bumpus, who at that moment came up.

Bumpus nodded intelligently, and seized the boy, who uttered a groan of anguish as he ceased a struggle which he felt was hopeless in such an iron gripe.

"Now, friends—all of you," shouted Henry, the moment he was relieved of his charge: "little Alice is in that house. We must pull it down. Who will lend a hand?"

He did not pause for an answer, but, seizing an ax, rushed through the smoke and began to cut down the door-posts. The whole party there assembled, numbering about fifty, rushed forward, as one man, to aid in the effort. The attempt was a wild one. Had Henry considered for a moment, he would have seen that, in the event of their succeeding in pulling down the blazing pile, they would in all probability smother the child in the ruins.

"The shell is in the outhouse," said Corrie, eagerly, to the giant who held him.

"Wot shell?" inquired Bumpus.

"The shell that they blow like a horn to call the people to work with."

"Ah! you're sane again," said the sailor releasing him; "go, find it, lad, and blow till yer cheeks crack."

Corrie was gone long before Jo had concluded even that short remark. In another second the harsh but loud sound of the shell rang over the hillside. The settlers, black and white, immediately ceased their pursuit of the savages, and from every side they came trooping in by dozens. Without waiting to inquire the cause of what was being done, each man, as he arrived, fell to work on the blazing edifice, and, urged on by Henry's voice and example, toiled and moiled in the midst of fire and smoke until the pastor's house was literally pulled to pieces.

Fortunately for little Alice, she had been carried out of the house long before by Keona, who, being subtle as well as revengeful, knew well how to strike at the tenderest part of the white man's heart.

While her friends were thus frantically endeavoring to deliver her from the burning house in which they supposed her to be, Alice was being hurried through the woods by a steep mountain path in the direction of the native village. Happily for the feelings of her father, the fact was made known, soon after the house had been pulled down, by the arrival of a small party of native settlers bearing one of the child's shoes. They had found it, they said, sticking in the mud, about a mile off, and had tracked the little footsteps a long way into the mountains by the side of the prints made by the naked feet of a savage. At length they had lost the tracks amid the hard lava rocks, and had given up the chase.

"We must follow them up instantly," said Mr. Mason, who had by this time recovered: "no time is to be lost."

"Aye, time is precious; who will go?" cried Henry, who, begrimed with fire and smoke, and panting vehemently from recent exertion, had just at that moment come towards the group.

"Take me! oh take me, Henry!" cried Corrie, in a beseeching tone, as he sprang promptly to his friend's side.

At any other time, Henry would have smiled at the enthusiastic offer of such a small arm to fight the savages; but fierce anger was in his breast at that moment. He turned from the poor boy and looked round with a frown, as he observed that, although the natives crowded round him at once, neither Gascoyne, nor Thorwald, nor Captain Montague showed any symptom of an intention to accompany him.

"Nay, be not angry, lad," said Gascoyne, observing the frown; "your blood is young and hot, as it should be; but it behooves us to have a council of war before we set out on this expedition, which, believe me, will be no trifling one, if I know anything of savage ways and doings."

"Mr. Gascoyne is right," said Montague, turning to the missionary, who stood regarding the party with anxious looks, quite unable to offer advice on such an occasion, and clasping the little shoe firmly in both hands; "it seems to me that those who know the customs of savage warfare should give their advice first. You may depend on all the aid that it is in my power to give."

"Ole Thorwald is our leader when we are compelled to fight in self-defense," said Mr. Mason; "would God that it were less frequently we were obliged to demand his services. He knows what is best to be done."

"I know what is best to do," said Thorwald, "when I have to lead men into action, or to show them how to fight. But, to say truth, I don't plume myself on possessing more than an average share of the qualities of the terrier dog. When niggers are to be hunted out of holes in the mountains like rabbits, I will do what in me lies to aid in the work; but I had rather be led than lead if you can find a better man."

Thorwald said this with a rueful countenance, for he had hoped to have settled this war in a pitched battle; and there were few things the worthy man seemed to enjoy more than a stand-up fight on level ground. A fair field and no favor was his delight; but climbing the hills was his mortal aversion. He was somewhat too corpulent and short of wind for that.

"Come, Gascoyne," said Henry; "you know more about the savages than anybody here; and if I remember rightly, you have told me that you are acquainted with most of the mountain passes."

"With all of them, lad," interposed Gascoyne; "I know every pass and cavern on the island."

"What, then, would you advise?" asked Montague.

"If a British officer can put himself under a simple trading skipper," said Gascoyne, "I may perhaps show what ought to be done in this emergency."

"I can co-operate with any one who proves himself worthy of confidence," retorted Montague, sharply.

"Well, then," continued the other, "it is vain to think of doing any good by a disorderly chase into mountains like these. I would advise that our forces be divided into three. One band under Mr. Thorwald should go round by the Goat's Pass, to which I will guide him, and cut off the retreat of the savages there; another party under my friend Henry Stuart should give chase in the direction in which little Alice seems to have been taken; and a third party, consisting of his Majesty's vessel the Talisman and crew; should proceed round to the north side of the island and bombard the native village."

"The Goat's Pass," growled Thorwald, "sounds unpleasantly rugged and steep in the ears of a man of my weight and years, Mister Gascoyne. But if there's no easier style of work to be done, I fancy I must be content with what falls to my lot."

"And truly," added Montague, "methinks you might have assigned me a more useful, as well as more congenial occupation, than the bombardment of a mud village full of women and children; for I doubt not that every able-bodied man has left it, to go on this expedition."

"You'll not find the Goat's Pass so bad as you think, good Thorwald," returned Gascoyne; "for I propose that the Talisman or her boats should convey you and your men to the foot of it, after which your course will be indeed rugged, but it will be short;—merely to scale the face of a precipice that would frighten a goat to think of, and then a plain descent into the valley, where, I doubt not, these villains will be found in force; and where, certainly, they will not look for the appearance of a stout generalissimo of half-savage troops. As for the bombarding of a mud village, Mr. Montague, I should have expected a well-trained British officer ready to do his duty, whether that duty were agreeable or otherwise."

"My *duty* certainly," interrupted the young captain, hotly; "but I have yet to learn that *your* orders constitute *my* duty."

The bland smile with which Gascoyne listened to this tended rather to irritate than to soothe Montague's feelings; but he curbed the passion which stirred his breast, while the other went on:

"No doubt the bombarding of a defenseless village is not pleasant work; but the result will be important, for it will cause the whole army of savages to rush to the protection of their women and children, thereby disconcerting their plans—supposing them to have any—and enabling us to attack them while assembled in force. It is the nature of savages to scatter, and so to puzzle trained forces; and no doubt those of His Majesty are well trained. But 'one touch of nature makes the whole world kin,' says a great authority; it is wonderful how useful a knowledge of various touches of nature is in the art of war.

"It may not have occurred to Mr. Montague that savages have a tendency to love and protect their wives and children, as well as civilized men, and that—"

"Pray, cease your irrelevant remarks; they are ill-timed," said Montague, impatiently. "Let us hear the remainder of your suggestions. I shall judge of their value, and act accordingly. You have not yet told us what part you yourself intend to play in this game."

"I mean to accompany Captain Montague, if he will permit me."

"How! go with me in the Talisman?" said Montague, surprised at the man's coolness, and puzzled by his impudence.

"Even so," said Gascoyne.

"Well, I have no objection, of course; but it seems to me that you would be more useful at the head of a party of your own men."

"Perhaps I might," replied Gascoyne; "but the coral reefs are dangerous on the north side of the island, and it is important that one well acquainted with them should guide your vessel. Besides, I have a trusty mate, and if you will permit me to send my old shipmate John Bumpus across the hills, he will convey all needful instructions to the Foam."

This was said in so quiet and straightforward a tone that Montague's wrath vanished. He felt ashamed of having shown so much petulance at a time when affairs of so great importance ought to have been calmly discussed; so he at once agreed to allow Bumpus to go. Meanwhile, Henry Stuart, who had been fretting with impatience at this conversation, suddenly exclaimed:

"It seems to me, sirs, that you are wasting precious time just now. I, at least, am quite satisfied with the duty assigned to me; so I'm off: ho! who will join me?"

"I'm your man," cried Corrie, starting up and flourishing

the broken saber above his head. At the same moment about a hundred natives ranged themselves round the youth, thus indicating that they, too, were his men.

"Well, lad, away you go," said Gascoyne, smiling; "but Master Corrie must remain with me."

"I'll do nothing of the sort," said Corrie, stoutly.

"Oh yes, you will, my boy, I want you to guide my man Bumpus over the mountains. You know the passes, and he don't. It's all for the good of the cause, you know,—the saving of little Alice."

Corrie wavered. The idea of being appointed, as it were, to a separate command, and of going with his new friend, was a strong temptation, and the assurance that he would in some way or other be advancing the business in hand settled the matter. He consented to become obedient.

In about half an hour all Gascoyne's plans were in course of being carried out. Ole Thorwald and his party proceeded on board the Talisman, which weighed, anchor, and sailed, with a light breeze, towards the north end of the island— guided through the dangerous reefs by Gascoyne. Henry and his followers were toiling nimbly up the hills in the direction indicated by the little footprints of Alice; and John Bumpus, proceeding into the mountains in another direction, pushed, under the guidance of Corrie, towards the bay, where the Foam still lay quietly at anchor.

It was evening when these different parties set out on their various expeditions. The sun was descending to the horizon in a blaze of lurid light. The slight breeze, which wafted his Britannic Majesty's ship slowly along the verdant shore, was scarcely strong enough to ruffle the surface of the sea. Huge banks of dark clouds were gathering in the sky, and a hot, unnatural closeness seemed to pervade the atmosphere, as if a storm were about to burst upon the scene. Everything, above and below, seemed to presage war—alike elemental and human;

and the various leaders of the several expeditions felt that the approaching night would tax their powers and resources to the uttermost.

It was, then, natural that in such circumstances the bereaved father should be distracted with anxiety as to which party he should join; and it was also natural that one whose life had been so long devoted to the special service of God should, before deciding on the point, ask, on his knees, his heavenly Father's guidance.

He finally resolved to accompany the party under command of Henry Stuart.

CHAPTER X

THE PURSUIT—POOPY, LED ON BY LOVE AND HATE, RUSHES TO THE RESCUE

The shades of night had begun to descend upon the island when Master Corrie reached the summit of the mountain ridge that divided the bay in which the Foam was anchored from the settlement of Sandy Cove.

Close on his heels followed the indomitable Jo Bumpus, who panted vehemently and perspired profusely from his unwonted exertions.

"Wot an object you are!" exclaimed Corrie, gazing at the hot giant with a look of mingled surprise and glee; for the boy's spirit was of that nature which cannot repress a dash of fun, even in the midst of anxiety and sorrow. We would not have it understood that the boy ever deliberately mingled the two things—joy and sorrow—at one and the same time; but he was so irresistibly alive to the ludicrous, that a touch of it was sufficient at any time to cause him to forget, for a brief space, his anxieties, whatever these might be.

Jo Bumpus smiled benignantly, and said that he "was glad to hear it." For Jo had conceived for the boy that species of fondness which large dogs are frequently known to entertain for small ones—permitting them to take outrageous liberties with their persons which they would resent furiously were they attempted by other dogs.

Presently the warm visage of Bumpus elongated, and his eyes opened uncommonly wide, as he stared at a particular spot in the ground; insomuch that Corrie burst into an uncontrollable fit of laughter.

"O Grampus! you'll kill me if you go on like that," said he; "I can't stand it,—indeed I can't. Sich a face! D'ye know what it's like?"

Jo expressed no desire to become enlightened on this point, but continued to gaze so earnestly that Corrie started up and exclaimed:

"What is it, Jo?"

"A fut," replied Jo.

"A footprint, I declare!" shouted the boy, springing forward and examining the print, which was pretty clearly defined in a little patch of soft sand that lay on the bare rock. "Why, Jo! it's Poopy's. I'd know it anywhere, by the bigness of the little toe. How *can* she have come up here?"

"I say, lad, hist!" said Bumpus, in a hoarse whisper; "here's another fut that don't belong to—what's her name,—Puppy, did ye say?"

"Why! it's Alice's," whispered the boy, his face becoming instantly grave, while an unwonted expression of anxiety crossed it; "and here's that of a savage beside it. He must have changed his intention; or, perhaps, he came this way to throw the people who were chasing them off the scent."

Corrie was right. Finding that he was hotly pursued, Keona had taken advantage of the first rocky ground he reached to diverge abruptly from the route he had hitherto followed in his flight; and, the further to confuse his pursuers, he had taken the almost exhausted child up in his arms and carried her a considerable distance, so that if his enemies should fall again on his track the absence of the little footprints might induce them to fancy they were following up a wrong scent.

In this he was so far successful; for the native settlers, as we have seen, soon gave up the chase, and returned with one of the child's shoes, which had fallen off unobserved by the savage.

But there was one of the pursuers who was far ahead of the others, and who was urged to continue the chase by the strongest of all motives,—love. Poor Kekupoopi had no sooner heard of the abduction of her young mistress than she had set off at the top of her speed to a well-known height in the mountains, whence, from a great distance, she could observe all that went on below. On the wings of affection she had flown, rather than walked, to this point of observation, and, to her delight, saw not only the pursuers, but the fugitives in the valley below. She kept her glowing eyes fixed on them, hastening from rock to rock and ridge to ridge, as intervening obstacles hid them from view, until she saw the stratagem, just referred to, practised by Keona. Then, feeling that she had no power of voice to let the pursuers know what had occurred, and seeing that they would certainly turn back on being baffled, she resolved to keep up the chase herself—trusting to accident to afford her an opportunity of rendering aid to Alice; or, rather, trusting to God to help her in her great difficulty; for the poor child had been well trained in the missionary's house, and love had been the teacher.

Taking a short cut down into the valley,—for she was well acquainted with all the wild and rugged paths of the mountains in the immediate neighborhood of the settlement,—she was so fortunate as to reach a narrow pass through which Keona and Alice must needs go. Arriving there a short time before they did, she was able to take a few minutes' rest before resuming the chase.

Little did the wily savage think that a pair of eyes as dark and bright, though not so fierce, as his own, were gazing at him from behind the bushes as he sped up that narrow gorge.

Poor Alice was running and stumbling by his side; for the monster held her by the hand and dragged her along, although she was scarcely able to stand. The heart of the black girl well-nigh burst with anger when she observed that both her shoes and stockings had been torn off in the hasty flight, and that her tender feet were cut and bleeding.

Just as they reached the spot near which Poopy was concealed, the child sank with a low wail to the ground, unable to advance another step. Keona seized her in his arms, and, uttering a growl of anger as he threw her rudely over his shoulder, bore her swiftly away.

But, quick though his step was, it could not outrun that of the poor little dark maiden who followed him like his shadow, carefully keeping out of view, however, while her mind was busy with plans for the deliverance of her young mistress. The more she thought, the more she felt how utterly hopeless would be any attempt that she could make, either by force or stratagem, to pluck her from the grasp of one so strong and subtle as Keona. At length she resolved to give up thinking of plans altogether, and take to prayer instead.

On reaching the highest ridge of the mountains, Keona suddenly stopped, placed Alice on a flat rock, and went to the top of a peak not more than fifty yards off. Here he lay down and gazed long and earnestly over the country through which they had just passed, evidently for the purpose of discovering, if possible, the position and motions of his enemies.

Poopy, whose wits were sharpened by love, at once took advantage of her opportunity. She crept on all fours towards the rock on which Alice lay, in such a manner that it came between her person and the savage.

"Missy Alice! O, Missy Alice! quick! look up! it's me—Poopy," said the girl, raising her head cautiously above the edge of the rock.

Alice started up on one elbow, and was about to utter a scream of delight and surprise, when her sable friend laid her black paw suddenly on the child's pretty mouth, and effectually shut it up.

"Hush! Alice; no cry. Savage hear and come back—kill Poopy bery much quick. Listen. Me all alone. You bery clibber. Dry up eyes, no cry any more. Look happy. God will save you. Poopy nebber leave you as long as got her body in her soul."

Just at this point, Keona rose from his recumbent position, and the girl, who had not suffered her eyes to move from him for a single instant, at once sunk behind the rock and crept so silently away that Alice could scarcely persuade herself she had not been dreaming.

The savage returned, took the child's hand, led her over the brow of the mountain, and began to descend, by a steep, rugged path, to the valleys lying on the other side of the island. But before going a hundred yards down the dark gorge—which was rendered all the darker by the approach of night—he turned abruptly aside, entered the mouth of a cavern, and disappeared.

Poopy was horrified at this unexpected and sudden change in the state of things. For a long time she lay closely hid among the rocks, within twenty yards of the cave's mouth, expecting every moment to see the fugitives issue from its dark recesses. But they did not reappear. All at once it occurred to the girl that there might possibly be an exit from the cavern at the other end of it, and that, while she was idly waiting there, her little mistress and her savage captor might be hastening down the mountain far beyond her reach.

Rendered desperate by this idea, she quitted her place of concealment, and ran recklessly into the cavern. But the place was dark as Erebus, and the ground was so rugged that she tripped and fell before she had advanced into it more than fifty yards.

Bruised by the fall, and overawed by the gloom of her situation, the poor girl lay still for some time where she had fallen, with bated breath, and listening intently; but no sound struck her ear save the beating of her own heart, which appeared to her unnaturally loud. Under an impulse of terror, she rose, and ran back into the open air.

Here it occurred to her that she might perhaps find the other outlet to the cave,—supposing that one really existed,—by going round the hill and carefully examining the ground on the other side. This, however, was a matter requiring considerable time, and it was not until a full hour had expired that she returned to the mouth of the cave, and sat down to rest and consider what should be done next.

To enter the dark recesses of the place without a light she knew would be impossible as well as useless, and she had no means of procuring a light. Besides, even if she had, what good could come of her exploration? The next impulse was to hasten back to the settlement at full speed and guide a party to the place; but, was it likely that the savage would remain long in the cave? This question suggested her former idea of the possible existence of another outlet; and as she thought upon Alice being now utterly beyond her reach, she covered her face with her hands and burst into tears. After a short time she began to pray. Then, as the minutes flew past, and her hopes sank lower and lower, she commenced—like many a child of Adam who thinks himself considerably wiser than a black girl—to murmur at her hard lot. This she did in an audible voice, having become forgetful of, as well as indifferent to, the chances of discovery.

"Oh! w'at for was me born?" she inquired, somewhat viciously; and not being able, apparently, to answer this question, she proceeded to comment in a wildly sarcastic tone on the impropriety of her having been brought into existence at all.

"Me should be dead. Wat's de use o'life w'en ums nothin' to live for? Alice gone! Darling Alice! Oh, dear! Me wish I wasn't never had been born; yes, me do! Don't care for meself! Wouldn't give nuffin for meself! Only fit to tend Missy Alice! Not fit for nuffin else. And now Alice gone—whar' to' nobody nose an' nobody care, 'xcept Poopy, who's not worth a brass button!"

Having given utterance to this last expression, which she had acquired from her friend Corrie, the poor girl began to howl in order to relieve her insupportable feelings.

It was at this point in our story that Master Corrie, and his companion the Grampus, having traced the before-mentioned footprints for a considerable distance, became cognizant of sundry unearthly sounds, on hearing which, never having heard anything like them before, these wanderers stood still in attitudes of breathless attention, and gazed at each other with looks of indescribable amazement, not altogether unmixed with a dash of consternation.

CHAPTER XI

A GHOST—A TERRIBLE COMBAT
ENDING IN A DREADFUL PLUNGE

"Corrie," said Jo Bumpus, solemnly, with a troubled expression on his grave face, "I've heer'd a many a cry in this life, both ashore and afloat; but, since I was half as long as a marlinespike, I've never heerd the likes o' that there screech nowhere."

At any other time the boy would have expressed a doubt as to the possibility of the Grampus having, at any period of his existence, been so short as "half the length of a marlinespike;" but, being very imaginative by nature, and having been encouraged to believe in ghosts by education, he was too frightened to be funny. With a face that might very well have passed for that of a ghost, and a very pale ghost too, he said, in a tremulous voice:

"Oh dear! Bumpus; what *shall* we do?"

"Dun know," replied Jo, very sternly; for the stout mariner also believed in ghosts, as a matter of course, although he would not admit it; and, being a man of iron mold and powerful will, there was at that moment going on within his capacious breast a terrific struggle between natural courage and supernatural cowardice.

"Let's go back," whispered Corrie. "I know another pass over the hills. It's a longer one, to be sure; but we can run, you know, to make for—"

He was struck dumb and motionless at this point by the recurrence of the dreadful howling, louder than ever, as poor Poopy's despair deepened.

"Don't speak to me, boy," said Bumpus, still more sternly, while a cold sweat stood in large beads on his pale forehead. "Here's wot I calls somethin' new; an' it becomes a man, specially a British seaman, d'ye see, to inquire into new things in a reasonable sort of way."

Jo caught his breath, and clutched the rock beside him power-fully, as he continued:

"It ain't a ghost, in course; it *can't* be that. Cause why? there's no sich a thing as a ghost."

"Ain't there?" whispered Corrie, hopefully.

The hideous yell that Poopy here set up seemed to give the lie direct to the skeptical seaman; but he went on deliberately, though with a glazed eye and a deathlike pallor on his face—

"No; there ain't no ghosts,—never wos, an' never will be. All ghosts is sciencrific dolusions, nothing more; and it's only the hignorant an' supercilious as b'lieves in 'em. I don't; an', wots more," added Jo, with tremendous decision, "I *won't!*"

At this point, the "sciencrific dolusion" recurred to her former idea of alarming the settlement; and with this view began to retrace her steps, howling as she went.

Of course, as Jo and his small companion had been guided by her footsteps, it followed that Poopy, in retracing them, grad-ually drew near to the terrified pair. The short twilight of those regions had already deepened into the shades of night; so that the poor girl's form was not at first visible, as she advanced from among the dark shadows of the overhanging cliffs and the large masses of scattered rock that lay strewn about that wild mountain pass.

Now, although John Bumpus succeeded, by an almost super-natural effort, in calming the tumultuous agitation of his spirit, while the wild cries of the girl were at some distance, he found himself utterly bereft of speech when the dreadful sounds unmistakably approached him. Corrie, too, became livid, and both were rooted to the spot in unutterable horror; but when the ghost at length actually came into view, and (owing to Poopy's body being dark, and her garments white) presented the appear-ance of a dimly luminous creature, without head, arms, or legs, the last spark of endurance in man and boy went out. The one gave a roar, the other a shriek of terror, and both turned and fled like the wind over a stretch of country, which, in happier circumstances, they would have crossed with caution.

Poopy helped to accelerate their flight by giving vent to a cry of fear, and thereafter to a yell of delight, as, from her point of view, she recognized the well-known outline of Corrie's figure clearly defined against the sky. She ran after them in frantic haste; but she might as well have chased a couple of wildcats. Either terror is gifted with better wings than hope, or males are better runners than females. Perhaps both propositions are true; but certain it is that Poopy soon began to perceive that the succor which had appeared so suddenly was about to vanish almost as quickly.

In this new dilemma, the girl once more availed herself of her slight knowledge of the place, and made a detour which enabled her to shoot ahead of the fugitives and intercept them in one of the narrowest parts of the mountain gorge. Here, instead of using her natural voice, she conceived that the likeliest way of making her terrified friends understand who she was, would be to shout with all the strength of her lungs. Accordingly, she planted herself suddenly in the center of their path, just as the two came tearing blindly round a corner of rock, and set up a series of yells, the nature of which utterly beggars description.

The result was, that, with one short wild cry of renewed horror, Bumpus and Corrie turned sharp round and fled in the opposite direction.

There is no doubt whatever that they would have succeeded in ultimately escaping from this pertinacious ghost, and poor Poopy would have had to make the best of her way to Sandy Cove alone, but for the fortunate circumstance that Corrie fell; and being only a couple of paces in advance of his companion, Bumpus fell over him.

The ghost took advantage of this to run forward, crying out, "Corrie! Corrie! Corrie!—it's me! *me*! ME!" with all her might.

"Eh! I do believe it knows my name!" cried the boy, scrambling to his feet, and preparing to renew his flight; but Bumpus laid his heavy hand on his collar, and held him fast.

"Wot! Did it speak?"

"Yes; listen! Oh dear! Come,—fly!"

Instead of flying, the seaman heaved a deep sigh; and, sitting down on a rock, took out a reddish brown cotton handkerchief, wherewith he wiped his forehead.

"My boy," said he, still panting; "it ain't a ghost. No ghost wos ever known to *speak*. They looks, an' they runs, an' they yells, an' they vanishes, but they never speaks; d'ye see? I told ye it was a sciencrific dolusion; though, I'm bound for to confess, I never heerd o' von o' them critters speakin', no more than the ghosts. Howsomedever, that's wot it is."

Corrie, who still hesitated, and held himself in readiness to bolt at a moment's notice, suddenly cried:

"Why! I *do* believe it's—No; it can't be—yes—I say, it's *Poopy*."

"Wot's Poopy?" inquired the seaman, in some anxiety.

"What! don't you know Poopy, Alice's black maid, who keeps her company, and looks after her; besides' doin' her and 'undoin' her (as she calls it), night and morning, and putting her to bed? Hooray! Poopy, my lovely black darling; where *have* you come from? You've frightened Bumpus here nearly out of his wits. I do believe he'd have bin dead by this time, but for me!"

So saying, Corrie, in the revulsion of his suddenly relieved feelings, actually threw his arms round Poopy, and hugged her.

"O Corrie!" exclaimed the girl, submitting to the embrace with as much indifference as if she had been a lamp-post, "w'at troble you hab give me! Why you run so? sure you know me voice."

"Know it, my sweet lump of charcoal; I'd know it among a thousand, if ye'd only use it in its own pretty natural tones; but if you *will* go and screech like a bottle-imp, you know," said

Corrie, remonstratively, "how can you expect a stupid feller like me to recognize it?"

"There ain't no sich things as bottle-imps, no more nor ghosts," observed Bumpus; "but hold your noise, you chatterbox, and let's hear wot the gal's got to say. Mayhap she knows summat about Alice?"

At this, Poopy manufactured an expression on her sable countenance which was meant to be intensely knowing and suggestive.

"Don't I? Yes, me do," said she.

"Out with it, then, at once, you pot of shoe-blacking," cried the impatient Corrie.

The girl immediately related all that she knew regarding the fugitives, stammering very much from sheer anxiety to get it all out as fast as she could, and delaying her communication very much in consequence, besides rendering her meaning rather obscure—sometimes unintelligible. Indeed, the worthy seaman could scarcely understand a word she said. He sat staring at the whites of her eyes, which, with her teeth, were the only visible parts of her countenance at that moment, and swayed his body to and fro, as if endeavoring by a mechanical effort to arrive at a philosophical conception of something exceedingly abstruse. But at the end of each period he turned to Corrie for a translation.

At length both man and boy became aware of the state of things, and Corrie started up crying:

"Let's go into the cave at once."

"Hold on, boy," cried Bumpus! "not quite so fast (as the monkey said to the barrel-organ w'en it took to playin' Scotch reels). We must have a council of war; d'ye see? The black monster Keona may have gone right through the cave and comed out at t'other end of it, in w'ich case it's all up with our chance o' finding 'em to-night. But if they've gone in to spend the night there, why we've nothing to do but watch at the mouth of it till mornin' an' nab 'em as they comes out."

"Yes; but how are we to know whether they're in the cave or not?" said Corrie, impatiently.

"Ah! that's the puzzler," replied Bumpus, in a meditative way; "but of course, we must look out for puzzlers ahead sometimes w'en we gets into a land storm, d'ye see; just as we looks out ahead for breakers in a storm at sea. Suppose now that I creeps into the cave and listens for 'em. They'd never hear me, 'cause I'd make no noise."

"You might as well try to sail into it in a big ship without making noise, you Grampus."

To this the Grampus observed, that if the cave had only three fathoms of water in the bottom of it he would have no objections whatever to try.

"But," added he, "suppose *you* go in."

Corrie shook his head, and looked anxiously miserable.

"Well, then," said Bumpus, "suppose we light two torches. I'll take one in one hand, and this here cutlash in the other; and you'll take t'other torch in one hand and your pistol in the other, and clap that bit of a broken sword 'tween yer teeth, and we'll give a 'orrid screech, and rush in, pell-mell—all of a heap like. You could fire yer pistol straight before you on chance (it's wonderful wot a chance shot will do sometimes); an' if it don't do nothin', fling it right into the blackguard's face: a brass-mounted tool like that ketchin' him right on the end of his peak would lay him flat over, like a ship in a white squall."

"And suppose," said Corrie, in a tone of withering sarcasm,— "suppose all this happened to Alice, instead of the dirty nigger?"

"Ah! to be sure. That's a puzzler,—puzzler number two."

Here Poopy, who had listened with great impatience to the foregoing conversation, broke in energetically.

"An' s'pose," said she, "dat Keona and Missy Alice come out ob cave w'en you two be talkerin' sich a lot of stuff?"

It may as well be remarked, in passing, that Poopy had

acquired a considerable amount of her knowledge of English from Master Corrie. Her remark, although not politely made, was sufficiently striking to cause Bumpus to start up, and exclaim:

"That's true, gal. Come, show us the way to this here cave."

There was a fourth individual present at this council of war who apparently felt a deep interest in its results, although he took no part in its proceedings. This was no other than Keona himself, who lay extended at full length among the rocks, not two yards from the spot where Bumpus sat, listening intently, and grinning from ear to ear with fiendish malice.

The series of shrieks, howls, and yells to which reference has been made had naturally attracted the attention of that wily savage when he was in the cave. Following the sounds with quick, noiseless step, he soon found himself within a few paces of the deliberating trio. The savage did not make much of the conversation, but he gathered sufficient to assure himself that his hiding-place had been discovered, and that plans were being laid for his capture.

It would have been an easy matter for him to have suddenly leaped on the unsuspecting Bumpus and driven a knife to his heart, after which poor Corrie and the girl could have been easily dealt with; but fortunately (at least for his enemies, if not for himself) indecision in the moment of action was one of Keona's besetting sins. He suspected that other enemies might be near at hand, and that the noise of the scuffle might draw them to the spot. He observed, moreover, that the boy had a pistol, which, besides being a weapon that acts quickly and surely, even in weak hands, would give a loud report and a bright flash that might be heard and seen at a great distance. Taking these things into consideration, he thrust back the knife which he had half unsheathed, and, retreating with the slow, gliding motion of a serpent, got beyond the chance of being detected, just as Bumpus rose to follow Poopy to the cave.

The savage entered its yawning mouth in a few seconds, and glided noiselessly into its dark recesses like an evil spirit. Soon after, the trio reached the same spot, and stood for some time silently gazing upon the thick darkness within.

A feeling of awe crept over them as they stood thus, and a shudder passed through Corrie's frame as he thought of the innumerable ghosts that might—probably did—inhabit that dismal place. But the thought of Alice served partly to drive away his fears and steel his heart. He felt that the presence of such a sweet and innocent child *must*, somehow or other, subdue and baffle the power of evil spirits, and it was with some show of firmness that he said:

"Come, Bumpus, let's go in. We are better without a torch; it would only show that we were coming; and as they don't expect us, the savage may perhaps kindle a light which will guide us."

Bumpus, who was not restrained by any thoughts of the supposed power or influence of the little girl, and whose super-stitious fears were again doing furious battle with his natural courage, heaved a deep sigh, ground his teeth together, and clenched his fists.

Even in that dreadful hour the seaman's faith in his physical invincibility, and in the terrible power of his fists, did not alto-gether fail. Although he wore a cutlass, and had used it that day with tremendous effect, he did not now draw it. He preferred to engage supernatural enemies with the weapons that nature had given him, and entered the cave on tiptoe with slow, cautious steps, his fists tightly clenched and ready for instant action, yet thrust into the pockets of his coatee in a deceptively peaceful way, as if he meant to take the ghosts by surprise.

Corrie followed him, also on tiptoe, with the broken saber in his right hand, and the cocked pistol in his left, his forefinger being on the trigger, and the muzzle pointing straight at the small of the seaman's back,—if one may be permitted to talk of such an enormous back having any "small" about it!

Poopy entered last, also on tiptoe, trembling violently, holding on with both hands to the waistband of Corrie's trousers, and only restrained from instant flight by her anxieties and her strong love for little Alice.

Thus, step by step, with bated breath and loudly beating hearts, pausing often to listen, and gasping in a subdued way at times, the three friends advanced from the gloom without into the thick darkness within, until their gliding forms were swallowed up.

Now it so happened that the shouts and yells to which we have more than once made reference in this chapter attracted a band of savages who had been put to flight by Henry Stuart's party. These rascals, not knowing what was the cause of so much noise up on the heights, and being much too well acquainted with the human voice in all its modifications to fancy that ghosts had anything to do with it, cautiously ascended towards the cavern, just a few minutes after the disappearance of John Bumpus and his companions.

Here they sat down to hold a palaver. While this was going on, Keona carried Alice in his unwounded arm to the other end of the cave, and, making his exit through a small opening at its inner extremity, bore his trembling captive to a rocky eminence, shaped somewhat like a sugarloaf, on the summit of which he placed her. So steep were the sides of this cone of lava, that it seemed to Alice that she was surrounded by precipices over which she must certainly tumble if she dared to move.

Here Keona left her, having first, however, said, in a low, stern voice:

"If you moves, you dies!"

The poor child was too much terrified to move, even had she dared; for she, too, had heard the unaccountable cries of Poopy, although, owing to distance and the wild nature of these cries, she had failed to recognize the voice. When, therefore, her jailer left her with this threat, she coiled herself up in the smallest possible space, and began to sob.

Meanwhile, Keona re-entered the cavern, with a diabolical grin on his sable countenance, which, although it savored more of evil than of any other quality, had in it, nevertheless, a strong dash of ferocious joviality, as if he were aware that he had got his enemies into a trap, and could amuse himself by playing with them as a cat does with a mouse.

Soon the savage began to step cautiously, partly because of the rugged nature of the ground and the thick darkness that surrounded him, and partly in order to avoid alarming the three adventurers who were advancing towards him from the other extremity of the cavern. In a few minutes he halted; for the footsteps and the whispering voices of his pursuers became distinctly audible to him, although all three did their best to make as little noise as possible.

"Wot a 'orrid place it is!" exclaimed Bumpus, in a hoarse, angry whisper, as he struck his shins violently, for at least the tenth time, against a ledge of rock. "I do b'lieve, boy, that there's nobody here, and that we'd as well 'bout ship and steer back the way we've comed; tho' it *is* a 'orrible coast for rocks and shoals."

To this, Corrie, not being in a talkative humor, made no reply.

"D'ye hear me, boy?" said Jo, aloud, for he was somewhat shaken again by the dead silence that followed the close of his remark.

"All right; I'm here;" said Corrie, meekly.

"Then why don't ye speak?" said Jo, tartly.

"I'd advise *you* not to speak so loud," retorted the boy.

"Is the dark 'un there?" inquired Bumpus.

"What d'ye say?"

"The dark 'un; the lump o' charcoal, you know."

"Oh! she's all safe," replied Corrie. "I only hope she won't haul the clothes right off my body; she grips at my waistband like a—"

Here he was cut short by Keona, who gave utterance to a low, dismal wail that caused the blood and marrow of all three to freeze up, and their hearts for a moment to leap into their throats and all but choke them.

"Poopy's gone," gasped Corrie, after a few seconds had elapsed.

There was no doubt of the fact; for besides the relief experienced by the boy, from the relaxing of her grip on his waistband, the moment the wail was heard, the sound of the girl's footsteps, as she flew back to the entrance of the cave was distinctly heard.

Keona waited a minute or two to ascertain the exact position of his enemies, then he repeated the wail, and swelled it gradually out into a fiendish yell that awoke all the echoes of the place. At the same time, guessing his aim as well as he could, he threw a spear and discharged a shower of stones at the spot where he supposed they stood.

There is no understanding the strange workings of the human mind! The very thing that most people would have expected to strike terror to the heart of Bumpus was that which infused courage into his soul. The frightful tones of the savage's voice in such a place did indeed almost prostrate the superstitious spirit of the seaman; but when he heard the spear whiz past within an inch of his ear, and received a large stone full on his chest, and several small ones on other parts of his person, that instant his strength returned to him, like that of Samson when the Philistines attempted to fall upon him. His curiously philosophical mind at once leaped to the conclusion that, although ghosts could yell, and look, and vanish, they could not throw spears or fling stones, and that, therefore, the man they were in search of was actually close beside them.

Acting on this belief, with immense subtlety Bumpus uttered a cry of feigned terror, and fled, followed by the panting Corrie, who uttered a scream of real terror at what he supposed must be the veritable ghost of the place.

But before he had run fifty yards, John Bumpus suddenly came to a dead halt, seized Corrie by the collar, dragged him down behind a rock, and laid his large hand upon his mouth, as being the shortest and easiest way of securing silence, without the trouble of explanation.

As he had anticipated, the soft tread of the savage was heard almost immediately after, as he passed on in full pursuit. He brushed close past the spot where Bumpus crouched, and received from that able-bodied seaman such a blow on the shoulder of his wounded arm as, had it been delivered in daylight, would have certainly smashed his shoulder-blade. As it was, it caused him to stagger, and sent him howling with pain to the mouth of the cavern, whither he was followed by the triumphant Jo, who now made sure of catching him.

But "there is many a slip 'twixt the cup and the lip." When Keona issued from the cave, he was received with a shout by the band of savages, who instantly recognized him as their friend by his voice. Poor Poopy was already in their hands, having been seized and gagged when she emerged before she had time to utter a cry. And now they stood in a semicircle, ready to receive all who might come forth into their arms, or on their spear-points, as the case might be.

Bumpus came out like an insane thunderbolt, and Corrie like a streak of lightning. Instantaneously the flash of the pistol, accompanied by its report and a deep growl from Bumpus, increased the resemblance to these meteorological phenomena, and three savages lay stunned upon the ground.

"This way, Corrie!" cried the excited seaman, leaping to a perpendicular rock, against which he placed his back, and raised his fists in a pugilistic attitude, "Keep one or two in play with your broken toothpick, an' I'll floor 'em one after another as they comes up. Now, then, ye black baboons, come on,—all at once, if you like,—an' Jo Bumpus'll show ye wot he's made of!"

Not perceiving very clearly, in the dim light caused by a few stars that flickered among the black and gathering clouds, the immense size and power of the man with whom they had to deal, the savages were not slow to accept this free and generous invitation to "come on." They rushed forward in a body, intending, no doubt, to take the man and boy prisoners; for if they had wished to slay them, nothing would have been easier than to have thrown one or two of their spears at their defense-less breasts.

Bumpus experienced a vague feeling that he had now a fair opportunity of testing and proving his invincibility; yet the desperate nature of the case did not induce him to draw his sword. He preferred his fists, as being superior and much more handy weapons. He received the first two savages who came within reach on the knuckles of his right and left hands, rendering them utterly insensible, and driving them against the two men immediately behind with such tremendous violence that they also were put *hors de combat*.

This was just what Bumpus had intended and hoped for. The sudden fall of so many gave him time to launch out his great fists a second time. They fell with the weight of sledge-hammers on the faces of two more of his opponents, flattening their noses, and otherwise disfiguring their features, besides stretching them on the ground. At the same time, Corrie flung his empty pistol in the face of a man who attempted to assault his companion on the right flank unawares, and laid him prone on the earth. Another savage, who made the same effort on the left, received a gash on the thigh from the broken saber that sent him howling from the scene of conflict.

Thus were eight savages disposed of in about as many seconds.

But there is a limit to the powers and the prowess of man. The savages, on seeing the fall of so many of their compan-ions, rushed in on Bumpus before he could recover himself for another blow. That is to say, the savages behind pushed forward those in front whether they would or no, and falling *en masse* on the unfortunate pair, well-nigh buried them alive in black human flesh.

Bumpus's last cry before being smothered was, "Down with the black varmints!" and Corrie's last shout was, "Hooray!"

Thus fell—despite the undignified manner of their fall—a couple of as great heroes as were ever heard of in the annals of war; not excepting even those of Homer himself.

Now, good reader, this maybe all very well for us to describe, and for you to read, but it was a terrible thing for Poopy to witness. Being bound hand and foot, she was compelled to look on; and, to say truth, she did look on with uncommon interest. When her friends fell, however, she expressed her regrets and fears in a subdued shriek, for which she received a sounding slap on the cheek from a young savage who had chosen for himself the comparatively dangerous post of watching her, while his less courageous friends were fighting.

Strange to say, Poopy did not shed more tears (as one might have expected) on receiving such treatment. She had been used to that sort of thing, poor child. Before coming to the service of her little mistress, she had been brought up (it would be more strictly correct to say that she had been kicked, and cuffed, and pinched, and battered up) by a step-mother, whose chief delight was to pull out handfuls of her woolly hair, beat her nose flat (which was adding insult to injury, for it was too flat by nature), and otherwise to maltreat her. When, therefore, Poopy received the slap referred to, she immediately dried her eyes and looked humble. But she did not by any means *feel* humble. No; a regard for truth compels us to state that, on this particular occasion, Poopy acted the part of a hypocrite. If her hands had been loose, and she had possessed a knife just then—we are afraid to think of the dreadful use to which she would have put it.

The natives spent a considerable time in securely binding their three captives, after which they bore them into the cavern.

Here they kindled a torch, and held a long palaver as to what was to be done with the prisoners. Some counseled instant death, others advised that they should be kept as hostages.

The debate was so long and fierce, that the day had begun to break before it was concluded. It was at length arranged that they should be conveyed alive to their village, there to be disposed of according to the instructions of their chiefs.

Feeling that they had already delayed too long, they placed the prisoners on their shoulders, and bore them swiftly away.

Poor Corrie and his sable friend were easily carried, coiled up like sacks, each on the shoulders of a stalwart savage; but Bumpus, who had required eight men to bind him, still remained unconvinced of his vincibility. He struggled so violently on the shoulders of the four men who bore him, that Keona, in a fit of passion, tinged no doubt with revenge, hit him such a blow on the head with the handle of an ax as caused his brains to sing, and a host of stars to dance before his eyes.

These stars were, however, purely imaginary; for at that time the dawn had extinguished the lesser lights. Ere long, the bright beams of the rising sun suffused the eastern sky with a golden glow. On passing the place where Alice had been left, a couple of the party were sent by Keona to fetch her. They took the unnecessary precaution of binding the poor child, and speedily rejoined their comrades with her in their arms.

The amazement of her friends on seeing Alice was only equaled by her surprise on beholding them. But they were not permitted to communicate with each other. Presently the whole party emerged from the wild mountain gorges, through which they had been passing for some time, and proceeded in single file along a narrow path that skirted the precipices of the coast. The cliffs here were nearly a hundred feet high. They descended sheer down into deep water; in some places even overhung the sea.

Here John Bumpus, having recovered from the stunning

effects of the blow dealt him by Keona, renewed his struggles, and rendered the passage of the place not only difficult but dangerous—to himself as well as to his enemies. Just as they reached a somewhat open space on the top of the cliffs, Jo succeeded, by almost superhuman exertion in bursting his bonds. Keona, foaming with rage, gave an angry order to his followers, who rushed upon Bumpus in a body as he was endeavoring to clear himself of the cords. Although John struck out manfully, the savages were too quick for him. They raised him suddenly aloft in their arms, and hurled him headlong over the cliff!

The horror of his friends on witnessing this may easily be imagined; but every other feeling was swallowed up in terror when the savages, apparently rendered bloodthirsty by what they had done, ran towards Alice, and, raising her from the ground, hastened to the edge of the cliff, evidently with the intention of throwing her over also.

Before they, had accomplished their fiendish purpose, however, a sound like thunder burst upon their ears and arrested their steps. This was immediately followed by another crash, and then came a series of single reports in rapid succession, which were multiplied by the echoes of the heights until the whole region seemed to tremble with the reverberation.

At first the natives seemed awe-stricken. Then, on becoming aware that the sounds which originated all this tumult came from the direction of their own village, they dropped Alice on the ground, fled precipitately down the rugged path that led from the heights to the valley, and disappeared, leaving the three captives, bound and helpless, on the cliffs.

CHAPTER XII

DANGEROUS NAVIGATION AND DOUBTFUL PILOTAGE — MONTAGUE IS HOT, GASCOYNE SARCASTIC

We now turn to the Talisman, which, it will be remembered, we left making her way slowly through the reefs toward the northern end of the island, under the pilotage of Gascoyne.

The storm, which had threatened to burst over the island at an earlier period of that evening, passed off far to the south. The light breeze which had tempted Captain Montague to weigh anchor soon died away, and before night a profound calm brooded over the deep.

When the breeze fell, Gascoyne went forward, and, seating himself on a forecastle carronade, appeared to fall into a deep reverie. Montague paced the quarter-deck impatiently, glancing from time to time down the skylight at the barometer which hung in the cabin, and at the vane which drooped motionless from the masthead. He acted with the air of a man who was deeply dissatisfied with the existing state of things, and who felt inclined to take the laws of nature into his own hands. Fortunately for nature and himself, he was unable to do this.

Ole Thorwald exhibited a striking contrast to the active, impatient commander of the vessel. That portly individual, having just finished a cigar which the first lieutenant had presented to him on his arrival on board, threw the fag end of it into the sea, and proceeded leisurely to fill a large-headed German pipe, which was the constant companion of his waking hours, and the bowl of which seldom enjoyed a cool moment.

Ole having filled the pipe, lighted it; then leaning over the taffrail, he gazed placidly into the dark waters, which were so perfectly calm that every star in the vault above could be compared with its reflection in the abyss below.

Ole Thorwald, excepting when engaged in actual battle, was phlegmatic, and constitutionally lazy and happy. When enjoying his German pipe he felt impressibly serene, and did not care to be disturbed. He therefore paid no attention to the angry manner of Montague, who brushed past him repeatedly in his hasty perambulations, but continued to gaze downwards and smoke calmly in a state of placid felicity.

"You appear to take things coolly, Mister Thorwald," said Montague, half in jest, yet with a touch of asperity in his manner.

"I always do" (puff) "when the weather's not warm." (Puff, puff.)

"Humph!" ejaculated Montague; "but the weather *is* warm just now; at least it seems so to me,—so warm that I should not be surprised if a thunder-squall were to burst upon us ere long."

"Not a pleasant place to be caught in a squall," returned the other, gazing through the voluminous clouds of smoke which he emitted at several coral reefs, whose ragged edges just rose to the level of the calm sea without breaking its mirror-like surface; "I've seen one or two fine vessels caught that way, just here abouts, and go right down in the middle of the breakers."

Montague smiled, and the commander-in-chief of the Sandy Cove army fired innumerable broadsides from his mouth with redoubled energy.

"That is not a cheering piece of information," said he, "especially when one has reason to believe that a false man stands at the helm."

Montague uttered the latter part of his speech in a subdued, earnest voice, and the matter-of-fact Ole turned his eyes slowly towards the man at the wheel; but observing that he who presided there was a short, fat, commonplace, and uncommonly jolly-looking seaman, he merely uttered a grunt, and looked at Montague inquiringly.

"Nay: I mean not the man who actually holds the spokes of the wheel, but he who guides the ship."

Thorwald glanced at Gascoyne, whose figure was dimly visible in the fore part of the ship, and then looking at Montague in surprise, shook his head gravely, as if to say, "I'm still in the dark; go on."

"Can Mr. Thorwald put out his pipe for a few minutes, and accompany me to the cabin? I would have a little converse on this matter in private."

Ole hesitated.

"Well, then," said the other, smiling, "you may take the pipe with you, although it is against rules to smoke in my cabin; but I'll make an exception in your case."

Ole smiled, bowed, and thanking the captain for his courtesy, descended to the cabin along with him, and sat down on a sofa in the darkest corner of it. Here he smoked vehemently, while his companion, assuming rather a mysterious air, said, in an undertone:

"You have heard, of course, that the pirate Durward has been seen, or heard of, in these seas?"

Ole nodded.

"Has it ever struck you that this Gascoyne, as he calls himself, knows more about the pirate than he chooses to tell?"

"Never," replied Ole. Indeed, nothing ever did *strike* the stout commander-in-chief of the forces. All new ideas came to him by slow degrees, and did not readily find admission to his perceptive faculties. But when they did gain an entrance into his thick head, nothing was ever known to drive them out again. As he did not seem inclined to comment on the hint thrown out by his companion, Montague continued, in a still more impressive tone:

"What would you say, if this Gascoyne himself turned out to be the pirate?"

The idea being a simple one, and the proper course to follow being rather obvious, Ole replied, with unwonted promptitude: "Put him in irons, of course, and hang him as soon possible."

Montague laughed. "Truly that would be a vigorous way of proceeding; but as I have no proof of the truth of my suspicions, and as the man is my guest at present, as well as my pilot, it behooves me to act more cautiously."

"Not at all; by no means; you're quite wrong, captain (which is the natural result of being young; all young people go wrong more or less); it is clearly your duty to catch a pirate anyhow you can, as fast as you can, and kill him without delay."

Here the sanguinary Thorwald paused to draw and puff into vitality the pipe which was beginning to die down, and Montague asked:

"But how d'you know he is the pirate?"

"Because you said so," replied his friend.

"Nay; I said that I *suspected* him to be Durward,—nothing more."

"And what more would you have?" cried Ole, whose calm spirit was ruffled with unusual violence at the thought of the hated Durward being actually within his reach. "For my part, I conceive that you are justified in taking him up on suspicion, trying him in a formal way (just to save appearances) on suspicion and hanging him at once on suspicion. Quite time enough to inquire into the matter after the villain is comfortably sewed up in a hammock with a thirty-pound shot at his heels, and sent to the bottom of the sea for the sharks and crabs to devour. Suspicion is nine points of the law in these regions, Captain Montague, and we never allow the tenth point to interfere with the course of justice one way or another. Hang him, or shoot him if you prefer it, at once; *that* is what I recommend."

Just as Thorwald concluded this amiable piece of advice, the deep, strong tones of Gascoyne's voice were heard addressing the first lieutenant.

"You had better hoist your royals and skyscrapers, Mr. Mulroy; we shall have a light air off the land presently, and it will require all your canvas to carry the ship round the north point, so as to bring her guns to bear on the village of the savages."

"The distance seems to me very short," replied the lieutenant, "and the Talisman sails faster than you may suppose with a light wind."

"I doubt not the sailing qualities of your good ship, though I could name a small schooner that would beat them in light wind or storm; but you forget that we have to land our stout ally Mr. Thorwald with his men at the Goat's Pass, and that will compel us to lose time,—too much of which has been lost already."

Without reply, the lieutenant turned on his heel, and gave the necessary orders to hoist the additional sails, while the captain hastened on deck, leaving Thorwald to finish his pipe in peace, and ruminate on the suspicions which had been raised in his mind.

In less than half an hour the light wind which Gascoyne had predicted came off the land, first in a series of what sailors term "cat's paws," and then in a steady breeze, which lasted several hours, and caused the vessel to slip rapidly through the still water. As he looked anxiously over the bow, Captain Montague felt that he had placed himself completely in the power of the suspected skipper of the Foam; for coral reefs surrounded him on all sides, and many of them passed so close to the ship's side that he expected every moment to feel the shock that would wreck his vessel and his hopes at the same time. He blamed himself for trusting a man whom he supposed he had such good reason to doubt, but consoled himself by thrusting his hand into his bosom an grasping the handle of a pistol, with which, in the event of the ship striking, he had made up his mind to blow out Gascoyne's brains.

About an hour later, the Talisman was hove-to off the Goat's Pass, and Ole Thorwald was landed with his party at the base of a cliff which rose sheer up from the sea like a wall.

"Are we to go up there?" inquired Ole, in a rueful tone of voice, as he surveyed a narrow chasm to which Gascoyne guided him.

"That is the way. It's not so bad at it looks. When you get to the top, follow the little path that leads along the cliffs northward, and you will reach the brow of a hill from which the native village will be visible. Descend and attack it at once, if you find men to fight with; if not, take possession quietly. Mind you don't take the wrong turn; it leads to places where a wildcat would not venture even in daylight. If you attend to what I have said, you can't go wrong. Good-night. Shove off."

The oars splashed in the sea at the word, and Gascoyne returned to the ship, leaving Ole to lead his men up the Pass as best he might.

It seemed as if the pilot had resolved to make sure of the destruction of the ship that night; for, not content with running her within a foot or two of innumerable reefs, he at last steered in so close to the shore that the beetling cliffs actually seemed to overhang the deck. When the sun rose, the breeze died away; but sufficient wind continued to fill the upper sails, and to urge the vessel gently onward for some time after the surface of the sea was calm.

Montague endeavored to conceal and repress his anxiety as long as possible; but when at length a line of breakers without any apparent opening presented themselves right ahead, he went up to Gascoyne and said, in a stern undertone:

"Are you aware that you forfeit your life if my vessel strikes?"

"I know it," replied Gascoyne, coolly throwing away the stump of his cigar, and lighting a fresh one; "but I have no desire either to destroy your vessel or to lose my life; although, to say truth, I should have no objection, in other circumstances, to attempt the one and to risk the other."

"Say you so?" said Montague, with a sharp glance at the countenance of the other, where, however, he could perceive nothing but placid good humor; "that speech sounds marvelously warlike, methinks in the mouth of a sandal-wood trader."

"Think you, then," said Gascoyne, with a smile of contempt, "that it is only your fire-eating men of war who experience bold impulses and heroic desires?"

"Nay; but traders are not wont to aspire to the honor of fighting the ships that are commissioned to protect them."

"Truly, if I had sought protection from the war-ships of the King of England, I must have sailed long and far to find it," returned Gascoyne. "It is no child's play to navigate these seas, where bloodthirsty savages swarm in their canoes like locusts. Moreover, I sail, as I have told your before, in the China Seas, where pirates are more common than honest traders. What would you say if I were to take it into my head to protect myself?"

"That you were well able to do so," answered Montague, with a smile; "but when I examined the Foam, I found no arms save a few cutlasses and rusty muskets that did not seem to have been in recent use."

"A few bold men can defend themselves with any kind of weapons. My men are stout fellows, not used to flinch at the sound of a round shot passing over their heads."

The conversation was interrupted here by the ship rounding a point and suddenly opening up a view of a fine bay, at the head of which, embosomed in trees and dense underwood, stood the native village of which they were in search.

Just in front of this village lay a small but high and thickly-wooded island, which, as it were, filled up the head of the bay, sheltering it completely from the ocean, and making the part of the sea which washed the shores in front of the houses resemble a deep and broad canal. This stripe of water was wide and deep enough to permit of a vessel of the largest size passing through it; but to any one approaching the place for the first time, there seemed to be no passage for any sort of craft larger than a native canoe. The island itself was high enough to conceal the Talisman completely from the natives until she was within half gunshot of the shore.

Gascoyne still stood on the fore part of the ship as she neared this spot, which was so beset with reefs and rocks that her escape seemed miraculous.

"I think we are near enough for the work that we have to do," suggested Montague, in some anxiety.

"Just about it, Mr. Montague," said Gascoyne, as he turned towards the helm and shouted, "Port your helm."

"Port it is," answered the man at the wheel.

"Steady."

"Back the topsails, Mr. Mulroy."

The sails were backed at once, and the ship became motionless, with her broadside to the village.

"What are we to do now, Mr. Gascoyne?" inquired Montague, smiling in spite of himself at the strange position in which he found himself.

"Fire away at the village as hard as you can," replied Gascoyne, returning the smile.

"What! do you really advise me to bombard a defenseless place, in which, as far as I can see, there are none but women and children."

"Even so," returned the other, carelessly. "At the same time I would advise you to give it them with a blank cartridge."

"And to what purpose such waste of powder?" inquired Montague.

"The furthering of the plans which I have been appointed to carry out," replied Gascoyne, somewhat stiffly, as he turned on his heel and walked away.

The young captain reddened and bit his lip, as he gave the order to load the guns with blank cartridge, and made preparation to fire this harmless broadside on the village. The word to "fire" had barely crossed his lips when the rocks around seemed to tremble with the crash of a shot that came apparently from the other side of the island; for its smoke was visible, although the vessel that discharged it was concealed behind the point.

The Talisman's broadside followed so quickly that the two discharges were blended in one.

CHAPTER XIII

DOINGS ON BOARD THE "FOAM"

The nature of this part of our story requires that we should turn back, repeatedly, in order to trace the movements of the different parties which coöperated with each other.

While the warlike demonstrations we have described were being made by the British cruiser, the crew of the Foam were not idle.

In consequence of the capture of Bumpus by the savages, Gascoyne's message was, of course, not delivered to Manton, and the first mate of the sandal-wood trader would have known nothing about the fight that raged on the other side of the island on the Sunday but for the three shots, fired by the first lieutenant of the Talisman, which decided the fate of the day.

Being curious to know the cause of the firing, Manton climbed the mountains until he gained the dividing ridge,—which, however, he did not succeed in doing till late in the afternoon, the way being rugged as well as long. Here he almost walked into the midst of a flying party of the beaten savages; but dropping suddenly behind a rock, he escaped their notice. The haste with which they ran, and the wounds visible on the persons of many of them, were sufficient to acquaint the mate of the Foam with the fact that a fight had taken place in which the savages had been beaten; and his knowledge of the state of affairs on the island enabled him to jump at once to the correct conclusion that the Christian village had been attacked.

A satanic smile played on the countenance of the mate as he watched the savages until they were out of sight; then, quitting his place of concealment, he hurried back to the schooner, which he reached some time after nightfall.

Immediately on gaining the deck he gave orders to haul the chain of the anchor short, to shake out the sails, and to make other preparations to avail himself without delay of the light breeze off the land which his knowledge of the weather and the locality taught him to look for before morning.

While his orders were being executed, a boat came alongside with that part of the crew which had been sent ashore by Gascoyne to escape the eye of the British commander. It was in charge of the second mate,—a short, but thick-set, and extremely powerful man, of the name of Scraggs,—who walked up to his superior the moment he came on board, and, in a tone somewhat disrespectful, asked what was going to be done.

"Don't you see?" growled Manton; "we're getting ready to sail."

"Of course I see that," retorted Scraggs, between whom and his superior officer there existed a feeling of jealousy as well as of mutual antipathy, for reasons which will be seen hereafter; "but I should like to know where we are going, and why we are going anywhere without the captain. I suppose I am entitled to ask that much."

"It's your business to obey orders," said Manton, angrily.

"Not if they are in opposition to the captain's orders," replied Scraggs, firmly, but in a more respectful tone; for in proportion as he became more mutinous, he felt that he could afford to become more deferential. "The captain's last orders to you were to remain where you are; I heard him give them, and I do not feel it my duty to disobey him at *your* bidding. You'll find, too, that the crew are of my way of thinking."

Manton's face flushed crimson, and, for a moment, he felt inclined to seize a handspike and fell the refractory second mate therewith; but the looks of a few of the men who were standing by and had overheard the conversation convinced him that a violent course of procedure would do him injury. Swallowing his passion, therefore, as he best could, he said:

"Come, Mr. Scraggs, I did not expect that *you* would set a mutinous example to the men; and if it were not that you do so out of respect for the supposed orders of the captain, I would put you in irons at once."

Scraggs smiled sarcastically at this threat, but made no reply, and the mate continued:

"The captain did indeed order me to remain where we are; but I have since discovered that the black dogs have attacked the Christian settlement, as it is called, and you know as well as I do that Gascoyne would not let slip the chance to pitch into the undefended village of the niggers, and pay them off for the mischief they have done to us more than once. At any rate, I mean to go round and blow down their log huts with Long Tom; so you can go ashore if you don't like the work."

Manton knew well, when he made this allusion to mischief formerly done to the crew of the Foam, that he touched a rankling sore in the breast of Scraggs, who in a skirmish with the natives some time before had lost an eye; and the idea of revenging himself on the defenseless women and children of his enemies was so congenial to the mind of the second mate, that his objections to act willingly under Manton's orders were at once removed.

"Ha!" said he, commencing to pace to and fro on the quarter-deck with his superior officer, while the men made the necessary preparations for the intended assault, "that alters the case, Mr. Manton. I don't think, however, that Gascoyne would have taken advantage of the chance to give the brutes what they deserve; for I must say he does seem to be unaccountably chicken-hearted. Perhaps it's as well that he's out of the way. Do you happen to know where he is, or what he's doing?"

"Not I. No doubt he is playing some sly game with this British cruiser, and I dare say he may be lending a hand to the settlers; for he's got some strange interests to look after there, you know" (here both men laughed), "and I shouldn't wonder if he was beforehand with us in pitching into the niggers. He is always ready enough to fight in self-defense, though we can never get him screwed up to the assaulting point."

"Aye, we saw something of the fighting from the hilltops; but as it is no business of ours, I brought the men down, in case they might be wanted aboard."

"Quite right, Scraggs. You're a judicious fellow to send on a dangerous expedition. I'm not sure, however, that Gascoyne would thank you for leaving him to fight the savages alone."

Manton chuckled as he said this, and Scraggs grinned maliciously as he replied:

"Well, it can't exactly be said that I've *left* him, seeing that I have not been with him since we parted aboard of this schooner; and as to his fightin' the niggers alone, hasn't he got ever so many hundred*Christian* niggers to help him to lick the others?"

"True," said Manton, while a smile of contempt curled his lip. "But here comes the breeze, and the sun wont be long behind it. All the better for the work we've got to do. Mind your helm there. Here, lads, take a pull at the topsail halyards; and some of you get the nightcap off Long Tom. I say, Mr. Scraggs, should we show them the *red*, by way of comforting their hearts?"

Scraggs shook his head dubiously. "You forget the cruiser. She has eyes aboard, and may chance to set them on that same red; in which case it's likely she would show us her teeth."

"And what then?" demanded Manton, "are *you* also growing chicken-hearted? Besides," he added, in a milder tone, "the cruiser is quietly at anchor on the other side of the island, and there's not a captain in the British navy who could take a pinnace, much less a ship, through the reefs at the north end of the island without a pilot."

"Well," returned Scraggs, carelessly, "do as you please. It's all one to me."

While the two officers were conversing, the active crew of the Foam were busily engaged in carrying out the orders of Manton; and the graceful schooner glided swiftly along the coast before the same breeze which urged the Talisman to the north end of the island. The former, having few reefs to avoid, approached her destination much more rapidly than the latter, and there is no doubt that she would have arrived first on the scene of action had not the height and form of the cliffs prevented the wind from filling her sails on two or three occasions.

Meanwhile, in obedience to Manton's orders, a great and very peculiar change was effected in the outward aspect of the Foam. To one unacquainted with the character of the schooner, the proceedings of her crew must have seemed unaccountable as well as surprising. The carpenter and his assistants were slung over the sides of the vessel upon which they plied their screw-drivers for a considerable time with great energy, but, apparently, with very little result. In the course of a quarter of an hour, however, a long narrow plank was loosened, which, when stripped off, discovered a narrow line of bright scarlet running quite round the vessel, a little more than a foot above the water-line. This having been accomplished, they next proceeded to the figurehead, and, unscrewing the white lady who smiled there, fixed in her place a hideous griffin's head, which, like the ribbon, was also bright scarlet. While these changes were being effected, others of the crew removed the boat that lay on the deck, bottom up between the masts, and uncovered a long brass pivot-gun, of the largest caliber, which shone in the saffron light of morning like a mass of burnished gold. This gun was kept scrupulously clean and neat in all its arrangements; the rammers, sponges, screws, and other apparatus belonging to it were neatly arranged beside it, and four or five of its enormous iron shot were piled under its muzzle. The traversing gear connected with it was well greased, and, in short, everything about the gun gave proof of the care that was bestowed on it.

But these were not the only alterations made in the mysterious schooner. Round both masts were piled a number of muskets, boarding-pikes, cutlasses, and pistols, all of which were perfectly clean and bright, and the men—fierce enough and warlike in their aspect at all times—had now rendered themselves doubly so by putting on broad belts with pistols therein, and tucking up their sleeves to the shoulders, thereby displaying their brawny arms as if they had dirty work before them. This strange metamorphosis was finally completed, when Manton, with his own hands, ran up to the peak of the mainsail a bright scarlet flag with the single word "AVENGER" on it in large black letters.

During one of those lulls in the breeze to which we have referred, and while the smooth ocean glowed in the mellow light that ushered in the day, the attention of those on board the Avenger (as we shall call the double-faced schooner when under red colors) was attracted to one of the more distant cliffs, on the summit of which human beings appeared to be moving.

"Hand me that glass," said Manton to one of the men beside him. "I shouldn't wonder if the niggers were up to some mischief there. Ah! just so," he exclaimed, adjusting the telescope a little more correctly, and again applying it to his eye. "They seem to be scuffling on the top of yonder precipice. Now there's one fellow down; but it's so far off that I can't make out clearly what they're about. I say, Mr. Scraggs, get the other glass and take a squint at them; you are further sighted than I am."

"You're right: they are killin' one another up yonder," observed Scraggs, surveying the group on the cliffs with calm indifference.

"Here comes the breeze," exclaimed Manton, with a look of satisfaction. "Now, look alive, lads; we shall be close on the nigger village in five minutes: it's just round the point of this small island close ahead. Come, Mr. Scraggs, we've other business on hand just now than squinting at the scrimmages of these fellows."

"Hold on," cried Scraggs, with a grin; "I do believe they're going to pitch a fellow over that cliff. What a crack he'll come down into the water with, to be sure. It's to be hoped the poor man is dead, for his own sake, before he takes that flight. Hallo!" added Scraggs, with an energetic shout and a look of surprise; "I say, that's one of *our* men; I know him by his striped flannel shirt. If he would only give up kicking for a second, I'd make out his—Humph! it's all up with him, now, poor fellow, whoever he is."

As he said the last words, the figure of a man was seen to shoot out from the cliff, and, descending with ever-increasing grapidity, to strike the water with terrific violence, sending up a jet of white foam as it disappeared.

"Stand by to lower the gig," shouted Manton.

"Aye, aye, sir," was the hearty response of the men, as some of them sprang to obey.

"Lower away!"

The boat struck water, and its crew were on the thwarts in a moment. At the same time the point of the island was passed, and the native village opened up to view.

"Load Long Tom—double shot!" roared Manton, whose ire was raised not so much at the idea of a fellow-creature having been so barbarously murdered as at the notion of one of the crew of his schooner having been so treated by contemptible niggers. "Away, lads, and pick up that man."

"It's of no use," remonstrated Scraggs; "he's done for by this time."

"I know it," said Manton, with a fierce oath; "bring him in, dead or alive. If the sharks leave an inch of him, bring it to me. I'll make the black villains eat it raw."

This ferocious threat was interlarded with and followed by a series of terrible oaths, which we think it inadvisable to repeat.

"Starboard!" he shouted to the man at the helm, as soon as the boat shot away on its mission of mercy.

"Starboard it is."

"Steady!"

While he gave these orders, Manton sighted the brass gun

carefully, and, just as the schooner's head came up to the wind, he applied the match.

Instantly a cloud of smoke obscured the center of the little vessel, as if her powder magazine had blown up, and a deafening roar went ringing and reverberating from cliff to cliff as two of the great iron shot were sent groaning through the air and pitched right into the heart of the village.

It was this tremendous shot from Long Tom, followed almost instantaneously by the broadside of the Talisman, that saved the life of Alice,—possibly the lives of her young companions also; that struck terror to the hearts of the savages, causing them to converge towards their defenseless homes from all directions, and that apprised Ole Thorwald and Henry Stuart that the assault on the village had commenced in earnest.

CHAPTER XIV

GREATER MYSTERIES THAN EVER—A BOLD MOVE AND A NARROW ESCAPE

We return now to the Talisman.

The instant the broadside of the cruiser burst with such violence, and in such close proximity, on Manton's ears, he felt that he had run into the very jaws of the lion; and that escape was almost impossible. The bold heart of the pirate quailed at the thought of his impending fate, but the fear caused by conscious guilt was momentary; his constitutional courage returned so violently as to render him reckless.

It was too late to put about and avoid being seen; for, before the shot was fired, the schooner had already almost run into the narrow channel between the island and the shore. A few seconds later, she sailed gracefully into view of the amazed Montague, who at once recognized the pirate vessel from Gascoyne's faithful description of her, and hurriedly gave orders to load with ball and grape, while a boat was lowered in order to slew the ship more rapidly so as to bring her broadside to bear on the schooner.

To say that Gascoyne beheld all this unmoved would be to give a false impression of the man. He knew the ring of his great gun too well to require the schooner to come in sight in order to convince him that his vessel was near at hand. When, therefore, she appeared, and Montague turned to him with a hasty glance of suspicion and pointed to her, he had completely banished every trace of feeling from his countenance, and sat on the taffrail puffing his cigar with an air of calm satisfaction. Nodding to Montague's glance of inquiry, he said:

"Aye, that's the pirate. I told you he was a bold fellow; but I did not think he was quite so bold as to attempt *this*!"

To do Gascoyne justice, he told the plain truth here; for,

having sent a peremptory order to his mate, by John Bumpus, not to move from his anchorage on any account whatever, he was not a little surprised as well as enraged at what he supposed was Manton's mutinous conduct. But, as we have said, his feelings were confined to his breast; they found no index in his grave face.

Montague suspected, nevertheless, that his pilot was assuming a composure which he did not feel; for from the manner of the meeting of the two vessels, he was persuaded that it was as little expected on the part of the pirates as of himself. It was with a feeling of curiosity, therefore, as to what reply he should receive, that he put the question, "What would Mr. Gascoyne advise me to do *now*?"

"Blow the villains out of the water," was the quick answer. "I would have done so before now, had I been you."

"Perhaps you might, but not *much* sooner," retorted the other, pointing to the guns which were ready loaded, while the men stood at their stations, matches in hand, only waiting for the broadside to be brought to bear on the little vessel, when an iron shower would be sent against her which must, at such short range, have infallibly sent her to the bottom.

The mate of the pirate schooner was quite alive to his danger, and had taken the only means in his power to prevent it. Close to where his vessel lay, a large rock rose between the shore of the large island and the islet in the bay which has been described as separating the two vessels from each other. Owing to the formation of the coast at this place, a powerful stream ran between the rock and this islet at low tide. It happened to be flowing out at that time like a mill-race. Manton saw that the schooner was being sucked into this stream. In other circumstances, he would have endeavored to avoid the danger; for the channel was barely wide enough to allow even a small craft to pass between the rocks; but now he resolved to risk it.

He knew that any attempt to put the schooner about would

only hasten the efforts of the cruiser to bring her broadside to bear on him. He also knew that, in the course of a few seconds, he would be carried through the stream into the shelter of the rocky point. He therefore ordered the men to lie down on the deck; while, in a careless manner, he slewed the big brass gun round, so as to point it at the man-of-war.

Gascoyne at once understood the intended maneuver of his mate; and, in spite of himself, a gleam of triumph shot from his eyes. Montague himself suspected that his prize was not altogether so sure as he had deemed it; and he urged the men in the boat to put forth their utmost efforts. The Talisman was almost slewed into position, when the pirate schooner was observed to move rapidly through the water, stern foremost, in the direction of the point. At first Montague could scarcely credit his eyes; but when he saw the end of the main boom pass behind the point, he became painfully alive to the fact that the whole vessel would certainly follow in the course of a few seconds. Although the most of his guns were still not sufficiently well pointed, he gave the order to fire them in succession. The entire broadside burst in this manner from the side of the Talisman, with a prolonged and mighty crash or roar, and tore up the waters of the narrow channel.

Most of the iron storm passed close by the head of the pirate. However, only one ball took effect; it touched the end of the bowsprit, and sent the jib-boom into the air in splinters. Manton applied the match to the brass gun almost at the same moment, and the heavy ringing roar of her explosion seemed like a prolonged echo of the broadside. The gun was well aimed; but the schooner had already passed so far behind the point that the ball struck a projecting part of the cliff, dashed it into atoms, and, glancing upwards, passed through the cap of the Talisman's mizzen-mast, and brought the lower yard, with all its gear, rattling down on the quarter-deck. When the smoke cleared away, the Avenger had vanished from the scene.

To put the ship about, and follow the pirate schooner, was the first impulse of Montague; but, on second thought, he felt that the risk of getting on the rocks in the narrow channel was too great to be lightly run. He therefore gave orders to warp the ship about, and steer round the islet, on the other side of which he fully expected to find the pirate. But time was lost in attempting to do this, in consequence of the wreck of the mizzen-mast having fouled the rudder. When the Talisman at last got under way, and rounded the outside point of the islet, no vessel of any kind was to be seen.

Amazed beyond measure, and deeply chagrined, the unfortunate captain of the man-of-war turned to Gascoyne, who still sat quietly on the taffrail smoking his cigar.

"Does this pirate schooner sport wings as well as sails?" said he; "for unless she does, and has flown over the mountains, I cannot see how she could disappear in so short a space of time."

"I told you the pirate was a bold man; and now he has proved himself a clever fellow. Whether he sports wings or no is best known to himself. Perhaps he can dive. If so, we have only to watch until he comes to the surface, and shoot him leisurely."

"Well, he is off; there is no doubt of that," returned Montague. "And now, Mr. Gascoyne, since it is vain to chase a vessel possessed of such mysterious qualities, you will not object, I dare say, to guide my ship to the bay where your own little schooner lies. I have a fancy to anchor there."

"By all means," said Gascoyne, coolly. "It will afford me much pleasure to do as you wish, and to have you alongside of my little craft."

Montague was surprised at the perfect coolness with which the other received his proposal. He was persuaded that there must be some mysterious connection between the pirate schooner and the sandal-wood trader, although his ideas were at this point somewhat undefined and confused; and he had expected that Gascoyne would have shown some symptoms of perplexity on being thus ordered to conduct the Talisman to a spot where, he suspected, no schooner would be found, or, if found, would appear under such a changed aspect as to warrant his seizing it on suspicion. As Gascoyne, however, showed perfect willingness to obey the order, he turned away, and left his strange pilot to conduct the ship through the reefs, having previously given him to understand that the touching of a rock and the termination of his (Gascoyne's) life would certainly be simultaneous events.

Meanwhile the Avenger, alias the Foam, had steered direct for the shore, into which she apparently ran, and disappeared like a phantom-ship. The coast of this part of the island, where the events we are narrating occurred, was peculiarly formed. There were several narrow inlets in the high cliffs which were exceedingly deep, but barely wide enough to admit of the passage of a large boat or a small vessel. Many of these inlets or creeks, which in some respects resembled the narrow fiords of Norway, though on a miniature scale, were so thickly fringed with trees, and the luxuriant undergrowth peculiar to southern climes, that their existence could not be detected from the sea. Indeed, even after the entrance to any one of them was discovered, no one would have imagined it to extend so far inland.

Two of those deep, narrow inlets, opening from opposite sides of the cape which lay close to the islet above referred to, had approached so close to each other at their upper extremities that they had at last met, in consequence of the sea undermining and throwing down the cliff that separated them. Thus the cape was in reality an island; and the two united inlets formed a narrow strait, through which the Avenger passed to her former anchorage by means of four pair of powerful sweeps or oars. This secret passage was well known to the pirates; and it was with a lurking feeling that it might some day prove of use to him, that Gascoyne invariably anchored near it when he visited the island as a sandal-wood trader.

During the transit, the carpenters of the schooner were not idle. The red streak and flag and griffin's head were removed; the big gun was covered with the long-boat, and the vessel which entered the one end of the channel as the warlike Avenger issued from the other side as the peaceful Foam; and, rowing to her former anchorage, dropped anchor. The shattered jib-boom had been replaced by a spare one, and part of the crew were stored away under the cargo, in an empty space of the hold reserved for this special purpose, and for concealing arms. A few of them were also landed, not far from the cliff over which poor Bumpus had been thrown, with orders to remain concealed, and be ready to embark at a moment's notice.

Soon after the schooner anchored, the boat which had been sent off in search of the body of our unfortunate seaman returned, having failed to discover the object for which it had been sent out.

The breeze had by this time died away almost entirely, so that three hours elapsed before the Talisman rounded the point, stood into the bay, and dropped anchor at a distance of about two miles from the suspected schooner.

CHAPTER XV

REMARKABLE DOINGS OF POOPY—
EXTRAORDINARY CASE OF RESUSCITATION

It is time now to return to our unfortunate friends, Corrie, Alice, and Poopy, who have been left long enough exposed on the summit of the cliff, from which they had expected to be tossed by the savages, when the guns of the Talisman so opportunely saved them.

The reader will observe that these incidents, which have taken so long to narrate, were enacted in a very brief space of time. Only a few hours elapsed between the firing of the broadside already referred to and the anchoring of the Talisman in the bay, where the Foam had cast anchor some time before her; yet in this short space of time many things occurred on the island which are worthy of particular notice.

As we have already remarked, Corrie and his two companions in misfortune had been bound, and in this condition were left by the savages to their fate. Their respective positions were by no means enviable. Poor Alice lay near the edge of the cliff, with her wrists and ankles so securely tied that no effort of which she was capable could set her free. Poopy lay about ten yards further up the cliff, flat on her sable back, with her hands tied behind her, and her ankles also secured; so that she could by no means attain to a sitting position, although she made violent and extraordinary efforts to do so. We say extraordinary, because Poopy, being ingenious, hit upon many devices of an unheard of nature to accomplish her object. Among others, she attempted to turn heels over head, hoping thus to get upon her knees; and there is no doubt whatever that she would have succeeded in this had not the formation of the ground been exceedingly unfavorable for such a maneuver.

Corrie had shown such an amount of desperate vindictiveness, in the way of kicking, hitting, biting, scratching, and pinching, when the savages were securing him, that they gave him five or six extra coils of the rope of cocoanut fiber with which they bound him. Consequently he could not move any of his limbs; and now he lay on his side between Alice and Poopy, gazing with much earnestness and no little astonishment at the peculiar contortions of the latter.

"You'll never manage it, Poopy," he remarked, in a sad tone of voice, on beholding the poor girl balanced on the small of her back, preparatory to making a spring that might have reminded one of the leaps of a trout when thrown from its native element upon the bank of a river. "And you'll break your neck if you go on like that," he added, on observing that, having failed in these attempts, she recurred to the heels-over-head process; but all in vain.

"O me!" sighed Poopy, as she fell back in a fit of exhaustion. "It's be all hup wid us."

"Don't say that, you goose," whispered Corrie; "you'll frighten Alice, you will."

"Will me?" whispered Poopy, in a tone of self-reproach; then in a loud voice, "Oh, no! it's not all hup yet. Miss Alice. See, me go at it again."

And "go at it" she did in a way that actually alarmed her companions. At any other time Corrie would have exploded with laughter, but the poor boy was thoroughly overwhelmed by the suddenness and the extent of his misfortune. The image of Bumpus, disappearing headlong over that terrible cliff, had filled his heart with a feeling of horror which nothing could allay, and grave thoughts at the desperate case of poor little Alice (for he neither thought of nor cared for Poopy or himself) sank like a weight of lead upon his spirit.

"Don't try it any more, dear Poopy," said Alice, entreatingly; "you'll only hurt yourself and tear your frock. I feel *sure* that some one will be sent to deliver us. Don't *you*, Corrie?"

The tone in which this question was put showed that the poor child did not feel quite so certain of the arrival of succor as her words implied. Corrie perceived this at once, and, with the heroism of a true lover, he crushed back the feelings of anxiety and alarm which were creeping over his own stout little heart in spite of his brave words, and gave utterance to encouraging expressions and even to slightly jovial sentiments, which tended very much to comfort Alice, and Poopy too.

"Sure?" he exclaimed, rolling on his other side to obtain a view of the child (for, owing to his position and his fettered condition, he had to turn on his right side when he wished to look at Poopy, and on his left when he addressed himself to Alice). "Sure? why, of course I'm sure. D'ye think your father would leave you lying out in the cold all night?"

"No, that I am certain he would not," cried Alice, enthusiastically; "but, then, he does not know we are here, and will never think of looking for us in such an unlikely place."

"Humph! that only shows your ignorance," said Corrie.

"Well, I dare say I *am* very ignorant," replied Alice, meekly.

"No, no! I don't mean *that*," cried Corrie, with a feeling of self-reproach. "I don't mean to say that you're ignorant in a general way, you know, but only about what men are likely to do, d'ye see, when they're hard put to it, you understand. *Our* feelings are so different from yours, you know, and—and—"

Here Corrie broke down, and in order to change the subject abruptly he rolled round towards Poopy, and cried, with considerable asperity.

"What on earth d'ye mean, Kickup, by wriggling about your black body in that fashion? If you don't stop it you'll fetch way down the hill, and go slap over the precipice, carrying Alice and me along with you. Give it up now; d'ye hear?"

"No, me won't," cried Poopy, with great passion, while tears sprang from her large eyes, and coursed over her sable cheeks. "Me *will* bu'st dem ropes."

"More likely to do that to yourself if you go on like that," returned Corrie. "But, I say, Alice, cheer up" (here he rolled round on his other side); "I've been pondering a plan all this time to set us free, and now I'm going to try it. The only bother about it is that these rascally savages have dropped me beside a pool of half soft mud that I can't help sticking my head into if I try to move."

"Oh! then, don't move, dear Corrie," said Alice, in an imploring tone of voice; "we can lie here quite comfortably till papa comes."

"Ah! yes," said Corrie, "that reminds me that I was saying we men feel and act so differently from you women. Now it strikes me that your father will go to all the most *unlikely* parts of the island first; knowin' very well that niggers don't hide in *likely* places. But as it may be a long time before he finds us" (he sighed deeply here, not feeling much confidence in the success of the missionary's search), "I shall tell you my plan, and then try to carry it out." (Here he sighed again, more deeply than before; not feeling by any means confident of the success of his own efforts.)

"And what is your plan?" inquired Alice, eagerly; for the child had unbounded belief in Corrie's ability to do almost anything he chose to attempt, and Corrie knew this, and was proud as a peacock in consequence.

"I'll get up on my knees," said he, "and then, once on them, I can easily rise to my feet and hop to you, and free you."

On this explanation of his elaborate and difficult plan Alice made no observation for some time, because, even to *her* faculties (which were obtuse enough on mechanical matters), it was abundantly evident that, the boy's hands being tied firmly behind his back, he could neither cut the ropes that bound her, nor untie them.

"What d'ye think, Alice?"

"I fear it won't do; your hands are tied, Corrie."

"Oh! that's nothing. The only difficulty is how to get on my knees."

"Surely that cannot be *very* difficult, when you talk of getting on your feet."

"Ha! that shows you're a—I mean, d'ye see, that the difficulty lies here; my elbows are lashed so fast to my side that I can't use them to prop me up; but if Poopy will roll down the hill to my side, and shove her pretty shoulder under my back when I raise it, perhaps I may succeed in getting up. What say you, Kickup?"

"Hee! Hee!" laughed the girl, "dat's fuss rate. Look out!"

Poopy, although sluggish by nature, was rather abrupt and violent in her impulses at times. Without further warning than the above brief exclamation, she rolled herself towards Corrie with such good-will that she went quite over him, and would certainly have passed onward to where Alice lay—perhaps over the cliff altogether—had not the boy caught her sleeve with his teeth, and held her fast.

The plan was eminently successful. By a series of jerks on the part of Corrie, and proppings on the part of Poopy, the former was enabled to attain a kneeling position, not, however, without a few failures, in one of which he fell forward on his face, and left a deep impression of his fat little nose in the mud.

Having risen to his feet, Corrie at once hopped towards Alice, after the fashion of those country wights who indulge in sack races, and, going down on his knees beside her, began diligently to gnaw the rope that bound her with his teeth. This was by no means an easy or a quick process. He gnawed and bit at it long before the tough rope gave way. At length Alice was freed, and she immediately set to work to undo the fastenings of the other two; but her delicate fingers were not well suited to such rough work, and a considerable time elapsed before the three were finally at large.

The instant they were so, Corrie said, "Now we must go

down to the foot of the cliff, and look for poor Bumpus. Oh, dear me! I doubt he is killed."

The look of horror which all three cast over the stupendous precipice showed that they had little hope of ever again seeing their rugged friend alive. But, without wasting time in idle remarks, they at once hastened to the foot of the cliff by the shortest route they could find. Here, after a short time, they discovered the object of their solicitude lying, apparently dead, on his back among the rocks.

When Bumpus struck the water, after being tossed over the cliff, his head was fortunately downward; and his skull, being the thickest and hardest bone in his body, had withstood the terrible shock to which it had been subjected without damage, though the brain within was, for a time, incapacitated from doing duty. When John rose again to the surface, after a descent into unfathomable water, he floated there in a state of insensibility. Fortunately the wind and tide combined to wash him to the shore, where a higher swell than usual launched him among the coral rocks, and left him there, with only his feet in the water.

"Oh! here he is,—hurrah!" shouted Corrie, on catching sight of the prostrate form of the seaman. But the boy's manner changed the instant he observed the color of the man's face, from which all the blood had been driven, leaving it like a piece of brown leather.

"He's dead," said Alice, wringing her hands in despair.

"P'raps not," suggested Poopy, with a look of deep wisdom, as she gazed on the upturned face.

"Anyhow, we must haul him out of the water," said Corrie, whose chest heaved with the effort he made to repress his tears.

Catching up one of Bumpus's huge hands, the boy ordered Alice to grasp the other. Poopy, without waiting for orders, seized hold of the hair of his head, and all three began to haul with might and main. But they might as well have tried to pull a line-of-battle ship up on the shore. The man's bulky form was immovable. Seeing this, they changed their plan, and, all three grasping his legs, slewed him partially round, and thus drew his feet out of the water.

"Now we must warm him," said Corrie, eagerly; for, the first shock of the discovery of the supposed dead body of his friend being over, the sanguine boy began to entertain hopes of resuscitating him. "I've heard that the best thing for drowned people is to warm them: so, Alice, do you take one hand and arm, Poopy will take the other, and I will take his feet, and we'll all rub away till we bring him to; for we must, we *shall* bring him round."

Corrie said this with a fierce look and a hysterical sob. Without more words he drew out his clasp-knife, and, ripping up the cuffs of the man's coat, laid bare his muscular arm. Meanwhile Alice untied his neckcloth, and Poopy tore open his Guernsey frock and exposed his broad, brown chest.

"We must warm that at once," said Corrie, beginning to take off his jacket, which he meant to spread over the seaman's breast.

"Stay! my petticoat is warmer," cried Alice, hastily divesting herself of a flannel garment of bright scarlet, the brilliant beauty of which had long been the admiration of the entire population of Sandy Cove. The child spread it over the seaman's chest, and tucked it carefully down at his sides, between his body and the wet garments. Then the three sat down beside him, and, each seizing a limb, began to rub and chafe with a degree of energy that nothing could resist. At any rate it put life into John Bumpus; for that hardy mariner gradually began to exhibit signs of returning vitality.

"There he comes!" cried Come, eagerly.

"Eh!" exclaimed Poopy, in alarm.

"Who? where?" inquired Alice, who thought that the boy referred to some one who had unexpectedly appeared on the scene.

"I saw him wink with his left eye,—look!"

All three suspended their labor of love, and, stretching forward their heads, gazed, with breathless anxiety, at the clay-colored face of Jo.

"I must have been mistaken," said Corrie, shaking his head.

"Go at him agin," cried Poopy, recommencing her work on the right arm with so much energy that it seemed marvelous how she escaped skinning that limb from fingers to shoulder.

Poor Alice did her best, but her soft little hands had not much effect on the huge mass of brown flesh they manipulated.

"There he comes again!" shouted Corrie.

Once more there was an abrupt pause in the process, and the three heads were bent eagerly forward watching for symptoms of returning life. Corrie was right. The seaman's left eye quivered for a moment, causing the hearts of the three children to beat high with hope. Presently the other eye also quivered; then the broad chest rose almost imperceptibly, and a faint sigh came feebly and broken from the cold blue lips.

To say that the three children were delighted at this would be to give but a feeble idea of the state of their feelings. Corrie had, even in the short time yet afforded him of knowing Bumpus, entertained for him feelings of the deepest admiration and love. Alice and Poopy, out of sheer sympathy, had fallen in love with him too, at first sight; so that his horrible death (as they had supposed), coupled with his unexpected restoration and revival through their united exertions, drew them still closer to him, and created within them a sort of feeling that he must, in common reason and justice, regard himself as their special property in all future time. When, therefore, they saw him wink, and heard him sigh, the gush of emotion that filled their respective bosoms was quite overpowering. Corrie gasped in his effort not to break down; Alice wept with silent joy as she continued to chafe the man's limbs; and Poopy went off into a violent fit of hysterical laughter, in which her "hee, hees" resounded with terrible shrillness among the surrounding cliffs.

"Now, then, let's to work again with a will," said Corrie. "What d'ye say to try punching him?"

This question he put gravely, and with the uncertain air of a man who feels that he is treading on new and possibly dangerous ground.

"What is punching?" inquired Alice.

"Why, *that*," replied the boy, giving a practical and by no means gentle illustration on his own fat thigh.

"Wouldn't it hurt him?" said Alice, dubiously.

"Hurt him! hurt the Grampus!" cried Corrie, with a look of surprise; "you might as well talk of hurting a hippopotamus. Come, I'll try."

Accordingly, Corrie tried. He began to bake the seaman, as it were, with his fists. As the process went on he warmed to the work, and did it so energetically, in his mingled anxiety and hope, that it assumed the character of hitting rather than punching—to the dismay of Alice, who thought it impossible that any human being could stand such dreadful treatment.

Whether it was owing to this process, or to the action of nature, or to the combined efforts of nature and his friends, that Bumpus owed his recovery, we cannot pretend to say; but certain it is, that, on Corrie's making a severer dab than usual into the pit of the seaman's stomach, he gave a gasp and a sneeze, the latter of which almost overturned Poopy, who chanced to be gazing wildly into his countenance at the moment. At the same time he involuntarily threw up his right arm, and fetched Corrie such a tremendous backhander on the chest that our young hero was laid flat on his back, half stunned by the violence of the fall, yet shouting with delight that his rugged friend still lived to strike another blow.

Having achieved this easy though unintentional victory, Bumpus sighed again, shook his legs in the air, and sat up, gazing before him with a bewildered air, and gasping from time to time in a quiet way.

"Wot's to do?" were the first words with which the restored seaman greeted his friends.

"Hurrah!" screamed Corrie, his visage blazing with delight, as he danced in front of him.

"Werry good," said Bumpus, whose intellect was not yet thoroughly restored; "try it again."

"Oh, how cold your cheeks are!" said Alice, placing her hands on them, and chafing them gently; then, perceiving that she did not communicate much warmth in that way, she placed her own fair, soft cheek against that of the sailor. Suddenly throwing both arms round his neck, she hugged him, and burst into tears.

Bumpus was somewhat taken aback by this unexpected explosion; but, being an affectionate man as well as a rugged one, he had no objection whatever to the peculiar treatment. He allowed the child to sob on his neck as long as she chose, while Corrie stood by, with his hands in his pockets, sailor-fashion, and looked on admiringly. As for Poopy, she sat down on a rock a short way off, and began to smile and talk to herself in a manner so utterly idiotical that an ignorant observer would certainly have judged her to be insane.

They were thus agreeably employed, when an event occurred which changed the current of their thoughts, and led to consequences of a somewhat serious nature. The event, however, was in itself insignificant. It was nothing more than the sudden appearance of a wild pig among the bushes close at hand.

CHAPTER XVI

A WILD CHASE—HOPE, DISAPPOINTMENT, AND DESPAIR—THE SANDAL-WOOD TRADER OUTWITS THE MAN-OF-WAR

When the wild pig, referred to in the last chapter, was first observed, it was standing on the margin of a thicket, from which it had just issued, gazing, with the profoundly philosophical aspect peculiar to that animal, at our four friends, and seeming to entertain doubts as to the propriety of beating an immediate retreat.

Before it had made up its mind on this point, Corrie's eye alighted on it.

"Hist!" exclaimed he with a gesture of caution to his companions. "Look there! We've had nothing to eat for an awful time,—nothing since breakfast on Sunday morning. I feel as if my interior had been amputated. Oh, what a jolly roast that fellow would make if we could only kill him!"

"Wot's in the pistol?" inquired Bumpus, pointing to the weapon which Corrie had stuck ostentatiously into his belt.

"Nothin'," answered the boy. "I fired the last charge in the face of a savage."

"Fling it at him," suggested Bumpus, getting cautiously up. "Here, hand it to me. I've seed a heavy horse-pistol like that do great execution when well aimed by a stout arm."

The pig seemed to have an intuitive perception that danger was approaching; for it turned abruptly round just as the missile left the seaman's hand, and received the butt with full force close to the root of its tail.

A pig's tendency to shriek on the receipt of the slightest injury is well known. It is therefore not to be wondered at that this pig went off into the bushes under cover of a series of yells so terrific they might have been heard for miles around.

"I'll after him," cried Bumpus, catching up a large stone, and leaping forward a few paces almost as actively as if nothing had happened to him.

"Hurrah!" shouted Corrie; "I'll go too."

"Hold on," cried Bumpus, stopping suddenly.

"Why?" inquired the boy.

"'Cause you must stop an' take care of the gals. It won't do to leave 'em alone again, you know, Corrie."

This remark was accompanied with an exceedingly huge wink, full of deep meaning, which Corrie found it convenient not to notice, as he observed gravely:

"Ah! true. One of us *must* remain with 'em, poor, helpless things; so—so *you* had better go after the squeaker."

"All right," said Bumpus, with a broad grin—"Hallo! why, here's a spear, that must ha' been dropped by one o' them savages. That's a piece o' good luck, anyhow, as the man said when he f'und the fi' pun' note. Now, then, keep an eye on them gals, lad, and I'll be back as soon as ever I can; though I does feel rather stiffish. My old timbers ain't used to such deep divin', d'ye see."

Bumpus entered the thicket as he spoke, and Corrie returned to console the girls with the feeling and the air of a man whose bosom is filled with a stern resolve to die, if need be, in the discharge of an important duty.

Now, the yell of this particular pig reached other ears beside those of the party whose doings we have attempted to describe. It rang in those of the pirates, who had been sent ashore to hide, like the scream of a steam-whistle, in consequence of their being close at hand, and it sounded like a faint cry in those of Henry Stuart and the missionary, who, with their party, were a long way off, slowly tracing the footsteps of the lost Alice, to which they had been guided by the keen scent of that animated scrap of door-mat, Toozle. The effect on both parties was powerful, but not similar. The pirates, supposing that a band of savages were near them, lay close, and did not venture forth until a prolonged silence and strong curiosity tempted them to creep, with slow movements and extreme caution, towards the place whence the sounds proceeded.

Mr. Mason and Henry, on the other hand, stopped and listened with intense earnestness, expecting, yet fearing, a recurrence of the cry, and then sprang forward with their party, under the belief that they had heard the voice of Alice calling for help.

Meanwhile, Bumpus toiled up the slopes of the mountain, keeping the pig well in view; for that animal having been some-what injured by the blow from the pistol, could not travel at its ordinary speed. Indeed, Jo would have speedily overtaken it but for the shaky condition of his own body after such a long fast, and such a series of violent shocks, as well mental as physical.

Having gained the summit of a hill, the pig, much exhausted, sat down on its hams, and gazed pensively at the ground. Bumpus took advantage of the fact, and also sat down on a stone to rest.

"Wot a brute it is" said he to himself. "I'll circumvent it yet, though."

Presently he rose, and made as if he had abandoned the chase, and were about to return the way he had come; but when he had effectually concealed himself from the view of the pig, he made a wide detour, and, coming out suddenly at a spot higher up the mountain, charged down upon the unsuspecting animal with a yell that would have done credit to itself.

The pig echoed the yell, and rushed down the hill towards the cliffs, closely followed by the hardy seaman, who, in the ardor of the chase, forgot or ignored his aches and pains, and ran like a greyhound, his hair streaming in the wind, his eyes blazing with excitement, and the spear ready poised for a fatal dart. Altogether, he was so wild and strong in appearance, and so furious in his onset, that it was impossible to believe he had been half dead little more than an hour before; but then, as we have before remarked, Bumpus was hard to kill!

For nearly half an hour did the hungry seaman keep up the chase, neither gaining nor losing distance; while the affrighted pig, having its attention fixed entirely on its pursuer, scrambled and plunged forward over every imaginable variety of ground, receiving one or two severe falls in consequence. Bumpus, being warned by its fate, escaped them. At last the two dashed into a gorge and out at the other end, scrambled through a thicket, plunged down a hill, and doubled a high rock, on the other side of which they were met in the teeth by Henry Stuart at the head of his band.

The pig attempted to double. Failing to do so, it lost its footing, and fell flat on its side. Jo Bumpus threw his spear with violent energy deep into the earth about two feet beyond it, tripped on a stump, and fell headlong on the top of the pig, squeezing the life out of its body with the weight of his ponderous frame, and receiving its dying yell into his very bosom.

"Hilloa! my stalwart chip of old Neptune," cried Henry, laughing, "you've bagged him this time effectually. Hast seen any of the niggers; or did you mistake this poor pig for one?"

"Aye, truly, I have seen them, and given a few of 'em marks that will keep 'em in remembrance of me. As for this pig," said Jo, throwing the carcass over his shoulder, "I want a bit of summat to eat—that's the fact; an' the poor children will be—"

"Children," cried Mr. Mason, eagerly; "what do you mean, my man; have you seen any?"

"In course I has, or I wouldn't speak of 'em," returned Jo, who did not at first recognize the missionary; and no wonder, for Mr. Mason's clothes were torn and soiled, and his face was bruised, bloodstained, and haggard.

"Tell me, friend, I entreat you," said the pastor, earnestly, laying his hand on Jo's arm; "have you seen my child?"

"Wot! are you the father of the little gal? Why, I've seed her only half an hour since. But hold on, lads; come arter me, an I'll steer you to where she is at this moment."

"Thanks be to God," said Mr. Mason, with a deep sigh of relief. "Lead on, my man, and, pray, go quickly."

Bumpus at once led the way to the foot of the cliffs, and went over the ground at a pace that satisfied even the impatience of the bereaved father.

While this was occurring on the mountain slopes, the pirates at the foot of the cliffs had discovered the three children, and finding, that no one else was near, had seized them and carried them off to a cave near to which their boat lay on the rocks. They hoped to have obtained some information from them as to what was going on at the other side of the island; but, while engaged in a fruitless attempt to screw something out of Corrie, who was peculiarly refractory, they were interrupted, first by the yells of Bumpus and his pig, and afterwards by the sudden appearance of Henry and his party on the edge of a cliff a short way above the spot where they were assembled. On seeing these, the pirates started to their feet and drew their cutlasses, while Henry uttered a shout and ran down the rocks like a deer.

"Shall we have a stand-up fight with 'em, Bill?" said one of the pirates.

"Not if I can help it; there's four to one," replied the other.

"To the boat," cried several of the men, leading the way; "and let's take the brats with us."

As Henry's party came pouring down the hill the more combatively disposed of the pirates saw at glance that it would be in vain to attempt a stand. They therefore discharged a scattering volley from their pistols (happily without effect), and, springing into their boat, pushed off from the shore, taking the children along with them.

Mr. Mason was the first to gain the beach. He had hit upon a shorter path by which to descend, and, rushing forward, plunged into the sea. Poor little Alice, who at once recognized her father, stretched out her arms towards him, and would certainly have leaped into the sea had she not been forcibly detained by one of the pirates, whose special duty it was to hold her with one hand, while he restrained the violent demonstrations of Corrie with the other.

The father was too late, however. Already the boat was several yards from the shore, and the frantic efforts he made, in the madness of his despair, to overtake it only served to exhaust him. When Henry Stuart reached the beach, it was with difficulty he prevented those members of his band who carried muskets from firing on the boat. None of them thought for a moment, of course, of making the mad attempt to swim towards her. Indeed, Mr. Mason himself would have hesitated to do so had he been capable of cool thought at the time; but the sudden rush of hope when he heard of his child being near, combined with the agony of disappointment on seeing her torn, as it were, out of his very grasp, was too much for him. His reasoning powers were completely overturned; he continued to buffet the waves with wild energy, and to strain every fiber of his being in the effort to propel himself through the water, long after the boat was hopelessly beyond reach.

Henry understood his feelings well, and knew that the poor missionary would not cease his efforts until exhaustion should compel him to do so, in which case his being drowned would be a certainty; for there was neither boat nor canoe at hand in which to push off to his rescue.

In these circumstances, the youth took the only course that seemed left to him. He threw off his clothes, and prepared to swim after his friend, in order to render the assistance of his stout arm when it should be needed.

"Here, Jakolu!" he cried to one of the natives who stood near him.

"Yes, mass'r," answered the sturdy young fellow, who has been introduced at an earlier part of this story as being one of the missionary's best behaved and most active church members.

"I mean to swim after him; so I leave the charge of the party to Mr. Bumpus there. You will act under his orders. Keep the men together, and guard against surprise. We don't know how many more of these blackguards may be lurking among the rocks."

To this speech Jakolu replied by shaking his head slowly and gravely, as if he doubted the propriety of his young commander's intentions. "You no can sweem queek nuff to save him," said he.

"That remains to be seen," retorted Henry, sharply; for the youth was one of the best swimmers on the island,—at least the best among the whites, and better than many of the natives, although some of the latter could beat him. "At any rate," he continued, "you would not have me stand idly by while my friend is drowning, would you?"

"Him's not drownin' yet," answered the matter-of-fact native. "Me 'vise you to let Jakolu go. Hims can sweem berer dan you. See, here am bit plank, too,—me take dat."

"Ha! that's well thought of," cried Henry, who was now ready to plunge; "fetch it me, quick; and mind, Jakolu, keep your eye on me; when I hold up both hands you'll know that I'm dead beat, and that you must come off and help us both."

So saying, he seized the small piece of driftwood which the native brought to him, and, plunging into the sea, struck out vigorously in the direction in which the pastor was still perseveringly, though slowly, swimming.

While Henry was stripping, his eye had quickly and intelligently taken in the facts that were presented to him on the bay. He had seen, on descending the hill, that the man-of-war had entered the bay and anchored there, a fact which surprised him greatly, and that the Foam still lay where he had seen her cast anchor on the morning of her arrival. This surprised him more for, if the latter was really a pirate schooner (as had been hinted more than once that day by various members of the settlement), why did she remain so fearlessly and peacefully within range of the guns of so dangerous and powerful an enemy? He also observed that one of the large boats of the Talisman was in the water alongside, and full of armed men, as if about to put off on some warlike expedition, while his pocket telescope enabled him to perceive that Gascoyne, who must needs be the pirate captain, if the suspicions of his friends were correct, was smoking quietly on the quarter-deck, apparently holding amicable converse with the British commander. The youth knew not what to think; for it was preposterous to suppose that a pirate captain could by any possibility be the intimate friend of his own mother.

These and many other conflicting thoughts kept rushing through his mind as he hastened forward; but the conclusions to which they led him—if, indeed, they led him to any—were altogether upset by the unaccountable and extremely piratical conduct of the seamen who carried off Alice and her companions, and whom he knew to be part of the crew of the Foam, both from their costume and from the direction in which they rowed their little boat.

The young man's perplexities were, however, neutralized for the time by his anxiety for his friend the pastor, and by the necessity of instant and vigorous effort for his rescue. He had just time, before plunging into the sea, to note with satisfaction that the man-of-war's boat had pushed off, and that if Alice really was in the hands of pirates, there was the certainty of her being speedily rescued.

In this latter supposition, however, Henry was mistaken.

The events on shore which we have just described had been witnessed, of course, by the crews of both vessels with, as may be easily conjectured, very different feelings.

In the Foam, the few men who were lounging about the deck looked uneasily from the war vessel to the countenance of Manton, in whose hands they felt that their fate now lay. The object of their regard paced the deck slowly, with his hands in his pockets and a pipe in his mouth, in the most listless manner, in order to deceive the numerous eyes which he knew full well scanned his movements with deep curiosity. The frowning brow and the tightly compressed lips alone indicated the storm of anger which was in reality raging in the pirate's breast at what he deemed the obstinacy of his captain in running into such danger, and the folly of his men in having shown fight on shore when there was no occasion for doing so. But Manton was too much alive to his own danger and interests to allow passion at such a critical moment to interfere with his judgment. He paced the deck slowly, as we have said, undecided as to what course he ought to pursue, but ready to act with the utmost energy and promptitude when the time for action should arrive.

On board the Talisman, on the other hand, the young commander began to feel certain of his prize; and when he witnessed the scuffle on shore, the flight of the boat's crew with the three young people, and the subsequent events, he could not conceal a smile of triumph as he turned to Gascoyne and said:

"Your men are strangely violent in their proceedings, sir, for the crew of a peaceable trader. If it were not that they are pulling straight for your schooner, where, no doubt, they will be received with open arms, I would have fancied they had been part of the crew of that wonderful pirate, who seems to be able to change *color* almost as quickly as he changes *position*."

The allusion had no effect whatever on the imperturbable Gascoyne, on whose countenance good humor seemed to have been immovably enthroned; for the worse his case became, the more amiable and satisfied was his aspect.

"Surely, Captain Montague does not hold me responsible for the doings of my men in my absence," said he, calmly. "I have already said that they are a wild set—not easily restrained even when I am present; and fond of getting into scrapes when they can. You see, we have not a choice of men in these out-of-the-way parts of the world."

"Apparently not," returned Montague; "but I hope to have the pleasure of seeing you order your men to be punished for their misdeeds; for, if not, I shall be under the necessity of punishing them for you. Is the boat ready, Mr. Mulroy?"

"It is, sir."

"Then, Mr. Gascoyne, if you will do me the favor to step into this boat, I will have much pleasure in accompanying you on board your schooner."

"By all means," replied Gascoyne, with a bland smile, as he rose and threw away the end of another cigar, after having lighted therewith the sixth or seventh in which he had indulged that day. "Your boat is well manned, and your men are well armed, Captain Montague; do you go on some cutting-out expedition, or are you so much alarmed at the terrible aspect of the broadside of my small craft that—"

Gascoyne here smiled with ineffable urbanity, and bowed slightly by way of finishing his sentence. Montague was saved the annoyance of having to reply by a sudden exclamation from his lieutenant, who was observing the schooner's boat through a telescope.

"There seems to be some one swimming after that boat," said he. "A man—evidently a European, for he is light-colored. He must have been some time in the water, for he is already a long way from shore, and seems much exhausted."

"Why! the man is drowning, I believe," cried Montague, quickly, as he looked through the glass.

At that moment Frederick Mason's strength had given way. He made one or two manful efforts to struggle after the retreating boat, and then, tossing his arms in the air, uttered a loud cry of agony.

"Ho! shove off and save him!" shouted Montague, the moment he heard it. "Look alive, lads! give way! and when you have picked up the man, pull straight for yonder schooner."

The oars at once fell into the water with a splash, and the

boat, large and heavy though it was, shot from the ship's side like an arrow.

"Lower the gig," cried the captain. "And now, Mr. Gascoyne, since you seem disposed to go in a lighter boat, I will accommodate you. Pray, follow me."

In a few seconds they were seated in the little gig, which seemed to fly over the sea under the vigorous strokes of her crew of eight stout men. So swift were her motions that she reached the side of the schooner only a few minutes later than the Foam's boat, and a considerable time before his own large boat had picked up Mr. Mason, who was found in an almost insensible condition, supported by Henry Stuart.

When the gig came within a short distance of the Foam, Gascoyne directed Montague's attention to the proceedings of the large boat, and at the same instant made a private signal with his right hand to Manton, who, still unmoved and inactive, stood at the schooner's bow awaiting and evidently expecting it.

"Ha!" said he aloud; "I thought as much. Now, lads, show the red; make ready to slip; off with Long Tom's nightcap; let out the skulkers; take these children down below, and a dozen of you stand by to receive the captain and his *friends*."

These somewhat peculiar orders, hurriedly given, were hastily obeyed, and in a few seconds more the gig of the Talisman ranged up alongside of the Foam.

CHAPTER XVII
THE ESCAPE

The instant that Captain Montague stepped over the side of the schooner, a handkerchief was pressed tightly over his mouth and nose. At the same time, he was seized by four strongmen and rendered utterly powerless. The thing was done so promptly and silently, that the men who remained in the gig heard no unusual sound.

"I'm sorry to treat a guest so roughly, Captain Montague," said Gascoyne, in a low tone, as the unfortunate officer was carried aft; "but the safety of my vessel requires it. They will carry you to my stateroom, where you will find my steward exceedingly attentive and obliging; but, *let me warn you*, he is peculiarly ready with the butt end of his pistol at times, especially when men are inclined to make unnecessary noise." He turned on his heel as he said this, and went forward, looking over the side in passing and telling the crew of the gig to remain where they were till their captain should call them.

This order the men felt constrained to obey, although they were surprised that the captain himself had not given it on quitting the boat; their suspicions were further awakened by the active operations going on upon deck. The sounds apprised them of these, for the bulwarks hid everything from view. At length, when they heard the cable slipping through the hawsehole, they could stand it no longer, but sprang up the side in a body. Of course they were met by men well prepared. As they were armed only with cutlasses, the pirates quickly overcame them, and threw them into the sea.

All further attempt at concealment was now abandoned. The man-of-war's boat, when it came up, was received with a shot from Long Tom, which grazed its side, carried away four of the starboard oars, and just missed dashing it to pieces by a mere hair's-breadth. At the same time the sails of the schooner were shaken out and filled by the light breeze, which, for nearly an hour, had been blowing off shore.

As the coming up of the gig and the large boat had occurred on that side of the schooner that was furthest from the Talisman, those on board of the latter vessel could not make out clearly what had occurred. That the schooner was a pirate was now clearly evident; for the red griffin and stripe were suddenly displayed, as well as the blood-red flag; but the first lieutenant did not dare to fire on her while the boats were so near. He slipped the cable, however, and made instant sail on the ship; and when he saw the large boat and the gig drop astern of the schooner, the former in a disabled condition, he commenced firing as fast as he could load; not doubting that his captain was in his own boat.

At such short range the shot flew around the pirate schooner like hail; but she appeared to bear a charmed existence; for, although they whistled between her spars and struck the sea all around her, very few indeed did her serious damage. The shots from Long Tom, on the other hand, were well aimed, and told with terrible effect on the hull and rigging of the frigate. Gascoyne himself pointed the gun, and his bright eye flashed, and a grim smile played on his lips as the shots whistled round his head.

The pirate captain seemed to be possessed by a spirit of fierce and reckless joviality that day. His usual calm, self-possessed demeanor quite forsook him. He issued his orders in a voice of thunder and with an air of what, for want of a better expression, we may term ferocious heartiness. He generally executed these orders himself, hurling the men violently out of his way as if he were indignant at their tardiness, although they sprang to obey as actively as usual; indeed, more so, for they were overawed and somewhat alarmed by this unwonted conduct on the part of their captain.

The fact was, that Gascoyne had for a long time past desired to give up his course of life and amend his ways; but he discovered, as all wicked men discover sooner or later, that, while it is easy to plunge into evil courses, it is by no means easy—on the contrary it is extremely difficult—to give them up. He had formed his resolution and had laid his plans; but all had miscarried. Being a man of high temper, he had been driven almost to desperation, and sought relief to his feelings in physical exertion.

Of all the men in the Avenger, however, no one was so much alarmed by the captain's conduct as the first mate, between whom and Gascoyne there had been a bitter feeling for some time past; and Manton knew (at least he believed) that it would be certain death to him if he should chance to thwart his superior in the mood in which he then was.

"That was a good shot, Manton," said Gascoyne, with a wild laugh, as the fore-topsail yard of the Talisman came rattling down on the deck, having been cut away by a shot from Long Tom.

"It was; but *that* was a better one," said Manton, pointing to the boom of the schooner's mainsail, which was cut in two by a round shot, just as the captain spoke.

"Good, very good," observed the latter, with an approving nod; "but that alters the game. Down with the helm! steady!"

"Get the wreck of that boom cleared away, Manton; we won't want the mainsail long. Here comes a squall. Look sharp. Close reef topsails."

The boom was swaying to and fro so violently that three of the men who sprang to order were hurled by it into the lee scuppers. Gascoyne darted towards the broken spar and held it fast, while Manton quickly severed the ropes that fastened it to the sail and to the deck, then the former hurled it over the side with as much ease as if it had been an oar.

"Let her away now."

"Why, that will run us right into the Long Shoal!" exclaimed Manton, anxiously, as the squall which had been approaching struck the schooner and laid her almost on her beam ends.

"I know it," replied Gascoyne, curtly, as he thrust aside the man at the wheel and took the spokes in his own hands.

"It's all we can do to find our way through that place in fine weather," remonstrated the mate.

"I know it," said Gascoyne, sternly.

Scraggs, who chanced to be standing by, seemed to be immensely delighted with the alarmed expression on Manton's face. The worthy second mate hated the first mate so cordially, and attached so little value to his own life, that he would willingly have run the schooner on the rocks altogether, just to have the pleasure of laughing contemptuously at the wreck of Manton's hopes.

"It's worth while trying it," suggested Scraggs, with a malicious grin.

"I mean to try it," said Gascoyne, calmly.

"But there's not a spot in the shoal except the Eel's Gate that we've a ghost of a chance of getting through," cried Manton, becoming excited as the schooner dashed towards the breakers like a furious charger rushing on destruction.

"I know it."

"And there's barely water on *that* to float us over," he added, striding forward, and laying a hand on the wheel.

"Half a foot too little," said Gascoyne, with forced calmness. Scraggs grinned.

"You shan't run us aground if I can prevent it," cried Manton, fiercely, seizing the wheel with both hands and attempting to move it, in which attempt he utterly failed; and Scraggs grinned broader than ever.

"Remove your hands," said Gascoyne, in a low, calm voice, which surprised the men who were standing near and witnessed these proceedings.

"I won't. Ho, lads! do you wish to be sent to the bottom by a—"

The remainder of this speech was cut short by the sudden descent of Gascoyne's knuckles on the forehead of the mate, who dropped on the deck as if he had been felled with a sledge-hammer. Scraggs laughed outright with satisfaction.

"Remove him," said Gascoyne.

"Overboard?" inquired Scraggs, with a bland smile.

"Below," said the captain; and Scraggs was fain to content himself with carrying the insensible form of his superior officer to his berth; taking pains, however, to bump his head carefully against every spar and corner and otherwise convenient projection on the way down.

In a few minutes more the schooner was rushing through the milk-white foam that covered the dangerous coral reef named the Long Shoal; and the Talisman lay to, not daring to venture into such a place, but pouring shot and shell into her bold little adversary with terrible effect, as the tattered sails and flying cordage showed. The fire was steadily replied to by Long Tom, whose heavy shots came crashing repeatedly through the hull of the man-of-war.

The large boat, meanwhile, had been picked up by the Talisman, after having rescued Mr. Mason and Henry, both of whom were placed in the gig. This light boat was now struggling to make the ship; but, owing to the strength of the squall, her diminished crew were unable to effect this; they therefore ran ashore, to await the issue of the fight and the storm.

For some time the Avenger stood on her wild course unharmed, passing close to huge rocks on either side of her, over which the sea burst in clouds of foam. Gascoyne still stood at the wheel, guiding the vessel with consummate skill and daring, while the men looked on in awe and in breathless expectation, quite regardless of the shot which flew around them, and altogether absorbed by the superior danger by which they were menaced.

The surface of the sea was so universally white, that there was no line of dark water to guide the pirate captain on his bold and desperate course. He was obliged to trust almost entirely to his intimate knowledge of the coast, and to the occasional patches in the surrounding waste where the comparative flatness of the boiling flood indicated less shallow water. As the danger increased, the smile left Gascoyne's lips; but the flashing of his bright eyes and his deepened color showed that the spirit boiled within almost as wildly as the ocean raged around him.

The center of the shoal was gained, and a feeling of hope and exultation began to rise in the breasts of the crew, when a terrific shock caused the little schooner to quiver from stem to stern, while an involuntary cry burst from the men, many of whom were thrown violently on the deck. At the same time a shot from the Talisman came in through the stern bulwarks, struck the wheel, and carried it away, with part of the tackle attached to the tiller.

"Another leap like that, lass, and you're over," cried Gascoyne, with a light smile, as he sprang to the iron tiller, and, seizing it with his strong hands, steered the schooner as if she had been a boat.

"Get new tackle rove, Scraggs," said he cheerfully. "I'll keep her straight for Eel's Gate with *this*. That was the first bar of the gate; there are only two altogether, and the second won't be so bad."

As the captain spoke, the schooner seemed to recover from the shock, and again rushed forward on her foaming course; but before the men had time to breathe, she struck again,—this time less violently, as had been predicted,—and the next wave lifting her over the shoals, launched her into deep water.

"There, that will do," said Gascoyne, resigning the helm to Scraggs. "You can keep her as she goes: there's plenty of water now, and no fear of that big bully following us. Meanwhile, I will go below, and see to the welfare of our passengers."

Gascoyne was wrong in supposing that the Talisman would not follow. She could not indeed follow in the same course; but the moment that Mulroy observed that the pirate had passed the shoals in safety, he stood inshore, and, without waiting to pick up the gig, traversed the channel by which they had entered the bay. Then, trusting to the lead and to his knowledge of the general appearance of shallows, he steered carefully along until he cleared the reefs, and finally stood out to sea.

In less than half an hour afterwards, the party on shore beheld the two vessels disappear among the black storm-clouds that gathered over the distant horizon.

CHAPTER XVIII

THE GOAT'S PASS—AN ATTACK, A BLOODLESS VICTORY, AND A SERMON

When Ole Thorwald was landed at the foot of that wild gorge in the cliffs which have been designated the Goat's Pass, he felt himself to be an aggrieved man, and growled accordingly.

"It's too bad o' that fire-eating fellow to fix on *me* for this particular service," said he to one of the settlers named Hugh Barnes, a cooper, who acted as one of his captains; "and at night, too; just as if a man of my years were a cross between a cat (which everybody knows can see in the dark) and a kangaroo, which is said to be a powerful leaper, though whether in the dark or the light I don't pretend to know, not being informed on the point. Have a care, Hugh. It seems to me you're going to step into a quarry hole, or over a precipice. How my old flesh quakes, to be sure! If it was only a fair, flat field and open day, with any odds you like against me, it would be nothing; but this abominable Goat's—Hah! I knew it! Help! hold on there! murder!"

Ole's sudden alarm was caused by his stumbling in the dark over the root of a shrub which grew on the edge of, and partly concealed, a precipice, over which he was precipitated, and at the foot of which his mangled and lifeless form would soon have reposed had not his warlike forefathers, being impressed with the advantage of wearing strong sword-belts, furnished the sword which Ole wore with such a belt as was not only on all occasions sufficient to support the sword itself, but which, on this particular occasion, was strong enough to support its owner when he was suspended from, and entangled with, the shrubs of the cliff.

A ray of light chanced to break into the dark chasm at the time, and revealed all its dangers to the pendulous Thorwald so powerfully that he positively howled with horror.

The howl brought Hugh and several of his followers to his side, and they with much difficulty, for he was a heavy man, succeeded in dragging him from his dangerous position and placing him on his feet, in which position he remained for some time, speechless and blowing.

"Now, I'll tell you what it is, boys," said he at length, "if ever you catch me going on an expedition of this sort again, flay me alive—that's all; don't spare me. Pull off the cuticle as if it were a glove; and if I roar don't mind—that's what I say."

Having said this, the veteran warrior smiled a ghastly smile, as if the idea of being so excruciatingly treated were rather pleasant than otherwise.

"You're not hurt, I hope?" inquired Hugh.

"Hurt; yes, I *am* hurt,—hurt in my feelings, not in my body, thanks to my good sword and belt; but my feelings are injured. That villain, that rascal, that pirate—as I verily believe him to be—selected me especially for this service, I am persuaded, just because he knew me to be unfit for it. Bah! but I'll pay him off for it. Come, boys, forward—perhaps, in the circumstances, it would be more appropriate to say upward! We must go through with it now, as our retreat is cut off. Lead the way, Hugh; your eyes are younger and sharper than mine; and if you chance to fall over a cliff, pray give a yell, like a good fellow, so that I may escape your sad fate."

In the course of half an hour's rough scramble, the party gained the crest of the Goat's Pass and descended in rear of the native village. The country over which they had to travel, however, was so broken and so beset with rugged masses of rock as to retard their progress considerably, besides causing them to lose their way more than once. It was thus daybreak before they reached the heights that overlooked the village; and the shot from the Avenger, with the broadside from the frigate, was delivered just as they began to descend the hill.

Ole, therefore, pushed on with enthusiasm to attack the village in rear; but he had not advanced half a mile when the peculiar and to him inexplicable movements of the two vessels, which have been already described, took place, leaving the honest commander of the land forces in a state of great perplexity as to what was meant by his naval allies, and in much doubt as to what he ought to do.

"It seems to me," said he to his chiefs, in a hastily-summoned council of war, "that we are all at sixes and sevens. I don't understand what maneuvers these naval men are up to, and I doubt if they know themselves. This being the case, and the fleet, if I may so name it, having run away, it behooves us, my friends, to show these sailors how we soldiers do our duty. I would advise, therefore, that we should attack at once. But as we are not a strong party, and as we know not how strong the savages may be, I think it my duty, before leading you on, to ask your opinions on the point."

The officers whose opinions were thus asked were Hugh Barnes, already mentioned, Terence Rigg the blacksmith of the settlement, and John Thomson the carpenter. These, being strong of body, powerful of will, and intelligent withal, had been appointed to the command of companies, and when on duty were styled "captain" by their commanding officer, who was, when on duty, styled "general" by them.

Ole Thorwald, be it remarked in passing, was a soldier at heart. Having gone through a moderate amount of military education, and possessing considerable talent in the matter of drill, he took special pride in training the natives and the white men of the settlement to act in concert and according to fixed principles. The consequence was that although his men were poorly armed, he had them in perfect command, and could cause them to act unitedly at any moment.

The captains having been requested to give their opinions, Captain Rigg, being senior, observed that he was for "goin' at 'em at wance, neck or nothing;" to which warlike sentiment he gave a peculiar emphasis by adding, "an' no mistake," in a very decided tone of voice.

"That's wot I says too, General," said Captain Thomson, the carpenter.

Captain Barnes being of the same opinion, General Thorwald said:

"Well, then, gentlemen, we shall attack without delay;" and proceeded to make the necessary arrangements.

When the Talisman fired her broadside of blank cartridge at the native village, there was not a solitary warrior in it—only aged men, women, and children. These, filled with unutterable consternation on hearing the thunderous discharge, sent up one yell of terror and forthwith took to their heels and made for the hills *en masse*, never once looking behind them, and, therefore, remaining in ignorance of the ulterior proceedings of the ship.

It was some time before they came in sight of Ole Thorwald and his men.

The moment they did so Ole gave the word to charge; and, whirling his sword round his head, set the example. The men followed with a yell. The poor savages turned at once and fled,—such of them at least as were not already exhausted by their run up hill,—and the rest, consisting chiefly of old men and children, fell on their knees and faces and howled for mercy.

As soon as the charging host became aware of the character of the enemy, they came to a sudden half.

"Sure, it's owld men and women we're about to kill!" cried Captain Rigg, lowering his formidable forehammer, with which, in default of a better weapon, he had armed himself; "but, hooray, Gineral! there may be lots o' the warrior reptiles in among the huts, and them poor craturs have been sent out to deceive us."

"That's true. Forward my lads!" shouted Ole, and again the army charged; nor did they stop short until they had taken possession of the village, when they found that all the fighting men were gone.

This being happily accomplished without bloodshed, Ole Thorwald, like a wise general, took the necessary steps to insure and complete his conquest. He seized all the women and children, and shut them up in a huge temple built of palm trees and roofed with broad leaves. This edifice was devoted to the horrible practise of cutting up human bodies that were intended to be eaten.

Ole had often heard of the cannibalism that is practised by most of the South Sea Islanders, though some tribes are worse than others; but he had never before this day come directly in contact with it. Here, however, there could be no doubt whatever of the fact. Portions of human bodies were strewn about this hideous temple,—some parts in a raw and bloody condition, as if they had just been cut from a lately slain victim; others in a baked state, as if ready to form part of some terrible banquet.

Sick at heart, Ole Thorwald turned from this sight with loathing. Concluding that the natives who practised such things could not be very much distressed by being shut up for a time in a temple dedicated to the gratification of their own disgusting tastes, he barricaded the entrance securely, placed a guard over it, and hurried away to see that two other buildings, in which the remainder of the women and children had been imprisoned, were similarly secured and guarded. Meanwhile the stalwart knight of the forehammer, to whom the duty had been assigned, placed sentries at the various entrances to the village, and disposed his men in such a way as to prevent the possibility of being taken by surprise.

These various arrangements were not made a moment too soon. The savages, as we have said in a former chapter, rushed towards their village from all quarters, on hearing the thunder of the great guns. They were now arriving in scores, and came rushing over the brow of the neighboring hill, and down the slopes that rose immediately in rear of their rude homes.

On finding that the place was occupied by their enemies, they set up a yell of despair, and retired to a neighboring height, where Ole could see, by their wild gesticulations, that they were hotly debating what should be done. It soon became evident that an attack would be made; for, as their comrades came pouring in, the party from the settlement was soon greatly outnumbered.

Seeing this, and knowing that the party under command of Henry Stuart would naturally hasten to his aid as soon as possible, Ole sought to cause delay by sending out a flag of truce.

The natives had been so long acquainted with the customs of the Europeans that they understood the meaning of this, and the chief of the tribe, at once throwing down his club, advanced fearlessly to meet the Christian native sent out with the flag.

The message was to the effect that if they, the enemy, should dare to make an attack, all the women and children then in the hands of the settlers should have their heads chopped off on the spot!

This was a startling announcement, and one so directly in opposition to the known principles of the Christians, that the heathen chief was staggered, and turned pale. He returned to his comrades with the horrifying message, which seemed to them all utterly unaccountable. It was quite natural for themselves to do such a deed, because they held that all sorts of cruelties were just in war. But their constant experience had been that, when a native became a follower of the Christian missionary, from that moment he became merciful, especially towards the weak and helpless. Counting upon this, they were stunned as well as astonished at Thorwald's message; for they believed implicitly that he meant to do what he threatened. They did not know that Ole, although a worthy man, was not so earnest a believer in all of Mr. Mason's principles but that he could practise on their credulity in time of need. Like the missionary, he would rather have died than have sacrificed the life of a woman or child; but, unlike him, he had no objection to deceive in order to gain time.

As it turned out, his threat was unnecessary, for Henry and his men were close at hand; and before the natives could make up their minds what to do, the whole band came pouring over the hill, with Jo Bumpus far ahead of the rest, leaping and howling like a maniac with excitement.

This decided the natives. They were now outnumbered and surrounded. The principal chief, therefore, advanced towards Bumpus with a piece of native cloth tied to the end of his war-club, which he brandished furiously by way of making it plain that his object was not war, but peace!

Naturally enough, the seaman misinterpreted the signal, and there is no doubt that he would have planted his knuckles on the bridge of the nose of the swarthy cannibal had not Henry Stuart made use of his extraordinary powers of speed. He darted forward, overtook Jo, and, grasping him around the neck with both arms, shouted:

"It's a flag of truce, man!"

"You don't say so?—well, who'd ha' thought it? It don't look like one; so it don't."

With this remark, Jo subsided into a peaceable man. Pulling a quid out of his pocket, he thrust it into his cheek, and, crossing his arms on his breast, listened patiently—though not profitably, seeing that he did not understand a word—to the dialogue that followed.

It will be remembered that poor Mr. Mason, after being saved by Henry, was taken into the gig of the Talisman and put ashore. After the two vessels had disappeared, as has been already described, Henry at once led his party towards the native village, knowing that Ole Thorwald would require support, all the more that the ship had failed to fulfil her part in the combined movement.

As the almost heartbroken father had no power to render further aid to his lost child, he suffered himself to be led, in a half-bewildered state, along with the attacking party under his young friend. He was now brought forward to parley with the native chief.

The missionary's manner and aspect at once changed. In the hope of advancing the cause of his Master, he forgot, or at least restrained, his own grief for a time.

"What would the chief say to the Christians?" he began, on being confronted with the savage and some of his warriors who crowded round him.

"That he wishes to have done with war," replied the man.

"That is a good wish; but why did the chief begin war?"

"Keona began it!" said the savage, angrily. "We thought our wars with the Christians were going to stop. But Keona is bad. He put the war spirit into my people."

Mr. Mason knew this to be true.

"Then," said he, "Keona deserves punishment."

"Let him die," answered the chief; and an exclamation of assent broke from the other natives. Keona himself, happening to be there, became pale and looked anxious; but remained where he stood, nevertheless, with his arms crossed on his dark breast. A bandage of native cloth was tied round his wounded arm. Without saying a word he undid this, tore it off, and allowed the blood to ooze from the reopened wound.

It was a silent appeal to the feelings and the sense of justice of his comrades, and created a visible impression in his favor.

"That wound was received by one who would have been a murderer!" said Mr. Mason, observing the effect of this action.

"He struck me!" cried Keona, fiercely.

"He struck you in defending his own home against a cowardly attack," answered the missionary.

At this point Ole Thorwald saw fit to interfere. Seeing that the natives were beginning to argue the case, and knowing that no good could come from such a course, he quietly observed:

"There will be neither wife nor child in this place if I do but hold up my hand."

The missionary and his party did not, of course, understand this allusion, but they understood the result; for the savages at once dropped their tones, and the chief sued earnestly for peace.

"Chiefs and warriors," said Mr. Mason, raising his hand impressively, "I am a man of peace, and I serve the Prince of peace. To stop this war is what I desire most earnestly; and I desire above all things that you and I might henceforth live in friendship, serving the same God and Saviour, whose name is Jesus Christ. But your ways are not like our ways. If I leave you now, I fear you will soon find another occasion to renew the war, as you have often done before. I have you in my power now. If you were to fight with us we could easily beat you, because we are stronger in numbers and well armed. Yes, I have you in my power, and, with the blessing of my God, I will keep you in my power *forever.*"

There was a visible fall in the countenances of the savages who regarded this strange announcement as their death-warrant. Some of them even grasped their clubs, and looked fiercely at their enemies: but a glance from Ole Thorwald quieted these restive spirits.

"Now, chiefs and warrior, I have two intentions in regard to you," continued Mr. Mason. "The one is that you shall take your clubs, spears, and other weapons, and lay them in a pile on this mound, after which I will make you march unarmed before us halfway to our settlement. From that point you shall return to your homes. Thus you shall be deprived of the power of treacherously breaking that peace which you know in your hearts you would break if you could.

"My second intention is that the whole of your tribe—men, women, and children—shall now assemble at the foot of this mound and hear what I have got to say to you. The first part of this plan I shall carry out by force, if need be. But for the second part, *I must have your own consent.* I may not force you to listen if you are not willing to hear."

At the mention of the women and children being required to assemble along with them, the natives pricked up their ears, and, as a matter of course, they willingly agreed to listen to all that the missionary had to say to them.

This being settled, and the natives knowing, from former experience, that the Christians never broke faith with them, they advanced to the mound pointed out and threw down their arms. A strong guard was placed over these; the troops of the settlement were disposed in such a manner as to prevent the possibility of their being recovered, and then the women and children were set free.

It was a noisy and remarkable meeting that which took place between the men and women of the tribe on this occasion; but soon surprise and expectation began to take the place of all other feelings as the strange intentions of the missionary were spoken of, and in a very short time Mr. Mason had a large and most attentive congregation.

Never before had the missionary secured such an opportunity. His eccentric method of obtaining a hearing had succeeded beyond his expectations. With a heart overflowing with gratitude to God, he stood up and began to preach the gospel.

Mr. Mason was not only eccentric, but able and wise. He made the most of his opportunity. He gave them a *very* long sermon that day; but he knew that the savages were not used to sermons, and that they would not think it long. His text was a double one,—"The soul that sinneth it shall die," and "Believe on the Lord Jesus Christ, and thou shalt be saved."

He preached that day as a man might who speaks to his hearers for the first and last time, and, in telling of the goodness, the mercy, and the love of God, the bitter grief of his own heart was sensibly abated.

After his discourse was over and prayer had been offered up, the savage warriors were silently formed into a band and marched off in front of the Christians to the spot where Mr.

Mason had promised to set them free. They showed no disinclination to go. They believed in the good faith of their captors. The missionary had, indeed, got them into his power that day. Some of them he had secured *forever*.

CHAPTER XIX

SORROW AND SYMPATHY—THE WIDOW
BECOMES A PLEADER AND HER SON
ENGAGES IN A SINGLE COMBAT

There are times in the life of every one when the heart seems unable to bear the load of sorrow and suffering that is laid upon it,—times when the anguish of the soul is such that the fair world around seems enshrouded with gloom, when the bright sun itself appears to shine in mockery, and when the smitten heart refuses to be comforted.

Such a time was it with poor Frederick Mason when, after his return to Sandy Cove, he stood alone, amid the blackened ruins of his former home, gazing at the spot which he knew, from the charred remnants as well as its position, was the site of the room which had once been occupied by his lost child.

It was night when he stood there. The silence was profound, for the people of the settlement sympathized so deeply with their beloved pastor's grief that even the ordinary hum of life appeared to be hushed, except now and then when a low wail would break out and float away on the night wind. These sounds of woe were full of meaning. They told that there were other mourners there that night,—that the recent battle had not been fought without producing some of the usual bitter fruits of war. Beloved, but dead and mangled forms, lay in more than one hut in Sandy Cove.

Motionless, hopeless, the missionary stood amid the charred beams and ashes, until the words "Call upon me in the day of trouble and I will deliver thee, and thou shalt glorify me," descended on his soul like sunshine upon ice. A suppressed cry burst from his lips, and, falling on his knees, he poured forth his soul in prayer.

While he was yet on his knees, a cry of anguish arose from

one of the huts at the foot of the hill. It died away in a low, heart-broken wail. Mr. Mason knew its meaning well. That cry had a special significance to him. It spoke reproachfully. It said, "There is comfort for *you*, for where life is there is hope; but here there is *death*."

Again the word of God came to his memory,—"Weep with them that weep." Starting up hastily, the missionary sprang over the black beams, and hurried down the hill, entered the village, and spent the greater part of the remainder of that night in comforting the bereaved and the wounded.

The cause of the pastor's grief was not removed thereby, but the sorrow itself was lightened by sympathy; and when he returned, at a late hour, to his temporary home, hope had begun to arise within his breast.

The widow's cottage afforded him shelter. When he entered it, Henry and his mother were seated near a small table on which supper was spread for their expected guest.

"Tom Armstrong will recover," said the missionary, seating himself opposite the widow, and speaking in a hurried, excited tone. "His wound is a bad one, given by a war-club, but I think it is not dangerous. I wish I could say as much for poor Simon. If he had been attended to sooner he might have lived; but so much blood has been already lost that there is now no hope. Alas for his little boy! He will be an orphan soon. Poor Hardy's wife is distracted with grief. Her young husband's body is so disfigured with cuts and bruises that it is dreadful to look upon; yet she will not leave the room in which it lies, nor cease to embrace and cling to the mangled corpse. Poor, poor Lucy! she will have to be comforted. At present she must be left with God. No human sympathy can avail just now; but she must be comforted when she will permit any one to speak to her. You will go to her to-morrow, Mrs. Stuart, won't you?"

As this was Mr. Mason's first meeting with the widow since the Sunday morning when the village was attacked, his words and manner showed that he dreaded any allusion to his own loss. The widow saw and understood this; but she had consolation for him as well as for others, and would not allow him to have his way.

"But what of Alice?" she said, earnestly. "You do not mention her. Henry has told me all. Have you nothing to say about yourself—about Alice?"

"Oh! what can I say?" cried the pastor, clasping his hands, while a deep sob almost choked him.

"Can you not say that she is in the hands of God—of a loving *Father*?" said Mrs. Stuart, tenderly.

"Yes, I can say that—I *have* said that; but—but—"

"I know what you would say," interrupted the widow; "you would tell me that she is in the hands of pirates,—ruthless villains who fear neither God nor man, and that, unless a miracle is wrought in her behalf, nothing can save her—"

"Oh! spare me, Mary; why do you harrow my broken heart with such a picture?" cried Mr. Mason, rising and pacing the room with quick, unsteady steps, while with both hands on his head he seemed to attempt to crush down the thoughts that burned up his brain.

"I speak thus," said the widow, with an earnestness of tone and manner that almost startled her hearers, "because I wish to comfort you. Alice, you tell me, is on board the Foam—"

"On board the *pirate schooner*!" cried Henry, almost fiercely; for the youth, although as much distressed as Mr. Mason, was not so resigned as he, and his spirit chafed at the thought of having been deceived so terribly by the pirate.

"She is on board the Foam," repeated the widow, in a tone so stern that her hearers looked at her in surprise, "and is therefore in the hands of Gascoyne, who will not injure a hair of her head. I tell you, Mr. Mason, that she is *perfectly safe* in the hands of Gascoyne."

"Of the pirate Durward!" said Henry, in a deep, angry voice.

"What ground have you for saying so?" asked the widow, quickly. "You only know him as Gascoyne the sandal-wood trader,—the captain of the Foam. He has been suspected, it is true; but suspicion is not proof. His schooner has been fired into by a war-vessel; he has returned the fire: any passionate man might be tempted to do that. His men have carried off some of our dear ones. That was *their* doing, not his. He knew nothing of it."

"Mother, mother," cried Henry, entreatingly, "don't stand up in that way for a pirate; I can't bear to hear it. Did he not himself describe the pirate schooner's appearance in this room, and when he was attacked by the Talisman did he not show out in his true colors, thereby proving that he is Durward the pirate?"

The widow's face grew pale and her voice trembled as she replied, like one who sought to convince herself rather than her hearer, "That is not *positive* proof, Henry, Gascoyne may have had some good reason for deceiving you all in this way. His description of the pirate may have been a false one. We cannot tell. You know he was anxious to prevent Captain Montague from impressing his men."

"And would proclaiming himself a pirate be a good way of accomplishing that end, mother?"

"Mary," said Mr. Mason, solemnly, as he seated himself at the table and looked earnestly in the widow's face, "your knowledge of this man and your manner of speaking about him surprise me. I have long thought that you were not acting wisely in permitting Gascoyne to be so intimate; for, whatever he may in reality be, he is a suspicious character, to say the best of him; and although *I* know that you think you are right in encouraging his visits, other people do not know that; they may judge you harshly. I do not wish to pry into secrets; but you have sought to comfort me by bidding me have perfect confidence in this man? I *must* ask what knowledge you have of him. How far are you aware of his character and employment? How do you know that he is so trustworthy?"

An expression of deep grief rested on the widow's countenance as she replied, in a sad voice;

"I *know* that you may trust Gascoyne with your child. He is my oldest friend. I have known him since we were children. He saved my father's life long, long ago, and helped to support my mother in her last years. Would you have me to forget all this because men say that he is a pirate?"

"Why, mother," cried Henry, "if you know so much about him you *must* know that, whatever he was in time past, he is the pirate Durward now."

"I do *not* know that he is the pirate Durward!" said the widow, in a voice and with a look so decided that Henry was silenced and sorely perplexed; yet much relieved, for he knew that his mother would rather die than tell a deliberate falsehood.

The missionary was also comforted; for although his judgment told him that the grounds of hope thus held out to him were very insufficient, he was impressed by the thoroughly confident tone of the widow, and felt relieved in spite of himself.

Soon after this conversation was concluded, the household retired to rest.

Next morning Henry was awakened out of a deep sleep by the sound of subdued voices in the room underneath his own. At first he paid no attention to these, supposing that, as it was broad daylight, some of their native servants were moving about. But presently the sound of his mother's voice induced him to listen more attentively. Then a voice replied, so low that he could with difficulty hear it at all. Its strength increased, however, and at last it broke forth in deep bass tones.

Henry sprang up and threw on his clothes. As he was thus engaged the front door of the opened, and the speakers went out. A few seconds sufficed for the youth to finish dressing him; then, seizing a pistol, he hurried out of the house. Looking quickly round, he just caught sight of the skirts of a woman's dress as they disappeared through the doorway of a hut which had been formerly inhabited by a poor native, who had subsisted on the widow's bounty until he died. The door was shut immediately after.

Going swiftly but cautiously round by a back way, Henry approached the hut. Strange and conflicting feelings filled his breast. A blush of deep shame and self-abhorrence mantled on his cheek when it flashed across him that he was about to play the spy on his own mother. But there was no mistaking Gascoyne's voice.

How the supposed pirate had got there, and wherefore he was there, were matters that he did not think of or care about at that moment. There he was; so the young man resolved to secure him and hand him over to justice.

Henry was too honorable to listen secretly to a conversation, whatever it might be, that was not intended for his ears. He resolved merely to peep in at one of the many chinks in the log but for one moment, to satisfy himself that Gascoyne really was there, and to observe his position. But as the latter now thought himself beyond the hearing of any one, he spoke in unguarded tones, and Henry heard a few words in spite of himself.

Looking through a chink in the wall at the end of the hut, he beheld the stalwart form of the sandal-wood trader standing on the hearth of the hut, which was almost unfurnished,—a stool, a bench, an old chest, a table, and a chair being all that it contained. His mother was seated at the table, with her hands clasped before her, looking up at her companion.

"Oh! why run so great a risk as this?" said she earnestly.

"I was born to run risks, I believe," replied Gascoyne, in a sad, low voice. "It matters not. My being on the island is the result of Manton's villainy; my being here is for poor Henry's sake and your own, as well as for the sake of Alice the missionary's child. You have been upright, Mary, and kind, and true as steel ever since I knew you. But for that I should have been lost long ago—"

Henry heard no more. These words did indeed whet his curiosity to the utmost; but the shame of acting the part of an "eavesdropper" was so great that, by a strong effort of will, he drew back, and pondered for a moment what he ought to do. The unexpected tone and tenor of Gascoyne's remark had softened him slightly; but, recalling the undoubted proofs that he had had of his really being a pirate, he soon steeled his heart against him. He argued that the mere fact of a man giving his mother credit for a character which everybody knew she possessed, was not sufficient to clear him of the suspicions which he had raised against himself. Besides, it was impertinence in any man to tell his mother his opinion of her to her face. And to call him "poor Henry," forsooth! This was not to be endured!

Having thus wrought himself up to a sufficient degree of indignation, the young man went straight to the door, making considerable noise in order to prepare those within for his advent. He had expected to find it locked. In this he was mistaken. It yielded to a push.

Throwing it wide open, Henry strode into the middle of the apartment, and, pointing the pistol at Gascoyne's breast, exclaimed:

"Pirate Durward, I arrest you in the king's name!"

At the first sound of her son's approach, Mrs. Stuart bent forward over the table with a groan, and buried her face in her hands.

Gascoyne received Henry's speech at first with a frown, and then with a smile.

"You have taken a strange time and way to jest, Henry," said he, crossing his arms on his broad chest and gazing boldly into the youth's face.

"You will not throw me off my guard thus," said Henry, sternly. "You are my prisoner. I know you to be a pirate. At any rate you will have to prove yourself to be an honest man before you quit this hut a free man. Mother, leave this place, that I may lock the door upon him."

The widow did not move, but Gascoyne made a step towards her son.

"Another step and I will fire. Your blood shall be on your own head, Gascoyne."

As Gascoyne still advanced, Henry pointed the pistol straight at his breast and pulled the trigger, but no report followed; the priming, indeed, flashed in the pan, but that was all!

With a cry of rage and defiance, Henry leaped upon Gascoyne like a young lion. He struck at him with the pistol; but the latter caught the weapon in his powerful hand, wrenched it from the youth's grasp, and flung it to the other end of the apartment.

"You shall not escape me," cried Henry, aiming a tremendous blow with his fist at Gascoyne's face. It was parried, and the next moment the two closed in a deadly struggle.

It was a terrible sight for the widow to witness these two herculean men exerting their great strength to the utmost in a hand-to-hand conflict in that small hut, like two tigers in a cage.

Henry, although nearly six feet in height, and proportionally broad and powerful, was much inferior to his gigantic antagonist; but to the superior size and physical force of the latter he opposed the lithe activity and the fervid energy of youth, so that to an unpractised eye it might have seemed doubtful at first which of the two men had the best chance.

Straining his powers to the utmost, Henry attempted to lift his opponent off the ground and throw him. In this he was nearly successful. Gascoyne staggered, but recovered himself instantly. They did not move much from the center of the room, nor was there much noise created during the conflict. It seemed too close—too full of concentrated energy, of heavy, prolonged straining—for much violent motion. The great veins in Gascoyne's forehead stood out like knotted cords; yet there was no scowl or frown on his face. Henry's brows, on the contrary, were gathered into a dark frown. His teeth were set, and his countenance flushed to deep red by exertion and passion.

Strange to say, the widow made no effort to separate the combatants; neither did she attempt to move from her seat to give any alarm. She sat with her hands on the table clasped tightly together, gazing eagerly, anxiously, like a fascinated creature, at the wild struggle that was going on before her.

Again and again Henry attempted, with all the fire of youth, to throw his adversary by one tremendous effort, but failed. Then he tried to fling him off, so as to have the power of using his fists or making an overwhelming rush. But Gascoyne held him in his strong arms like a vice. Several times he freed his right arm and attempted to plant a blow; but Gascoyne caught the blow in his hand, or seized the wrist and prevented its being delivered. In short, do what he would, Henry Stuart could neither free himself from the embrace of his enemy nor conquer him. Still he struggled on; for, as this fact became more apparent, the youth's blood became hotter from mingled shame and anger.

Both men soon began to show symptoms of fatigue. It was not in the nature of things that two such frames, animated by such spirits, could prolong so exhausting a struggle. It was not doubtful now which of the two would come off victorious. During the whole course of the fight Gascoyne had acted entirely on the defensive. A small knife or stiletto hung at his left side, but he never attempted to use it, and he never once tried to throw his adversary. In fact, it now became evident, even to the widow's perceptions, that the captain was actually playing with her son.

All along, his countenance, though flushed and eager, exhibited no sign of passion. He seemed to act like a good-humored man who had been foolishly assaulted by a headstrong boy, and who meant to keep him in play until he should tire him out.

Just then the tinkling of a bell and other sounds of the people of the establishment beginning to move were heard outside.

Henry noticed this.

"Ha!" he exclaimed, in a gasping voice, "I can at least hold you until help comes."

Gascoyne heard the sounds also. He said nothing, but he brought the strife to a swift termination. For the first time he bent his back like a man who exerts himself in earnest, and lifted Henry completely off the ground.

Throwing him on his back, he pressed him down with both arms so as to break from his grasp. No human muscles could resist the force applied. Slowly but surely the iron sinews of Henry's arms straightened out, and the two were soon at arms' length.

But even Gascoyne's strength could not unclasp the grip of the youth's hands, until he placed his knee upon his chest; then, indeed, they were torn away.

Of course, all this was not done without some violence; but it was still plain to the widow that Gascoyne was careful not to hurt his antagonist more than he could help.

"Now, Henry, my lad," said he, holding the youth down by the two arms, "I have given you a good deal of trouble this morning, and I mean to give you a little more. It does not just suit me at present to be tried for a pirate, so I mean to give you a race. You are reputed one of the best runners in the settlement. Well, I'll give you a chance after me. If you overtake me, boy, I'll give myself up to you without a struggle. But I suspect you'll find me rather hard to catch!"

As he uttered the last words he permitted Henry to rise. Ere the youth had quite gained his footing, he gave him a violent push and sent him staggering back against the wall. When Henry recovered his balance, Gascoyne was standing in the open doorway.

"Now, lad, are you ready?" said he, a sort of wild smile lighting up his face.

Henry was so taken aback by this conduct, as well as by the

rough handling which he had just received, that he could not collect his thoughts for a few seconds; but, when Gascoyne nodded gravely to his mother, and walked quietly away, saying, "Good-by, Mary," the exasperated youth darted through the doorway like an arrow.

If Henry Stuart's rush may be compared to the flight of an arrow from a bow, not less appropriately may Gascoyne's bound be likened to the leap of the bolt from a cross-bow: The two men sprang over the low fences that surrounded the cottage, leaped the rivulet that brawled down its steep course behind it, and coursed up the hill like mountain hares.

The last that Widow Stuart saw of them, as she gazed eagerly from the doorway of the hut, was, when Gascoyne's figure was clearly defined against the sky as he leaped over a great chasm in the lava high up the mountain-side. Henry followed almost instantly, and then both were hidden from view in the chaos of rocks and gorges that rose above the upper line of vegetation.

It was a long and a severe chase that Henry had undertaken, and ably did his fleet foot sustain the credit which he had already gained. But Gascoyne's foot was fleeter. Over every species of ground did the sandal-wood trader lead the youth that morning. It seemed, in fact, as if a spirit of mischief had taken possession of Gascoyne; for his usually grave face was lighted up with a mingled expression of glee and ferocity. It changed, too, and wore a sad expression at times, even when the man seemed to be running for his life.

At last, after running until he had caused Henry to show symptoms of fatigue, Gascoyne turned suddenly round, and shouting "Good-by, Henry, my lad!" went straight up the mountain, and disappeared over the dividing ridge on the summit.

Henry did not give in. The insult implied in the words renewed his strength. He tightened his belt as he ran, and rushed up the mountain almost as fast as Gascoyne had done; but when he leaped upon the ridge, the fugitive had vanished!

That he had secreted himself in one of the numerous gorges or caves with which the place abounded was quite clear; but it was equally clear that no one could track him out in such a place unless he were possessed of a dog's nose. The youth did indeed attempt it; but, being convinced that he was only searching for what could not by any possibility be found, he soon gave it up, and returned, disconsolate and crestfallen, to the cottage.

CHAPTER XX

MYSTERIOUS CONSULTATIONS AND PLANS — GASCOYNE ASTONISHES HIS FRIENDS, AND MAKES AN UNEXPECTED CONFESSION

"A pretty morning's work I have made of it, mother," said Henry, as he flung himself into a chair in the cottage parlor, on his return from the weary and fruitless chase which has just been recorded.

The widow was pale and haggard; but she could not help smiling as she observed the look of extreme disappointment which rested on the countenance of her son.

"True, Henry," she replied, busying herself in preparing breakfast, "you have not been very successful; but you made a noble effort."

"Pshaw! a noble effort, indeed! Why, the man has foiled me in the two things in which I prided myself most,—wrestling and running. I never saw such a greyhound in my life."

"He is a giant, my boy; few men could hope to overcome him."

"True, as regards wrestling, mother; I am not much ashamed of having been beaten by him at that; but running,—that's the sore point. Such a weight he is, and yet he took the north gully like a wildcat; and you know, mother, there are only two of us in Sandy Cove who can go over that gully. Aye, and he went a full yard further than ever I did. I measured the leap as I came down. Really, it is too bad to have been beaten so completely by a man who must be nearly double my age. But, after all, the worst of the whole affair is, that a pirate has escaped me after I actually had him in my arms!—the villain!"

"You do not *know* that he is a villain," said the widow in a subdued tone.

"You are right, mother," said Henry, looking up from the plate of bacon, to which he had been devoting himself with much assiduity, and gazing earnestly into his mother's face,—"you are right and, do you know, I feel inclined to give the fellow the benefit of the doubt; for, to tell you the truth, I have a sort of liking for him. If it had not been for the way in which he has treated you, and the suspicious character that he bears, I do believe I should have made a friend of him."

A look of evident pleasure crossed the widow's face while her son spoke; but as that son's eyes were once more riveted on the bacon, which his morning exercise rendered peculiarly attractive, he did not observe it.

Just then the door opened, and Mr. Mason entered. His face wore a dreadfully anxious expression.

"Ha! I'm glad to see you, Henry," said he; "of course you have not caught your man. I have been waiting anxiously for you to consult about our future proceedings. It is quite evident that the pirate schooner cannot be far off. Gascoyne must either have swam ashore, or been landed in a boat. In either case the schooner must have been within the reef at the time, and there has been little wind since the squall blew itself out yesterday."

"Quite enough, however, to blow such a light craft pretty far out to sea in a few hours," said Henry, shaking his head.

"No matter," replied Mr. Mason, with a sigh; "*something* must be done, at any rate. I have borrowed the carpenter's small cutter, which is now being put in order for a voyage. Provisions and water for a few days are already on board, and I have come to ask you to take command of her, as you know something of navigation. I will go, of course, but will not take any management of the little craft, as I know nothing about the working of vessels."

"And where do you mean to go?" asked Henry.

"That remains to be seen. I have some ideas running in my head, of course; but before letting you know them, I wish to hear what you would advise."

"I would advise, in the first place, that you should provide one or two thorough sailors to manage the craft. By the way, that reminds me of Bumpus. What of him? Where is he? In the midst of all this bustle I have not had time for much thought; and it has only just occurred to me that if this schooner is really a pirate, and if Gascoyne turns out to be Durward, it follows that Bumpus is a pirate too, and ought to be dealt with accordingly."

"I have thought of that," said Mr. Mason, with a perplexed look, "and intended to speak to you on the subject; but events have crowded so fast upon each other of late that it has been driven out of my mind. No doubt, if the Foam and the Avenger are one and the same vessel, as seems too evident to leave much room for doubt, then Bumpus is a pirate; for he does not deny that he was one of the crew. But he acts strangely for a pirate. He seems as much at his ease amongst us as if he were the most innocent of men. Moreover, his looks seem to stamp him a thoroughly honest fellow. But, alas! one cannot depend on looks."

"But where is the man?" asked Henry.

"He is asleep in the small closet off the kitchen," said Mrs. Stuart, "where he has been lying ever since you returned from the heathen village. Poor fellow, he sleeps heavily, and looks as if he had been hurt during all this fighting."

"Hurt! say you?" exclaimed Henry, laughing; "it is a miracle that he is now alive after the flight he took over the north cliff into the sea."

"Flight!—over the north cliff!" echoed Mrs. Stuart, in surprise.

"Aye, and a fearful plunge he had." Here Henry detailed poor Jo's misadventure. "And now," said he, when he had finished, "I must lock his door and keep him in. The settlers have forgotten him in all this turmoil; but, depend upon it, if they see him they will string him up for a pirate to the first handy branch of a tree, without giving him the benefit of a trial; and that would not be desirable."

"Yet you would have shot Gascoyne on mere suspicion, without a thought of trial or justice," said Mrs. Stuart.

"True, mother; but that was when I was seizing him, and in hot blood," said Henry, in a subdued voice. "I was hasty there, no doubt. Lucky for us both that the pistol missed fire."

The widow looked as if she were about to reply, but checked herself.

"Yes," said Mr. Mason, recurring to the former subject; "as we shall be away a few days, we must lock Bumpus up to keep him out of harm's way. Meanwhile—"

The missionary was interrupted here by the sudden opening of the door. An exclamation of surprise burst from the whole party as they sprang up, for Gascoyne strode into the room, locked the door, and taking out the key handed it to Henry, who stood staring at him in speechless amazement.

"You are surprised to see me appear thus suddenly," said he; "but the fact is that I came here this morning to fulfil a duty; and although Master Henry there has hindered me somewhat in carrying out my good intentions, I do not intend to allow him to frustrate me altogether."

"I do not mean to make a second attempt, Gascoyne, after what has occurred this morning," said Henry, seating himself doggedly on his chair. "But it would be as well that you should observe that Mr. Mason is a stout man, and, as we have seen, can act vigorously when occasion offers. Remember that we are two to one now."

"There will be no occasion for vigorous action, at least as regards me, if you will agree to forget your suspicions for a few minutes and listen to what I have got to say. Meanwhile, in order to show you how thoroughly in earnest I am, and how regardless of my personal safety, I render myself defenseless—thus."

Gascoyne pulled a brace of small pistols from their place of concealment beneath the breast of his shirt, and drawing the knife that hung at his girdle, hurled them all through the open window into the garden. He then took a chair, planted it in the middle of the room, and sat down. The sadness of his deep voice did not change during the remainder of that interview. The bold look which usually characterized this peculiar man had given place to a grave expression of humility which was occasionally varied by a troubled look.

"Before stating what I have come for," said Gascoyne, "I mean to make a confession. You have been right in your suspicions,— *I am Durward the pirate!* Nay, do not shrink from me in that way, Mary. I have kept this secret from you long, because I feared to lose the old friendship that has existed between us since we were children. I have deceived you in *this thing only.* I have taken advantage of your ignorance to make you suppose that I was merely a smuggler, and that, in consequence of being an outlaw, it was necessary for me to conceal my name and my movements. You have kept my secret, Mary, and have tried to win me back to honest ways; but you little knew the strength of the net I had wrapped around me. You did not know that I was a pirate!"

Gascoyne paused, and bent his head as if in thought. The widow sat with clasped hands, gazing at him with a look of despair on her pale face. But she did not move or speak. The three listeners sat in perfect silence, until the pirate chose to continue his confession.

"Yes, I have been a pirate," said he; "but I have not been the villain that men have painted me." He looked steadily in the widow's face as he said these words deliberately.

"Do not try to palliate your conduct, Gascoyne," said Mr. Mason, earnestly. "The blackness of your sin is too great to be deepened or lightened by what men may have said of you. You are a pirate. Every *pirate is a murderer.*"

"*I am not a murderer,*" said Gascoyne, slowly, in reply, but still fixing his gaze on the widow's face, as if he addressed himself solely to her.

"You may not have committed murder with your own hand," said Mr. Mason, "but the man who leads on others to commit the crime is a murderer, in the eye of God's law as well as in that of man."

"I never led on men to commit murder," said Gascoyne, in the same tone, and with the same steadfast gaze. "This hand is free from the stain of human blood. Do you believe me, Mary?"

The widow did not answer. She sat like one bereft of all power of speech or motion.

"I will explain," resumed the pirate captain, drawing a long breath, and directing his looks to Henry now.

"For reasons which it is not necessary that you should know, I resolved some years ago to become a pirate. I had been deceived—shamefully deceived and wronged—by wealthy and powerful men. I had appealed to the law of my country, and the law refused to right me. No, not the law, but those who sat on the judgment-seat to pervert the law. It matters not now; I was driven mad at the time, for the wrong done was not done so much to me as to those whom I loved. I vowed that I should be avenged.

"I soon found men as mad as myself, who only wanted a leader to guide them in order to run full swing to destruction. I seized the Foam, of which schooner I was mate, called her the Avenger, and became a pirate. No blood was shed when I seized the schooner. Before an opportunity occurred of trying my hand at this new profession, my anger had cooled. *I repented* of what I had done; but I was surrounded by men who were more bent on mischief than I was. I could not draw back, but I modified my plan. I determined to become merely a *robber*, and use the proceeds of my trade to indemnify those to whom injustice had been done. I thought at the time that there was some justice in this. I called myself, in jest, a tax-gatherer of the sea. I ordered the men aft one day, and explained to them my views. I said that

I abhorred the name and the deeds of pirates; that I would only consent to command them if they agreed never to shed human blood except in fair and open fight.

"They liked the idea. There were men among them who had never heartily agreed to the seizing of the schooner, and who would have left her if I would have allowed them; these were much relieved to hear my proposal. It was fixed that we should *rob*, but not *murder*. Miserable fool that I was! I thought it was possible to go just so far and no farther into sin. I did not know at that time the strength of the fearful current into which I had plunged.

"But we stuck to our principles. We never did commit murder. And as our appearance was always sufficient to cause the colors of any ship we ever came across to be hauled down at once, there has been no occasion for shedding blood, even in fair and open fight. Do you believe me, Mary?" said Gascoyne, pausing at this point.

The widow was still silent; but a slight inclination of her head satisfied the pirate, who was about to resume, when Mr. Mason said: "Gascoyne, do you call warfare in the cause of robbery by the name of 'fair and open fight?'"

"No, I do not. Yet there have been great generals and admirals in this world who have committed wholesale murder in this same cause, and whose names stand high on the roll of fame!"

A look of scorn rested on the pirate's face as he said this, but it passed away quickly.

"You tell me that there were some of the men in the schooner whom you kept aboard against their will!" said Mr. Mason. "Did it never occur to you, Gascoyne, that you may have been the murderer of the *souls* of these men?"

The pirate made no reply for some time, and the troubled, anxious look that had more than once crossed his face returned.

"Yes," said he, at length, "I have thought of that. But it is done now, and cannot be undone. I can do no more now than give myself up to justice. You see, I have thrown away my arms and stand here defenseless. But I did not come here to plead for mercy. I came to make to you all the reparation I can for the wrong I have done you. When that last act is completed, you may do with me what you please. I deserve to die, and I care not to live."

"O Gascoyne! speak not thus!" exclaimed the widow, earnestly. "However much and deeply you have sinned against man, if you have not taken life you do not deserve to die. Besides, there is a way of pardon open to the very chief of sinners."

"I know what you mean, Mary, I know what you mean; but— well, well, this is neither the time nor place to talk of such things. Your little girl, Mr. Mason, is in the hands of the pirates."

"I know that," said the missionary, wincing as if he had received a deep wound; "but she is not in *your* power now."

"More's the pity; she would have been safer with me than with my first mate, who is the greatest villain afloat on the high seas. He does not like our milk-and-water style of robbing. He is an out-and-out pirate in heart, and has long desired to cut my throat. I have to thank him for being here to-night. Some of the crew who are like himself seized me while I was asleep, bound and gagged me, put me into a boat, and rowed me ashore; for we had easily escaped the Talisman in the squall, and, doubling on our course, came back here. The mate was anxious to clear off old scores by cutting my throat at once, and pitching me into the sea. Luckily some of the men, not so bloodthirsty as he, objected to this; so I was landed and cast loose."

"But what of Alice?" cried Mr. Mason, anxiously. "How can we save her?"

"By taking my advice," answered Gascoyne. "You have a small cutter at anchor off the creek at the foot of the hill. Put a few trusty men aboard of her, and I will guide you to the island where the Avenger has been wont to fly when hard pressed."

"But how do you know that Manton will go there?" inquired

Henry, eagerly.

"Because he is short of powder, and all our stores are concealed there, besides much of our ill-gotten wealth."

"And how can you expect us to put ourselves so completely in your power?" said Mr. Mason.

"Because you *must* do so if you would save your child. She is safe now, I know, and will be until the Avenger leaves the island where our stores are concealed. If we do not save her before that happens, *she is lost to you forever!*"

"That no man can say. She is in the hands of God," cried Mr. Mason, fervently.

"True, true," said Gascoyne, musing. "But God does not work by miracles. We must be up and doing at once. I promise you that I shall be faithful, and that, after the work is done, I will give myself up to justice."

"May we trust him, mother?" said Henry.

"You may trust him, my son," replied the widow, in a tone of decision that satisfied Henry, while it called forth a look of gratitude from the pirate.

The party now proceeded to arrange the details of their plan for the rescue of Alice and her companions. These were speedily settled, and Henry rose to go and put them in train. He turned the key of the door, and was on the point of lifting the latch, when this was done for him by some one on the outside. He had just time to step back, when the door flew open, and he stood face to face with Hugh Barnes the cooper.

"Have you heard the news, Henry?—hallo!"

This abrupt exclamation was caused by the sight of Gascoyne, who rose quietly the moment he heard the door open, and turning his back towards it, walked slowly into a small apartment that opened off the widow's parlor, and shut the door.

"I say, Henry, who's that big fellow?" said the cooper, casting a suspicious glance towards the little room into which he had disappeared.

"He is a *friend* of mine," replied Mrs. Stuart, rising hastily, and welcoming her visitor.

"Humph! it's well he's a *friend*," said the man, as he took a chair; "I shouldn't like to have him for an enemy."

"But what is the news you were so anxious to tell us?" inquired Henry.

"That Gascoyne, the pirate captain, has been seen on the island by some of the women, and there's a regular hunt organizing. Will you go with us?"

"I have more important work to do, Hugh," replied Henry; "besides, I want you to go with me on a hunt which I'll tell you about if you'll come with me to the creek."

"By all means. Come along."

Henry and the cooper at once left the cottage. The latter was let into the secret, and prevailed on to form one of the crew of the Wasp, as the little cutter was named. In the course of the afternoon everything was in readiness. Gascoyne waited till the dusk of evening, and then embarked along with Ole Thorwald; that stout individual having insisted on being one of the party, despite the remonstrances of Mr. Mason, who did not like to leave the settlement, even for a brief period, so completely deprived of all its leading men. But Ole entertained a suspicion that Gascoyne intended to give them the slip; and having privately made up his mind to prevent this, he was not to be denied.

The men who formed the crew—twelve in number—were selected from among those natives and settlers who were known never to have seen the pirate captain. They were chosen with a view to their fighting qualities; for Gascoyne and Henry were sufficient for the management of the little craft. There were no large guns on board, but all the men were well armed with cutlasses, muskets, and pistols.

Thus equipped, the Wasp stood out to sea with a light breeze, just as the moon rose on the coral reef and cast a shower of sparkling silver across the bay.

CHAPTER XXI

A TERRIBLE DOOM FOR AN INNOCENT MAN

"So, you're to be hanged for a pirate, Jo Bumpus, ye are. That's pleasant to think of, anyhow."

Such was the remark which our stout seaman addressed to himself when he awoke on the second morning after the departure of the Wasp. If the thought was really as pleasant as he asserted it to be, his visage must have been a bad index to the state of his mind; for at that particular moment Joe looked uncommonly miserable.

The wonted good-humored expression of his countenance had given place to a gaze of stereotyped surprise and solemnity. Indeed, Bumpus seemed to have parted with much of his reason, and all of his philosophy; for he could say nothing else during at least half an hour after awaking except the phrase, "So you're going to be hanged for a pirate." His comments on the phrase were, however, a little varied, though always brief; such as, "Wot a sell! Who'd ha' thought it! It's a dream, it is,—an 'orrible dream! *I* don't believe it; who does? Wot'll your poor mother say?" and the like.

Bumpus had, unfortunately, good ground for making this statement.

After the cutter sailed it was discovered that Bumpus was concealed in Mrs. Stuart's cottage. This discovery had been the result of the seaman's own recklessness and indiscretion; for when he ascertained that he was to be kept a prisoner in the cottage until the return of the Wasp, he at once made up his mind to submit with a good grace to what could not be avoided. In order to prove that he was by no means cast down, as well as to lighten the tedium of his confinement, Jo entertained himself by singing snatches of sea songs; such as, "My tight little craft,"—"A life on the stormy sea,"—"Oh for a draught of the howling blast!" etc.; all of which he delivered in a bass voice so powerful that it caused the rafters of the widow's cottage to ring again.

These melodious, not to say thunderous, sounds also caused the ears of a small native youth to tingle with curiosity. This urchin crept on his brown little knees under the window of Bumpus's apartment, got on his brown and dirty little tip-toes, placed his brown little hands on the sill, hauled his brown and half-naked little body up by sheer force of muscle, and peeped into the room with his large and staring brown eyes, the whites of which were displayed to their full extent.

Jo was in the middle of an enthusiastic "Oh!" when the urchin's head appeared. Instead of expressing his passionate desire for a "draught of the howling blast," he prolonged the "Oh!" into a hideous yell, and thrust his blazing face close to the window so suddenly that the boy let go his hold, fell backwards, and rolled head over heels into a ditch, out of which he scrambled with violent haste, and ran with the utmost possible precipitancy to his native home on the sea-shore.

Here he related what he had seen to his father. The father went and looked in upon Jo's solitude. He happened to have seen Bumpus during the great fight, and knew him to be one of the pirates. The village rose *en masse*. Some of the worst characters in it stirred up the rest, went to the widow's cottage, and demanded that the person of the pirate should be delivered up.

The widow objected. The settlers insisted. The widow protested. The settlers threatened force. Upon this the widow reasoned with them; besought them to remember that the missionary would be back in a day or two, and that it would be well to have his advice before they did anything, and finally agreed to give up her charge on receiving a promise that he should have a fair trial.

Bumpus was accordingly bound with ropes, led in triumph through the village, and placed in a strong wooden building which was used as the jail of the place.

The trial that followed was a mere mockery. The leading spirits of it were those who had been styled by Mr. Mason, "enemies within the camp." They elected themselves to the offices of prosecutor and judge, as well as taking the trouble to act the part of jurymen and witnesses. Poor John Bumpus's doom was sealed before the trial began. They had prejudged the case, and only went through the form to ease their own consciences and to fulfil their promise to the widow.

It was in vain that Bumpus asserted, with a bold, honest countenance, that he was not a pirate, that he never had been, and never would be a pirate; that he didn't believe the Foam was a pirate—though he was free to confess its crew "*wos* bad enough for anything a'most;*" that he had been hired in South America (where he had been shipwrecked) by Captain Gascoyne, the sandal-wood trader; that he had made the voyage straight from that coast to this island without meeting a single sail; and that he had never seen a shot fired or a cutlass drawn aboard the schooner.

To all this there was but one coarsely-expressed answer,—"It is a lie!" Jo had no proof to give of the truth of what he said, so he was condemned to be hanged by the neck till he should be dead; and as his judges were afraid that the return of the Wasp might interfere with their proceeding, it was arranged that he should be I executed on the following day at noon.

It must not be imagined, that, in a Christian village such as we have described, there was no one who felt that this trial was too hastily gone into, and too violently conducted. But those who were inclined to take a merciful view of the case, and who plead for delay, were chiefly natives, while the violent party was composed of most of the ill-disposed European settlers.

The natives had been so much accustomed to put confidence in the wisdom of the white men since their conversion to Christianity, that they felt unable to cope with them on this occasion; so that Bumpus, after being condemned, was led away to his prison, and left alone to his own reflections.

It chanced that there was one friend left, unintentionally, in the cell with the condemned man. This was none other than our friend Toozle, the mass of ragged door-mat on which Alice doted so fondly. This little dog had, during the course of events which have taken so long to recount, done nothing worthy of being recorded. He had, indeed, been much in every one's way, when no one had had time or inclination to take notice of him. He had, being an affectionate dog, and desirous of much sympathy, courted attention frequently, and had received many kicks and severe rebuffs for his pains; and he had also, being a tender-hearted dog, howled dreadfully when he lost his young mistress; but he had not in any way promoted the interests of humanity, or advanced the ends of justice. Hence our long silence in regard to him.

Recollecting that he had witnessed evidences of a friendly relation subsisting between Alice and Bumpus, Toozle straightway sought to pour the overflowing love and sorrow of his large little heart into the bosom of that supposed pirate. His advances were well received, and from that hour he followed the seaman like his shadow. He shared his prison with him, trotted behind him when he walked up and down his room in the widow's cottage; lay down at his feet when he rested; looked up inquiringly in his face when he paused to meditate; whined and wagged his stump of a tail when he was taken notice of, and lay down to sleep in deep humility when he was neglected.

Thus it came to pass that Toozle attended the trial of Bumpus, entered his cell along with him, slept with him during the night, accompanied him to the gallows in the morning, and sat under him when they were adjusting the noose, looking up with feelings of unutterable dismay, as clearly indicated by the lugubrious and woebegone cast of his ragged countenance. But we are anticipating.

It was on the morning of his execution that Bumpus sat on the edge of his hard pallet, gazed at his manacled wrists, and gave vent to the sentiments set down at the beginning of this chapter.

Toozle sat down at his feet, looking up in his face sympathetically.

"No, I *don't* believe it's possible," said Bumpus, for at least the hundredth time that morning. "It's a joke; that's wot it is. Ain't it, Toozle, my boy?"

Toozle whined, wagged his tail, and said, as plainly as if he had spoken:

"Yes, of course it is,—an uncommonly bad joke, no doubt; but a joke, undoubtedly; so keep up your heart, my man."

"Ah! you're a funny dog," continued Bumpus; "but you don't know what it is to be hanged, my boy. Hanged! why it's agin all laws o' justice, moral an' otherwise, it is. But I'm dreamin'; yes, it's dreamin' I am; but I don't think I ever did dream that I thought I was dreamin' an' yet wasn't quite sure. Really, it's perplexin', to say the least on it. Ain't it, Toozle?"

Toozle wagged his tail.

"Ah, here comes my imaginary jailer to let me out o' this here abominably real-lookin' imaginary lockup. Hang Jo Bumpus!—why, it's—"

Before Jo could find words sufficiently strong to express his opinion of such a murderous intention, the door opened, and a surly-looking man—a European settler—entered with his breakfast. This meal consisted of a baked breadfruit and a can of water.

"Ha! you've come to let me out, have you?" cried Jo, in a tone of forced pleasantry, which was anything but cheerful.

"Have I though!" said the man, setting down the food on a small deal table that stood at the head of the bedstead; "don't think it, my man; your time's up in another two hours. Hallo! where got ye the dog?"

"It came in with me last night,—to keep me company, I fancy, which is more than the human dogs o' this murderin' place had the civility to do."

"If it had know'd you was a murderin' pirate," retorted the jailer, "it would ha' thought twice before it would ha' chose *you* for a comrade."

"Come, now," said Bumpus, in a remonstrative tone; "you don't really b'lieve I'm a pirate, do you?"

"In coorse I do."

"Well, now, that's 'xtror'nary. Does everybody else think that too?"

"Everybody."

"An' am I *really* goin' to be hanged?"

"Till you're dead as mutton."

"That's entertainin', ain't it, Toozle?" cried poor Bumpus, with a laugh of desperation; for he found it utterly impossible to persuade himself to believe in the reality of his awful position.

As he said nothing more, the jailer went away, and Bumpus, after heaving two or three very deep sighs, attempted to partake of his meager breakfast. The effort was a vain one. The bite stuck in his throat; so he washed it down with a gulp of water, and, for the first time in his life, made up his mind to go without his breakfast.

A little before twelve o'clock the door again opened, and the surly jailer entered, bearing a halter, and accompanied by six stout men. The irons were now removed from Bumpus's wrists, and his arms pinioned behind his back. Being almost stupefied with amazement at his position, he submitted without a struggle.

"I say, friends," he at last exclaimed, "would any amount of oaths took before a maginstrate convince ye that I'm not a pirate, but a true-blue seaman?"

"If you were to swear from this time till doomsday it would make no difference. You admit that you were one of the Foam's crew. We now know that the Foam and the Avenger are the same schooner. Birds of a feather flock together. A pirate would swear anything save his life. Come,—time's up."

Bumpus bent his head for a minute. The truth forced itself upon him now in all its dread reality. But no unmanly terrors filled his breast at that moment. The fear of man or of violent death was a sensation which the seaman never knew. The feeling of the huge injustice that was about to be done filled him with generous indignation; the blood rushed to his temples, and, with a bound like a tiger, he leaped out of the jailer's grasp, hurling him to the ground in the act.

With the strength almost of a Samson he wrestled with his cords for a few seconds; but they were new and strong. He failed to burst them. In another moment he was overpowered by the six men who guarded him. True to his principles, he did his utmost to escape. Strong in the faith that while there is life there is hope, he did not cease to struggle, like a chained giant, until he was placed under the limb of the fatal tree which had been selected, and round which an immense crowd of natives and white settlers had gathered.

During the previous night the Widow Stuart had striven to save the man whom she knew to be honest; for Gascoyne had explained to her all about his being engaged in his service. But those to whom she appealed, even on her knees, were immovable. They considered the proof of the man's guilt quite conclusive, and regarded the widow's intercession as the mere weakness of a tender-hearted woman.

On the following morning, and again beside the fatal tree itself, the widow plead for the man's life with all her powers of eloquence; but in vain. When all hope appeared to have passed away, she could not stand to witness so horrible a murder, she fled to her cottage, and, throwing herself on her bed, burst into an agony of tears and prayer.

But there were some among the European settlers there who, now that things had come to a point, felt ill at ease, and would fain have washed their hands of the whole affair. Others there were who judged the man from his countenance and his acts, not from circumstances. These remonstrated even to the last, and advised delay. But the half-dozen who were set upon the man's death—not to gratify a thirst for blood, but to execute due justice on a pirate whom they abhorred—were influential and violent men. They silenced all opposition at last, and John Bumpus finally had the noose put round his neck.

"O Susan! Susan!" cried the poor man, in an agony of intense feeling, "it's little ye thought your Jo would come to such an end as this when ye last sot eyes on him—an' sweet blue eyes they wos, too!"

There was something ludicrous as well as pathetic in this cry. It did more for him than the most eloquent pleading could have done. Man in a crowd is an unstable being. At any moment he will veer right round and run in an opposite direction. The idea that the condemned man had a Susan who would mourn over his untimely end touched a chord in the hearts of many among the crowd. The reference to her sweet blue eyes at such a moment raised a smile, and an extremely dismal but opportune howl from poor Toozle raised a laugh.

Bumpus started and looked sternly on the crowd.

"You may think me a pirate," said he; "but I know enough of the feelin's of honest men to expect no mercy from those wot can laugh at a fellow-creetur in such an hour. You had better get the murder over as soon as you can. I am ready—Stay! one moment more. I had almost forgot it. There's a letter here that I want one o' you to take charge of. It's the last I ever got from my Susan; and if I had taken her advice to let alone havin' to do with all sandal-wood traders, I'd never ha' bin in such a fix as I am this day. I want to send it back to her with my blessin' and a lock o' my hair. Is there an honest man among ye who'll take in hand to do this for me?"

As he spoke, a young man, in a costume somewhat resembling that of a sailor, pushed through the crowd, leaped upon the deal table on which Jo stood, and removed the noose from his neck.

An exclamation of anger burst from those who surrounded the table; but a sound something like applause broke from the crowd, and restrained any attempt at violence. The young man at the same time held up his hand, and asked leave to address them.

"Aye! aye! let's hear what he has got to That's it: speak up, Dan!"

The youth, whose dark olive complexion proclaimed him to be a half-caste, and whose language showed that he had received at least the rudiments of education, stretched out his hand and said:

"Friends, I do not stand here to interfere with justice. Those who seek to give a pirate his just reward do well. But there has been doubt in the minds of some that this man may not be a pirate. His own word is of no value; but if I can bring forward anything to show that perhaps his word is true, then we have no right to hang him till we have given him a longer trial."

"Hear! hear!" from the white men in the crowd, and "Ho! ho!" from the natives.

Meanwhile the young man, or Dan, as some one called him, turned to Bumpus and asked for the letter to which he had referred. Being informed that it was in the inside pocket of his jacket, the youth put his hand in and drew it forth.

"May I read it? Your life may depend on what I find here."

"Sartinly,—by all manner of means," replied Jo, not a little surprised at the turn affairs were taking.

Dan opened and perused the epistle for a few minutes, during which intense silence was maintained in the crowd, as if they expected to *hear* the thoughts of the young man as they passed through his brain.

"Ha! I thought so," exclaimed Dan, looking up and again

addressing the crowd. "At the trial yesterday you heard this man say that he was engaged at San Francisco by Gascoyne on the 12th of April last, and that he believed the schooner to be a sandal-wood trader when he shipped."

"Yes, yes,—ho!" from the crowd.

"If this statement of his be true, then he was not a pirate when he shipped, and he has not had much time to become one between that time and this. The letter which I hold in my hand proves the truth of this statement. It is dated San Francisco, 11th April, and is written in a female hand. Listen,—I will read it; and you shall judge for yourselves."

The young man then read the following letter, which, being a peculiar as well as an interesting specimen of a love-letter, we give *verbatim et literatim:*

"Peelers farm near Sanfransko Aprile 11
"For John bumpuss, aboord the Schooner fome
"my darlin Jo,

"ever sins you towld me yesterday that youd bin an gaged yerself into the fome, my mind has been Onaisy. Ye no, darlint, from the our ye cald me yer own Susan, in clare county, More betoken, iv bin onaisy about ye yer so bowld an Rekles. but this is wurst ov all. iv no noshun o them sandle-wood skooners. the Haf ov thems pirits and The other hafs no better, whats wus is that my owld master was drownded in wan, or out o wan, but shure its All the Saim. down he wint and that wos the Endd.

"now Deer jo dont go to say in that skooner i beseech ye, jo. Ye towld me that ye liked the looks o the cappen and haited the looks o the Krew. Now deer, take warnin think ov me. think ov the words in the coppie book weev writ so often together at owld makmahons skool, eevil cmunishakens Krupt yer maners, i misrember it, but ye no wot id be sayin' to ye.

"o jo Dont go, but cum an see me as soon as iver ye can
"yours til deth.
"SUSAN."

"p.s. the piggs is quite livly but ther not so hansum heer as in the owld country, don't forgit to rite to your susan."

No one can conceive the indignation that swelled the broad chest of honest John Bumpus when he listened to the laughter with which some parts of this letter were received.

"Now," said Dan, "could any man want better proof than this that John Bumpus *is not* a pirate?"

This question was answered by a perfect yell from the crowd.

"Set him free! cut his cords!" cried a voice.

"Stop, friends," cried a big, coarse-looking man, leaping on the table and jostling Dan out of the way. "Not quite so fast. I don't pretend to be a learned feller, and I can't make a speech with a buttery tongue like Dan here. But wot I've got to say is—Justice forever!"

"Hurrah!" from some of the wild spirits of the crowd. "Go on, Burke," from others.

"Yes, wot I say is—Justice forever! Fair play an' no favor: *that's* wot I say!"

Another cheer greeted the bold assertion of these noble sentiments.

"Now, here it is," continued Burke, becoming much excited, "wot's to hinder that there letter bein' a forgery?—aye, that's the word, a forgery? (Hear! hear!), got up apurpose to bamboozle us chaps that ain't lawyers. D'ye see?"

Burke glanced at Dan, and smote his thigh triumphantly as he said this.

"It does not *look* like a forgery," said Dan, holding up the letter and pointing to the writing. "I leave it to yourselves to say if it *sounds* like a forgery—"

"I don't care a farthin' dip for yer *looks* and *sounds*," cried Burke, interrupting the other. "No man is goin' for to tell me that anybody can trust to *looks* and *sounds*. Why, I've know'd the greatest villain that ever chewed the end of a smuggled cigar *look* as innocent as the babe unborn. An' is there a man here wot'll tell me he hasn't often an' over again mistook the crack of a big gun for a clap o' thunder?"

This was received with much approval by the crowd, which had evidently more than half-forgotten the terrible purpose for which it had assembled there, and was now much interested in what bade fair to be a keen dispute. When the noise abated, Dan raised his voice and said:

"If Burke had not interrupted me, I was going to have said that another thing which proves the letter to be no forgery is, that the postmark of San Francisco is on the back of it, with the date all right."

This statement delighted the crowd immensely, and caused Burke to look disconcerted for a few seconds; he rallied, however, and returned to the charge.

"Postmarks! wot do I care for postmarks? Can't a man forge a postmark as easy as any other mark?"

"Ah! that's true," from a voice in the crowd.

"No, not so easily as *any* other mark," retorted Dan; "for it's made with a kind of ink that's not sold in shops. Everything goes to prove that the letter is no forgery. But, Mr. Burke, will you answer me this. If it *was* a forgery, got up for the purpose of saving this man's life,*at what time was it forged?* for Bumpus could not know that he would ever need such a letter until yesterday afternoon, and between that time and this there was but little time to forge a letter from San Francisco, postmark and all, and make it soiled and worn at the edges like an old letter. ['Hear!' and sensation.] More than that," cried Dan, waxing eager and earnest, "if it was a forgery, got up for the purpose, *why was it not produced at the trial?* ['Hear! hear!' and cheers] And, last of all why, if this forgery was so important to him, did John Bumpus forget all about it until he stood on this table; aye, *until the rope was round his neck?*"

A perfect storm of cheers and applause followed this last

sentence, in the midst of which there were cries of "You're floored, Burke! Hurrah for Bumpus! Cut the ropes!"

But although John's life was now safe, his indignation at Susan's letter having been laughed at was not altogether allayed.

"I'll tell ye wot it is," said he, the instant there was a lull in the uproar of voices. "If you think that I'll stand here and see my Susan's letter insulted before my eyes, you're very far out o' your reckoning. Just cut them ropes, an' put any two o' yer biggest men, black or white, before me, an' if I don't show them a lot o' new stars as hasn't been seed in no sky wotiver since Adam was a little boy, my name's—"

Up to this point Jo was heard; but the conclusion of his defiance was drowned in roars of laughter.

"Cut the ropes!" shouted the crowd.

Dan drew a clasp-knife from his pocket, and with one stroke set Bumpus free.

"Shoulder high!" yelled a voice; "Hurrah!"

A wild rush was made at the table. Jo's executioners were overturned and trampled under foot, and the table, with himself and his young advocate sprawling on it, was raised on the shoulders of the crowd and borne off in triumph.

Half an hour later, Bumpus was set down at the widow's door. Mrs. Stuart received him with a scream of surprise and joy, for she had given him up as a lost man.

"Now, then, Mrs. Stuart," said Jo, throwing himself on a chair and wiping the perspiration from his forehead, "don't make such a fuss about me, like a good creetur. But do get me a bit o' bacon, and let's be thankful that I'm here to eat it. Cut it fat, Mrs. Stuart; cut it fat; for it's wonderful wot a appetite I've got after such a mornin's work as I've gone through. Well, well, after all that yer friends have said of ye, Jo Bumpus, I do believe that yer *not* born to be hanged!"

CHAPTER XXII

THE RENDEZVOUS — AN EPISODE — PECULIAR CIRCUMSTANCES — OTHER MATTERS

About five or six days' sail from the scene of our tale there lies one of those small rocks or islets with which the breast of the Pacific is in many places thickly studded.

It is a lonely coral isle, far removed from any of its fellows, and presenting none of those grand features which characterize the island on which the settlement of Sandy Cove was situated. In no part does it rise more than thirty feet above the level of the sea; in most places it is little more than a few feet above it. The coral reefs around it are numerous; and as many of them rise to within a few feet of the surface, the navigation in its neighborhood is dangerous in the extreme.

At the time of which we write, the vegetation of the isle was not very luxuriant. Only a few clusters of cocoanut palms grew here and there over its otherwise barren surface. In this respect it did not resemble most of the other islands of the Pacific. Owing partly to its being out of the usual course of ships, and partly to the dangerous reefs already referred to, the spot was never approached by vessels, or, if a ship happened to be driven towards it, she got out of its way as speedily as possible.

This was the rendezvous of the pirates, and was named by them the Isle of Palms.

Here, in caverns hollowed out of the coral rock, Gascoyne had been wont to secrete such goods and stores as were necessary for the maintenance of his piratical course of life; and to this lone spot did Manton convey his prisoners after getting rid of his former commander. Towards this spot, also, did Gascoyne turn the prow of the cutter Wasp in pursuit of his mutinous first mate.

Manton, for reasons best known to himself (certainly not

from goodness of heart), was kind to his captives to the extent of simply letting them alone. He declined to hold any intercourse whatever with Captain Montague, and forbade him to speak with the men upon pain of being confined to his berth. The young people were allowed to do as they pleased, so long as they kept out of the way.

On reaching the Isle of Palms the pirates at once proceeded to take in those stores of which they stood in need. The harbor into which the schooner ran was a narrow bay, on the shores of which the palm trees grew sufficiently high to prevent her masts being seen from the other side of the island. Here the captives were landed; but as Manton did not wish them to witness his proceedings, he sent them across the islet under the escort of a party who conveyed them to the shores of a small bay. On the rocks in this bay lay the wreck of what once had been a noble ship. It was now completely dismantled. Her hull was stove in by the rocks. Her masts and yards were gone, with the exception of their stumps and the lower part of the main-mast, to which the mainyard still hung with a ragged portion of the mainsail attached to it.

A feeling of depression filled the breast of Montague and his companions as they came in sight of this wreck, and the former attempted to obtain some information in regard to her from his conductors; but they sternly bade him ask no questions. Some time afterwards he heard the story of this vessel's fate. We shall record it here.

Not many months prior to the date of our tale, the Avenger happened to have occasion to run down to the Isle of Palms. Gascoyne was absent at the time. He had been landed at Sandy Cove, and had ordered Manton to go to the rendezvous for supplies. On nearing the isle a storm arose. The wind was fair, however, and the schooner ran for her destination under close-reefed sails. Just before reaching it they fell in with a large full-rigged ship, which, on sighting the schooner, ran up her flag half-mast high, as a signal of distress. She had sprung a leak, and was sinking.

Had the weather been calmer, the pirates would have at once boarded the vessel and carried her as a prize into the harbor; but the sea ran so high that this was impossible. Manton therefore ran down as close to the side of the merchantman (for such she seemed to be) as enabled him to hail her through the speaking-trumpet. When sufficiently near he demanded her name and destination.

"The Brilliant, from Liverpool, bound for the Sandwich Islands. And you?"

"The Foam—from the Feejees—for Calcutta. What's wrong with you?"

"Sprung a leak; is there anchorage in the bay?" sang out the captain of the merchantman.

"No; it's too shoal for a big ship. Bear away round to the other side of the island. You'll find good holding ground there. I'll show you the way."

The pirate accordingly conducted the unsuspecting stranger away from the only safe harbor in the island, and led him through a complete labyrinth of reefs and rocks, to the bay on the other side, in which he knew full well there was scarcely enough of water to float his own little schooner.

With perfect confidence in his guide, the unfortunate captain of the merchantman followed until both vessels were in the comparatively still and sheltered waters of the bay. Here Manton suddenly put down the helm, brought his vessel up to the wind, and allowed the stranger to pass in.

"Hold on about sixty fathoms further, and then let go your anchor," he shouted, as the ship went steadily on to her doom.

"Aye, aye, and thank'ee," cried the captain, who had already taken in nearly all sail and was quite prepared to anchor.

But Manton knew that before twenty fathoms more should be passed over by the ship she would run straight on a coral reef, which rose to within about five feet of the surface of the sea. In an exposed place this reef would have formed a line of breakers; but in its sheltered position the water gave no indication of its existence. The gale, though not blowing direct into the bay, entered it in a sufficiently straight line to carry the ship onward with great speed, notwithstanding the reduction made in her canvas.

"Stand by to let go the anchor," cried her captain.

That was his last order. Scarcely had the words passed his lips when the ship struck with a shock that caused her to quiver like a leaf from stem to stern. All the top-masts with their yards and rigging went over the side, and in one instant the fine vessel was a total wreck.

The rest of the story is soon told. The pirates, showing their true colors, ran alongside and took possession without opposition; for the crew of the merchantman were so overwhelmed by the suddenness and appalling nature of the calamity that had befallen them that they had no heart to resist.

Of course it was out of the question that the crew of the Brilliant could be allowed to remain on the island. Some of the pirates suggested that they should be put on a raft, towed to leeward of the island, and, when out of sight of it, be cast adrift to float about until they should be picked up or get blown on one of the numerous islands that lay to the southward of the rendezvous. Manton and Scraggs advocated this plan, but the better-disposed among the men protested against such needless cruelty, and suggested that it would be better to put them into the long-boat of the ship, bandage their eyes, then tow them out of sight of land, and cast them loose to steer where they pleased.

This plan was adopted and carried into execution. Then the pirates returned, and at their leisure unloaded and secured the cargo of their prize. It was richer than they had anticipated, being a miscellaneous cargo of valuable commodities for the trading stores of some of the South Sea merchants and settlers.

The joy felt by the pirates on making this discovery was all the benefit that was ever derived from these ill-gotten gains by any one of those who had a hand in that dastardly deed. Long before they had an opportunity of removing the goods thus acquired, the career of the Avenger had terminated. But we must not anticipate our story.

On a green knoll near the margin of this bay, and in full view of the wreck, a rude tent or hut was constructed by the pirates out of part of an old sail which had been washed ashore from the wreck, and some broken spars. A small cask of biscuit and two or three blankets were placed in it, and here the captives were left to do as they pleased until such time as Manton chose to send for them. The only piece of advice that was given to them by their surly jailer was that they should not on any pretense whatsoever cross the island to the bay in which the schooner lay at anchor.

"If ye do," said the man who was the last of the party to quit them, "ye'll wish ye hadn't—that's all. Take my advice, and keep yer kooriosity in yer breeches pockets."

With this caution they were left to their own devices and meditations.

It was a lovely, calm evening, at sunset, when our four unfortunate friends were thus left alone in these strange circumstances. The effect of their forlorn condition was very different on each. Poopy flung herself down on the ground, inside the tent, and began to sob; Alice sat down beside her, and wept silently; whilst Montague, forgetting his own sorrows in his pity for the poor young creatures who had been thus strangely linked to him in affliction, sat down opposite to Alice, and sought to comfort her.

Will Corrie, feeling that he could do nothing to cheer his companions in the circumstances, and being unable to sit still, rose, and going out at the end of the tent, both sides of which were open, stood leaning on a pole, and contemplated the scene before him.

In a small creek, or indentation of the shore, close to the knoll on which the tent stood, two of the pirates were working at a boat which lay there. Corrie could not at first understand what they were about; but he was soon enlightened; for, after hauling the boat as far out of the water as they could, they left her there, and followed, their comrades to the other side of the island, carrying the oars along with them.

The spirit that dwelt in Corrie's breast was a very peculiar one. Up to this point in his misfortunes the poor boy had been subdued,—overwhelmed by the suddenness and the terrible nature of the calamity that had befallen him, or, rather, that had befallen Alice; for, to do him justice, he only thought of her. Indeed, he carried this feeling so far that he had honestly confessed to himself, in a mental soliloquy, the night on which he had been captured, he did not care one straw for himself, or Poopy, or Captain Montague; that his whole and sole distress of mind and body was owing to the grief into which Alice had been plunged. He had made an attempt to comfort her one night on the voyage to the Isle of Palms, when she and Poopy and he were left alone together; but he failed. After one or two efforts he ended by bursting into tears, and then, choking himself violently with his own hands, said that he was ashamed of himself, that he wasn't crying for himself but for her (Alice), and that he hoped she wouldn't think the worse of him for being so like a baby. Here he turned to Poopy, and in a mostunreasonable manner began to scold her for being at the bottom of the whole mischief, in the middle of which he broke off, said that he believed himself to be mad, and vowed he would blow out his own brains first, and those of all the pirates afterwards. Whereupon he choked, sobbed again, and rushed out of the cabin as if he really meant to execute his last awful threat.

But poor Corrie only rushed away to hide from Alice the irrepressible emotions that nearly burst his heart. Yes, Corrie was thoroughly subdued by grief. But the spring was not broken; it was only crushed flat by the weight of sorrow that lay like a millstone on his youthful bosom.

The first thing that set his active brain agoing once more—thereby overturning the weight of sorrow and causing the spring of his peculiar spirit to rebound—was the sight of the two pirates hauling up the boat and carrying off the oars.

"Ha! that's your game, is it?" muttered the boy, between his teeth, and grasping the pole with both hands as if he wished to squeeze his fingers into the wood. "You don't want to give us a chance of escaping, don't you, eh! is that it? You think that because we're a small party, and the half of us females, that we're cowed, and wont think of trying any other way of escaping, do you? Oh yes, that's what you think; you know it, you do, *but you're mistaken*" (he became terribly sarcastic and bitter at this point); "you'll find that you've got *men* to deal with, that you've not only caught a tartar, but *two* tartars—one o' them being ten times tartarer than the other. Oh, if—"

"What's all that you're saying, Corrie?" said Montague, stepping out of the tent at that moment.

"O Captain!" said the boy, vehemently, "I wish I were a giant!"

"Why so, lad?"

"Because then I would wade out to that wreck, clap my shoulder to her bow, shove her into deep water, carry you, and Alice, and Poopy aboard, haul out the main-mast by the roots, make an oar of it, and scull out to sea, havin' previously fired off the biggest gun aboard of her to let the pirates know what I was doing."

Corrie's spirit was in a tumultuous and very rebellious state. He was half inclined to indulge in hysterical weeping, and more than half disposed to give way to a burst of savage glee. He spoke with the mantling blood blazing in his fat cheeks, and his two eyes glittering like those of a basilisk. Montague could not repress a smile and a look of admiration as he said to our little hero:

"Why, Corrie, if you were a giant it would be much easier to go to the other side of the island, wring off the heads of all the pirates, and, carrying me on your shoulders, and Alice and Poopy in your coat pockets, get safely aboard the Foam, and ho! for Sandy Cove."

"So it would," said Corrie gravely. "I did not think of that; and it would be a far pleasanter way than the other."

"Ah, Corrie, I fear that you are a very bloodthirsty fellow."

"Of course I am when I have pirates to deal with. I would kill them every man, without a thought."

"No, you wouldn't, my boy. You couldn't do it in cold blood, even although they are bad men."

"I don't know that," said Corrie, dubiously. "I would do it without more feeling than I would have in killing a cat."

"Did you ever kill a cat?" asked Montague.

"Never," answered Corrie.

"Then how can you tell what your feelings would be if you were to attempt to do it. I remember once, when I was a boy, going out to hunt cats."

"O Captain Montague! surely *you* never hunted cats," exclaimed Alice, who came out of the tent with a very pale face, and uncommonly red eyes.

"Yes, indeed, I did *once*; but I never did it again. I caught one, a kitten, and set off with a number of boys to kill it; but as we went along it began to play with my necktie, and to *purr*. Our hearts were softened, so we let it go. Ah, Corrie, my boy, never go hunting cats!" said Montague, earnestly.

"Did I say I was going to?" replied Corrie indignantly.

Montague laughed, and so did Alice, at the fierce look the boy put on.

"Come," said the former, "I'm sure that you would not kill a pirate in cold blood any more than you would kill a kitten—

would you?"

"I'm not sure o' that," said Corrie, half laughing, but still looking fierce. "In the first place, my blood is never cold when I've to do with pirates; and, in the second place, pirates are not innocent creatures covered with soft hair, and—they don't purr!"

This last remark set Alice into a fit of laughter, and drew a faint "hee! hee!" from Poopy, who had been listening to the conversation behind the canvas of the tent.

Montague took advantage of this improved state of things. "Now, Alice," said he cheerfully, "do you and Poopy set about spreading our blanket tablecloth, and getting supper laid out. It is but a poor one,—hard biscuit and water,—but there is plenty of it, and, after all, that is the main thing. Meanwhile, Corrie and I will saunter along shore and talk over our plans. Cheer up, my little girl; we will manage to give these pirates the slip somehow or other, you may depend upon it."

"Corrie," said Montague, when they were alone. "I have spoken cheeringly to Alice, because she is a little girl and needs comfort, but you and I know that our case is a desperate one, and it will require all our united wisdom and cleverness to effect oar escape from these rascally pirates."

The commander of the Talisman paused, and smiled in spite of himself at the idea of being placed in circumstances that constrained him to hold a consultation, in matters that might involve life and death, with a mere boy! But there was no help for it; besides, to say truth, the extraordinary energy and courage that had been displayed by the lad, combined with a considerable amount of innate sharpness in his character, tended to create a feeling that the consultation might not be altogether without advantage. At all events, it was better to talk over their desperate position even with a boy than to confine his anxieties to his own breast.

But although Montague had seen enough of his young

companion to convince him that he was an intelligent fellow, he was not prepared for the fertility of resource, the extremity of daring, and the ingenuity of device that were exhibited by him in the course of that consultation.

To creep over, in the dead of night, knife in hand, and attack the pirates while asleep, was one of the least startling of his daring propositions; and to swim out to the wreck, set her on fire, and get quietly on board the Avenger, while all the amazed pirates should have rushed over to see what could have caused such a blaze, cut the cable and sail away, was among the least ingenious of his devices.

These two talked long and earnestly while the shades of evening were descending on the Isle of Palms; and in the earnestness of their talk, and the pressing urgency of their case, the man almost forgot that his companion was a boy, and the boy never for a moment doubted that he himself, in everything but years, was a man.

It was getting dark when they returned to the tent, where they found that Alice and Poopy had arranged their supper with the most scrupulous care and nicety. These, too, with the happy buoyancy of extreme youth, had temporarily forgotten their position, and, when their male companions entered, were deeply engaged in a private game of a "tea-party," in which hard biscuit figured as bun, and water was made to do duty for tea. In this latter part of the game, by the way, the children did but carry out in jest a practise which is not altogether unknown in happier circumstances and in civilized society.

CHAPTER XXIII

PLANS PARTIALLY CARRIED OUT—THE CUTTER'S FATE—AND A SERIOUS MISFORTUNE

The cutter was a fast sailer, and, although the pirate schooner had left Sandy Cove nearly two days before her, the Wasp, having had a fair wind, followed close on her heels. The Avenger cast anchor in the harbor of the Isle of Palms on the morning of her fifth day out; the Wasp sighted the island on the evening of the same day.

It was not Gascoyne's purpose to run down at once and have a hand-to-hand fight with his own men. He felt that his party was too weak for such an attempt, and resolved to accomplish by stratagem what he could not hope to compass by force. He therefore hove-to the instant the tops of the palm trees appeared on the horizon, and waited till night should set in and favor his designs.

"What do you intend to do?" inquired Henry Stuart, who stood on the deck watching the sun as it sank into the ocean behind a mass of golden clouds, in which, however, there were some symptoms of stormy weather.

"I mean to wait till it is dark," said Gascoyne, "and then run down and take possession of the schooner."

Henry looked at the pirate captain in surprise, and not without distrust. Ole Thorwald, who was smoking his big German pipe with great energy, looked at him with undisguised uneasiness.

"You speak as if you had no doubt whatever of succeeding in this enterprise, Mr. Gascoyne," said the latter.

"I *have* no doubt," replied Gascoyne.

"I do believe you're right," returned Thorwald, smoking furiously as he became more agitated "I make no question but your villains will receive you with open arms. What guarantee have we, Mister Gascoyne, or Mister Durward, that we shall not be seized and made to walk the plank, or perform some similarly fantastic feat—in which, mayhap, our feet will have less to do with the performance than our necks—when you get into power?"

"You have no guarantee whatever," returned Gascoyne, "except the word of a pirate!"

"You say truth," cried Ole, springing up and pacing the deck with unwonted energy, while a troubled and somewhat fierce expression settled on his usually good-humored countenance. "You say truth, and I think we have been ill-advised when we took this step; for my part, I regard myself as little better than a maniac for putting myself obstinately, not to say deliberately, into the very jaws of a lion,—perhaps I should say a tiger. But, mark my words, Gascoyne, *alias* Durward" (here he stopped suddenly before the pirate, who was leaning in a careless attitude against the mast, and looked him full in the face), "if you play us false, as I have no hesitation in saying I believe that you fully intend to do, your life will not be worth a pewter shilling."

"I am yet in your power, Mr. Thorwald," said Gascoyne; "if your friends agree to it, I cannot prevent your putting about and returning to Sandy Cove. But in that case the missionary's child *will be lost!*"

"I do not believe that my child's safety is so entirely dependent on you," said Mr. Mason, who had listened in silence to the foregoing dialogue; "she is in the hands of that God on whom you have turned your back, and with whom all things are possible. But I feel disposed to trust you, Gascoyne; and I feel thus because of what was said of you by Mrs. Stuart, in whose good sense I place implicit confidence. I would advise Mr. Thorwald to wait patiently until he sees more cause than he does at present for distrust."

Gascoyne had turned round, and, during the greater part of this speech, had gazed intently towards the horizon.

"We shall have rough weather to-night," said he; "but our

work will be done before it comes, I hope. Up with the helm now, Henry, and slack off the sheets; it is dark enough to allow us to creep in without being observed. Manton will of course be in the only harbor in the island; we must therefore go round to the other side, and take the risk of running on the reefs."

"Risk!" exclaimed Henry; "I thought you knew all the passages about the island!"

"So I do, lad—all the passages; but I don't profess to know every rock and reef in the bottom of the sea. Our only chance is to make the island on the south side, where there are no passages at all except one that leads into a bay; but if we run into that, our masts will be seen against the southern sky, even from the harbor where the schooner lies. If we are seen they will be prepared for us, in which case we shall have a desperate fight with little chance of success and the certainty of much bloodshed. We must therefore run straight for another part of the shore, not far from the bay I have referred to, and take our chance of striking. I *think* there is enough of water to float this little cutter over the reefs, but I am not sure."

"Think! sure!" echoed Thorwald, in a tone of exasperated surprise; "and if we *do* strike, Mr. Gascoyne, do you mean us to go beg for mercy at the hands of your men, or to swim back to Sandy Cove?"

"If we strike, I shall take the boat, land with the men, and leave the cutter to her fate. The Avenger will suffice to take us back to Sandy Cove."

Ole was rendered speechless by the coolness of this remark; so he relieved himself by tightening his belt, and spouting forth volcanoes of smoke.

Meanwhile, the cutter had run to within a short distance of the island. The night was rendered doubly dark by the rapid spreading of those heavy clouds which indicated the approach of a squall, if not a storm.

"This is well," said Gascoyne, in a low tone, to Henry Stuart, who stood near him; "the worse the storm is to-night the better for the success of our enterprise. Henry lad, I'm sorry you think so badly of me."

Henry was taken aback by this unexpected remark, which was made in a low, sad tone.

"Can I think too badly of one who confesses himself to be *pirate*?" said Henry.

"The confession is at least in my favor. I had no occasion to confess, nor to give myself up to you."

"Give yourself up! It remains to be seen whether you mean to do that or not."

"Do you not believe me, Henry? Do you not believe the account that I gave of myself to you and your mother?"

"How can I?" said the young man, hesitatingly.

"Your mother believed me."

"Well, Gascoyne, to tell you the plain truth, I *do* feel more than half inclined to believe you; and I'm sorry for you; I am, from my soul. You might have led a different life, you might even do so yet."

"You forget," said Gascoyne, smiling sadly. "I have given myself up, and you are bound to prevent my escaping."

Henry was perplexed by this reply. In the enthusiasm of his awakened pity he had for a moment forgotten the pirate in the penitent. Before he could reply, however, the cutter struck violently on a rock, and an exclamation of alarm and surprise burst from the crew, most of whom were assembled on deck.

"Silence!" cried Gascoyne, in a deep, sonorous tone, that was wonderfully different from that in which he had just been speaking to Henry; "get out the boat. Arm yourselves, and jump in. There is no time to lose."

"The cutter is hard and fast," said Henry; "if this squall does not come on, or if it turns out to be a light one, we may get her off."

"Perhaps we may, but I have little hope of that," returned

Gascoyne. "Now, lads, are you all in the boat? Come, Henry, get in at once."

"I will remain here,", said Henry.

"For what end?" said Gascoyne, in surprise.

"The cutter belongs to a friend; I do *not* choose to forsake her in this off-hand manner."

"But nothing can save her, Henry."

"Perhaps not. Nevertheless, I will do what I can. She moves a little. If she is lifted over this reef while we are on shore, she will be carried out to sea and lost, and that must not be allowed. Leave me here till you land the men, and then send the boat back with two of them. We will put some of the cutter's ballast into it, and try to tow her off. It won't take half an hour, and that will not interfere with your plans, I should think, for the whole night lies before us."

Seeing that he was determined, Gascoyne agreed, and left the cutter, promising to send off the boat directly. But it took half an hour to row from the Wasp to the shore, and before the half of that time had elapsed, the storm which had been impending burst over the island.

It was much more violent than had been expected. The cutter was lifted over the reef by the first wave, and struck heavily as she slid into deep water. Then she rushed out to sea before the gale. Henry seized the helm and kept the little vessel right before the wind. He knew nothing of the sea around, and the intense darkness of the night prevented his seeing more than a dozen yards beyond the bow.

It was perhaps as well that he was kept in ignorance of what awaited him; for he was thus spared at least the anticipation of what appeared certain destruction. He fancied that the rock over which he had been carried was the outer reef of the island. In this he was mistaken. The whole sea around and beyond him was beset with reefs, which at that moment were covered with foam. Had daylight revealed the scene, he would have been appalled. As it was, he stood stoutly and hopefully to the helm, while the cutter rushed wildly on to her doom.

Suddenly she struck with terrific violence, and Henry was hurled to the deck. Leaping up, he sprang again to the helm and attempted to put about, but the shock had been so great that the whole framework of the little craft was dislocated. The fastenings of the rudder had been torn out, and she was unmanageable. The next wave lifted her over the reef, and the gale swept her away.

Even then the hopes of the young man did not quite fail him. He believed that the last reef had now been passed, and that he would be driven out to the open sea, clear at least of immediate danger. It was a vain hope. In another moment the vessel struck for the third time, and the mast went over the side. Again and again she rose and fell with all her weight on the rocks. The last blow burst out her sides, and she fell to pieces, a total wreck, leaving Henry struggling with the waves.

He seized the first piece of wood that came in his way, and clung to it. For many hours he was driven about and tossed by the winds and waves until he began to feel utterly exhausted; but he clung to the spar with the tenacity of a drowning man. In those seas the water is not so cold as in our northern climes, so that men can remain in it for a great length of time without much injury. There are many instances of the South Sea islanders having been wrecked in their canoes, and having spent not only hours but days in the water, clinging to broken pieces of wood, and swimming for many miles, pushing these before them.

When, therefore, the morning broke, and the bright sun shone out, and the gale had subsided, Henry found himself still clinging to the spar, and, although much weakened, still able to make some exertion to save himself.

On looking round he found that numerous pieces of the wreck floated near him, and that the portion to which he clung was the broken lower mast. A large mass of the deck, with part of the gunwale attached to it, lay close beside him, held to the mast by one of the shrouds. He at once swam to this, and found it sufficiently large to sustain his weight, though not large enough to enable him to get quite out of the water. While here, half in and half out of the water, his first act was to fall on his knees and thank God for sparing his life, and to pray for help in that hour of need.

Feeling that it would be impossible to exist much longer unless he could get quite out of the water so as to allow the sun to warm his chilled frame, he used what strength remained in him to drag towards him several spars that lay within his reach. These he found to be some of the rough timbers that had lain on the deck of the cutter to serve as spare masts and yards. They were, therefore, destitute of cordage, so that it was not possible to form a secure raft. Nevertheless, by piling them together on the top of the broken portion of the deck; he succeeded in constructing a platform which raised him completely out of the water.

The heat of the sun speedily dried his garments, and as the day wore on the sea went down sufficiently to render the keeping of his raft together a matter of less difficulty than it was at first. In trying to make some better arrangement of the spars on which he rested, he discovered the corner of a sail sticking between two of them. This he hauled out of the water, and found it to be a portion of the gaff. It was a fortunate discovery; because, in the event of long exposure, it would prove to be a most useful covering. Wringing it out, he spread it over the logs to dry.

The doing of all this occupied the shipwrecked youth so long that it was nearly midday before he could sit down on his raft and think calmly over his position. Hunger now began to remind him that he was destitute of food; but Henry had been accustomed, while roaming among the mountains of his island home, to go fasting for long periods of time. The want of break-fast, therefore, did not inconvenience him much; but before he had remained inactive more than ten minutes, the want of sleep began to tell upon him. Gradually he felt completely over-powered by it. He laid his head on one of the spars at last, and resigned himself to an influence he could no longer resist.

It was evening before he awoke from that slumber. The sun had just disappeared below the horizon, and the red clouds that remained behind were beginning to deepen, as night prepared to throw her dark mantle over the sea. A gull wheeled over the youth's head and uttered a wild cry as he awoke, causing him to start up with a feeling of bewildered uncertainty as to where he was.

The true nature of his position was quickly forced upon him. A dead calm now prevailed. Henry gazed eagerly, wist-fully round the horizon. It was an unbroken line; not a speck that resembled a sail was to be seen. Remembering for the first time that his low raft would be quite invisible at a very short distance, he set about erecting a flag. This was easily done. Part of his red shirt was torn off and fastened to a light spar, the end of which he stuck between the logs. Having set up his signal of distress, he sat down beside it, and, drawing part of the sail over his shoulders, leaned on the broken part of the bulwark, and pondered his forlorn condition.

It was a long, sad reverie into which poor Henry Stuart fell that evening. Hope did not, indeed, forsake his breast; for hope is strong in youth; but he was too well acquainted with the details of a sailor's life and risks to be able to shut his eyes to the real dangers of his position. He knew full well that if he should be cast on any of the inhabited islands of the South Seas (unless it might be one of the very few that had at that time accepted the gospel) he would certainly be killed by the savages, whose practise it is to slay and eat all unfortunates who chance to be wrecked and cast upon their shores. But no islands were in sight; and it was possible that he might be left to float on the boundless ocean until the slow and terrible process of starvation did its work, and wore away the life which he felt to be so fresh and strong within him.

When he thought of this he shuddered, and reverted, almost with a feeling of pleasure, to the idea that another storm might spring up ere long, and, by dashing his frail raft to pieces, bring his life to a speedy termination. His hopes were not very clear even to his own mind. He did indeed hope, because he could not help it; but what it was that he hoped for would have puzzled him to state. A passing ship finding him in a part of the Pacific where ships were not wont to pass was perhaps among the least animating of all his hopes.

But the thoughts that coursed through the youth's brain that night were not centered alone upon the means or the prospects of deliverance. He thought of his mother,—her gentleness, her goodness, her unaccountable partiality for Gascoyne; but, more than all, he thought of her love for himself. He thought, too, of his former life,—his joys, his sorrows, and his sins. As he remembered these last, his soul was startled, and he thought of his God and his Saviour as he had never thought before. Despite his efforts to restrain them, tears, but not unmanly tears,*would* flow down his cheeks as he sat that evening on his raft; meditated on the past, the present, and the future, and realized the terrible solemnity of his position,—without water or food— almost without hope—alone on the deep.

CHAPTER XXIV

AN UNEXPECTED MEETING—DOINGS ON THE ISLE OF PALMS—GASCOYNE'S DESPAIR

It was not without some difficulty that the boat reached the shore after the squall burst upon them. On landing, the party observed, dark though it was, that their leader's countenance wore an expression of the deepest anxiety; yet there were lines upon it that indicated the raging of conflicting passions which he found it difficult to restrain.

"I fear me," said Ole Thorwald, in a troubled voice, "that our young friend Henry Stuart is in danger."

"Lost!" said Gascoyne, in a voice so low and grating that it startled his hearers.

"Say not so," said Mr. Mason, earnestly. "He is a brave and a clever youth, and knows how to manage the cutter until we can row back and fetch him ashore."

"Row back!" exclaimed Gascoyne, almost fiercely. "Think you that I would stand here idly if our boat could live in such a sea as now rolls on the rocks? The Wasp must have been washed over the reef by this time. She may pass the next without being dashed to pieces, but she is too rickety to stand the third. No, there is no hope!"

While he spoke the missionary's eyes were closed, and his lips moved as if in silent prayer. Seizing Gascoyne nervously by the arm, he said; "You cannot tell that there is no hope. That is known only to One who has encouraged us to 'hope against hope.' Henry is a stout youth and a good swimmer. He may succeed in clinging to some portion of the wreck."

"True, true," cried Gascoyne, eagerly grasping at this hope, slight though it was. "Come; we waste time. There is but one chance. The schooner must be secured without delay. Lads, you will follow Mr. Thorwald. Do whatever he bids you. And now," he added, leading the merchant aside, "the time for action has come. I will conduct you to a certain point on the island, where you will remain concealed among the bushes until I return to you."

"And suppose you never return to us, Mister Gascoyne!" said Ole, who regarded every act of the pirate captain with suspicion.

"Then you will remain there till you are tired," answered Gascoyne, with some asperity, "and after that do what you please."

"Well, well, I am in your power," retorted the obdurate Norseman; "make what arrangements you please. I will carry them out until—"

Here Ole thought fit to break off, and Gascoyne, without taking notice of the remark, went on in a few hurried sentences to explain as much of his plan as he thought necessary for the guidance of his suspicious ally.

This done, he led the whole party to the highest part of the island, and made them lie in ambush there while he went forward alone to reconnoiter. The night was admirably suited to their purpose. It was so dark that it was difficult to perceive objects more than a few yards off, and the wind howled so furiously among the palms that there was no danger of being overheard in the event of their speaking too loud or stumbling over fallen trees.

Gascoyne, who knew every rock and tree on the Isle of Palms, went rapidly down the gentle slope that intervened between him and the harbor in which the Foam lay at anchor. Dark though it was, he could see the taper masts and yards of his vessel traced dimly against the sky.

The pirate's movements now became more cautious. He stepped slowly, and paused frequently to listen. At last he went down on his hands and knees and crept forward for a considerable distance in that position, until he reached a ledge of rocks that overhung the shore of the bay. Here he observed an object like a round lump of rock, lying a few yards before him, on a spot where he was well aware no such rock had previously existed. It moved after a moment or two. Gascoyne knew that there were no wild animals of any kind on the island, and, therefore, at once jumped to the conclusion that this must needs be a human being of some sort. Drawing his knife he put it between his teeth, and creeping noiselessly towards the object in question, laid his strong hand on the neck of the horrified Will Corrie.

That adventurous and desperate little hero having lain sleepless and miserable at the feet of Alice until the squall blew the tent over their heads, got up and assisted Montague to erect it anew in a more sheltered position, after which, saying that he meant to take a midnight ramble on the shore to cool his fevered brow, he made straight for the sea, stepped knee-deep into the raging surf, and bared his breast to the furious blast.

This cooled him so effectually that he took to running along shore in order to warm himself. Then it occurred to him that the night was particularly favorable for a sly peep at the pirates. Without a moment's hesitation, he walked and stumbled towards the high part of the island, at which he arrived just half an hour before Gascoyne reached it. He had seen nothing, however, and was on the point of advancing still further in his explorations, when he was discovered as we have seen.

Gascoyne instantly turned the boy over on his back, and nipped a tremendous yell in the bud by grasping his wind-pipe.

"Why, Corrie!" exclaimed Gascoyne, in surprise, at the same time loosening his grip, though still holding the boy down.

"Ah! you villain, you rascally pirate. *I* know you; I—"

The pipe was gently squeezed at this point, and the sentence abruptly cut short.

"Come, boy, you must not speak so loud. Enemies are near. If you don't behave I'll have to throttle you. I have come from Sandy Cove with a party to save you and your friends."

Corrie did not believe a word of this. He knew, or at least he supposed, that Gascoyne had left the schooner, not having seen him since they sailed from Sandy Cove; but he knew nothing of the manner in which he had been put ashore.

"It won't do, Gascoyne," gasped poor Corrie, on being permitted again to use his windpipe. "You may kill me, but you'll never cow me. I don't believe you, you cowardly monster."

"I'll have to convince you then," said Gascoyne, suddenly catching the boy in his arms, and bearing him swiftly away from the spot.

Corrie struggled like a hero, as he was. He tried to shout, but Gascoyne's right hand again squeezed the windpipe; he attempted to bite, but the same hand easily kept the refractory head in order; he endeavored to kick and hit, but Gascoyne's left hand encircled him in such a comprehensive embrace, and pressed him so powerfully to his piratical bosom, that he could only wriggle. This he did without ceasing, until Gascoyne suddenly planted him on his feet, panting and disheveled, before the astonished faces of Frederick Mason and Ole Thorwald.

It is not necessary to describe in detail the surprise of all then and there assembled, the hurried conversation, and the cry of joy with which the missionary received the information that Alice was safe and within five minutes' walk of the spot on which he stood. Suffice it to say that Corrie was now convinced of the good faith of Gascoyne, whom he at once led, along with Mr. Mason, to the tent where Alice and her friends slept, leaving Thorwald and his men where they were to await further orders.

The cry of wild delight with which Alice sprang into her father's arms might have been destructive of all Gascoyne's plans had not the wind carried it away from the side of the island where the pirate schooner lay. There was now no time to be lost. After the first embrace, and a few hurried words of blessing and thanksgiving, the missionary was summoned to a consultation.

"I will join you in this enterprise, Mr. Gascoyne," said Montague. "I believe what you say to be true; besides, the urgency of our present danger leaves me no room for choice. I am in your power. I believe that in your present penitent condition you are willing to enable us to escape from your former associates; but I tell you frankly that, if ever I have an opportunity to do so, I will consider it my duty to deliver you over to justice."

"Time is too precious to trifle thus," said Gascoyne, hurriedly. "I have already said that I will deliver myself up—not, however, to *you*, but to Mr. Mason—after I have rescued the party, so that I am not likely to claim any consideration from you on account of the obligation which you seem to think my present act will lay you under. But you must not accompany me just now."

"Why not?"

"Because your presence may be required here. You and Mr. Mason will remain where you are to guard the girls, until I return. All that I have to ask is, that you be in readiness to follow me at a moment's notice when the time comes."

"Of course what you arrange *must* be agreed to," said Montague.

"Come, Corrie, I will require your assistance. Follow me," said the pirate captain, as he turned and strode rapidly away.

Corrie was now thoroughly convinced of the good intentions of Gascoyne; so he followed him without hesitation. Indeed, now that he had an opportunity of seeing a little more of his gigantic companion, he began to feel a strange kind of pity and liking for him, but he shuddered and felt repelled when he thought of the human blood in which his hands must have been imbrued; for as yet he had not heard of the defense of himself which Gascoyne had made in the widow's cottage. But he had not much time to think; for in a few minutes they came upon Ole Thorwald and his party.

"Follow me quietly," said Gascoyne. "Keep in single file and close together; for if we are separated here, we shall not easily get together again."

Leading them over the same ground that he had formerly traversed, Gascoyne conducted his party to the shores of the bay where the Foam lay at anchor. Here he made them keep close in the bushes, with directions to be ready to act the instant he should call on them to do so.

"But it would comfort me mightily, Mister Gascoyne," said Thorwald, in a somewhat troubled voice, "if you would give some instructions or advice as to what I am to do in the event of your plans miscarrying. I care naught for a fair fight in open field; but I do confess to a dislike of being brought to the condition of *not knowing what to do.*"

"It won't matter much what you do, Mr. Thorwald," said Gascoyne, gravely. "If my plans miscarry, you will be killed every soul of you. You'll not have the ghost of a chance of escaping."

Ole opened his eyes uncommonly wide at this.

"Well," said he, at length, with a sigh of resignation, "it's some comfort to know that one can only be killed once."

Gascoyne now proceeded leisurely to strip off his shirt, thereby displaying a chest, back, and arms in which the muscles were developed to an extent that might have made Hercules himself envious. Kicking off his boots, he reduced his clothing to a pair of loose knee-breeches.

"'Tis a strange time to indulge in a cold bath!" murmured Thorwald, whose state of surprise was beginning to render him desperately ironical.

Gascoyne took no notice of the remark, but calling Corrie to his side, said:

"Can you swim, boy?"

"Yes, like a duck."

"Can you distinguish the stem of the schooner?"

"I can."

"Listen, then. When you see a white sheet waved over the taffrail, throw off your jacket and shirt and swim out to the schooner. D'ye understand?"

"Perfectly," replied the boy, whose decision of manner and action grew with the occasion.

"And now, Mr. Thorwald," said Gascoyne, "I shall swim off to the schooner. If, as I expect, the men are on shore in a place that I wot of, and with which you have nothing to do, well and good. I will send a boat for you with muffled oars; but, mark you, let there be no noise in embarking or in getting aboard the schooner. If, on the other hand, the men are aboard, I will bring a boat to you myself, in which case silence will not be so necessary, and your fighting powers shall be put to the proof."

Without waiting for a reply, the pirate captain walked down the sloping beach and waded slowly into the dark sea. His motions were so noiseless and stealthy that those who watched him with eager eyes could only discern a figure moving gradually away from them and melting into the thick gloom.

Fierce though the storm was outside, the sheltered waters of the bay were almost calm, so that Gascoyne had no difficulty in swimming off to the Foam without making any noise. As he drew near, a footstep on the deck apprised him that there was at least a watch left. A few seconds later a man leaned over the low bulwarks of the vessel on the side on which the swimmer approached.

"Hist! what sort o' brute's that!" he exclaimed, seizing a handspike that chanced to be near him and hurling it at the head of the brute.

The handspike fell within a yard of Gascoyne, who, keeping up his supposed character, made a wild splash with his arms and dived like a genuine monster of the deep. Swimming under water as vigorously as he could, he endeavored to gain the other side of the vessel before he came up; but, finding that this was impossible, he turned on his back and allowed himself to rise gently until nothing but his face appeared above the surface. By this means he was enabled to draw a full breath, and then, causing himself to sink, he swam under water to the other side of the schooner, and rose under her quarter.

Here he paused a minute to breathe, then glided with noiseless strokes to the main chains, which he seized hold of, and, under their shelter, listened intently for at least five minutes.

Not a sound was to be heard on board save the footsteps of the solitary watchman who slowly paced the deck, and now and then beguiled the tedium of his vigil by humming a snatch of a sea song.

Gascoyne now felt assured that the crew were ashore, enjoying themselves, as they were wont to do, in one of the artificial caverns where their goods were concealed. He knew, from his own former experience, that they felt quite secure when once at anchor in the harbor of the Isle of Palms; it was therefore probable that all of them had gone ashore except this man, who had been left to take care of the vessel.

Gascoyne now drew himself slowly up into the chains, and remained there for a few seconds in a stooping position, keeping his head below the level of the bulwarks while he squeezed the water out of his lower garments. This done, he waited until the man on deck came close to where he stood, when he sprang on him with the agility of a tiger, threw him down, and placed his hand on his mouth.

"It will be your wisest course to be still, my man," said Gascoyne, sternly. "You know who I am, and you know what I can do when occasion requires. If you shout when I remove my hand from your mouth, you die."

The man seemed to be quite aware of the hopelessness of his case; for he quietly submitted to have his mouth bound with a handkerchief, and his hands and feet tied with cords. A few seconds sufficed to accomplish this, after which Gascoyne took him up in his arms as if he had been a child, carried him below, and laid him on one of the cabin lockers. Then, dragging a sheet off one of the beds, he sprang up on deck and waved it over the stern.

"That's the signal for me," said Corrie, who had watched for it eagerly. "Now, Uncle Ole, mind you obey orders: you are rather inclined to be mutinous, and that won't pay to-night. If you don't look out, Gascoyne will pitch into you, old boy."

Master Corrie indulged in these impertinent remarks while he was stripping off his jacket and shirt. The exasperated Thorwald attempted to seize him by the neck and shake him, but Corrie flung his jacket in his face, and sprang down the beach like a squirrel. He had wisdom enough, however, to say and do all this in the quietest possible manner; and when he entered the sea he did so with as much caution as Gascoyne himself had done, insomuch that he seemed to melt away like a mischievous sprite.

In a few minutes he was alongside of the Foam; caught a rope that was thrown to him, and quickly stood on the deck.

"Well done, Corrie. Clamber over the stern, and slide down by that rope into the little boat that floats there. Take one of the oars, which you will find muffled, and scull to the shore, and bring off Thorwald and his men. And, hark'ee, boy, bring off my shirt and boots. Now, look alive; your friend Henry Stuart's life may depend on it."

"Henry's life!" exclaimed Corrie, in amazement.

"Come, no questions. His life may depend on your promptitude."

Corrie wanted no stronger motive for speed. In a state of surprise mingled with anxious forebodings, he leaped over the stern and was gone in a moment.

The distance between the shore and the schooner being very short, the boat was quickly alongside, and the party under stout Ole Thorwald took possession of their prize.

Meanwhile Gascoyne had set the jib and fore-topsail, which latter had been left hanging loose from the yard, so that by hauling out the sheets slowly and with great care, the thing was done without noise. The cable was then cut, the boat manned, and the Foam glided out of the bay like a phantom ship.

The moment she got beyond the shelter of the palms her sails filled, and in a few minutes she was rushing through the water at the rate of ten or eleven knots an hour.

Gascoyne stood at the helm and guided her through the intricacies of the dangerous coast with consummate skill, until he reached the bay where the wrecked ship lay. Here he lay to, and sent the boat ashore for the party that had been left at the tent. They were waiting; anxiously for his return. Great, therefore, was their astonishment when he sent them a message inviting them to go on board the Foam!

The instant they embarked, Gascoyne put about, and, ordering the mainsail to be hoisted, and one of the reefs to be shaken out of the topsail, ran round to the windward of the island, with the foam flying in great masses on either side of the schooner, which lay over so much before the gale that it was scarcely possible to stand on the deck.

The manner in which the pirate captain now acted was calculated to fill the hearts of those whose lives seemed to hang in his hands with alarm if not dismay. His spirit seemed to be stirred within him. There was indeed no anger, either in his looks or tones; but there was a stern fixedness of purpose in his manner and aspect which aroused, yet repelled, the curiosity of those around him. Even Ole Thorwald and Montague agreed that it was best to let him alone; for although they might overcome his great physical force by the united strength of numbers, the result would certainly be disastrous, as he was the only one who knew the locality.

On reaching the windward side of the island he threw the schooner up into the wind, and ordered the large boat to be hoisted out and put in the water. Gascoyne issued his commands in a quick, loud voice, and Ole shook his head as if he felt that this overbearing manner proved what he had expected; namely, that when the pirate got aboard his own vessel, he would come out in his true colors.

Whatever men felt or thought, there was no hesitation in rendering prompt obedience to that voice. The large boat was hoisted off the brass pivot gun amidships and lowered into the water. Then Gascoyne gave the helm to one of the men, with directions to hold it exactly as it then lay, and, hurrying down below, speedily returned, to the astonishment of every one, with a man in his arms.

"Now, Connway," said Gascoyne, as he cut the cords that bound the man and removed the handkerchief from his mouth, "I'm a man of few words, and to-night have less time than usual to speak. I set you free. Get into that boat; one oar will suffice to guide it; the wind will drive it to the island. I send it as a parting gift to Manton and my former associates. It is large enough to hold them all. Tell them that I repent of my sins, and the sooner they do the same the better. I cannot now undo the evil I have done them. I can only furnish the means of escape, so that they may have time and opportunity to mend their ways; and, hark'ee, the sooner they leave this place the better. It will no longer be a safe retreat. Farewell!"

While he was speaking he led the man by the arm to the side of the schooner, and constrained him to get into the boat. As he uttered the last word he cut the rope that held it, and let it drop astern.

Gascoyne immediately resumed his place at the helm, and once more the schooner was running through the water, almost gunwale under, towards the place where the Wasp had been wrecked.

Without uttering a word of explanation, and apparently forgetful of every one near him, the pirate continued during the remainder of that night to steer the Foam out and in among the roaring breakers, as if he were trying how near he could venture to the jaws of destruction without actually plunging into them. As the night wore on the sky cleared up, and the scene of foaming desolation that was presented by the breakers in the midst of which they flew, was almost enough to appal the stoutest heart.

The crew looked on in moody silence. They knew that their lives were imperiled; but they felt that they had no resource! No one dared to address the silent, stern man who stood like an iron statue at the helm the whole of that night. Towards morning, he steered out from among the dangerous coral reefs, and ran south straight before the wind.

Then Corrie summoned up courage, and, going aft to Gascoyne, looked up in his face and said:

"You're searching for Henry, I think?"

"Yes, boy, I am," answered the pirate, and a gleam of kindliness crossed his face for a moment; but it was quickly chased away by a look of deep anxiety, and Corrie retired.

Now that the danger of the night was over, all the people on board became anxious to save Henry, or ascertain his fate; but although they searched the ocean far and wide, they saw not a vestige of him or of the Wasp. During this period Gascoyne acted like a bewildered man. He never quitted the helm night or day. He only ate a biscuit now and then when it was brought to him, and he did not answer when he was spoken to.

Every one felt sympathy with the man who seemed to mourn so deeply for the lost youth.

At last Montague went up to him and said, in a gentle voice: "I fear that Henry is gone."

Gascoyne started as if a sword had pierced him. For one moment he looked fiercely in the young captain's face; then an expression of the deepest sadness overspread his countenance as he said: "Do you think there is no hope?"

"None," said Montague. "I grieve to give pain to one who seems to have been an intimate friend of the lad."

"He was the son of my oldest and best friend. What would

you advise, Mr. Montague?"

"I think—that is to say, don't *you* think—that it would be as well to put about now?"

Gascoyne's head dropped on his chest, and for some moments he stood speechless, while his strong hands played nervously with the tiller that they had held so long and so firmly. At last he looked up and said, in a low voice: "I resign the schooner into your hands, Mr. Montague."

Then he went slowly below, and shut himself up in his cabin.

Montague at once put down the helm, and, pointing the schooner's prow northward, steered for the harbor of Sandy Cove.

CHAPTER XXV

SURLY DICK THE RESCUE

We must turn aside here for a short time to follow the fortunes of the Talisman.

When that vessel went in chase of the Foam, after her daring passage across the reefs, she managed to keep her in view until the island was out of sight astern. Then the increasing darkness caused by the squall hid the two vessels from each other, and before the storm passed away the superior sailing qualities of the Foam carried her far beyond the reach of the cruiser.

But Mr. Mulroy was not a man to be easily baffled. He resolved to continue the chase, and, supposing that his commander must have got safely to the shore, he made up his mind to proceed southward for a short time, thinking it probable that the pirate would run for the shelter of those remote islands which he knew were seldom visited by the merchant ships. The importance of keeping the chase in view as long as possible, and following it up without delay, he felt would be accepted as a sufficient excuse by Montague for not putting back to take him on board.

The squalls which happened to prevail at that time drove the Talisman further south than her first lieutenant had intended to go, and she failed to fall in with the pirate schooner. Mulroy cruised far and wide for fully a week; then he gave up the chase as hopeless. Two days after the breaking of the storm that wrecked the Wasp the Talisman's prow was turned northward towards Sandy Cove.

It was the close of a calm, beautiful evening when this was done. A gentle breeze fanned the topsails, although it failed to ruffle the sea.

"I don't like to be baffled in this way," said Mulroy to his second lieutenant, as they paced the quarter-deck together.

"It is very unfortunate," returned the other. "Would it not be well to examine the man called Surly Dick before leaving these waters? You know he let out that there is some island hereabout at which the pirates are wont to rendezvous. Perhaps by threats, if not by persuasion, he may be induced to tell us where it lies."

"True. I had forgotten that fellow altogether. Let him be sent for."

In a few minutes Surly Dick stepped on the quarter-deck and touched his cap. He did not appear to have grown less surly since his introduction on board the frigate. Discipline had evidently a souring effect on his temper.

"Your late comrades have escaped me," said the first lieutenant; "but you may depend upon it, I will catch the villains in the long run."

"It'll be a pretty long run before you do," remarked the man, sulkily.

Mulroy looked sternly at him. "You forget," said he, "that you are a prisoner. Let me advise you to be at least *civil* in your manner and tone. Whether the run shall be a long or a short one remains to be seen. One thing is pretty certain; namely, that your own run of life will be a *very* short one. You know the usual doom of a, pirate when he is caught."

Surly Dick moved uneasily. "I was made a pirate against my will," said he, in a still more sulky tone and disrespectful manner.

"You will find it difficult to prove that," returned Mulroy. "Meanwhile I shall put you in irons, and treat you as you deserve, until I can place you in the hands of the civil authorities."

Surly Dick stood first on one leg and then on the other; moved his fingers about nervously, and glanced in the lieutenant's face furtively. It was evident that he was ill at ease.

"I never committed murder, sir," said he, in an improved tone. "It wasn't allowed on board of the Avenger, sir. It's a hard case that a fellow should be made a pirate by force, and then be scragged for it, though he's done none o' the bloody work."

"This may be true," rejoined the lieutenant; "but, as I have said, you will find it difficult to convince your judges of it. But you will receive a fair trial. There is one thing, however, that will stand in your favor, and that is a full and free confession. If you make this, and give me all the information you can in order to bring your late comrades to justice, your judges will perhaps be disposed to view your case leniently."

"Wot more *can* I confess, sir?" said Dick, beginning to look a little more interested. "I've already confessed that I was made a pirate against my will, and that I've never done no murder; though I *have* plundered a little, just like the rest. As for helpin' to bring my comrades to justice, I only wish as I know'd how, and I'd do it right off, I would."

Surly Dick's expression of countenance when he said this was a sufficient guarantee that he was in earnest.

"There is an island somewhere hereabout," said the lieutenant, "where the pirates are in the habit of hiding sometimes, is there not?"

Surly Dick looked at his questioner slyly, as he replied, "There is, sir."

"Do you not think it very likely that they may have run there now,—that they may be there at this moment?"

"It's *oncommon* likely," replied Dick, with a grin.

"Can you direct me how to steer, in order to reach that island?"

Surly Dick's aspect changed. He became morose again, and looked silently at his feet for a few moments, as if he were debating something in his own mind. He was, in truth, perplexed; for, while he was extremely anxious to bring his hated comrades to justice, he was by no means so anxious to let the lieutenant into the secret of the treasures contained in the caverns of the Isle of Palms, all of which he knew would be at once swept hopelessly beyond his grasp if they should be discovered. He also reflected that if he could only manage to get his late companions comfortably hanged, and himself set free for having turned King's evidence against them, he could return to the island and abstract the wealth it contained by degrees. The brilliant prospect thus opened up to him was somewhat marred, however, by the consideration that some of the pirates might make a confession and let this secret be known, in which case his golden dreams would vanish. The difficulty of making up his mind was so great that he continued for some time to twist his fingers and move his feet uneasily in silence.

Mulroy observed the pirate's indecision, and, although he knew not its cause to the he Was sufficiently acquainted with human nature to know that now was the moment to overcome the man, if he was to be overcome at all.

"Well, well," he said, carelessly; "I'm sorry to see you throw away your only chance. As for the information you refuse to give. I can do without it. Perhaps I may find some of your late comrades when we make the island, who will stand witness against *you*. That will do, my man; you may go. Mr. Geoffrey" (turning to a midshipman), "will you accompany that pirate forward, and see that he is put in irons?"

"But you don't know where the island is," said Surly Dick, anxiously, as the lieutenant was turning away.

Mulroy turned back: "No," said he; "but you ought to know that when a seaman is aware of the existence of an island, and knows that he is near it, a short time will suffice to enable him to find it."

Again he was about to turn away, when Dick cried out, "Stay, sir; will you stand by me if I show you the way?"

"I will not deceive you," said Mulroy bluntly. "If you show me how to steer for this island, and assist me in every way that you can to catch these villains, I will report what you have done, and the judges at your trial will give what weight they please to the facts; but if you suppose that I will plead for such a rascal as you are, you very much mistake me."

A look of deep hatred settled on the pirate's countenance as he said, briefly, "Well, I'll show you how to steer."

Accordingly, Surly Dick, after being shown a chart, and being made aware of the exact position of the ship, ordered the course to be altered to "north-half-east." As this was almost dead in the eye of the light breeze that was blowing the Talisman had to proceed on her course by the slow process of tacking.

While she was in the act of putting about on one of these tacks, the look-out reported "a boat on the lee bow."

"Boat on the lee bow!" was passed from mouth to mouth, and the order was immediately given to let the frigate fall off. In another moment, instead of ploughing her way slowly and doggedly to windward, the Talisman ran swiftly before the breeze toward a dark object which at a distance resembled a boat with a mast and a small flag flying from it.

"It is a raft, I think," observed the second lieutenant, as he adjusted the telescope more perfectly.

"You are right; and I think there is some one on it," said Mulroy. "I see something like a man lying on it; but whether he is dead or alive I cannot say. There is a flag, undoubtedly; but no one waves a handkerchief or a rag of any kind. Surely, if a *living* being occupied the raft, he would have seen the ship by this time. Stay; he moves! No; it must have been imagination. I fear that he is dead, poor fellow. Stand by to lower a boat."

The lieutenant spoke in a sad voice; for he felt convinced that he had come too late to the aid of some unfortunate who had died in perhaps the most miserable manner in which man can perish.

Henry Stuart did indeed lie on the raft a dead man to all appearance. Towards the evening of his third day, he had suffered very severely from the pangs of hunger. Long and earnestly had he gazed round the horizon, but no sail appeared. He felt that his end was approaching, and, in a fit of despair and increasing weakness, he fell on his face in a state of half-consciousness. Then he began to pray, and gradually he fell into a troubled slumber.

It was while he was in this condition that the Talisman hove in sight. Henry had frequently fallen into this species of sleep during the last few hours, but he never continued in it long; for the pains of thirst, as well as hunger, now racked his frame. Nevertheless, he was not much reduced in strength or vigor. A long, slow process of dying would have still lain before the poor youth, had it been his lot to perish on that raft.

A delightful dream came over him as he lay. A rich banquet was spread before him. With wolfish desire he grasped the food, and ate as he never ate before. Oh! it was a rare feast, that! Each morsel was delicious; each draught nectar. But he could not devour enough. There was a strange feeling in him that he could by no means eat to satisfaction.

While he was thus feasting in dreams, the Talisman drew near. Her bulwarks were crowded with faces gazing earnestly at the bit of red rag that fluttered in the breeze, and the pile of loose spars on which the man's form lay extended and motionless.

Suddenly Henry awoke, with a start, to find that his rich banquet was a terrible delusion; that he was starving to death; and that a large ship was hove to within a few yards of him!

Starting up on his knees, he uttered a wild shriek. Then, as the truth entered his soul, he raised his hand and gave a faint cheer.

The revulsion of feeling in the crew of the Talisman was overpowering. A long, loud, tremendous cheer burst from every heart!

"Lower away!" was shouted to the men who stood at the fall-tackles of the boat.

As the familiar sounds broke on Henry's ears, he leaped to his feet, and, waving his hand above his head, again attempted to cheer; but his voice failed him. Staggering backwards, he fell fainting into the sea.

Almost at the same instant, a man leaped from the bulwark of the frigate, and swam vigorously towards the raft. It was Richard Price, the boatswain of the frigate. He reached Henry before the boat did, and, grasping his inanimate form, supported him until it came up and rescued them both. A few minutes later Henry Stuart was restored to consciousness, and the surgeon of the frigate was administering to him such restoratives as his condition seemed to require.

CHAPTER XXVI

THE CAPTURE AND THE FIRE

Eight days after the rescue of Henry Stuart from a horrible death, as related in the last chapter, the Talisman found herself, late in the afternoon, within about forty hours' sail of Sandy Cove.

Mulroy had visited the Isle of Palms, and found that the pirates had flown. The mate of the Avenger and his companions had taken advantage of the opportunity of escape afforded them by Gascoyne, and had hastily quitted their rendezvous, with as much of the most valuable portion of their booty as the boat could carry. As this is their last appearance in these pages, it may be as well to say that they were never again heard of. Whether they perished in a storm, or gained some distant land, and followed their former leader's advice,—to repent of their sins,—or again took to piracy, and continued the practise of their terrible trade under a more bloody-minded captain, we cannot tell. They disappeared as many a band of wicked men has disappeared before, and never turned up again. With these remarks, we dismiss them from our tale.

Surly Dick now began to entertain sanguine hopes that he would be pardoned, and that he would yet live to enjoy the undivided booty which he alone knew lay concealed in the Isle of Palms; for, now that he had heard Henry's account of the landing of Gascoyne on the island, he never doubted that the pirates would fly in haste from a spot that was no longer unknown to others, and that they would be too much afraid of being captured to venture to return to it.

It was, then, with a feeling of no small concern, that the pirate heard the lookout shout on the afternoon referred to, "Sail ho!"

"Where away?"

"On the lea beam."

The course of the frigate was at once changed, and she ran down towards the strange sail.

"A schooner, sir," observed the second lieutenant to Mr. Mulroy.

"It looks marvelously like the Foam, *alias* the Avenger," observed the latter. "Beat to quarters. If this rascally pirate has indeed been thrown in our way again, we will give him a warm reception. Why, the villain has actually altered his course, and is standing towards us."

"Don't you think it is just possible," suggested Henry Stuart, "that Gascoyne may have captured the vessel from his mate, and now comes to meet us as a friend?"

"I don't know that," said Mulroy, in an excited tone; for he could not easily forget the rough usage his vessel had received at the hands of the bold pirate. "I don't know that. No doubt Gascoyne's mate was against him; but the greater part of the crew were evidently in his favor, else why the secret manner in which he was deprived of his command? No, no. Depend upon it, the villain has got hold of his schooner and will keep it. By a fortunate chance we have again met; I will see to it that we do not part without a close acquaintance. Yet why he should throw himself into my very arms in this way, puzzles me. Ha! I see his big gun amidships. It is uncovered. No doubt he counts on his superior sailing powers, and means to give us a shot and show us his heels. Well, we shall see."

"There goes his flag," observed the second lieutenant.

"What! eh! It's the Union Jack!" exclaimed Mulroy.

"I doubt not that your own captain commands the schooner," said Henry, who had, of course, long before this time, made the first lieutenant of the Talisman acquainted with Montague's capture by the pirate, along with Alice and her companions. "You naturally mistrust Gascoyne; but I have reason to believe that, on this occasion at least, he is a true man."

Mulroy returned no answer; for the two vessels were now

almost near enough to enable those on board to distinguish faces with the telescope. A very few minutes sufficed to remove all doubts; and a quarter of an hour later, Montague stood on his own quarter-deck, receiving the congratulations of his officers, while Henry Stuart was seized upon and surrounded by his friends Corrie, Alice, Poopy, the missionary, and Ole Thorwald.

In the midst of a volley of excited conversation, Henry suddenly exclaimed, "But what of Gascoyne? Where is the pirate captain?"

"Why, we've forgotten him" exclaimed Thorwald, whose pipe was doing duty like a factory chimney. "I shouldn't wonder if he took advantage of us just now to give us the slip!"

"No fear of that," said Mr. Mason. "Poor fellow, he has felt your loss terribly, Henry; for we all believed that you were lost; but I am bound to confess that none of us have shown a depth of sorrow equal to that of Gascoyne. It seems unaccountable to me. He has not shown his face on deck since the day he gave up all hope of rescuing you, and has eaten nothing but a biscuit now and then, which he would suffer no one but Corrie to take to him."

"Poor Gascoyne! I will go and relieve his mind," said Henry, turning to quit the quarter-deck.

Now, the noise created by the meeting of the two vessels had aroused Gascoyne from the lethargic state of mind and body to which he had given way. Coming on deck, he was amazed to find himself close to the Talisman. A boat lay alongside the Foam, into which he jumped, and, sculling towards the frigate, he stepped over the bulwarks just as Henry turned to go in search of him.

The pirate captain's face wore a haggard, careworn, humbled look, that was very different from its usual bold, lion-like expression. No one can tell what a storm had passed through the strong man's breast while he lay alone on the floor of his cabin,—the deep, deep sorrow; the remorse for sin; the bitterness of soul, when he reflected that his present misery was chargeable only to himself. A few nights had given him the aspect of a much older man.

For a few seconds he stood glancing round the quarter-deck of the Talisman with a look of mingled curiosity and sadness. But when his eye fell on the form of Henry he turned deadly pale, and trembled like an aspen leaf.

"Well, Gascoyne, my—my—*friend*," said the youth, with some hesitation, as he advanced.

The shout that Gascoyne uttered on hearing the young man's voice was almost superhuman. It was something like a mingled cheer and cry of agony. In another moment he sprang forward, and, seizing Henry in his arms, pressed him to his breast with a grasp that rendered the youth utterly powerless.

Almost instantly he released him from his embrace, and, seizing his hand, said, in a wild, gay, almost fierce manner:

"Come, Henry, lad; I have somewhat to say to you. Come with me."

He forced rather than led the amazed youth into the boat, sculled to the schooner, hurried him into the cabin, and shut and locked the door.

We need scarcely say that all this was a matter of the deepest curiosity and interest to those who witnessed it; but they were destined to remain with their curiosity unsatisfied for some time after that.

When Henry Stuart issued from the cabin of the Avenger after that mysterious interview, his countenance wore a surprised and troubled expression. Gascoyne's on the contrary, was grave and calm, yet cheerful. He was more like his former self.

The young man was, of course eagerly questioned as to what had been said to him, and why the pirate had shown such fondness for him; but the only reply that could be got from him was, "I must not tell. It is a private matter. You shall know time enough."

With this answer they were fain to be content. Even Corrie failed to extract anything more definite from his friend.

A prize crew was put on board the Foam, and the two vessels proceeded towards the harbor of Sandy Cove in company.

Henry and his friends went in the Foam; but Gascoyne was detained a prisoner on board the Talisman. Montague felt that it was his duty to put him in irons; but he could not prevail on himself to heap unneccessary indignity on the head of one who had rendered him such good service; so he left him at large, intending to put him in irons only when duty compelled him to do so.

During the night a stiff breeze, amounting almost to a gale, of fair wind sprang up, and the two vessels flew towards their destination; but the Foam left her bulky companion far behind.

That night a dark and savage mind was engaged on board the Talisman in working out a black and desperate plot. Surly Dick saw, in the capture of Gascoyne and the Foam, the end of all his cherished hopes, and in a fit of despair and rage he resolved to be avenged.

This man, when he first came on board the frigate, had not been known as a pirate, and afterwards, as we have seen, he had been treated with leniency on account of his offer to turn informant against his former associates. In the stirring events that followed, he had been overlooked, and, on the night of which we are writing, he found himself free to retire to his hammock with the rest of the watch.

In the night, when the wind was howling mournfully through the rigging, and the greater part of the crew were buried in repose, this man rose stealthily from his hammock, and, with noiseless tread, found his way to a dark corner of the ship where the eyes of the sentries were not likely to observe him. Here he had made preparations for his diabolical purpose. Drawing a flint and steel from his pocket, he proceeded to strike a light. This was procured in a few seconds; and as the match flared up in his face, it revealed the workings of a countenance in which all the strongest and worst passions of human nature had stamped deep and terrible lines.

The pirate had taken the utmost care, by arranging an old sail over the spot, to prevent the reflection of the light being seen. It revealed a large mass of oakum and tar. Into the heart of this he thrust the match, and instantly glided away, as he had come, stealthily and without noise.

For a few seconds the fire smoldered: for the sail that covered it kept it down, as well as hid it from view. But such combustible material could not be smothered long. The smell of burning soon reached one of the marines stationed on the lower deck, who instantly gave the alarm; but almost before the words had passed his lips the flames burst forth.

"Fire! fire! fire!"

What a scene ensued! There was confusion at first; for no sound at sea rings so terribly in the ear as the shout of "Fire!"

But speedily the stern discipline on board a man-of-war prevailed. Men were stationed in rows; the usual appliances for the extinction of fire were brought into play; buckets of water were passed down below as fast as they could be drawn. No miscellaneous shouting took place; but the orders that were necessary, and the noise of action, together with the excitement and the dense smoke that rolled up the hatchway, produced a scene of the wildest and most stirring description.

In the midst of this, the pirate captain, as might have been expected, performed a prominent part. His great physical strength enabled him to act with a degree of vigor that rendered his aid most valuable. He wrought with the energy of a huge mechanical power, and with a quick promptitude of perception and a ready change of action which is denied to mere mechanism. He tore down the bulkheads that rendered it difficult to get at the place where the fire was; he hurled bucket after bucket of water on the glowing mass, and rushed, amid clouds of hot steam and suffocating smoke, with piles of wet blankets to smother it out.

Montague and he wrought together. The young captain issued his orders as calmly as if there were no danger, yet with a promptitude and vigor that inspired his men with confidence. Gascoyne's voice was never heard. He obeyed orders, and acted as circumstances required; but he did not presume, as men are apt to do on such occasions, to give orders and advice when there was a legitimate commander. Only once or twice were the deep tones of his bass voice heard, when he called for more water, or warned the more daring among the men when danger from falling timber threatened them.

But all this availed not to check the flames. The men were quickly driven upon deck, and it soon became evident that the vessel must perish. The fire burst through the hatchways, and in a short time began to leap up the rigging.

It now became necessary to make arrangements for the saving of the crew.

"Nothing more can be done, Mr. Mulroy," said Montague, in a calm voice, that accorded ill with the state of his mind. "Get the boats ready, and order the men to assemble on the quarter-deck."

"If we were only nearer the island," said Gascoyne, in a low tone, as if he were talking to himself, "we might run her on the reef, and the breakers would soon put out the fire."

"That would be little consolation to me," said Montague, with a bitter smile. "Lower the boats, Mr. Mulroy. The Foam has observed our condition, I see. Let them row to it. I will go in the gig."

The first lieutenant hastened to obey the order, and the men embarked in the boats, lighted by the flames, which were now roaring high up the masts.

Meanwhile the man who had been the cause of all this was rushing about the deck, a furious maniac. He had wrought at the fire almost as fiercely as Gascoyne himself, and now that all hope was past, he continued, despite the orders of Montague to the contrary, to draw water and rush with bucket after bucket into the midst of the roaring flames. At last he disappeared, no one knew where, and no one cared; for in such a scene he was soon forgotten.

The last man left the ship when the heat on the poop became so great that it was scarcely possible to stand there. Still Montague and Gascoyne stood side by side near the taffrail, and the gig with her crew floated just below them. The last boatful of men pulled away from the burning vessel and then Montague turned, with a deep sigh, and said:

"Now, Mr. Gascoyne, get into the boat. I must be the last man to quit the ship."

Without a word, Gascoyne swung himself over the stern, and, sliding down by a rope, dropped into the boat. Montague followed, and they rowed away.

Just at that moment Surly Dick sprang on the bulwarks, and, holding on by the mizzen-shrouds, took off his hat and cheered:

"Ha! ha!" he shrieked, with a fiendish laugh, "I've escaped you, have I? escaped you—hurrah!" and with another wild shriek he leaped on the hot deck, and, seizing a bucket, resumed his self-imposed duty of deluging the fire with water.

"Pull, pull lads! We can't leave the miserable man to perish," cried Montague, starting up, while the men rowed after the frigate with their utmost might. But in vain. Already she was far from them, and ever increased the distance as she ran before the gale.

As long as the ship lasted the poor maniac was seen diligently pursuing his work; stopping now and then to spring on the bulwarks and give another cheer.

At last the blazing vessel left boats and schooner far behind, and the flames rose in great flakes and tongues above her topmasts, while the smoke rolled in dense black volumes away to leeward.

While the awe-stricken crew watched her, there came a sudden flash of bright white flame, as if a volcano had leaped out of the ocean. The powder-magazine had caught. It was followed by a roaring crash that seemed to rend the very heavens. A thick darkness settled over the scene; and the vessel that a few hours before had been a noble frigate was scattered on the ocean a mass of blackened ruins.

CHAPTER XXVII
PLEADING FOR LIFE

The Pacific is not always calm, but neither is it always stormy. We think it necessary to make this latter observation because the succession of short-lived gales and squalls which have been prominently and unavoidably brought forward in our tale might lead the reader to deem the name of this ocean inappropriate.

The gale blew itself out a few hours after the destruction of the Talisman, and left the Foam becalmed within sight of Sandy Cove island, almost on the same spot of ocean where she lay when we introduced her to the reader in the first chapter.

Although the sea was not quite so still now, owing to the swell caused by the recent gale, it was quite as glassy as it was then. The sun, too, was as hot, and the sky as brilliant; but the aspect of the Foam was much changed. The deep quiet was gone. Crowded on every part of the deck, and even down in her hold, were the crew of the man-of-war, lolling about listlessly and sadly, or conversing with grave looks about the catastrophe which had deprived them so suddenly of their floating home. Gascoyne and Henry leaned over the stern, to avoid being over- heard by those around them, and conversed in low tones.

"But why not attempt to escape?" said the latter, in reply to some observation made by his companion.

"Because I am pledged to give myself up to justice."

"No; not to justice," replied the youth quickly. "You said you would give yourself up to me and Mr. Mason, I for one won't act the part of a—a—"

"Thief-catcher," suggested Gascoyne.

"Well, put it so if you will; and I am certain that the missionary will not have anything to do with your capture. He will say that the officers of justice are bound to attend to such matters. It would be perfectly right in you to try to escape."

"Ah, Henry! your feelings have warped your judgment," said Gascoyne, shaking his head. "It is strange how men will prevaricate and deceive themselves when they want to reason themselves into a wrong course or out of a right one. But what you or Mr. Mason think or will do has nothing to do with my course of action."

"But the law holds, if I mistake not, that a man is not bound to criminate himself," said Henry.

"I know not and care not what the law of man holds," replied the other sadly. "I have forfeited my life to my country, and I am willing to lay it down."

"Nay, not your life," said Henry; "you have done no murder."

"Well, then, at least my liberty is forfeited. I shall leave it to those who judge me whether my life shall be taken or no. I sometimes wish that I could get away to some distant part of the world, and there, by living the life of an honest man, try to undo, if possible, a little of what I have done. But, woe's me, wishes and regrets come too late. No; I must be content to reap what I have sown."

"They will be certain to hang you," said the youth, bitterly.

"I think it likely they will," replied his companion.

"And would you call that justice?" asked Henry, sharply. "Whatever punishment you may deserve, you do not deserve to die. You know well enough that your word will go for nothing, and no one else can bear witness in your favor. You will be regarded simply as a notorious pirate. Even if some of the people whose lives you have spared while taking their goods should turn up, their testimony could not prove that you had not murdered others; so your fate is certain if you go to trial. Have you any right, then, to compass your own death by thus giving yourself up?"

"Ah, boy, your logic is not sound."

"But answer my question," said the youth, testily.

"Henry, plead with me no longer," said Gascoyne, in a deep,

stern tone. "My mind is made up. I have spent many years in dishonesty and self-deception. It is perhaps possible that by a life devoted to doing good I might in the long run benefit men more than I have damaged them. This is just possible, I say, though I doubt it; but I have *promised* to give myself up whenever this cruise is at an end, and I won't break the last promise I am likely to give in this world; so do not attempt to turn me, boy."

Henry made no reply, but his knitted brows and compressed lips showed that a struggle was going on within him. Suddenly he stood erect, and said, firmly:

"Be it so, Gascoyne. I will hold you to your promise. You shall *not* escape me!"

With this somewhat singular reply, Henry left his surprised companion, and mingled with the crowd of men who stood on the quarter-deck.

A light breeze had now sprung up, and the Foam was gliding rapidly towards the island. Gascoyne's deep voice was still heard at intervals issuing a word of command, for, as he knew the reefs better than any one else on board, Montague had intrusted him with the pilotage of the vessel into harbor.

When they had passed the barrier-reef, and were sailing over the calm waters of the enclosed lagoon in the direction of Sandy Cove, the young officer went up to the pirate captain with a perplexed air and a degree of hesitation that was very foreign to his character.

Gascoyne flushed deeply when he observed him. "I know what you would say to me," he said, quickly. "You have a duty to perform. I am ready."

"Gascoyne," said Montague, with deep earnestness of tone and manner, "I would willingly spare you this, but, as you say, I have a duty to perform. I would, with all my heart, that it had fallen to other hands. Believe me, I appreciate what you have done within the last few days, and I believe what you have said in regard to yourself and your career. All this, you may depend upon it, will operate powerfully with your judges. But you know I cannot permit you to quit this vessel a *free man*."

"I know it," said Gascoyne, calmly.

"And—and—" (here Montague stammered and came to an abrupt pause).

"Say on, Captain Montague. I appreciate your generosity in feeling for me thus; but I am prepared to meet whatever awaits me."

"It is necessary," resumed Montague, "that you be manacled before I take you on shore."

Gascoyne started. He had not thought of this. He had not fully realized the fact that he was to be deprived of his liberty so soon. In the merited indignity which was now to be put upon him, he recognized the opening act of the tragedy which was to terminate with his life.

"Be it so," he said, lowering his head, and sitting down on a carronade, in order to avoid the gaze of those who surrounded him.

While this was being done, the youthful Corrie was in the fore part of the schooner whispering eagerly to Alice and Poopy.

"O Alice! I've seen him!" exclaimed the lad.

"Seen who?" inquired Alice, raising her pretty little eyebrows just the smallest morsel.

"Why, the boatswain of the Talisman, Dick Price, you know, who jumped overboard to save Henry when he fell off the raft. Come, I'll point him out."

So saying, Corrie edged his way through the crowd until he could see the windlass. Here, seated on a mass of chain cable, sat a remarkably rugged specimen of the British boatswain. He was extremely short, excessively broad, uncommonly jovial, and remarkably hairy. He wore his round hat so far on the back of his head that it was a marvel how it managed to hang there, and smoked a pipe so black that the most powerful imagination could hardly conceive of its ever having been white, and so short that it seemed all head and no stem.

"That's him!" said Corrie, eagerly.

"Oh! is it?" replied Alice, with much interest.

"Hee! hee!" observed Poopy.

"Stand by to let go the anchor!" shouted Montague.

Instantly bustle and noise prevailed everywhere. The crew of the lost frigate had started up on hearing the order, but having no stations to run to, they expended the energy that had been awakened, in shuffling about and opening an animated conversation in undertones.

Soon the schooner swept round the point that had hitherto shut out the view of Sandy Cove, and a few minutes later the rattling of the chain announced that the voyage of the Foam had terminated.

Immediately after, a boat was lowered, and Gascoyne was conveyed by a party of marines to the shore, and lodged in the prison which had been but recently occupied by our friend John Bumpus.

Mrs. Stuart had purposely kept out of the way when she heard of the arrival of the Foam. She knew Gascoyne so well that she felt sure he would succeed in recapturing his schooner. But she also knew that in doing this he would necessarily release Montague from his captivity, in which case it was certain that the pirate captain, having promised to give himself up, would be led on shore a prisoner. She could not bear to witness this; but no sooner did she hear of his being lodged in jail than she prepared to visit him.

As she was about to issue from her cottage, Henry met her, and clasped her in his arms. The meeting would have doubtless been a warmer one had the mother known what a narrow escape her son had so recently had. But Mrs. Stuart was accustomed to part from Henry for weeks at a time, and regarded this return in much the same light as former home-comings, except in so far as he had news of their lost friends to give her. She welcomed him therefore with a kiss and a glad smile, and then hurried him into the house to inquire about the result of the voyage.

"I have already heard of your success in finding Alice and our friends. Come, tell me more."

"Have you heard how nearly I was lost, mother?"

"Lost!" exclaimed the widow, in surprise; "no, I have heard nothing of that."

Henry rapidly narrated his escape from the wreck of the Wasp, and then, looking earnestly in his mother's anxious face he said, slowly: "But you do not ask for Gascoyne, mother. Do you know that he is now in the jail?"

The widow looked perplexed. "I know it," said she, "I was just going to see him when you came in."

"Ah, mother," said Henry, reproachfully, "why did you not tell me sooner about Gascoyne?"

He was interrupted here by Corrie and Alice rushing into the room, the latter of whom threw herself into the widow's arms and burst into tears, while Master Corrie indulged in some eccentric bounds and cheers by way of relieving his feelings. For some time Henry allowed them to talk eagerly to each other; then he told Corrie and Alice that he had something of importance to say to his mother, and led her into an adjoining room.

Corrie had overheard the words spoken by Henry just as he entered, and great was his curiosity to know what was the mystery connected with the pirate captain. This curiosity was intensified when he heard a half-suppressed shriek in the room where mother and son were closeted. For one moment he was tempted to place his ear to the keyhole! But a blush covered his fat cheeks at the very thought of acting such a disgraceful part. Like a wise fellow, he did not give the tempter a second opportunity, but, seizing the hand of his companion, said:

"Come along, Alice; we'll go seek for Bumpus."

Half an hour afterwards the widow stood at the jail door. The jailer was an intimate friend, and considerately retired during the interview.

"O Gascoyne! has it come to this?" She sat down beside the pirate, and grasped one of his manacled hands in both of hers.

"Even so, Mary; my hour has come. I do not complain of my doom. I have brought it on myself."

"But why not try to escape?" said Mrs. Stuart, earnestly. "There are some here who could aid you in the matter."

Here the widow attempted to reason with Gascoyne, as her son had done before, but with similar want of success. Gascoyne remained immovable. He did indeed betray deep emotion while the woman reasoned with him, in tones of intense earnestness; but he would not change his mind. He said that if Montague, as the representative of the law, would set him free in consideration of what he had recently done, he would accept of liberty; but nothing could induce him to escape.

Leaving him in this mode, Mrs. Stuart hurried to the cottage where Montague had taken up his abode.

The young captain received her kindly. Having learned from Corrie all about the friendship that existed between the widow and Gascoyne, he listened with the utmost consideration to her.

"It is impossible," said he, shaking his head; "I *cannot* set him free."

"Do his late services weigh nothing with you?" pleaded the widow.

"My dear madam," replied Montague, sorrowfully, "you forget that I am not his judge. I have no right to weigh the circumstances of his case. He is a convicted and self-acknowledged pirate. My only duty is to convey him to England, and hand him over to the officers of justice. I sympathize with you, indeed I do; for you seem to take his case to heart very much; but I cannot help you. I *must* do my duty. The Foam will be ready for sea in a few days. In it I shall convey Gascoyne to England."

"O Mr. Montague! I do take his case to heart, as you say, and no one on this earth has more cause to do so. Will it interest you more in Gascoyne, and induce you to use your influence in his favor, if I tell you that—that—*he is my husband*?"

"Your husband!" cried Montague, springing up, and pacing the apartment with rapid strides.

"Aye," said Mrs. Stuart, mournfully, covering her face with her hands. "I had hoped that this secret would die with me and him; but in the hope that it may help, ever so little, to save his life, I have revealed it to you."

"Believe me, the secret shall be safe in my keeping," said Montague, tenderly, as he sat down again, and drew his chair near to that of Mrs. Stuart. "But, alas! I do not see how it is possible for me to help your husband. I will use my utmost influence to mitigate his sentence; but I cannot, I *dare* not set him free."

The poor woman sat pale and motionless while the captain said this. She began to perceive that all hope was gone, and felt despair settling down on her heart.

"What will be his doom," said she, in a husky voice, "if his life is spared?"

"I do not know. At least I am not certain. My knowledge of criminal law is very slight, but I should suppose it would be transportation for—"

Montague hesitated, and could not find it in his heart to add the word "life."

Without uttering a word, Mrs. Stuart rose, and, staggering from the room, hastened with a quick, unsteady step toward her own cottage.

CHAPTER XXVIII

A PECULIAR CONFIDANT—MORE DIFFICULTIES, AND VARIOUS PLANS TO OVERCOME THEM

When Alice Mason was a little child, there was a certain tree near her father's house to which, in her hours of sorrow, she was wont to run and tell it all the grief of her overflowing heart. She firmly believed that this tree heard and understood and sympathized with all that she said. There was a hole in the stem into which she was wont to pour her complaints; and when she had thus unburdened her heart to her silent confidant, she felt comforted, as one feels when a human friend has shared one's sorrows.

When the child became older, and her sorrows were heavier, and, perhaps, more real, her well-nurtured mind began to rise to a higher source for comfort. Habit and inclination led her indeed to the same tree; but when she kneeled upon its roots and leaned against its stem, she poured out her heart into the bosom of Him who is ever present, and who can be touched with a feeling of our infirmities.

Almost immediately after landing on the island, Alice sought the umbrageous shelter of her old friend and favorite, and on her knees thanked God for restoring her to her father and her home.

To the same place the missionary directed his steps; for he knew it well, and doubtless expected to find his daughter there.

"Alice, dear, I have good news to tell you," said the missionary, sitting down beside her.

"I know what it is!" cried Alice, eagerly.

"What do you think it is, my pet?"

"Gascoyne is to be forgiven! Am I right?"

Mr. Mason shook his head sadly. "No, that is not what I have to tell you. Poor fellow, I would that I had some good news to give you about him; but I fear there is no hope for him,—I mean as regards his being pardoned by man."

Alice sighed, and her face expressed the deepest tenderness and sympathy.

"Why do you take so great an interest in this man, dear?" said her father.

"Because Mary Stuart loves him, and I love Mary Stuart. And Corrie seems to like him, too, since he has come to know him better. Besides, has he not saved my life, and Captain Montague's, and Corrie's? Corrie tells me that he is very sorry for the wicked things he has done, and he thinks that if his life is spared he will become a good man. Has he been very wicked, papa?"

"Yes, very wicked. He has robbed many people of their goods, and has burnt and sunk their vessels."

Alice looked horrified.

"But," continued her father, "I am convinced of the truth of his statement,—that he has never shed human blood. Nevertheless, he has been very wicked, and the fact that he has such a powerful will, such commanding and agreeable manners, only makes his guilt the greater; for there is less excuse for his having devoted such powers and qualities to the service of Satan. I fear that his judges will not take into account his recent good deeds and his penitence. They will not pardon him."

"Father," said Alice, earnestly, "God pardons the chief of sinners; why will not man do so?"

The missionary was somewhat perplexed as to how he should reply to such a difficult question.

"My child," said he, "the law of God and the law of man must be obeyed, or the punishment must be inflicted on the disobedient: both laws are alike in this respect. In the case of God's law, Jesus Christ our Lord obeyed it, bore the punishment for us, and set our souls free. But in the case of man's law, who is to bear Gascoyne's punishment and set *him* free?"

As poor Alice could not answer this, she cast down her

tearful eyes, sighed again and looked more miserable than ever.

"But come, my pet," resumed Mr. Mason, you must guess again. "It is really good news,—try."

"I can't," said Alice, looking up in her father's face with animation and shaking her head. "I never could guess anything rightly."

"What would you think the best thing that could happen?" said her father.

The child looked intently at the ground for a few seconds, and pursed her rosy little mouth, while the smallest possible frown—the result of intellectual exertion—knitted her fair brow.

"The best thing that could happen," said she, slowly, "would be that all the whole world should become good."

"Well done, Alice!" exclaimed her father, laughing; "you have certainly taken the widest possible view of the subject. But you have soared a little too high; yet you have not altogether missed the mark. What would you say if, the chiefs of the heathen village were to cast their idols into the fire, and ask me to come over and teach them how to become Christians?"

"Oh! have they *really* done this?" cried Alice, in eager surprise.

"Indeed they have. I have just seen and had! a talk with some of their chief men, and have promised to go over to their village to-morrow. I came up here just to tell you this, and to say that your friend the widow will take care of you while I am away."

"And shall we have no more wars,—no more of these terrible deeds of blood?" inquired the child, while a shudder passed through her frame at the recollection of what she had heard and seen during her short life on that island.

"I trust not, my lamb. I believe that God has heard our prayers, and that the Prince of peace will henceforth rule in this place. But I must go and prepare for this work. Come, will you go with me?"

"Leave me here for a little, papa; I wish to think it over all alone."

Kissing her forehead, the missionary left her. When he was out of sight the little girl sat down, and, nestling between two great roots of her favorite tree, laid her head against the stem and shut her eyes.

But poor Alice was not left long to her solitary meditations. There was a peculiarly attractive power about her which drew other creatures around her, wherever she might chance to be.

The first individual who broke in upon her was that animated piece of ragged door-mat, Toozle. This imbecile little dog was not possessed of much delicacy of feeling. Having been absent on a private excursion of his own into the mountain when the schooner arrived, he only became aware of the return of his lost, loved, and deeply-regretted mistress, when he came back from his trip. The first thing that told him of her presence was his own nose, the black point of which protruded with difficulty a quarter of an inch beyond the mass of matting which totally extinguished his eyes, and, indeed, every other portion of his head.

Coming down the hill immediately behind Sandy Cove at a breakneck scramble, Toozle happened to cross the path by which his mistress had ascended to her tree. The instant he did so, he came to a halt so sudden that one might have fancied he had been shot. In another moment he was rushing up the hill in wild excitement, giving an occasional yelp of mingled surprise and joy as he went along. The footsteps led him a little beyond the tree, and then turned down towards it, so that he had the benefit of the descent in making the final onset.

The moment he came in sight of Alice he began to bark and yelp in such an eager way that the sounds produced might be described as an intermittent scream. He charged at once with characteristic want of consideration, and, plunging headlong into Alice's bosom, sought to cover her face with kisses; that is, with *licks*, that being the well-known canine method of doing the thing!

"O Toozle! how glad, glad, glad, I am to see you! my own darling Toozle!" cried Alice, actually shedding tears.

Toozle screamed with delight. It was almost too much for him. Again and again he attempted to lick her face, a familiarity which Alice gently declined to permit; so he was obliged to content himself with her hand.

It has often struck us as surprising, that little dogs—usually so intelligent and apt to learn in other matters—should be so dull of apprehension in this. Toozle had the experience of a lifetime to convince him that Alice objected to have her face licked, and would on no account permit it, although she was extremely liberal in regard to her hands; but Toozle ignored the authority of experience. He was at this time a dog of mature years; but his determination to kiss Alice was as strong as it had been when, in the tender years of his infancy, he had entertained the mistaken belief that she was his own mother.

He watched every unguarded moment to thrust forward his black, not to say impertinent, little snout; and although often reproved, he still remained unconvinced, resolutely returned to the charge, and was not a bit ashamed of himself.

On the present occasion, Toozle behaved like a canine lunatic, and Alice was beginning to think of exercising a little tender violence in order to restrain his superabundant glee, when another individual appeared on the scene, and for a time, at least, relieved her.

The second comer was our dark friend, Kekupoopi. She by some mischance had got separated from her young mistress, and immediately went in search of her. She found her at once, of course; for, as water finds its level, so love finds its object, without much loss of time.

"O Toozle!—bee! hee!—am dat you?" exclaimed Poopy, who was as much delighted in her way to see the dog as Alice had been.

Toozle was, in his way, as much delighted to see Poopy as he had been to see Alice;—no, we are wrong, not quite so much as that, but still extremely glad to see her, and evinced his joy by extravagant sounds and actions. He also evinced his scorn for the opinion that some foolish persons hold, namely, that black people are not as good as white, by rushing into Poopy's arms and attempting to lick her black face as he had tried to do to Alice. As the dark-skinned girl had no objection (for tastes differ, you see), and received the caresses with a quiet "Hee! hee!" Toozle was extremely gratified.

Now, it happened that Jo Bumpus, oppressed with a feeling of concern for his former captain, and with a feeling of doubt as to the stirring events in which he was an actor being waking realities, had wandered up the mountain-side in order to indulge in profound philosophical reflections.

Happening to hear the noise caused by the joyful meeting which we have just described, he turned aside to see what all the "row" could be about, and thus came unexpectedly on Alice and her friends.

About the same time it chanced (for things sometimes do happen by chance in a very remarkable way, it chanced that Will Corrie, being also much depressed about Gascoyne), resolved to take into his confidence Dick Price, the boatswain, with whom during their short voyage together he had become intimate.

He found that worthy seated on a cask at the end of the rude pile of coral rocks that formed the quay of Sandy Cove, surrounded by some of his shipmates, all of whom, as well as himself, were smoking their pipes and discussing things in general.

Corrie went forward and pulled Dick by the sleeve.

"Hallo, boy! what do you want with me?" said the boatswain.

"I want to speak to you."

"Well, lad, fire away."

"Yes, but I want you to come with me," said the boy, with an anxious and rather mysterious look.

"Very good—heave ahead," said the boatswain, getting up, and following Corrie with a peculiarly nautical roll.

After he had been led through the settlement and a considerable way up the mountain in silence, the boatswain suddenly stopped and said: "Hallo! hold on; my timbers won't stand much more o' this sort o' thing. I was built for navigatin' the seas,—I was not for cruisin' on the land. We're far enough out of ear-shot, I s'pose in this here bit of a plantation. Come, what have ye got to say to me? You ain't a goin' to tell me the Freemason's word, are ye? For, if so, don't trouble yourself; I wouldn't listen to it on no account w'atever. It's too mysterious, that is, for me."

"Dick Price," said Corrie, looking up in the face of the seaman, with a serious expression that was not often seen on his round countenance, "you're a man."

The boatswain looked down at the youthful visage in some surprise.

"Well, I s'pose I am," said he, stroking his beard complacently.

"And you know what it is to be misunderstood, misjudged, don't you?"

"Well, now I come to think on it, I believe I *have* had that misfortune—'specially w'en I've ordered the powder-monkeys to make less noise; for them younkers never do seem to understand me. As for misjudgin', I've often an' over again heard 'em say I was the crossest feller they ever did meet with; but they *never* was more out in their reckoning."

Corrie did not smile; he did not betray the smallest symptom of power either to appreciate or to indulge in jocularity at that moment. But feeling that it was useless to appeal to the former experience of the boatswain, he changed his plan of attack.

"Dick Price," said he, "it's a hard case for an innocent man to be hanged."

"So it is, boy,—oncommon hard. I once know'd a poor feller as was hanged for murderin' his old grandmother. It was afterwards found out that he never done the deed; but he was the most incorrigible thief and poacher in the whole place; so it wasn't such a mistake, after all."

"Dick Price," said Corrie, gravely, at the same time laying his hand impressively on his companion's arm, "I'm a *tremendous* joker—*awful* fond o' fun and skylarkin'."

"'Pon my word, lad, if you hadn't said so yourself, I'd scarce have believed it. You don't look like it just now, by no manner o' means."

"But I am, though," continued Corrie; "and I tell you that in order to show you that I am very, *very* much in earnest at this moment, and that you *must* give your mind to what I've got to say."

The boatswain was impressed by the fervor of the boy. He looked at him in surprise for a few seconds, then nodded his head, and said, "Fire away!"

"You know that Gascoyne is in prison!" said Corrie.

"In course I does. That's one rascally pirate less on the seas, anyhow."

"He is not so bad as you think, Dick."

"Whew!" whistled the boatswain. "You're a friend of his, are ye?"

"No, not a friend; but neither am I an enemy. You know he saved my life, and the lives of two of my friends, and of your own captain, too."

"Well, there's no denying that; but he must have been the means of takin' away more lives than what he has saved."

"No, he hasn't," cried Corrie, eagerly. "That's it, that's just the point; he has saved more than ever he took away, and he's sorry for what he has done; yet they're going to hang him. Now, I say, that's sinful—it's not just. It shan't be done, if I can prevent it; and you must help me to get him out of this scrape,—you must, indeed, Dick Price."

The boatswain was quite taken aback. He opened his eyes wide with surprise, and putting his head to one side, gazed earnestly and long at the boy, as if he had been a rare old painting.

Before he could reply, the furious barking of a dog attracted Corrie's attention. He knew it to be the voice of Toozle. Being well acquainted with the locality of Alice's tree, he at once concluded that she was there; and knowing that she would certainly side with him, and that the side she took *must* necessarily be the winning side, he resolved to bring Dick Price within the fascination of her influence.

"Come, follow me," said he; "we'll talk it over with a friend of mine."

The seaman followed the boy obediently, and in a few minutes stood beside Alice.

Corrie had expected to find her there, but he had not counted on meeting with Poopy and Jo Bumpus.

"Hallo, Grampus! is that you?"

"Wot! Corrie, my boy, is it yourself? Give us your flipper, small though it be. I didn't think I'd niver see ye agin, lad."

"No more did I, Grampus; it was very nearly all up with us."

"Ah, my boy!" said Bumpus, becoming suddenly very grave, "you've no notion, how near it was all up with *me*. Why, you won't believe it, I was all but scragged."

"Dear me! what is scragged?" inquired Alice.

"You don't mean to say you don't know!" exclaimed Bumpus.

"No, indeed, I don't."

"Why, it means being hanged. I was so near hanged, just a day or two back, that I've had an 'orrible pain in my neck ever since at the bare thought of it! But who's your friend?" said Bumpus, turning to the boatswain.

"Oh! I forgot him,—he's the boatswain of the Talisman. Dick Price, this is my friend John Bumpus."

"Glad to know you, Dick Price."

"Same to you, and luck, John Bumpus."

The two sea-dogs joined their enormous palms, and shook hands cordially.

After these two had indulged in a little desultory conversation, Will Corrie, who, meanwhile, consulted with Alice in an undertone, brought them back to the point that was uppermost in his mind.

"Now," said he, "it comes to this,—we must not let Gascoyne be hanged."

"Why, Corrie!" cried Bumpus, in surprise, "that's the very thing I was a-thinkin' of w'en I comed up here and found Miss Alice under the tree."

"I'm glad to hear that, Jo; it's what has been on my own mind all the morning. But Dick Price, he is not convinced that he deserves to escape. Now you tell him all *you* know about Gascoyne, and I'll tell him all *I* know; and if he don't believe us, Alice and Poopy will tell him all *they* know; and if that won't do, you and I will take him up by the legs and pitch him into the sea!"

"That bein' how the case stands, fire away," said Dick Price, with a grin, sitting down on the grass and busily filling his pipe.

Dick was not so hard to be convinced as Corrie had feared. The glowing eulogiums of Bumpus, and the earnest pleadings of Alice, won him over very soon. He finally agreed to become one of the conspirators.

"But how is the thing to be done?" asked Corrie, in some perplexity.

"Ah! that's the p'int," observed Dick, looking profoundly wise.

"Nothing easier," said Bumpus, whose pipe was by this time keeping pace with that of his new friend. "The case is as clear as mud. Here's how it is. Gascoyne is in limbo; well, we are out of limbo. Good. Then, all we've got for to do is to break into limbo and shove Gascoyne out of limbo, and help him to escape. It's all square, you see, lads."

"Not so square as you seem to think," said Henry Stuart, who at that moment stepped from behind the stem of the tree, which had prevented the party from observing his approach.

"Why not?" said Bumpus, making room for the young man to sit beside Alice on the grass.

"Because," said Henry, "Gascoyne won't agree to escape."

"Not agree for to escape!"

"No. If the prison doors were opened at this moment, he would not walk out."

Bumpus became very grave, and shook his head. "Are ye sartin sure o' this?" said he.

"Quite sure," replied Henry, who now detailed part of his recent conversation with the pirate captain.

"Then it's all up with him!" said Bumpus; "and the pirate will meet his doom, as I once heard a feller say in a play—though I little thought to see it acted in reality."

"So he will," added Dick Price.

Corrie's countenance fell, and Alice grew pale, Even Poopy and Toozle looked a little depressed.

"No; it is *not* all up with him," cried Henry Stuart, energetically. "I have a plan in my head which I think will succeed, but I must have assistance. It won't do, however, to discuss this before our young friends. I must beg of Alice and Poopy to leave us. I do not mean to say I could not trust you, Alice, but the plan must be made known only to those who have to act in this matter. Rest assured, dear child, that I shall do my best to make it successful."

Alice sprang up at once. "My father told me to follow him some time ago," said she. "I have been too long of doing so already. I *do* hope you will succeed."

So saying, and with a cheerful "Good-by!" the little girl ran down the mountain-side, closely followed by Toozle and Poopy.

As soon as she was gone, Henry turned to his companions

and unfolded to them his plan,—the details and carrying out of which, however, we must reserve for another chapter.

CHAPTER XXIX
BUMPUS IS PERPLEXED — MYSTERIOUS COMMUNINGS, AND A CURIOUS LEAVE-TAKING

"It's a puzzler," said Jo Bumpus to himself,—for Jo was much in the habit of conversing with himself; and a very good habit it is, one that is often attended with much profit to the individual, when the conversation is held upon right topics and in a proper spirit,—"it's a puzzler, it is; that's a fact."

Having relieved his mind of this observation, the seaman proceeded to cut down some tobacco, and looked remarkably grave and solemn as if "it" were not only a puzzler, but an alarmingly serious puzzler.

"Yes, it's the biggest puzzler as ever I comed across," said he, filling his pipe; for John, when not roused, got on both mentally and physically by slow stages.

"Niver know'd its equal," he continued, beginning to smoke, which operation, as the pipe did not "draw" well at first, prevented him from saying anything more.

It was early morning when Bumpus said all this, and the mariner was enjoying his morning pipe in a reclining attitude on the grass beneath Alice Mason's favorite tree, from which commanding position he gazed approvingly on the magnificent prospect of land and sea which lay before him, bathed in the light of the rising sun.

"It *is* wery koorious," continued John, taking his pipe out of his mouth and addressing himself to *it* with much gravity— "*wery* koorious. Things *always* seems wot they isn't, and turns out to be wot they didn't appear as if they wasn't; werry odd indeed, it is! Only to think that this here sandal-wood trader should turn out for to be Henry's father and the widow's mother,—or, I mean, the widow's husband,—an' a pirate an' a deliverer o' little boys and girls out o' pirate's hands,—his own hands, so to speak,—not to mention captings in the Royal Navy, an' not sich a bad feller after all, as won't have his liberty on no account wotiver, even if it was gived to him for nothin', and yet wot can't get it if he wanted it iver so much; and to think that Jo Bumpus should come for to lend hisself to—Hallo! Jo, back yer tops'ls! Didn't Henry tell ye that ye wasn't to converse upon that there last matter even with yerself, for fear o' bein' overheard and sp'ilin' the whole affair? Come, I'll refresh myself."

The refreshment in which Jo proposed to indulge was of a peculiar kind which never failed him,—it was the perusal of Susan's love-letter.

He now sat up, drew forth the precious and much-soiled epistle, unfolded and spread it out carefully on his knees, placed his pipe very much on one side of his mouth, in order that the smoke might not interfere with his vision, and began to read.

"'*Peeler's Farm,*'—ah! Susan, darlin', it's Jo Bumpus as would give all he has in the world, includin' his Sunday clo's, to be anchored alongside o' ye at that same farm!—'*Sanfransko.*' I misdoubt the spellin' o' that word, Susan, dear; it seems to me raither short, as if ye'd docked off its tail. Howsomdever—'*For John bumpuss*'—O Susan, Susan! if ye'd only remember the big B, and there ain't two esses. I'm sure it's not for want o'tellin' ye, but ye was never great in the way ov memry or spellin'. Pr'aps it's as well. Ye'd ha' bin too perfect, an' that's not desirable by no means,—'*my darlin' Jo,*'—ay, *them's* the words. It's that as sets my 'art a b'ilin' over like."

Here Jo raised his eyes from the letter, and revelled silently in the thought for at least two minutes, during which his pipe did double duty in half its usual time. Then he recurred to his theme; but some parts he read in silence, and without audible comment.

"Aye," said he, "'*sandle-wood skooners, the Haf ov thems pirits*'—so they is, Susan. It's yer powers o' prophesy as amazes me; '*an' The other hafs no beter*;' a deal wus, Susan, if ye only know'd it. Ah! my sweet gal, if ye knew wot a grief that word *'beter'* was to me before I diskivered wot it wos, ye'd try to improve yer hand o' write, an' make fewer blots!"

At this point Jo was arrested by the sound of footsteps behind him. He folded up his letter precipitately, thrust it into his left breast-pocket, and jumped up with a guilty air about him.

"Why, Bumpus! we have startled you out of a morning nap, I fear," said Henry Stuart, who, accompanied by his mother, came up at that moment. "We are on our way to say good-by to Mr. Mason. As we passed this knoll I caught sight of you, and came up to ask about the boat."

"It's all right," said Bumpus, who quickly recovered his composure,—indeed, he had never lost much of it. "I've bin down to Saunder's store and got the ropes for your—"

"Hush, man I there is no need of telling what they are for," said Henry, with a mysterious look at his mother.

"Why not tell me all, Henry?" said Mrs. Stuart; "surely, you can trust me?"

"Trust you, mother!" replied the youth, with a smile. "I should think so; but there are reasons for my not telling you everything just now. Surely, you can trust *me*? I have told you as much as I think advisable in the meantime. Ere long I will tell you all."

The widow sighed, and was fain to rest content. She sat down beside the tree, while her companions talked together, apart, in low tones.

"Now Jo, my man," continued Henry, "*one* of our friends must be got out of the way."

"Wery good; I'm the man as'll do it."

"Of course I don't mean that he's to be killed!"

"In coorse not. Who is he?"

"Ole Thorwald."

"Wot! the descendant o' the Sea Kings, as he calls himself?"

"The same," said Henry, laughing at the look of surprise with which Bumpus received this information.

"What has *he* bin an' done?"

"He has done nothing as yet," said Henry; "but he will certainly thwart our schemes if he hears of them. He has an inveterate ill-will to my poor father (Henry lowered his voice as he proceeded), and I know has suspicions that we are concocting some plan to enable him to escape, and watches us accordingly. I find him constantly hanging about the jail. Alas! if he knew how thoroughly determined Gascoyne is to refuse deliverance unless it comes from the proper source, he would keep his mind more at ease."

"Don't you think if you wos to tell him that Gascoyne *is* yer father he would side with us?" suggested Bumpus.

"Perhaps he would. I *think* he would; but I dare not risk it. The easier method will be to outwit him."

"Not an easy thing for to do, I'm afraid; for he's a cute old feller. How is it to be done?" asked Bumpus.

"By telling him the truth," said Henry; "and *you* must tell it to him."

"Well, that *is* a koorious way," said Bumpus, with a broad grin.

"But not the whole truth," continued Henry. "You must just tell him as much as it is good for him to know, and nothing more; and as the thing must be done at once, I'll tell you what you have got to say."

Here the young man explained to the attentive Bumpus the course that he was to follow, and, having got him thoroughly to understand his part, he sent him away to execute it. Meanwhile he and his mother went in search of Mr. Mason, who at the time was holding a consultation with the chiefs of the native village, near the site of his burnt cottage. The consultation had just been concluded when they reached the spot, and the missionary was conversing with the native carpenter who superintended the erection of his new home.

After the morning greeting, and a few words of general

conversation, Mrs. Stuart said: "We have come to talk with you in private; will you walk to Alice's tree with us?"

"Certainly, my friend; I hope no new evils are about to befall us," said the missionary, who was startled by the serious countenances of the mother and son; for he was ignorant of the close relation in which they stood to Gascoyne, as, indeed, was every one else in the settlement, excepting Montague and his boat-swain and Corrie, all of whom were enjoined to maintain the strictest secrecy on the point.

"No; I thank God, all is well," replied Mrs. Stuart; "but we have come to say that we are going away."

"Going away!" echoed the missionary, in surprise. "When?— where to?—why? You amaze me, Mary."

"Henry will explain."

"The fact is, Mr. Mason?" said Henry, "circumstances require my absence from Sandy Cove on a longer trip than usual, and I mean to take my mother with me. Indeed, to be plain with you, I do not think it likely that we shall return for a long time, perhaps not at all; and it is absolutely necessary that we should go secretly. But we could not go without saying good-by to you."

"We owe much to you, dear Mr. Mason," cried the widow, grasping the missionary's hand and kissing it. "We can never, never forget you; and will always pray for God's best blessings to descend on you and yours."

"This is overwhelming news!" exclaimed Mr. Mason, who had stood hitherto gazing from the one to the other in mute astonishment. "But, tell me, Mary" (here he spoke in earnest tones), "is not Gascoyne at the bottom of this?"

"Mr. Mason," said Henry, "we never did, and never will deceive you. There is a good reason for neither asking nor answering questions on this subject *just now*. I am sure you know us too well to believe that we think of doing what is wrong, and you can trust us—at least my mother—that we will not do what is foolish."

"I have perfect confidence in your hearts, my dear friends," replied Mr. Mason; "but you will forgive me if I express some doubt as to your ability to judge between right and wrong when your feelings are deeply moved, as they evidently are, from some cause or other, just now. Can you not put confidence in me? I can keep a secret, and may, perhaps, give you good counsel."

"No, no," said Henry, emphatically; "it will not do to involve you in our affairs. It would not be right in us *just now* to confide even in you. I cannot explain why—you must accept the simple assurance in the meantime. Wherever we go, we can communicate by letter, and I promise, ere long, to reveal all."

"Well, I will not press you further; but I will commend you in prayer to God. I do not like to part thus hurriedly, however. Can we not meet again before you go?"

"We shall be in the cottage at four this afternoon, and will be very glad if you will come to us for a short time," said the widow.

"That is settled, then; I will go and explain to the natives that I cannot accompany them to the village till to-morrow. When do you leave?"

"To-night."

"So soon! Surely it is not—But I forbear to say more on a subject which is forbidden. God bless you, my friends; we shall meet at four. Good-by!"

The missionary turned from them with a sad countenance, and went in search of the native chiefs; while Henry and his mother separated from each other, the former taking the path that led to the little quay of Sandy Cove, the latter that which conducted to her own cottage.

CHAPTER XXX
MORE LEAVING—DEEP DESIGNS—
BUMPUS IN A NEW CAPACITY

On the particular day of which we are writing, Alice Mason felt an unusual depression of spirits. She had been told by her father of the intended departure of the widow and her son, and had been warned not to mention it to any one. In consequence of this, the poor child was debarred her usual consolation of pouring her grief into the black bosom of Poopy. It naturally followed, therefore, that she sought her next favorite,—the tree.

Here, to her surprise and comfort, she found Corrie, seated on one of its roots, with his head resting on the stem, and his hands clasped before him. His general appearance was that of a human being in the depths of woe. On observing Alice, he started up, and assuming a cheerful look, ran to meet her.

"Oh! I'm so glad to find you here, Corrie," cried Alice, hastening forward; "I'm in such distress! Do you know that— Oh! I forgot papa said I was to tell nobody about it!"

"Don't let that trouble you, Alice," said Corrie, as they sat down together under the tree. "I know what you were about to say,—Henry and his mother are going away."

"How do you know that? I thought it was a great secret!"

"So it is, a *tremendous* secret," rejoined Corrie, with a look that was intended to be very mysterious; "and I know it, because I've been let into the secret for reasons which I cannot tell even to you. But there is another secret which you don't know yet, and which will surprise you perhaps, *I* am going away, too."

"You!" exclaimed the little girl, her eyes dilating to their full size.

"Aye—me!"

"You're jesting, Corrie."

"Am I? I wish I was; but it's a fact."

"But where are you going to?" said Alice, her eyes filling with tears.

"I don't know."

"Corrie!"

"I tell you, I don't know; and if I did know, I couldn't tell. Listen, Alice; I will tell you as much as I am permitted to let out."

The boy became extremely solemn at this point, took the little girl's hand, and gazed into her face as he spoke.

"You must know," he began, "that Henry and his mother and I go away to-night—"

"To-night?" cried Alice, quickly.

"To-night," repeated the boy. "Bumpus and Jakolu go with us. I have said that I don't know where we are going to, but I am pretty safe in assuring you that we are going somewhere. Why we are going I am forbidden to tell,—divulge, I think Henry called it; but what that means I don't know. I can only guess it's another word for tell; and yet it can't be that either, for you can speak of *telling* lies, but you can't speak of *divulging* them. However, that don't matter. But I'm not forbidden to tell you why I'm going away. In the first place, then, I'm going to seek my fortune! Where I'm to find it remains to be seen. The only thing I know is, that I mean to find it somewhere or other, and then" (here Corrie because very impressive) "come back and live beside you and your father,—not to speak of Poopy and Toozle."

Alice smiled sadly at this. Corrie looked graver than ever, and went on:

"Meanwhile, during my absence I will write letters to you, and you'll write ditto to me. I am going away because I ought to go and be doing something for myself. You know quite well that I would rather stop beside you than go anywhere in this wide world, Alice; but that would be stupid. I'm getting to be a man now, and mustn't go on showin' the weaknesses of a boy.

In the second, or third place,—I forget which, but no matter,—I am going with Henry, because I could not go with a better man; and in the fourth—if it's not the fifth—place, I'm going because Uncle Ole Thorwald has long wished me to go to sea; and, to tell you the truth, I would have gone long ago had it not been for you, Alice. There's only one thing that bothers me." Here Corrie looked at his fair companion with a perplexed air.

"What is that?" asked Alice, sympathetically.

"It is that I must go without saying good-by to Uncle Ole. I am *very* sorry about it. It will look so ungrateful to him; but it *can't* be helped."

"Why not?" inquired Alice. "If he has often said he wished you to go sea, would he not be delighted to hear that you are going?"

"Yes; but he must not know that I am going to-night, and with Henry Stuart."

"Why not?"

"Ah! that's the point. Mystery! Alice—mystery! What a world of mystery this is!" observed the precocious Corrie, shaking his head with profound solemnity. "I've been involved (I think that's the word), rolled up, drowned, and buried in mystery for more than three weeks, and I'm beginning to fear that I'll never again git into the unmysteriously happy state in which I lived before this abominable man-of-war came to the island. No, Alice: I dare not say anything more on that point, even to you *just now*. But *won't* I give it you all in my first letter? and*won't* you open your eyes until they look like two blue saucers?"

Further conversation between the friends was interrupted at this point by the inrushing of Toozle, followed up by Poopy, and a short time after, by Mr. Mason, who took Alice away with him, and left poor Corrie disconsolate.

While this was going on, John Bumpus was fulfilling his mission to Ole Thorwald.

He found that obstinate individual in his own parlor, deep in the investigation of the state of his books of business, which had been allowed to fall into arrears during his absence.

"Come in, Bumpus. So I hear you were half-hanged when we were away."

Ole wheeled round on his stool, and hooked his thumbs into the armholes of his vest, as he said this, leaned his back against his desk, and regarded the seaman with a facetious look.

"*Half*-hanged, indeed!" said Bumpus, indignantly. "I was more than half—three-quarters, at least. Why, the worst of it's over w'en the rope's round your neck."

"That is a matter which you can't speak to, John Bumpus, seeing that you've never gone beyond the putting of the rope round your neck."

"Well, I'm content with wot I does happen to know about it," remarked Jo, making a wry face; "an' I hope that I'll never git the chance of knowin' more. But I comed here on business, Mr. Thorwald" (here John became mysterious, and put his finger to his lips.) "I've comed here, Mr. Thorwald, to—*split.*"

As Ole did not quite understand the meaning of this word, and did not believe that the seaman actually meant to rend himself from head to foot, he said, "Why, Bumpus! what d'ye mean?"

"I mean as how that I've comed to split on my comrades; w'ich means, I'm goin' to tell upon 'em."

"Oh!" exclaimed Ole, eying the man with a look of distrust.

"Yes," pursued Bumpus; "I'm willin' to tell ye all about it, and prevent his escape, if you'll only promise, on your word as a gin'lmun, that ye won't tell nobody else but six niggers, who are more than enough to sarve your turn."

"Prevent whose escape?" said Thorwald, with an excited look.

"Gascoyne's."

Ole jumped off his stool, and hit his left palm a sounding blow with his right fist.

"I knew it!" he exclaimed, staring into the face of the seaman.

"I was sure of it! I said it! But how d'ye know, my man?"

"Ah! I'll not say another word if ye don't promise to let me go free, and only take six niggers with ye."

"Well, Bumpus, I do promise, on the word of a true Norseman, which is much better than that of a gentleman, that no harm shall come to you if you tell me all you know of this matter. But I will promise nothing more; because if you won't tell me, you have told me enough to enable me to take such measures as will prevent Gascoyne from escaping."

"No, ye can't prevent it," said Bumpus, with an air of indifference. "If you don't choose to come to my way o' thinkin', ye can take yer own coorse. But, let me tell you, there's more people on the island that will take Gascoyne's part than ye think of. There's the whole crew of the Talisman, whose cap'n he saved, and a lot besides; an' if ye do come to a fight about it, ye'll have a pretty tough scrimmage. There'll be blood spilt, Mr. Thorwald, an' it was partly to prevent that as I comed here for. But you know best. You better take yer own way, an' I'll take mine."

The cool impudence of manner with which John Bumpus said this had its effect on Ole, who, although fond enough of fighting against enemies, had no sort of desire to fight against friends, especially for the sake of a pirate.

"Come, Bumpus," said he, "you and I understand each other. Let us talk the thing over calmly. I've quite as much objection to see unnecessary bloodshed as you have. We have had enough of that lately. Tell me what you know, and I promise to do what you recommend as far as I can in reason."

"Do you promise to let no one else know wot I tell ye?"

"I do."

"An' d'ye promise to take no more than six niggers to prewent this escape?"

"Will six be enough?"

"Plenty; but, if that bothers ye, say twelve,—I'm not

partic'lar,—say twelve. That's more than enough; for they'll only have four to fight with."

"Well, I promise that too."

"Good. Now I'll tell ye all about it," said Bumpus. "You see, although I'm splittin', I don't want to get my friends into trouble, and so I got you to promise; an' I trust to yer word, Mr. Thorwald—you being a gen'lmun. This is how it is: Young Henry Stuart thinks that although Gascoyne is a pirate, or rather *was* a pirate, he don't deserve to be hanged. Cause why? Firstly, he never committed no murder; secondly, he saved the lives o' some of your people—Alice Mason among the rest; and, thirdly, he is an old friend o' the family as has done 'em good sarvice long ago. So Henry's made up his mind that, as Gascoyne's sure to be hanged if he's tried, it's his duty to prewent that there from happenin' of. Now, ye see, Gascoyne is quite willin' to escape—"

"Ha! the villain!" exclaimed Ole; "I was sure of that. I knew well enough that all his smooth-tongued humility was hypocrisy. I'm sorry for Henry, and don't wish to thwart him; but it's clearly my duty to prevent this escape if I can."

"So I think, sir," said Bumpus; "so I think. That's just w'at I said to meself w'en I made up my mind for to split. Gascoyne bein' willin', then, Henry has bribed the jailer, and he intends to open the jail door for him at twelve o'clock this night, and he'll know w'at to do with his legs w'en he's got 'em free."

"But how am I to prevent his escape if I do not set a strong guard over the prison?" exclaimed Ole, in an excited manner. "If he once gets into the mountains, I might as well try to catch a hare."

"All fair and softly, Mr. Thorwald. Don't take on so. It ain't two o'clock yet; we've lots o' time. Henry has arranged to get a boat ready for him. At twelve o'clock to-night the doors will be opened, and he'll start for the boat. It will lie concealed among the rocks off the Long Point. There's no mistakin' the spot, just west of the village; an' if you place your niggers there, you'll have as good chance as need be to nab 'em. Indeed, there's *two* boats to be in waitin' for the pirate captain and his friends—set 'em up!"

"And where is the second boat to be hidden?" asked Ole.

"I'm not sure of the exact spot; but it can't be very far off from the tother, cer'nly not a hundred miles," said Bumpus, with a grin. "Now, wot I want is, that if ye get hold of the pirate ye'll be content, an' not go an' peach on Henry an' his comrades. They'll be so ashamed o' themselves at bein' nabbed in the wery act that they'll give it up as a bad job. Besides, ye can then go an' give him in charge of Capting Montague. But if ye try to *prewent* the escape bein' attempted, Henry will take the bloody way of it; for I tell *you*, his birse is up, an' no mistake."

"How many men are to be with Gascoyne?" asked Thorwald, who, had he not been naturally a stupid man, must have easily seen through this clumsy attempt to blind him.

"Just four," answered Bumpus; "an' I'm to be one of 'em."

"Well, Bumpus, I'll take your advice. I shall be at the Long Point before twelve, with a dozen niggers, and I'll count on you lending us a hand."

"No, ye mustn't count on that, Mr. Thorwald. Surely, it's enough if I run away and leave the others to fight."

"Very well; do as you please," said Thorwald, with a look of contempt.

"Good day, Mr. Thorwald. You'll be sure to be there?"

"Trust me."

"An' you'll not a word about it to nobody?"

"Not a syllable."

"That's all square. You'll see the boat w'en ye git there, and as long as ye see that boat yer all right. Good day, sir."

John Bumpus left Thorwald's house chuckling, and wended his way to the widow's cottage, whistling the "Groves of Blarney."

CHAPTER XXXI

THE AMBUSH—THE ESCAPE—RETRIBUTIVE JUSTICE—AND CONCLUSION

An hour before the appointed time, Ole Thorwald, under cover of a dark night, stole out of his own dwelling, with slow and wary step, and crossed the little plot of ground that lay in front of it, with the sly and mysterious air of a burglar rather than that of an honest man.

Outside his gate he was met in the same cautious manner by a dark-skinned human being, the character of whose garments was something between those of a sailor and a West India planter. This was Sambo, Thorwald's major-domo, clerk, overseer, and right-hand man. Sambo was not his proper name; but his master, regarding him as being the embodiment of all the excellent qualities that could by any possibility exist in the person of a South Sea islander, had bestowed upon him the generic name of the dark race, in addition to that wherewith Mr. Mason had gifted him on the day of his baptism.

Sambo and his master exchanged a few words in low whispers, and then gliding down the path that led from the stout merchant's house to the south side of the village, they entered the woods that lined the shore, like two men bent on a purpose which might or might not be of the blackest possible kind.

"I don't half like this sort of work, Sambo," observed Thorwald, speaking and treading with less caution as they left the settlement behind them. "Ambushments, surprises, and night forages, especially when they include Goat's Passes, don't suit me at all. I have a strong antipathy to everything in the way of warfare, save a fair field and no favor, under the satisfactory light of the sun."

"Ho!" said Sambo, quietly; as much as to say, "I hear and appreciate, but having no observation to make in reply, I wait for more from your honored lips."

"Now, you see," pursued Thorwald, "if I were to follow my own tastes, which, it seems to me, I am destined not to be allowed to do any more in the affairs of this world, if I may judge by the events of the past month,—if I were to follow my own tastes, I say, I would go boldly to the prison where this pestiferous pirate captain lies, put double irons on him, and place a strong guard round the building. In this case I would be ready to defend it against any odds, and would have the satisfaction of standing up for the rights of the settlement like a man, and of hurling defiance at the entire British navy, at least such portions of it as happens to be on the island at this time, if they were to attempt a rescue—as this Bumpus hints they are likely to do. Yet it seems to me strange and unaccountable that they should thus interest themselves in a vile pirate. I verily believe that I have been deceived; but it is too late now to alter my plans, or to hesitate. Truly, it seemeth to me that I might style myself an ass, without impropriety."

"Ho!" remarked Sambo; and the grin with which the remark was accompanied seemed to imply that he not only appreciated his master's sentiment, but agreed with it entirely.

"You've got eleven men, I trust. Sambo?"

"Yes, mass'r."

"All good and true, I hope—men who can be trusted both in regard to their fighting qualities and their ability to hold their tongues."

"Dumb as owls, ebery von," returned Sambo.

"Good! You see, my man, I *must* not permit that fellow to escape; at the same time I do not wish to blazon abroad, that it is my friend Henry Stuart who is helping him. Neither do I wish to run the risk of killing my friends in a scrimmage, if they are so foolish as to resist me; therefore I am particular about the men you have told off for this duty. Where did you say they are to meet us?"

"Close by de point, mass'r."

A few minutes' walk brought them to the point, where the men were awaiting them. As far as Ole could judge, by the dim light of a few stars that struggled through the cloudy sky, they were eleven as stout fellows as any warrior could desire to have at his back in a hand-to-hand conflict. They were all natives, clothed much in the same manner as Sambo, and armed with heavy clubs; for, as we have seen, Thorwald was resolved that this should be a bloodless victory.

"Whereabouts is the boat?" whispered Ole to his henchman, as he groped his way down the rocky slopes toward the shore.

"'Bout two hondr'd yards more farder in front," said Sambo.

"Then I'll place the men here," said Ole, turning to the natives, who were following close at his heels. "Now, boys, remain under cover of this rock till I lead you on to the attack; and, mind what I say to you,—*no killing*! Some of the party are my friends; d'ye understand? I don't want to do them a damage; but I do want to prevent their letting off as great a villain, I believe, as ever sailed the ocean under a black flag—only his was a red one, because of his extreme bloody-mindedness, no doubt, which led him to adopt the color of blood. We will attack them in the rear; which means, of course, by surprise; though I must confess that style of warfare goes much against the grain with me. There are just four men, I am told, besides the pirate. Our first onset will secure the fall of at least two of the party by my own cudgel; and, mark me, lads, I don't say this in a spirit of boasting. He would indeed be but a poor warrior who could not fell two men when he took them unawares and in the dark. No; I feel half ashamed o' the work; but I suppose it is my duty. So you see there will be just two men and the pirate left for us to deal with. Four of you ought to be able to overcome the two men without drawing blood, except, it may be, a little surface fluid. The remaining nine of us will fall on the pirate captain in a body. You will easily know him by his great size; and I have no manner of doubt but that he will make himself further known by the weight of his blows. If I happen to fall, don't look after me till you have overcome and bound the pirate. The ropes are all ready, and my man Sambo will carry them."

Having delivered this address to his followers, who by their "Ho's" and grins indicated their perfect readiness to do as they were bid, Ole Thorwald left them in ambush, and groped his way down to the beach, accompanied by Sambo.

"Did you bring the chain and padlock. Sambo?"

"Yis, mass'r. But you no tink it am berer to take boat away— pull him out ob sight?"

"No, Sambo; I have thought on that subject already, and have come to the conclusion that it is better to let the boat remain. You see they have placed it in such a way that as long as daylight lasted it could be seen from the settlement, and even now it is visible at some distance, as you see. If we were to remove it, they would at once observe that it was gone, and thus be put on their guard. No, no, Sambo. I may not be fond of ambushments, but I flatter myself that I have some talent for such matters."

The master and servant had reached the beach by this time, where they found the boat in the exact position that had been indicated by John Bumpus. It lay behind a low piece of coral rock, fastened to an iron ring by means of a rope, while the oars lay in readiness on the thwarts.

Sambo now produced a heavy iron chain, with which the boat was speedily fastened to the ring. It was secured with a large padlock, the key of which Ole placed in his pocket.

This being satisfactorily accomplished, they returned to the place of ambush.

"Now, Mister Gascoyne," observed Thorwald, with a grim smile, as he sat down beside his men and pulled out his watch, "I will await your pleasure. It is just half-past eleven; if you are a punctual man, as Jo Bumpus led me to believe, I will try your metal in half an hour, and have you back in your cage before one o'clock! What say you to that, Sambo?"

The faithful native opened his huge mouth wide, and shut his eyes, thereby indicating that he laughed; but he said nothing, bad, good, or indifferent, to his master's facetious observation. The other natives also grinned, in a quiet but particularly knowing manner, after which the whole party relapsed into profound silence, and kept their midnight watch with exemplary patience and eager expectation.

At this same hour the pirate captain was seated in his cell on the edge of the low bedstead, with his elbows resting on his knees and his face buried in his hands.

The cell was profoundly dark,—so dark that the figure of the prisoner could scarcely be distinguished.

Gascoyne did not move for many minutes; but once or twice a deep sigh escaped him, showing that, although his body was at rest, his thoughts were busy. At last he moved, and clasped his hands together violently, as if under a strong impulse. In doing so, the clank of his chains echoed harshly through the cell. This seemed to change the current of his thoughts; for he again covered his face with both hands, and began to mutter to himself.

"Aye," said he, "it has come at last. How often I have dreamed of this when I was free and roaming over the wide ocean! I would say that I have been a fool did I not feel that I have more cause to bow my head and confess that I am a sinner. Ah, what a thing pride is! How little do men know what it has cost me to humble myself before them as I have done! yet I feel no shame in confessing it here, where I am all alone. Alone?—*am* I alone?"

For a long time Gascoyne sat in deep silence, as if he were following out the train of thought which had been suggested by the last words. Presently his ideas again found vent in muttered speech.

"In my pride I have said that there is no God. I don't think I ever believed that; but I tried to believe it, for I knew that my deeds were evil. Surely my own words will condemn me; for I have said that I think myself a fool, and does not the Bible say that 'the fool hath said in his heart there is no God?' Aye, I remember it well. The words were printed in my brain when I learned the Psalms of David at my mother's knee, long, long ago. My mother! what bitter years have passed since that day! How little did ye dream, mother, that your child would come to *this*! God help me!"

The pirate relapsed into silence, and a low groan escaped him. But his thoughts seemed too powerful to be restrained within his breast; for they soon broke forth again in words.

"Your two texts have come true, Pastor Mason. You did not mean them for me; but *they were sent* to me. 'There is no rest, saith my God, to the wicked.'—No rest! I have not known rest since I was a boy.—'Be sure your sin shall find you out.' I laughed at those words once; they laugh at me now. I have found them out to be true, and found it out too late. Too late! *Is* it too late? If these words be true, are not all the words of God equally true? 'The blood of Jesus Christ his Son cleanseth us from *all* sin.' That was what you said, Pastor Mason, on that Sunday morning when the savages were stealing down on us. It gave me comfort then; but, ah me! it seems to give me no comfort now. Oh that I had resisted the tempter when he *first* came to me! Strange! I often heard this said long, long ago; but I laughed at it,—not in scorn; no, it was an easy indifference. I did not believe it had anything to do with *me*. And now, I suppose, if I were to stand in the public streets and cry that I had been mistaken, with all the fervor of a bursting heart, men would laugh at me in an easy way—as I did then.

"I don't fear death. I have often faced it, and I don't remember ever feeling afraid of death. Yet I shrink from death *now*. Why is this? What a mystery my thoughts and feelings are to me! I know not what to think. But it will soon be over; for I feel certain that I shall be doomed to die. God help me!"

Gascoyne again became silent. When he had remained thus a few minutes, his attention was roused by the sound of footsteps and of whispering voices close under his window. Presently the key was put in the lock, the heavy bolt shot back, and the door creaked on its hinges as it opened slowly.

Gascoyne knew by the sound that several men entered the cell, but, as they carried no light, he could not tell how many there were. He was of course surprised at a visit at such an unusual hour, as well as at the stealthy manner in which his visitors entered; but, having made up his mind to submit quietly to whatever was in store for him, and knowing that he could not hope for much tenderness at the hands of the inhabitants of Sandy Cove, he was not greatly disturbed. Still, he would not have been human had not his pulse quickened under the influence of a strong desire to spring up and defend himself.

The door of the cell was shut and locked as quietly as it had been opened; then followed the sound of footsteps crossing the floor.

"Is that you, jailer?" demanded Gascoyne.

"Ye'll know that time enough," answered a gruff voice, that was not unfamiliar to the prisoner's ear.

The others who had entered along with this man did not move from the door,—at least, if they did so, there was no sound of footsteps. The man who had spoken went to the window and spread a thick cloth over it. Gascoyne could see this, because there was sufficient light outside to make the arms of the man dimly visible as he raised them up to accomplish his object. The cell was thus rendered, if possible, more impenetrably dark than before.

"Now, pirate," said the man, turning round and suddenly flashing a dark lantern full on the stern face of the prisoner, "you and I will have a little converse together—by yer leave or without yer leave. In case there might be pryin' eyes about, I've closed the porthole, d'ye see."

Gascoyne listened to this familiar style of address in surprise, but did not suffer his features to betray any emotion whatever. The lantern which the seaman (for such he evidently was) carried in his hand threw a strong light wherever its front was turned, but left every other part of the cell in partial darkness. The reflected light was, however, quite sufficient to enable the prisoner to see that his visitor was a short, thick-set man, of great physical strength, and that three men of unusual size and strength stood against the wall, in the deep shadow of a recess, with their straw hats pulled very much over their eyes.

"Now, Mr. Gascoyne," began the seaman, sitting down on the edge of a small table beside the low pallet, and raising the lantern a little, while he gazed earnestly into the prisoner's face, "I've reason to believe—"

"Ha! you are the boatswain of the Talisman!" exclaimed Gascoyne, as the light reflected from his own countenance irradiated that of Dick Price, whom, of course, he had seen while they were on board the frigate together.

"No, Mister Pirate," said Dick; "I am *not* the bo's'n of the Talisman, else I shouldn't be here this night. I *wos* the bo's'n of that unfortunate frigate, but I is so no longer."

Dick said this in a melancholy tone, and thereafter meditated for a few moments in silence.

"No," he resumed with a heavy sigh, "the Talisman's blow'd up, an' her bo's'n's out on the spree, so to speak—though it ain't a cheerful spree, by no means. But to come back to the p'int (w'ich was wot the clergyman said w'en he'd got so far away from the p'int that he never*did* get back to it), as I wos sayin', or was goin' to say w'en you prewented me, I've reason to b'lieve you're agoin' to try for to make yer escape."

"You are mistaken, my man," said Gascoyne, with a sad smile; "nothing is further from my thoughts."

"I don't know how far it's from yer thoughts," said Dick, sternly, "but it's pretty close to your intentions, so I'm told."

"Indeed you are mistaken," replied Gascoyne. "If Captain Montague has sent you here to mount guard, he has only deprived you of a night's rest needlessly. If I had intended to make my escape, I would not have given myself up."

"I don't know that,—I'm not so sure o' that," rejoined the boatswain, stoutly. "You're said to be a obstinate feller, and there's no sayin' what obstinate fellers won't do or will do. But I didn't come here for to argify the question with *you*, Mister Gascoyne. Wot I com'd here for wos to do my duty; so, now, I'm agoin' to do it."

Gascoyne, who was amused in spite of himself by the manner of the man, merely smiled, and awaited in silence the pleasure of his eccentric visitor.

Dick now set down the lantern, went to the door, and returned with a coil of stout rope.

"You see," observed the boatswain, as he busied himself in uncoiling-and making a running noose on the rope, "I'm ordered to prewent you from carrying out your intentions— wotiver these may be—by puttin' a coil or two o' this here rope round you. Now, wot I've got to ask of you is, Will ye submit peaceable like to have it done?"

"Surely, this is heaping unnecessary indignity upon me!" exclaimed Gascoyne, flushing crimson with anger.

"It *may* be unnecessary, but it's got to be done," returned Dick, with cool decision, as he placed the end of a knot between his powerful teeth, and drew it tight. "Besides, Mister Gascoyne, a pirate must expect indignities to be heaped upon him. However, I'll heap as few as possible on ye in the discharge of my duty."

Gascoyne had started to his feet; but he sat down, abashed on being thus reminded of his deserts.

"True," said he; "true. I will submit."

He added in his mind, "I deserve this;" but nothing more escaped his lips, while he stood up and permitted the boatswain to pass the cord round his arms, and lash them firmly to his sides.

Having bound him in a peculiarly tight and nautical manner, Dick once more went to his accomplices at the door, and returned with a hammer and chisel, and a large stone. The latter he placed on the table, and, directing Gascoyne to raise his arms—which were not secured below the elbows—and placed his manacles on the stone, he cut them asunder with a few powerful blows, and removed them.

"The darbies ain't o' no use, you see, as we've got you all safe with the ropes. Now, Mister Gascoyne, I'm agoin' to heap one more indignity on ye. I'm sorry to do it, d'ye see; but I'm bound for to obey orders. You'll be so good as to sit down on the bed,—for I ain't quite so long as you, though I won't say that I'm not about as broad,—and let me tie this napkin over yer mouth."

"Why!" exclaimed Gascoyne, again starting and looking fiercely at the boatswain; "this, at least, must be unnecessary. I have said that I am willing to submit quietly to whatever the law condemns me. You don't take me for a woman or a child, that will be apt to cry out when hurt?"

"Certainly not; but as I'm goin' to take ye away out o' this here limbo, it is needful that I should prewent you from lettin' people know that yer goin' on yer travels; for I've heerd say there's some o' yer friends as is plottin' to help you to escape."

"Have I not said already that I do not wish to escape, and therefore will not take advantage of any opportunity afforded me by my friends? Friends! I have no friends! Even those whom I thought were my friends have not been near my prison all this day."

Gascoyne said this bitterly, and in great anger.

"Hush!" exclaimed Dick; "not quite so loud, Mister Pirate. You see there *is* some reason in my puttin' this on your mouth. It'll be as well to let me do it quietly, else I'll have to get a little help."

He pointed to the three stout men who stood motionless and silent in the dark recess.

"Oh, it was cowardly of you to bind my arms before you told me this," said Gascoyne, with flashing eyes. "If my hands were free now—"

He checked himself by a powerful effort, and crushed back the boastful defiance which rose to his lips.

"Now, I'll tell ye what it is, Mister Gascoyne," said Dick Price, "I do believe yer not such a bad feller as they say ye are, an' I'm disposed to be marciful to ye. If yell give me your word of honor that you'll not holler out, and that you'll go with us peaceably, and do wot yer bid, I'll not trouble you with the napkin, nor bind ye up more than I've done already. But" (here Dick spoke in tones that could not be misunderstood), "if ye won't give me that promise, I'll gag ye and bind ye neck and heels, and we'll carry ye out o' this, shoulder high. Now, wot say ye to that?"

Gascoyne had calmed his feelings while the boatswain was speaking. He even smiled when he replied, "How can you ask me to give my word of honor? What honor has a pirate to boast of, think you?"

"Not much, pr'aps," said Dick; "howsomdever, I'll be content with wot's left of it; and if there ain't none, why, then, give us yer word. It'll do as well."

"After all, it matters little what is done with me," said Gascoyne, in a resigned-voice. "I am a fool to resist thus. You need not fear that I will offer any further resistance, my man. Do your duty, whatever that may be."

"That won't do," said Dick, stoutly; "ye must promise not to holler out."

"I promise," said Gascoyne, sternly. "Pray cease this trifling; and, if it is not inconsistent with your duty, let me know where I am to be taken to."

"That's just wot I'm not allowed for to tell. But you'll find it out in the coorse of time. Now, all that you've got to do is to walk by my side, and do wot I tell ye."

The prisoner made no answer. He was evidently weary of the conversation, and his thoughts were already wandering on other subjects.

The door was now unlocked by one of the three men who stood near it. As its hinges creaked, Dick shut the lantern, and threw the cell at once into total darkness. Taking hold of Gascoyne's wrist gently, as if to guide, not to force him away, he conducted him along the short passage that led to the outer door of the prison. This was opened, and the whole party stood in the open air.

Gascoyne looked with feelings of curiosity at the men who surrounded him; but the night was so intensely dark that their features were invisible. He could just discern the outlines of their figures, which were enveloped in large cloaks. He was on the point of speaking to them, when he remembered his promise to make no noise; so he restrained himself, and followed his guard in silence.

Dick and another man walked at his side, the rest followed in rear. Leading him round the outskirts of the village, towards its northern extremity, Gascoyne's conductors soon brought him to the beach, at a retired spot, where was a small bay. Here they were met by one whose stature proved him to be a boy. He glided up to Dick, who said, in a low whisper:

"Is all ready?"

"All right," replied the boy, in a whisper.

"The ooman aboard?"

"Aye."

"Now, Mr. Gascoyne," said Dick, pointing to a large boat floating beside the rocks on which they stood, "you'll be so good as to step into that 'ere boat, and sit down beside the individual you see a-sitting in the stern-sheets."

"Have you authority for what you do?" asked Gascoyne,

hesitating.

"I have power to enforce wot I command," said Dick, quietly. "Remember yer promise, Mister Pirate, else—"

Dick finished his sentence by pointing to the three men who stood near—still maintaining a silence worthy of Eastern mutes; and Gascoyne, feeling that he was completely in their power, stepped quickly into the boat, and sat down beside the "individual" referred to by Dick, who was so completely enveloped in the folds of a large cloak as to defy recognition. But the pirate captain was too much occupied with his own conflicting thoughts and feelings to bestow more than a passing glance on the person who sat at his side. Indeed, it was not surprising that Gascoyne was greatly perplexed by all that was going on at that time; for he could not satisfactorily account to himself for the mystery and secrecy which his guards chose to maintain. If they were legitimate agents of the law, why these muffled oars, with which they swept the boat across the lagoon, through the gap in the coral reef, and out to sea? And if they were *not* agents of the law, who were they, and where were they conveying him?

The boat was a large one, half-decked, and fitted to stand a heavy sea and rough weather. It would have moved sluggishly through the water had not the four men who pulled the oars been possessed of more than average strength. As soon as they passed the barrier reef, the sails were hoisted, and Dick took the helm. The breeze was blowing fresh off the land, and the water rushed past the boat as she cut swiftly out to sea, leaving a track of white foam behind her. For a few minutes the mass of the island was dimly seen rising like a huge shade on the dark sky, but soon it melted away, and nothing remained for the straining eyes to rest upon save the boat with its silent crew and the curling foam on the black sea.

"We've got him safe now, lads," said Dick Price, speaking for the first time that night in unguarded tones. "You'd better do the deed. The sooner it's done the better."

While he was speaking, one of the three men opened a large clasp-knife, and advanced towards Gascoyne.

"Father," said Henry, cutting the rope that bound him, "you are free at last!"

Gascoyne started; but before he had time to utter the exclamation of surprise that sprang to his lips, his hand was seized by the muffled figure that sat at his side.

"O, Gascoyne! forgive us—forgive *me*!" said Mary Stuart, in a trembling voice. "I did, indeed, know something of what they meant to do, but I knew nothing of the cruel violence that these bonds—"

"Violence!" cried Dick Price. "I put it to yourself, Mister Gascoyne, if I didn't treat ye as if ye wos a lamb?"

"Wot a blissin it is for a man to git his mouth open agin, and let his breath go free," cried Jo Bumpus, with a deep sigh. "Come, Corrie, give us a cheer—hip! hip! hip!—"

The cheer that followed was stirring, and wonderfully harmonious; for it was given in a deep bass and a shrill treble, with an intermediate baritone "Ho!" from Jakolu.

"I know it, Mary—I know it," said Gascoyne; and there was a slight tremor in his deep voice as he drew his wife towards him, and laid her head upon his breast.

"You have never done me an evil turn—you have done me nothing but good—since you were a little child. Heaven bless you, Mary!"

"Now, father," said Henry, "I suppose you have no objection to make your escape?"

"No need to raise that question, lad," said Gascoyne, with a perplexed smile. "I am not quite clear as to what my duty is, now that I am free to go back again and give myself up."

"Go back!—free!" exclaimed John Bumpus, in a tone of withering sarcasm. "So, Mister Gascoyne, ye've got sich an uncommon cargo o' conceit in ye yet, that you actually think ye could go back without so much as saying, By your leave!"

While Jo was speaking, he bared to the shoulder an arm that was the reverse of infantine, and, holding it up, said, slowly:

"I've often had a sort o' desire, d'ye see, to try whether this bit of a limb or the one that's round Mrs. Stuart's waist is the strongest. Now, if *you* have any desire to settle this question, just try to put, to shove, this boat's head up into the wind— that's all!"

This was said so emphatically by the pugnacious Bumpus that his companions laughed, and Corrie cheered in admiration.

"You see," observed Henry, "you need not give yourself any concern as to this point; you have no option in the matter."

"No, not a bit o' poption in it wotiver; though wot that means I ain't rightly sure," said Dick Price.

"Perhaps I ought to exercise my parental authority over you, Henry," said Gascoyne, "and *command* you to steer back to Sandy Cove."

"But we wouldn't let him, Mister Pirate," said Dick Price, who, now that his difficult duties were over, was preparing to solace himself with a pipe; an example that was immediately followed by Bumpus, who backed his friend by adding:

"No more we would."

"Nay, then, if Henry joins me," said Gascoyne, "I think that we two will not have a bad chance against you three."

"Come, that's good: so *I* count for nothing!" exclaimed Corrie.

"Ha! stick up, lad," observed Bumpus. "The niggers wot you pitched into at the mouth o' yon cave didn't think that—eh! didn't they not?"

"Well, well; if Corrie sides with you, I feel that my wisest course is to submit. And now, Henry," said Gascoyne, resuming his wonted gravity of tone and demeanor, "sit down here and let me know where we are going, and what you mean to do. It is natural that I should feel curious on these points, even although I *have* perfect confidence in you all."

Henry obeyed, and their voices sank into low tones as they mingled in earnest converse about their future plans.

Thus did Gascoyne, with his family and friends, leave Sandy Cove in the dead of that dark night, and sail away over the wide waste of the great Pacific Ocean.

* * * *

Reader, our tale is nearly told. Like a picture it contains but a small portion of the career of those who have so long engaged your attention, and, I would fain hope, your sympathy. The life of man may be comprehensively epitomized almost to a point, or expanded out *ad infinitum*. He was born, he died, is its lowest term. Its highest is not definable.

Innumerable tomes, of encyclopedic dimensions, could not contain, much less exhaust, an account of all that was said and done, and all that might be said about what was said and done, by our *ci-devant*sandal-wood trader and his friends. Yet there are main points, amid the little details of their career, which it would be unpardonable to pass over in silence. To these we shall briefly refer before letting the curtain fall.

There is a distant isle of the sea, a beautiful spot, an oceanic gem, which has been reclaimed by the word of God from those regions that have been justly styled "the dark places of the earth." We will not mention its name; we will not even indicate its whereabouts, lest we should furnish a clue to the unromantic myrmidons of the law, whose inflexible justice is only equaled by their pertinacity in tracking the criminal to his lair!

On this beautiful isle, at the time of our tale, the churches and houses of Christian men had begun to rise. The natives had begun to cultivate the arts of civilization, and to appreciate, in some degree, the inestimable blessings of Christianity. The plow had torn up the virgin soil, and the anchors of merchant-ships had begun to kiss the strand. The crimes peculiar to civilized men had not yet been developed. The place had all the romance and freshness of a flourishing infant colony.

Early one fine morning, a half-decked boat rowed into the harbor of this isle, and ran alongside the little quay, where the few natives who chanced to be lounging there were filled with admiration at the sight of five stalwart men who leaped upon the rocks, an active lad who held the boat steady, and a handsome middle-aged woman, who was assisted to land with much care by the tallest of her five companions.

There were a few small bales of merchandise in the boat. These being quickly tossed ashore, one of the natives was asked to show the way to the nearest store, where they might be placed in safekeeping.

This done, the largest man of the party, who was clad in the rough garments of a merchant captain, offered his arm to the female, who was evidently his wife, and went off in search of the chief magistrate of the settlement, leaving his companions to look after the boat and smoke their pipes.

The handsome stranger introduced himself to the magistrate as Mr. Stuart; stated that he intended to settle on the island as a general merchant, having brought a few bales of merchandise with him; that he had been bred an engineer and a shipwright, and meant also to work at his old trade, and concluded by asking for advice and general information in regard to the state of trade on the island.

After having obtained all the information on these subjects that the magistrate could give,—insomuch that that functionary deemed him a perfect marvel of catechetical wisdom and agreeable address,—the stalwart stranger proceeded to inquire minutely into the state of religion and education among the natives and settlers, and finally left the charmed magistrate rejoicing in the belief that he was a most intelligent philanthropist, and would be an inestimable acquisition to the settlement.

A small trading-store was soon built. The stranger was not a rich man. He began in a humble way, and sought to eke out his subsistence by doing the ordinary work of a wright. In this latter occupation he was ably assisted by his stout son, Henry; for the duties of the store were attended to chiefly by the lad Corrie, superintended by Mr. Stuart.

The mysterious strangers were a source of much gossip and great speculation, of course, to the good people of Green Isle, as we shall style this gem of the Pacific, in order to thwart the myrmidons of the law! They found them so reserved and uncommunicative, however, on the subject of their personal affairs, that the most curious gossip in the settlement at last gave up speculating in despair.

In other respects, the new family were noted for kindliness and urbanity. Mrs. Stuart, especially, became an intimate friend of the missionary who dwelt there, and one of his hardest working parishioners. Mr. Stuart also became his friend; but the stern gravity of countenance, and reserved, though perfectly well-bred and even kindly manner of the stranger forbade close intimacy. He was a most regular attendant at church, not only on Sundays, but at the weekly-prayer meetings and occasional festivals, and the missionary noticed that his Bible looked as if it were a well-thumbed one.

At first the two seamen, whom people soon found out, were named respectively Jo and Dick, wrought in the wright's workshop, and at all kinds of miscellaneous jobs; besides making frequent and sometimes long voyages in their boat to the neighboring islands. As time flew by, things seemed to prosper with the merchant. The keel of a little schooner was laid. Father, and son, and seamen (as well as the native servant, who was called Jako) toiled at this vessel incessantly until she was finished— then Henry was placed in command of her, Jo and Dick were appointed first and second mates, two or three natives completed the crew, and she went to sea under the somewhat peculiar name of the Avenger.

This seemed to be the first decided advance in the fortunes of the new family. Business increased in a wonderful way. The

Avenger returned again and again to the Green Isle laden with rich and varied commodities for the successful merchant. In course of time the old store was taken down, and a new one built; the Avenger was sold, and a large brig purchased; the rather pretty name of which—"Evening Star"—was erased, and the mysterious word Avenger put in its place. Everything, in short, betokened that Mr. Stuart was on the high road to fortune.

But there were some mysteries connected with the merchant which sorely puzzled the wisest heads in the place, and which would have puzzled still wiser heads had they been there. Although it soon became quite evident to the meanest capacity that Mr. Stuart was the richest man on the island, yet he and his family continued to occupy the poor, shabby, little, ill-furnished cottage which they had erected with their own hands when they first landed; and although they sold the finest silks and brocades to the wives and daughters of the other wealthy settlers, they themselves wore only the plainest and most somber fabrics that consisted with respectability.

People would have called them a family of misers but for their goodness of character in other respects, and for the undeniable fact that they were by far the most liberal contributors to the church and to the poor—not only in their own island, but in all the other islands around them.

Another thing that puzzled the mercantile men of the place extremely was the manner in which Mr. Stuart kept his books of business. They soon began to take note that he kept two ledgers and two distinct sets of books—the one set small, the other set very bulky. Some of the more audacious among his customers ventured to peep over his shoulder, and discovered that the small set contained nothing but entries of boats made, and repairs to shipping executed, and work connected exclusively with the shipwright department of his business—while the large books contained entries of those silks, and sugars, and teas, and spices, etc., which turned so much gold into his coffers.

It thus became evident to these men of business that the merchant kept the two departments quite separate, in order to ascertain the distinct profits on each. They were the more amazed at this when they considered that the shipwright work must necessarily be a mere driblet, altogether unworthy the attention of one so wealthy. But that which amazed them most of all was, that such a man, in such circumstances, could waste his time in doing with his own hands the work of an ordinary mechanic—thus (as they concluded) entailing on himself the necessity of devoting much of the night to his more lucrative concern.

These long-headed men of business little knew the man. They did not know that he was *great* in the highest sense of the term, and that, among other elements of his greatness, he possessed the power of seizing the little things—the little opportunities— of life, and turning them to the best account; and that he not only knew what should be done; and how to do it, but was gifted with that inflexible determination of purpose to carry out a design, without which knowledge and talent can never accomplish great things. The merchant did not, as they supposed, work late at night. He measured his time, and measured his work. In this he was like many other men in this struggling world; but he *stuck* to his time and to his work, in which respect he resembled the great few whose names stand prominent on the page of history.

In consequence of this, Mr. Stuart wrought with success at both departments of his business, and while in the one he coined thousands, in the other he earned more than the average wages of a working-man.

The Avenger was erratic and uncertain in her voyages. She evidently sailed to the principal islands of the South Seas, and did business with them all. From one of these voyages, Henry, her captain, returned with a wife,—a dark-haired, dark-eyed, lady-like girl,—for whom he built a small cottage beside his father's, and left her there while he was away at sea.

It was observed by the clerks in Mr. Stuart's counting-room, that their chief accountant, Mr. Corrie, was a great letter-writer,—that when one letter was finished, he invariably began another, and kept it by him, adding sheet after sheet to it until the Avenger returned and carried it off. Once Mr. Corrie was called hurriedly away while in the act of addressing one of these epistles. He left it lying on his desk, and a small, contemptible, little apprentice allowed his curiosity so far to get the better of him, that he looked at the address, and informed his companions that Mr. Corrie's correspondent was a certain Miss Alice Mason!

Of course, Mr. Corrie received voluminous replies from this mysterious Alice; and, if one might judge from his expression on reading these epistles (as that contemptible little apprentice *did* judge), the course of *his* love ran smoother than usual; thus, by its exceptionality, proving the truth of the rule.

Years passed away. The merchant's head became gray, but his gigantic frame was as straight and his step as firm as ever. His wife, strange to say, looked younger as she grew older! It seemed as if she were recovering from some terrible illness that had made her prematurely old, and were now renewing her youth. The business prospered to such an extent that, by becoming altogether too wonderful, it ceased to be a matter of wonder altogether to the merchants of the Green Isle. They regarded it as semi-miraculous,—the most unprecedented case of "luck" that had ever been heard of in the annals of mercantile history.

But the rich merchant still dwelt in the humble, almost mean cottage, and still wrought as an engineer and shipwright with his own hands.

In the little cottage beside his own there were soon seen (and *heard*) three stout children, two boys and a girl, the former being named respectively Gascoyne and Henry, the latter Mary. It is needless to say that these were immense favorites with the eccentric merchant.

During all this time there was a firm in Liverpool which received periodical remittances of money from an unknown source. The cashier of that firm, a fat little man, with a face like a dumpling and a nose like a cherry, lived, as it were, in a state of perpetual amazement in regard to these remittances. They came regularly, from apparently nowhere, were acknowledged to nobody, and amounted, in the course of time, to many thousands. This firm had, some years previously, lost a fine vessel. She was named the Brilliant; had sailed for the South Sea Islands with a rich cargo, and was never more heard of. The fat cashier knew the loss sustained by this vessel to a penny. He had prepared and calculated all the papers and sent duplicates on board; and as he had a stake in the venture, he never forgot the amount of the loss sustained.

One day the firm received a remittance from the unknown, with a note to the following effect at the foot of it: "This is the last remittance on account of the Brilliant. The value of the cargo, including compound interest, and the estimated value of the vessel, have now been repaid to the owners."

The fat cashier was thunderstruck! He rushed to his ledger, examined the account, calculated the interest, summed up the whole, and found it correct. He went home to bed, and fell sound asleep in amazement; awoke in amazement; went back to the office in amazement; worked on day after day in amazement; lived, and eventually died, in a state of unrelieved amazement In regard to this incomprehensible transaction!

About the same time that this occurred, Mr. Stuart entered his poor cottage, and finding his wife there, said:

"Mary, I have sent off the last remittance to-day. I have made amends for that evil deed. It has cost me a long and hard struggle to realize the thousands of pounds that were requisite; for some of the goods had got damaged by damp in the cavern of the Isle of Palms; but the profits of my engineering and shipwright business have increased of late, and I have managed to square it all off, with interest. And now, Mary, I can do no more. If I knew of any others who have suffered at my hands. I would restore what I took tenfold; but I know of none. It therefore remains that I should work this business for the good of mankind. Of all the thousands that have passed through my hands, I have not used one penny. You know that I have always kept the business that has grown out of the labors of my own hands distinct from that which has been reared on the stolen goods. I have lived and supported you by it, and now, through God's blessing, it has increased to such an extent that I think we may afford to build a somewhat more commodious house, and furnish it a little better.

"As for the mercantile business, it *must* go on. It has prospered and still prospers. Many mouths are dependent on it for daily bread. I will continue to manage it, but every penny of profit shall go in charity as long as I live. After that, Henry may do with it as he pleases. He has contributed largely to make it what it is, and deserves to reap where he has sown so diligently. Do you think I am right in all this, Mary?"

We need scarcely remark that Mary did think it all right; for she and Gascoyne had no differences of opinion *now*.

Soon after this, Corrie went off on a long voyage in the Avenger. The vessel touched at San Francisco, and while there, some remarkable scenes took place between Jo Bumpus and a good-looking woman whom he called Susan. This female ultimately went on board the Avenger, and sailed in her for Green Isle.

On the way thither they touched at one of the first of the South Sea Islands that they came in sight of, where scenes of the most unprecedented description took place between Corrie and a bluff old gentleman named Ole Thorwald, and a sweet, blue-eyed, fair-haired maiden named Alice Mason!

Strange to say, this fair girl agreed to become a passenger in the Avenger; and, still more strange to say, her father and

Ole Thorwald agreed to accompany her; also an ancient piece of animated door-matting called Toozle, and a black woman named Poopy, whose single observation in regard to every event in sublunary history was, "Hee! hee!"

On reaching Green Isle, Corrie and Alice were married, and on the same day Bumpus and Susan were also united. There was great rejoicing on the occasion. Ole Thorwald and Dick Price distinguished themselves by dancing an impromptu and maniacal *pas de deux* at the double wedding!

Of Captain Montague's future career we know nothing. He may have been killed in the wars of his country, or he may have become an admiral in the British navy, for all we know to the contrary. One thing only we are certain of, and that is, that he sailed for England, in the pirate schooner, and seemed by no means to regret the escape of the pirate captain!

Years rolled away. The head of Gascoyne became silvery white; but Time seemed impotent to subdue the vigor of his stalwart frame, or destroy the music of his deep bass voice. He was the idol of numerous grandchildren as well as of a large circle of juveniles, who, without regard to whether they had or had not a right to do so, styled him "Grandfather."

Little did these youngsters think, as they clambered over his huge frame, and listened with breathless attention to his wild stories of the sea, that "grandfather" had once been the celebrated and much-dreaded Durward, the pirate!

Nothing could induce Gascoyne to take a prominent part in the public affairs of his chosen home; but he did attempt to teach a class of the very smallest boys and girls in the missionary's Sunday-school, and he came in time to take special delight in this work.

He was never so happy as when telling to these little ones the story of redeeming love. In the choice of subjects for his class, he was somewhat peculiar as well as in his manner of treating them. He was particularly emphatic and earnest, used to fill his little hearers with awe, when he spoke of the danger of sin and the importance of resisting its beginnings. But his two favorite themes of all—and those which dwelt most frequently on his lips—were, "God is love," and, "Love is the fulfilling of the law."

THE END